PATRICK A. DAVIS

THE SHATTERED BLUE LINE

POCKET STAR BOOKS
New York   London   Toronto   Sydney

This book is a work of fiction. Names, characters, places and incidents are products of the author's imagination or are used fictitiously. Any resemblance to actual events or locales or persons living or dead is entirely coincidental.

An *Original* Publication of POCKET BOOKS

 A Pocket Star Book published by
POCKET BOOKS, a division of Simon & Schuster, Inc.
1230 Avenue of the Americas, New York, NY 10020

Copyright © 2005 by Patrick A. Davis

ISBN-13: 978-0-7434-9975-0
ISBN-10: 0-7434-9975-1

First Pocket Books printing September 2005

10 9 8 7 6 5 4 3 2 1

POCKET STAR BOOKS and colophon are registered trademarks of Simon & Schuster, Inc.

Cover design by Jae Song
Cover image by Myron/GettyImages

Manufactured in the United States of America

For information regarding special discounts for bulk purchases, please contact Simon & Schuster Special Sales at 1-800-456-6798 or business@simonandschuster.com.

To Colonel Neal Barlow, USAFA '78,
the officer every cadet should aspire to be

Acknowledgments

This book wouldn't have been possible without the contributions of so many people who labored selflessly in the hope that I would create something readable. First, I'd like to thank my informal editing team of Bob and Katie Sessler for their patience and friendship, and my parents, Bill and Betty Davis, for their love and support. I'd also like to express my gratitude to my ever-growing circle of readers: Ginny, Chuck, and Dave Markl; Bobby and Kathy Baker; Kevin, Kyla and Kaila Davis; Cecil and Barb Fuqua; Michael Roche; Chris Wells; Pat and Marva Dryke; Colonel Dennis Hilley; Michael Garber; and Nathan Green. As always, I need to thank my medical team of Dr. Carey Page and Dr. Bill Burke for imparting their wisdom into a form a layman can understand.

Heartfelt appreciation goes to my Air Force Academy experts who kept me straight on the many changes since I once walked those hallowed halls: Lt. Col. Carl Hawkins, '79 classmate and test pilot extraordinaire; Lt. Col Tim Scully and his wife, Marsha, the gurus of the Aeronautics lab; Shirley Orlofsky, who runs the Aero Department, though she's too modest to admit it; Dave Lindsay, who is continuing proof that USAFA graduates men and women of honor and character; Steve Archeletta, the only man I'd trust to pack my parachute; and Diana Barlow, the best cook and the kindest literary critic I know. In particular, I need to thank the cadets who were crucial to enlightening me on the insights of Academy life: Kaitlin Barlow, Mary Zinnel, Rachel Owen, and Christina Smith.

I'd also like to thank my editor, Kevin Smith, for his astute guidance, and my agent Karen Solem, for her faith in my books. Finally, I'd like to express my love to my wife, Helen, who makes everything possible.

Prologue

SHE AWOKE WITH A VIOLENT START, HER SLEEP-dulled mind reacting with confusion. Then came the panic as her head was roughly pulled back and something was jammed into her mouth. A cloth. She tried to scream but gagged. Dark figures descended upon her and strong hands pinned her to the bed. She attempted to kick, wrench free, but the grips were too powerful.

There were two of them. They looked enormous. Her eyes darted wildly and for an instant, she thought she was having a nightmare. It had to be a nightmare. From the moonlight filtering in through the window, she recognized the surreal faces of her attackers. Cartoon faces.

Donald Duck and Pluto.

She flinched at a sudden tearing sound. A third figure materialized.

It was Mickey Mouse and he held a knife.

As the blade moved toward her, she screamed to herself, *This can't be happening! Not here!*

The blade pressed against her throat. She began to whimper.

Mickey Mouse whispered a guttural command: "Move and you die."

She nodded numbly.

Mickey Mouse produced a cloth laundry bag and threw it over the girl's head. The sudden blackness enhanced her feeling of powerlessness and terror. Her arms were pulled high above her head. More tearing sounds; her hands were quickly duct-taped together.

Mickey Mouse went to the door, opened it a crack, then cautiously stepped outside. Donald and Pluto grasped the girl by her legs and armpits and carried her after Mickey.

The hallway was still and silent. A clock on a wall read 3:32. The procession crept past a line of closed doors, entering a corner room containing two sofas, several chairs, and a television.

Donald and Pluto lay the girl on the carpeted floor, securing her taped hands to a metal sofa leg with rope. When they finished, they each grabbed one of her thighs and pried them apart.

The girl twisted and writhed, trying vainly to resist.

She again felt the knife against her throat and relaxed, accepting her fate. At some point, she began to cry.

Mickey Mouse straddled her torso and cut away her T-shirt. She wore no bra and he fondled her large breasts, squeezing each nipple. His breathing became labored and excited. When he could stand it no longer, he cut off her panties and undid his zipper.

"You cocksucking tease," he whispered. "We're going to show you, bitch."

Forty minutes later, Mickey, Pluto, and Donald emerged from the room. Mickey carried a small vacuum while Donald held a trash bag. As they closed the door behind them, they traded silent high fives and playful punches. None took notice of the large mural on the opposite wall, which showed a female pilot standing beside an F-15 fighter.

"The New Air Force," the caption read.

Chapter 1

No one familiar with the military would have mistaken the lone occupant of the Security Forces holding cell to be a field-grade Air Force officer. He appeared a few years too young, no more than late twenties, and his disheveled black hair pressed the limits of military grooming. Instead of a blue uniform, he wore an expensive silk suit—slightly wrinkled since he'd spent the night in it—that far surpassed the budgetary constraints of an officer of his rank.

Major Nathan Malone lay on a cot, a tie folded over his eyes to block the light, his breathing deep and regular. Since it was only 7:00 A.M., he could have been asleep, but he wasn't. For the past five minutes, he'd been listening to muffled shouts and the squawking of radios, trying to determine the cause. Twice, he'd been on the verge of asking someone, but decided to wait. If they needed him, they'd let him know . . . assuming he still had a job.

Malone felt a twinge of regret over what had transpired last night, but there was nothing he could do about it now. Officers arrested for a DWI rarely get a second chance. Officers who commanded the local Office of Special Investigations detachment, the Air Force's equivalent of the FBI, never do. As the base's top criminal investigator, he more than anyone should know better than to drink and drive.

As usual, a woman was responsible for his predicament. As long as Malone could remember, they'd found his chiseled good looks and spare, six-five frame irresistible. And his affluent lifestyle certainly didn't hurt, funded by an inheritance courtesy of his grandfather, a former military officer who'd made a fortune on Wall Street. At thirty-four, Malone had never come close to settling down because he knew he'd never be able to resist the temptations that swirled around him.

For once, he should have tried.

The woman at the Officers' Club bar last night had been a stunner. A brunette captain with a body to die for and a face like an angel. She struck up a conversation, batted her lashes and cooed all the right things in his ear. How was he supposed to know she had a light colonel boyfriend, and the guy would show up—

Footsteps coming toward him.

Outside, the commotion had died off. When the footsteps stopped, Malone removed the tie and focused on the one-way mirror installed in the solid cell door. His head throbbed dully against the brightness of the fluorescent lights, a reminder that tequila and beer don't mix. At the click of the lock, he eased his long frame off the cot.

The door opened, revealing a baby-faced security

cop and a compact major in Class A service blues. Malone frowned at the major. He'd expected to be released into the custody of his boss, the air base wing commander. Instead, he was looking at Seth Wilson, the executive officer to—

"I'll take it from here, Airman Crotter," Major Wilson ordered.

"Yes, sir."

As the cop departed, Wilson entered, cryptically eyeing Malone, who towered above him. "Jeez, you look like a bag of shit, Malone." Wilson sounded pleased. Years earlier, Wilson had been an upperclassman in Malone's basic cadet training squadron; he'd resented Malone's lack of military bearing then and cared for him even less now.

"Heard about the altercation at the club," Wilson went on. "The lieutenant colonel must have been the one who tipped off the security cops that you were driving drunk. Hell, it had to be him. You were hitting on his girl. Hope she was worth it."

"I love you, too, Seth," Malone grunted warily. "What are you doing here?"

"The boss wants to see you."

Wilson's boss was Lieutenant General Neal Crenshaw, the Academy superintendent.

"Why?"

Wilson shrugged. "No clue. I was told to spring you from custody."

"Cut the shit, Seth. He going to fire me?"

A thin smile was the only response. It was enough. Malone felt stung by the realization that General

Crenshaw wanted to personally fire him instead of letting the air base wing commander handle it. Obviously, the general sought to extract his pound of flesh, not that Malone blamed him.

This was another bridge he burned long ago.

Following Wilson into the hallway, Malone remarked on the near-empty Security Forces squadron building. Normally it should be bustling with activity. He asked, "Mind telling me what's going on, Seth?"

Wilson walked away as if he hadn't heard him.

Malone sighed, shaking his head. The little prick was determined to play I-got-a-secret.

At the duty desk, Malone signed for a packet containing his wallet and personal items, including his cell phone. His badge, holster, and nine-millimeter weapon were turned over to Wilson.

Wilson said, "You might want to clean up a little."

"Why?" Malone asked mildly.

"For chrissakes, you're about to see a three-star general."

"So?"

"Didn't you learn anything while you were a cadet, Malone? It's about respect. You show up looking like that and you're telling General Crenshaw you don't respect him."

"You have a razor or a toothbrush, Seth?"

"Well, no—"

"A change of clothes, maybe an extra sports coat?"

"Of course not—"

"I got an overcoat in the car. Best I can do." He brushed past Wilson and headed out the door.

*   *   *

Another spectacular Colorado morning. The snow had stopped, the air was crisp and cold, and the sun hung low on the horizon, framed against an easel of brilliant blue. Wilson drove off in a staff car, Malone trailing in a black BMW turbo that he'd bought for cash. Early in his career, he'd resisted flaunting his wealth, figuring that would make it easier to be accepted by his fellow officers. It was wishful thinking. Working for the OSI was like being an IRS auditor. It seemed everyone had a guilt complex and once they learned what Malone did, they'd take off. It got to be a joke with Malone. He'd hold out his hand and say, "I work for the OSI," and mentally start a time hack. It rarely took more than two minutes before the person beat a retreat.

Not that Malone particularly cared. If he was looked upon as a black hat who got his rocks off busting people, so be it. Besides, he was free to enjoy his toys.

Two blocks later, Malone eased behind Wilson, who'd stopped at the intersection across from wing/base headquarters, the building where the OSI offices were located. After his arrest, Malone had phoned the night duty officer, to notify him what happened.

"I'll call Mother, sir," the DO said. "She might know someone who could smooth things over."

"No."

"Sir, Mother has contacts who might—"

"Don't call her. That's an order."

The DO sounded confused when he hung up. But Malone wasn't up to facing Mother. Besides, this was the military, not some civilian cop force where favors could be called in.

Wilson turned west on South Gate Boulevard, heading toward the cadet area nestled at the base of the Rampart Range mountains. Since it was early on a Saturday morning, traffic was nonexistent. In a few hours, that would change when the crowd arrived for the game against Utah. It was another sellout; for the first time in a quarter-century, Air Force was undefeated, with two games left in the season, and was ranked in the top five.

Settling in for the short drive, Malone felt his trepidation grow, recalling the last time he'd faced the full wrath of General Crenshaw. Even though it was almost fourteen years earlier, the memory was still vivid. He'd been a sophomore or third-class cadet and Major Crenshaw was the Air Officer Commanding, in charge of Malone's squadron.

Crenshaw had put him in a brace and was holding up a bottle of Scotch, saying, "So you admit this is yours and your roommate Cadet Wasdin knew nothing about it?"

"Yes, sir."

"You know this means you're gone? You're already on conduct probation."

"I understand, sir."

Crenshaw contemplated him disgustedly "You don't really give a damn, do you? You want to leave."

Malone was silent.

"You figure a rich, pampered kid like yourself doesn't have any reason to put up with the hassle. That it? You going to work in the family firm? Get some cushy job on Wall Street where you can sit at a big desk and play grab-ass with your secretary?"

Malone still said nothing.

"What I don't understand, Malone," Crenshaw went on, "is why you did it this way. You've played by the rules for almost two years, yet lately you've been screwing up by the numbers. If you wanted to leave, you could have quit. Why make us throw you out?"

"It's the only way, sir."

"Only way for what?"

It was too complicated to explain, so Malone didn't bother.

Two days later, he was out-processed and escorted off the base. Before he left, Crenshaw told him he would regret leaving. "Maybe not now, but eventually. They all do."

"I doubt it, sir."

"You will. You're better than this. You're not a quitter, but that's what you did. You quit, took the easy way out."

Crap, Malone had thought. But in the ensuing years, Crenshaw's words gnawed at him. He told himself he had nothing to prove, but the compulsion grew. After graduating from Colorado State, he'd applied for Officer Candidate School with no expectation of being accepted. After all, he'd been tossed from the Academy and the last thing he thought was that the Air Force would take him back now.

They did.

Even then, he almost didn't join. Among the reasons

he'd orchestrated his departure from the Academy was he'd tired of the rigidity and blind obedience to the seemingly senseless regulations. Still, he had to admit it was the one place where he'd found acceptance and a sense of camaraderie he'd never before experienced. What finally swayed him was the realization that he had no other good options, nowhere else to go. His grandfather had passed away and with his mother's recent death from cancer, he had no family except for a father he barely knew. Malone was two when his father left and other than the generous court-mandated support checks, he'd had almost no contact from him. On his fourteenth birthday, Malone's mother finally explained his father's abandonment; he'd believed she'd tricked him into the marriage by becoming pregnant.

"He thinks I was after his money. It's me he's angry with, not you."

"Then why doesn't he want anything to do with me? I'm still his son."

"He will. Someday. Give him time."

But someday never came.

After his mother's funeral, Malone was surprised to see his father waiting for him in a limo. He was accompanied by his fourth wife, Molly, a big-haired redhead with a drop-dead figure and a reputation for using it. Molly sipped a martini and greeted Malone with a sloppy smile. She looked like she'd put on a little weight.

As usual, his father was all business, not even bothering with condolences over his ex-wife's death. With a trace of irritation, he announced, "You haven't returned my calls."

As if he actually expected Malone to do so.

Malone debated whether to tell him to go to hell or simply walk away. Before he could decide, his father thrust a folder through the window.

"What's this?"

"A quit-claim agreement for you to sign over your voting rights in the firm's board."

His father had tried once before to deny Malone his legacy, but his grandfather had intervened. "And if I don't sign . . ."

"I'll contest the terms of your grandfather's will."

"You'll lose. I satisfied his conditions."

"His intent was for you to graduate from a service academy. Since you never—"

"His terms stated I couldn't resign. I didn't."

An icy smile. "It doesn't matter. My lawyers will tie up your money with injunctions. You'll be an old man before you can spend another dime."

Malone had no doubt that his father would carry out his threat. He supposed he should have been angry; but he wasn't. He'd used up his anger long ago.

He took the file. "If everything is in order—"

"It is."

Watching him sign the documents, his father said, "I'm sorry it never worked out between us."

But he didn't look sorry. Malone shrugged. "I'm not. This way I don't feel guilty."

"Guilty?"

Malone stooped down, so he could see Molly. She

noticed him looking and giggled. Malone said to his father, "Remember when I was in New York to sign the acceptance of the will—"

"Yes."

He winked at Molly. "I invited her to my hotel and she accepted. I fucked her."

Molly gave a gasp and dropped her glass. His father turned bright red and snarled, "Why, you miserable son of—"

Malone tossed the folder into the car and calmly walked away.

Two months later, he was in Officer Candidate School. Because of his Academy experience, Malone breezed through training and had his pick of assignments. Since he was too tall to fly—he exceeded the ejection-seat height requirement—he chose the only other profession that held any interest.

Military criminal investigator.

What attracted him to the job was that it freed him from the usual military protocol. OSI investigators worked in civilian clothes and acted with an autonomy their uniformed counterparts could only dream about. To Malone, these benefits far outweighed his exclusion from the base social scene.

Over the years, Malone had solved a number of big cases and moved up the chain. While his superiors criticized his less-than-military demeanor and overly aggressive methods—he'd received letters of reprimand for insubordination and use of excessive force—they couldn't deny his results. Whenever a big case came down, it was invariably entrusted to Malone.

Upon receiving the assignment to head the Academy office—a job he'd lobbied hard for—Malone felt he'd come full circle. He'd never intended to make the military a career and considered separating when he learned Crenshaw would be the new superintendent. Crenshaw's appointment was made in response to a growing scandal in which one hundred forty-four women, mostly female cadets, alleged they'd been sexually harassed, intimidated, and/or raped. In the subsequent uproar, the majority of the Academy leadership—none who had been present when the incidents occurred—had been summarily dismissed. Crenshaw was being installed to conduct damage control, revamp the training system, and determine the extent of the sexual misconduct.

At the Officers' Club reception the night Crenshaw assumed command, Malone made a point of walking right up to him. When they came face to face, there was no look of shock or surprise on Crenshaw's face. Just the opposite; the general seemed to expect him.

He immediately drew Malone off to the side and blindsided him with the pronouncement: "I'm relieving you, Malone."

Just like that, after all these years. Malone was floored. "But why—"

The general was already telling him. "It's the scandal, Malone. Congress, the public, and the media are up in arms. As the OSI chief, you're going to be caught right in the middle. The pressure will be intense. You'll be investigated and your conclusions will be second-guessed. The bottom line is I need someone I can trust. Someone who won't cave in to the pressure when—"

"You mean quit," Malone said.

Crenshaw gave him a long look. "You quit once before."

"I was dismissed, sir."

"Still sticking to that song and dance, huh? Well, your reliability isn't my only concern. I've studied your record. Over 90 percent of your cases solved, but you're still a loose cannon. Jesus, you broke a suspect's arm—"

"He killed two people and resisted arrest."

"I don't give a damn. There's simply no justification for—"

"One victim was a child, General," Malone said. "The bastard raped and strangled her. The girl was five years old."

Crenshaw swallowed. "Jesus . . ."

A female colonel with a clipboard came over. "General, Senator Smith and Congressman Martin have arrived."

Crenshaw eyed Malone. "They're here to provide guidance on the scandal. That's the kind of scrutiny you'll be under."

"A chance, sir. I'm only asking for a chance to prove you're wrong about me."

"I'm sorry, but I can't afford—"

"You were wrong about me before. If I am a quitter, would I be here, sir? Would I?"

Crenshaw didn't reply. Malone realized he'd planted a seed of doubt.

The colonel said, "General, the senator wants to get started right away. He's on a tight schedule—"

Crenshaw shot her a look and she clammed up.

"All right, Malone," he said reluctantly. "You can remain in place for now. You check out each allegation and report directly to me. You cross every *i* and dot every *t*. You give no one an opportunity to second-guess your findings, you understand?"

"I understand, sir."

"One fuck-up and you're gone."

"Yes, sir."

Since that conversation last summer, Malone had investigated eight of the most serious allegations. In each case, his methods had been thorough and above reproach. Only last week, Crenshaw had complimented his work.

Only last week . . .

"Shit," Malone muttered.

He followed Major Wilson up Interior Drive. They were on the back side of the Academy, against the mountains, the planetarium and the chapel's gleaming aluminum spires just ahead. In between stood a long building resembling a bread pan with feet.

It was Harmon Hall, the office of the superintendent. As Malone pulled into the parking area and retrieved his overcoat from the backseat, he recalled a popular military ditty, one that explained his predicament.

All it takes is one fuck-up to wipe out a hundred 'atta-boys.

Chapter 2

SPARTAN. FUTURISTIC. ANGULAR.

Those words described the Air Force Academy architecture and Harmon Hall mirrored that theme. It was a chrome-and-glass three-story rectangle covered by glittering red tiles. The ground level consisted of two square pedestals, which supported the upper floors and housed the stairs and elevators. From the exterior, it was easy to pick out the superintendent's third-floor office. It overlooked the cadet area and was the only one with a balcony.

Seated behind his desk in a spacious paneled office and surrounded by two full colonels, a one-star general, and a woman in a business suit, Lieutenant General Neal Crenshaw made no attempt to hide his anger as he hunched over a speaker, listening to a tinny voice. A rail-thin black man with closely mowed gray hair and intense eyes, the general was not someone accustomed to being talked down to, but that was precisely what was occurring now.

The honorable Kevin Smith, the senior senator from

Colorado and the person behind the Senate panel investigating the Academy's sex scandal, was ticking off a list of demands. With each one, the general's jaw knotted perceptibly. Glancing at the woman, he noted her look of satisfaction.

Bitch, Crenshaw thought.

When the senator fell silent, a hiss of expectation followed. Crenshaw said nothing; Smith wasn't waiting for his response.

The Secretary of Defense's voice cracked over the speaker. "Senator, we can agree to most of your conditions—"

"*All*, Mr. Secretary. The American people need assurances there won't be a cover-up."

"Senator, that charge is out of line—"

"Is it? Your people covered up dozens of rapes."

"*Unproven* charges of rape. You've seen the reports. We didn't have the evidence to pursue—"

"Reports written by your investigators. Look, you do what you have to do. But if you go against me on this, I'll go on the floor and demand a complete investigation into *your* handling of this affair."

"Now just a damn minute—"

"I also intend to contact the president and the majority leader. I'm sure I can convince them to appoint an independent counsel. In my estimation, that's the preferable approach, but it will take time. Still, if you force my hand . . ."

"Okay. *Okay*. Your representative can monitor the investigation."

"Monitor? I want her raised to the level of a coinvestigator. She'll have full authority to request documents, conduct interviews—"

"She already has that authority."

"Through the subcommittee panel's subpoena power. Again that takes time. I'm talking about immediate access. Passwords, entry badges, the works."

A long hiss. The woman in the business suit resisted the urge to smile. The four officers traded worried glances. The senator had the SECDEF by the nuts and was squeezing hard.

The SECDEF sighed audibly. "Okay. She's on the team."

"I knew you'd see it my way. You don't want to be caught in the middle of this thing, believe me." Senator Smith paused, adding ominously, "Oh, one more thing. Tell your people not to fuck with her or I'll have their asses." He clicked off.

"You heard the man, General," the SECDEF said. "We cooperate fully. Any questions?"

Crenshaw looked to the one-star, Brigadier General Timothy Scully, the commandant of cadets and the person responsible for overseeing cadet discipline. The Com shook his head.

"No, sir," Crenshaw said.

"Answers, General. I want answers and fast."

"Yes, sir."

Another click and the SECDEF was gone.

Crenshaw punched off his speaker, looking at the woman. Even though she'd been conducting her investigation for several weeks, he couldn't get used to the sight of her. It was unnerving.

"There are more reliable investigators," he said to her. "Certainly ones with less professional baggage. In light of this latest incident, his character could be an issue. I suggest you reconsider—"

"I read through his personnel file, General. He's the perfect choice."

Crenshaw tensed at her remark. He'd suspected her presence here hadn't been mere coincidence, and now there seemed little doubt. The Academy was in serious trouble.

"Come in," he said, reacting to the knock on the door.

Overkill.

When Malone followed Major Wilson into the office and saw the other senior officers, he was convinced General Crenshaw intended to dress him down in front of the Academy's hierarchy, thoroughly humiliate him before firing him.

Then his eyes drifted to the right and he saw the woman. His knees almost buckled and he told himself he had to be mistaken. It was impossible, it couldn't be her.

Dead people don't come back to life.

Christina Barlow had been a cheerleader, a fourth-class cadet in his squadron. Malone could still recall almost the precise moment when he last saw her. It was in late October of his third-class year, and they lived across the hall from each other. When Malone heard hysterical crying, he rushed from his room and found a crowd outside her door. Pushing through, he saw Christina sitting on her bed, sobbing uncontrollably and hugging a blanket around her bare shoulders. She appeared nude underneath and there were bruises on her wrists, where ropes had cut into the flesh. A upper-class female cadet was kneeling beside her, asking her what happened, but Christina wouldn't answer.

Until she saw all the faces staring at her. Male faces.

"They raped me," she screamed. "They raped me."

"Who raped you, Christina?" the female cadet asked. "Which ones?"

"All of them. All of them."

Later, Malone realized she had been right. In a way, they all *had* raped her.

When he heard about her death from a mutual friend a few years later, Malone assumed she'd committed suicide. Christina had been so traumatized by the rape that she'd suffered a massive breakdown and had been institutionalized.

"All I know," the friend had said, "is she died in a car accident. Drove off a cliff or something."

The woman smiled broadly, enjoying Malone's reaction. She looked as beautiful as he remembered. Shoulder-length auburn hair cascaded down the side of her face, hugging wide cheekbones and flawless skin. Her eyes were still an opaque green, matching the business suit that clung to her willowy frame. But what finally convinced Malone was her height. The one characteristic that was undeniable.

She was an Amazon who stood over six feet.

Major Wilson went over to General Crenshaw, handed him Malone's weapon, holster, and credentials, and quickly withdrew. For several beats, no one spoke. Malone became aware of disapproving stares, a reaction to his stubble and roadmap eyes. It took him two attempts before he formed a response. "My God, it can't be . . ."

"No," General Crenshaw said. "It's not Christina."

"Kaitlin," the woman said. "I'm Kaitlin Barlow, Christina's twin. She probably mentioned me."

Fourteen years was a long time, and Malone tried to recall—

"It doesn't matter."

Kaitlin came forward and they shook hands. Her grip was firm, lingering on his longer than necessary. She wore designer gloves and hadn't bothered to remove them. She said, "Christina spoke of you, how you tried to help her. Thank you."

Malone was surprised by the familiarity of her perfume. "I wish . . . I wish I could have done more."

"We all did."

An awkward silence fell upon the room. Everyone was familiar with Christina's story, but then they should be. It was the worst sexual assault incident in Academy history and had come to be known as the Mickey Mouse rape. In the early morning hours, Christina had been accosted in her dorm room, threatened with a knife, bound and gagged, carried to the soundproofed TV room, and gang raped. When it was over, her attackers left her tied between two large sofas, where she was found the next morning. Despite the brutality of the rape, it had been conducted with precision. To lessen the chances they could be identified, her attackers had worn masks of Disney characters, covered her head with a laundry bag, spoken in unrecognizable whispers, and used rubbers. They had also been careful to vacuum her pubic area and the carpet, ensuring they left behind no hairs that could be linked to them.

Their efforts proved successful. Not a single rapist was ever identified.

They all got away.

Kaitlin briefly closed her eyes as if willing away the memory. Refocusing on Malone, her tone became clipped and professional. "I'm an attorney on Senator Smith's staff. He assigned me to replace Todd Jensen as the primary investigator for the sexual misconduct panel."

"I see." But of course Malone didn't see, not completely. Like Crenshaw, he found it more than coincidental that she would be placed in this role.

Kaitlin Barlow stepped back and addressed Crenshaw. "I'd like to get going, General. I'll brief Agent Malone on the way."

Crenshaw nodded, but didn't look happy about it.

"On the way?" Malone said. "Where?"

Kaitlin continued talking to Crenshaw. "To avoid confusion, General, I'd like the appropriate agencies informed of my status. Hospital personnel, Security Forces, local law enforcement—"

"We'll see to it," Crenshaw said.

She fingered the access badge clipped to her lapel. "I also need this proxy card upgraded to one without restrictions." Proxy cards were a post-9/11 security enhancement—digitized swipe cards that allowed entry into the various buildings in the cadet area.

"Chuck," Crenshaw said.

One of the colonels pivoted and left the room. Crenshaw said to Kaitlin, "You can pick up a temporary badge from Admin on your way out. Anything else?"

"Not at the moment."

Malone's curiosity meter was pegged out on high. Not only hadn't anyone mentioned his DWI, but Crenshaw appeared to be taking orders from Kaitlin. Another sexual incident? Had to be. Why else would Kaitlin be calling the shots?

"We're conducting an investigation," Kaitlin said to Malone. "You'll need your credentials. I assume you have a car, Nathan? You go by Nathan?"

"Yes. I prefer Malone."

"Fine. You drive." She snatched a coat, purse, and briefcase from a chair and turned for the door.

Malone moved toward Crenshaw's desk and found himself confronted by a piercing scowl. "If it was up to me," Crenshaw growled, "you'd be out of a job. As far as I'm concerned, you still might."

"Yes, sir."

"Next time, you better have a shave. You're not a civilian; quit trying to act like one."

"Yes, sir."

Crenshaw shook his head and pushed over Malone's credentials, holster, and weapon. As Malone donned the items the general's irritation faded.

"Don't quit on me. I'm counting on you."

Malone was struck by the emotional undercurrent in his voice. He nodded slowly. "The case we're investigating, sir? I imagine it's—"

Kaitlin called out, "Let's go, Malone. We're wasting time."

He glanced back, saw her motioning impatiently. As he hurried toward her, Crenshaw made a parting remark, but it wasn't the response he expected.

"Watch her," he said. "She thinks you're perfect for this job."

Chapter 3

THE INSTANT MALONE AND KAITLIN LEFT, THE Com swung around to Crenshaw. "Sir, how the hell did she get hold of Malone's personnel file?"

"Base personnel. She handed them a subpoena and a list of names."

"A list?" the Com said.

"Seven names, Tim. All but Malone were senior Academy leadership."

It took the Com a second. "She's got *my* personnel records."

"Mine and Marv's, too," Crenshaw said, glancing at the remaining colonel, Colonel Marvin Greenley, a vice commandant of cadets. "And it gets worse. DIS also turned over their background investigations for our security clearances."

The Com's face darkened. The Defense Investigative Service exhaustively researched a person's past, to ensure his or her reliability. Kaitlin Barlow would know extremely private details about his professional and personal life.

"Sir," the Com snapped, "this is a violation of our rights. She's out of control."

"Don't act so surprised, Tim. Why the hell do you think she took over the investigation? The damn thing is stalled and they're desperate to find evidence to support a conviction. Something to parade in front of the cameras. Well, they've got what they wanted now. If it turns out a cadet is responsible . . ." He grimaced without finishing the thought.

"Sir, she pulled *our* records. We're not the ones under investigation."

"It's another power play, like Senator Smith's conference call. To make sure we know who's in charge." Crenshaw addressed the colonel. "Marv, better tell Public Affairs to arrange a press conference ASAP. If we don't make an announcement soon—"

"Smith will," the Com said angrily. "He's probably slapping high fives over what happened."

Crenshaw voiced no disagreement; there was truth in the Com's damning indictment. A vacillating politician with no core values to guide him, Smith had lost the confidence of his constituency and was given little chance to win a third term. When the Academy scandal broke, Smith saw an opportunity for political salvation and seized upon it, painting himself as the champion of women's rights. For months, he relentlessly criticized the Air Force as being unresponsive and uncaring, and accused the Academy leadership of a well-orchestrated cover-up. His public onslaught achieved the desired effect; within weeks, the Academy leadership was replaced and Smith's poll numbers began to climb.

Did the senator truly believe that the plight of female cadets who'd been assaulted was a worthy cause? Probably. But what angered Crenshaw and the Air Force was the blatant manner with which Smith twisted the truth. He continually cited the number 144, as if that represented proven cases of sexual assault. In reality, the majority of those incidents—over 80 percent—were *anonymous* allegations made to a hotline. The actual numbers supported by evidence were far lower, no more than twenty. And even those had little chance of getting an actual conviction.

In a private meeting with Smith, Crenshaw had asked the senator what he would have done when confronted with cases of "he said, she said," where there was no corroborating evidence.

"Do you want us to arbitrarily accept the word of the female, Senator?"

"Of course not. My issue is fairness. I would expect a thorough and objective investigation."

"We've done that. There is no semen, no torn clothing, no witnesses, nothing."

"Come now, General. Surely there must be some supporting evidence—"

"In most instances, the attacks went unreported, often for years. All we have is her word against his. What would *you* do, Senator? Who would *you* punish?"

Passing on a response, Smith informed the general that he empathized with the difficulty of the military's position. The senator made the statement with a smile, his tone completely sincere.

The next day, he stood on the Senate floor and

accused Crenshaw of stonewalling the investigation.

Crenshaw rubbed his eyes, feeling suddenly tired. He'd worked so hard to turn things around. Now, when he was so close . . .

Colonel Greenley gave a little cough. Crenshaw sighed, squinting at him. "What'd I forget, Marv?"

"The game, sir. If you've made a decision, we need to inform Public Affairs."

"Postpone it." The Com nodded his agreement; no choice.

As Greenley left, the Com said, "What about the AD and Coach Ralston, sir?"

His tone held a note of caution, making it clear what he was really asking. While the generals had no concerns about the athletic director, Ralston was another matter. A young coach who'd gotten the job because he'd been an Academy football star, his team's success had inflated his ego to the point where he'd become impossible to deal with. If Ralston considered a policy detrimental to his players, he immediately voiced a complaint to Crenshaw or the Com; if he didn't receive satisfaction, he went over their heads to the Air Force chief. Crenshaw had put up with Ralston's antics out of necessity; the football team provided a necessary distraction from the scandal.

"You notify the AD," Crenshaw said. "I'll handle Coach Ralston."

The Com remained dubious. "He'll call the Chief, sir. You know he will. There isn't enough time to make up the game. It'll cost the team a chance to play for the BCS."

"Ralston," Crenshaw said grimly, "won't call the chief. He'll do exactly what I damn well tell him. Now give me a couple minutes, Tim. And have Mrs. Weaver hold my calls."

"Yes, sir."

As the Com headed off, Crenshaw's eyes dropped to the two blue files on his desk. Each was stamped with an Academy crest and a name. Opening the topmost one, he saw a smiling face. He slowly, almost reverentially touched the image, unaware the Com had paused in the doorway and was watching him.

"Bullshit rumors," the Com said.

But he looked uneasy as he left.

As Malone and Kaitlin exited Harmon Hall, he kept waiting for her to give him a chance to speak, but she continued with a running commentary on a subject he was already knowledgeable about—himself.

Kaitlin seemed to know everything about him. She spoke of his mother's death, his estrangement from his father, his family's wealth, practically his entire history. She'd obviously done her homework, and thanks to Crenshaw's remark, Malone had a growing suspicion why.

He gestured to his car and they walked toward it. Kaitlin kept up her nonstop chatter. She discussed his short-lived Academy stay and assessed his OSI career. Specifically, she focused on the less-than-favorable comments found in his performance evaluations and his letters of reprimand.

"There's a definite pattern," she said. "While you're a

solid investigator, you don't give a damn about proper procedure and tend to overreact. You also have trouble with authority. I can't believe you told off a two-star general. That's a trip. It really is."

Malone's second letter of reprimand. He started to explain that the general had been obstructing his investigation, but Kaitlin talked right over him.

"From your record," she said, "I'm surprised the military ever promoted you. I thought they wanted team players and that's something you're not. You're not a member of the team."

As easy as that. The confirmation Malone had been seeking.

Crossing the road onto the parking lot, Kaitlin abruptly faced him. "Mind a personal question?"

"You serious?" he said dryly.

She ignored him. "It's something General Crenshaw mentioned. He was trying to convince me why you shouldn't be on the case—"

"Surprise, surprise."

"You arranged to be kicked out of the Academy. Why?"

She knew his grandfather had willed him money, so he explained the conditions. She said, "Nice granddad. He tried to make up for your dad, huh?"

"Somewhat."

"Why tie the money to your attendance at an academy?"

They resumed walking. "He wanted me to get discipline."

"Obviously, that didn't work."

He let it go.

"So," she pressed, "how much money did you inherit? Several million? Five? Ten?"

"Quite a bit."

"I can find out with a couple phone calls."

"Quite a bit."

She surrendered with a smile. Dimpled, like her sister's. Looking at her, Malone had to remind himself that she wasn't Christina.

Approaching the car, Malone dug out his keys and thumbed the door release. "A BMW," Kaitlin said, shaking her head. "It's all image with you, isn't it? The car, the clothes. That Rolex."

Behave, Malone. "I like nice things."

"Including women?"

Malone heard the challenge in her voice. She had him pegged and couldn't resist baiting him. He went with it and said, "Especially women."

And he ran his eyes over her in a suggestive way.

Her face flushed. She was flustered and had no idea how to react. Twice she appeared on the verge of speaking, but nothing came out. She gave up and hurried around him to get to the passenger door. As she did, she caught a heel on the curb and stumbled, banging her knee against the bumper. She swore.

"You okay?" Malone asked, reaching out to her.

She jerked back as if scalded.

"Hey, hey," he said. "I don't bite."

She rubbed her knee, glowering. "Let's get one thing straight. I'm not interested."

"In?"

"*You.*"

Malone gazed over the parking area with amusement. "You think I'm going to jump you right here?"

She straightened warily. "I know you, Malone. I *know* you."

Malone smiled pleasantly. "Crap," he announced loudly.

She blinked.

"Your research is crap. I'm not some oversexed, undisciplined Neanderthal—"

"If the shoe fits—"

"What I *am* is an Air Force officer. I *obey* orders. I don't buck the system unless I have a helluva good reason. I'm also not some ticked-off former cadet bearing a grudge; I *wanted* to be kicked out of the Academy, remember? All in all, I'd say you blew it. I'm not your perfect choice."

Understanding swam across her beautiful face. "General Crenshaw?"

Malone nodded. "You took this job because of what happened to your sister. The more dirt you can dig up against the Academy, the better." Her eyes turned cold. "Look," he said, "I'm not judging you—"

"Like hell."

"You deny you have an agenda?"

A silence. She did a slow burn and Malone waited for an eruption. None came.

In a controlled voice—a lawyer's voice—she said, "I could express the same concerns about you. For all I know, you'd cover up a crime to protect the Academy."

"Only to get laid." She had asked for it.

Kaitlin stiffened, but kept her composure. "Agent Malone," she said formally, "do you believe the panel's investigation is a waste of time?"

"*Agent* Malone?"

"Answer the question."

Malone hesitated. "No. It led to needed changes. Female cadets now feel free to report any harassment."

"I'm referring to the past harassment allegations. Should they be investigated?"

"I'm *conducting* those investigations, remember?"

"With a notable lack of success."

"You're the attorney. You know we can't prosecute without evidence, but that isn't for lack of trying."

"It isn't?" Her eyes measured him. "How do you explain what happened to my sister and her treatment by the administration?"

Malone had known this question was coming. He was tempted to say Christina was partly at fault; she'd played with fire by throwing her sexuality around. But that didn't excuse what had happened to her.

Nothing did.

"The Academy tried to find those responsible—"

She snorted.

He said, "Could they have done more? You better believe it. But the truth is—"

"*The truth* is the investigation failed because the administration *wanted* it to fail. An arrest would have meant a trial and a scandal. To save the Academy's precious reputation and their even more precious careers, the generals let my sister's attackers walk. You deny it?"

Christ. "Listen, the OSI did everything possible to

find your sister's rapists—" She was about to interrupt and he added quickly, "I'm not saying your concerns aren't valid. But you're talking about something that took place in 1991. The culture was different. What happened to your sister would never—"

He broke off. She was giving him a superior smile and he realized he'd strolled into her set-up line. "Okay, okay," he said. "There's been another rape, but that doesn't necessarily reflect—"

"That was only the motive."

"Motive?"

"A double homicide. The bodies of two female cadets were found in Jack's Valley. Near a place called Dead Man's Lake."

"Oh, Jesus—"

"One victim was a girl who confided in me that she'd been raped. The second was her roommate. I'd say that throws a wrench into your change-of-culture theory." She opened the passenger door, looking at him coolly. "By the way, you're also wrong about why I wanted you. It's because my sister said you were the one person who tried to protect her. I guess I made a mistake. Now do me a favor and get in the fucking car, *Agent* Malone."

She climbed inside and shut the door with a bang.

As Malone climbed behind the wheel, he was still reeling from the stunning revelation. He felt her watching him and waited for her to say something.

But she just sat there, staring.

He sat in silence until they turned north onto

Academy Drive, heading down the sweeping hill toward Jack's Valley. "You going to tell me the rest of it?"

"I haven't decided."

"If we're going to work together—"

"I haven't decided."

"Little late to have me removed, isn't it?"

"I haven't decided."

A power play to prove her clout? Or did she really harbor doubts about him?

Malone realized there was one thing he could say to convince her. It was related to the ground rules the Senate panel negotiated. To prevent their investigation from being a complete witch hunt, they could only look at cases dating back to 1995.

Four years too late for Kaitlin.

"I've opened Christina's file," Malone said. "I run down leads in my free time."

No response. He saw her suspicion.

"It's one of the reasons I came here. I liked your sister and promised myself I'd find the bastards who raped her."

Kaitlin's suspicion slowly faded. She even managed a tiny smile.

"I knew I was right about you."

She finally told him about the murders.

Chapter 4

WHEN GENERAL CRENSHAW CALLED COACH RALston and informed him the game was postponed because two cadets had been murdered, the coach reacted precisely as anticipated. He exploded in a stream of profanity, calling Crenshaw's decision unnecessary and asinine, and demanding the general reconsider. It was a shockingly callous response, but one Crenshaw understood. It came down to money; the greater the team's success, the more big-name schools would be throwing high dollar contracts in Coach Ralston's face.

As Ralston ranted, Crenshaw tried to tell him to be quiet, but the coach was too incensed to listen. He said, "I'm sorry two cadets are dead, but this is a goddamn overreaction. *You're* overreacting, General. Canceling the game serves no fucking purpose. My boys busted their asses and have an opportunity to play in the national championship. *The national championship.* Now you're punishing them because you believe it's somehow inappropriate—"

Crenshaw interrupted him angrily. "Coach, you don't know the facts—"

"Have you told the Chief? I'm betting you haven't.

He knows how important we are to Air Force morale. There's no way he'd agree to—"

"*Shut the hell up, Coach.*"

That finally got through to Ralston. On the other end of the phone, Crenshaw finally heard silence.

"Now listen to me," Crenshaw growled. "You're in trouble. If you're not careful, everything will come out."

"Come out? What are you talking about?" His tone was insolent.

Crenshaw revealed the names of the victims. That was all that was necessary. There was a sharp intake of breath on the other end. When Ralston spoke, his voice was strained, his insolence gone.

"What do we do, General?" he asked.

Jack's Valley.

To Air Force Academy grads, it's a hallowed place, remembered with equal parts trepidation and pride in achievement. Home to the assault course, pugil stick wars, and endless marches, Jack's Valley was where new cadets spent much of their first summer having their civilian veneer ground away and resurfaced with the base coat of a military officer. The sense of achievement comes not from conquering the valley or even having performed adequately, but having simply endured.

A dirt road abeam the western edge of the athletic fields marked the entrance to Jack's. Normally, it wouldn't be guarded, but this morning a Security Forces SUV with flashing lights was parked ominously by the turnoff.

A burly security cop wearing a technical sergeant's

chevrons on his blue beret stepped forward as Malone drove up. The cop appeared surprised by the sight of the OSI chief and immediately waved the car through. A couple of hundred yards later, Kaitlin and Malone arrived at another checkpoint blocking the apex of the road, where it forked. To the right lay the winding heart of the valley; straight ahead, their destination. Two security policemen motioned them to the shoulder, where almost a dozen vehicles—civilian and military— were wedged in a haphazard line. One was a base hospital ambulance and two were El Paso County SUVs— the local police forensic teams supported the OSI during major crimes investigations. Malone didn't spot the county coroner's van, but he did notice a battered pickup. Its presence saved him a phone call.

"Preserving tire tracks?" Kaitlin said, remarking on the obvious. Unlike General Crenshaw and the Com, she hadn't previously visited the crime scene.

"Footprints, too." Malone nosed in behind the ambulance. "The trail to Dead Man's Lake is just around the bend."

Leaving the car, they heard voices filtering toward them. Through the bare trees, they glimpsed movement in a clearing where the left fork dead-ended. Malone walked up to the ambulance and rapped on the driver's window. He returned with packets of aspirin and several pairs of latex gloves.

He choked down two of the aspirin packets dry. Watching him, Kaitlin said lightly, "A little hungover?"

"A lot hungover," Malone corrected unapologetically. He snapped on latex gloves and offered her a pair.

She shook him off, holding up her hands. She wore driving gloves, with leather palms and fabric fingers.

"Don't touch anything," he said. "You could contaminate the scene with fibers."

"I *am* an attorney."

"You ever investigated a murder?"

"Of course not."

"Investigated *any* crime?"

"No, but—"

"Don't touch anything unless you clear it with me."

She spun and walked away. Malone shrugged. She had to know he was in charge.

Crossing the snow toward the security cops, they passed a group of people leaning against a county van. Malone recognized Britt Dixon, a criminalist he'd worked with in the past.

Britt threw up a hand. "Hey, Malone, tell Mother to hurry it up. We're freezing our asses off."

"It won't do any good, Britt." Mother never let anyone poke around a crime scene until she was done checking it out.

"Humor me. My kid's got a hockey game at one."

Malone threw up a dismissive wave.

"For the middle-school *championship*."

"Who is Mother?" Kaitlin asked Malone.

"My senior civilian investigator. Mother spent a career in the Air Force before—"

He broke off; they reached the two security cops. Like their counterpart, both were mystified to see Malone. Obviously, the Security Forces betting pool had given heavy odds that he would be canned.

"The crime scene is over there, sir," one of the cops said, pointing to the clearing that had come into view.

"Thank you," Malone said.

"For crying out loud, Malone!" an exasperated voice called out. "How could you do something so *stupid?*"

In the clearing, Malone saw the wooden sign marking the trail to Dead Man's Lake. Several of his men were standing nearby, inspecting the snowy ground. To their right, wearing a bulky yellow coat, stood a stout woman with flaming red hair. Her hands were on her hips and she was glaring disgustedly at Malone.

"Meet Mother," Malone said to Kaitlin.

When Marva "Mother" Hubbard left the Air Force after a twenty-three-year career, she never envisioned returning as a civilian investigator. To her, the position would have been a demotion, essentially the reason she'd retired in the first place. A tireless investigator, Mother had the drive and ambition to become the first woman to rise to the top of the OSI pecking order. By rights, she should have succeeded, but her combative nature and brutally caustic personality got in the way. Over the years, she bruised too many egos—male egos—ultimately sealing her professional fate. When she was passed over for that final promotion, she retired rather than accept the second-best offer.

It was a mistake. Twice divorced and childless—she was called Mother precisely because no one could be any less nurturing—Mother's job was how she'd come to define her life. When that was gone, so was her reason for existing.

Swallowing her considerable pride, Mother made phone calls, inquiring about the possibility of civilian OSI billets. Initially, everyone turned her down; she'd made too many enemies and no one wanted her back in the service. After a year, a general who'd owed her a favor finally pulled a few strings on her behalf, but only after he judged her sincerity to a question he posed.

"Can you do it, Mother? Can you take orders?"

"Yes, sir. Absolutely."

"I mean it. You won't be in charge. You'll only be an agent."

"I understand completely, sir. Believe me, it's not a problem."

Mother, of course, had lied through her teeth.

"The *big* head," Mother said, as Malone and Kaitlin started over. "How many times have I told you to think with the big head? You're a *commander*, Malone. You're supposed to set an example for the men."

The OSI men grinned. "Now her," Kaitlin announced cheerfully, "I like already."

Malone said nothing. They kept walking. The snow wasn't deep, no more than an inch or so.

"How come you let her talk to you this way?"

"Implying I have a choice?"

"You don't? You're the boss, right?"

"Mother," Malone said, "retired as a full colonel."

Kaitlin stared at him.

By now they were almost to Mother. "Maturity, Malone," Mother said sarcastically. "Look it up sometime. You can't spend your life chasing skirts in bars."

"She wasn't wearing a skirt," Malone deadpanned.

"Treat it like a joke. You're damn lucky you weren't relieved—" She squinted at Kaitlin. "I know you?"

"The Barlow case," Malone said. "Kaitlin was the victim's twin sister. She's working for Senator Smith."

"Right," Mother said to Kaitlin. "We got the word. Small world. I never made a connection when I heard your name. Malone tell you I was the investigator initially assigned to your sister's case? No? I'm sorry about Christina. Believe me, if there was any chance of finding the bastards—"

Kaitlin interrupted her. "Agent Malone said he's reopened the case."

Mother appeared surprised at the remark. She frowned at Malone before answering Kaitlin.

"We've reopened the case," she said. "But I wouldn't get your hopes up. We had over a dozen suspects, but they all had rock-solid alibis. That's not likely to change."

"My sister believed her attackers were athletes."

"Football players," Mother corrected. "As a cheerleader, she traveled with the team, so they would have known her. Her attackers were also pretty big guys, which fit. She gave us the names of eight players who hit on her, made comments. But they all had alibis. It was over a weekend and five were crashed out at the same house, after a party."

"Convenient," Kaitlin said.

Mother studied her, her voice turning quiet. "I tried to break their stories. I . . . tried."

The two women gazed at each other and something unspoken passed between them.

"I'm sure you did," Kaitlin said.

She sounded as if she meant it, but as she turned away, her expression became troubled. Noticing, Malone said, "It's true, Kaitlin. Mother did all she could."

"Even questioned Malone," Mother said.

Kaitlin looked at Malone in surprise. "You were a suspect?"

"His size," Mother said, "and he lived across the hall."

Kaitlin said, "Surely my sister never accused Malone."

"No, and Malone didn't play football. But we had to check out everyone in the squadron. Like I said, it's a small world. You, Malone, me, all turning up here. Wish it was under better circumstances. Well, I suppose you'll want to take a look. I warn you, it's pretty rough."

Without waiting for a reply, Mother headed off to show them the bodies.

The sign by the footpath said "Dead Man's Lake." Kaitlin grimly shook her head at the irony. She was following Mother, Malone bringing up the rear.

Since the lake was only a quarter-mile away, it would be a short trek, which was good news for Kaitlin. She wore boots with heels, placing fashion above practicality. On the trail, they saw footprints in the snow and were careful to stay off to the side.

"Bodies are about twenty yards before the lake," Mother explained. "Found by a couple of fourth classmen around 0500. Kranski's up in the dorms, interviewing them now. Won't get much. They were sneaking onto the lake ice to spray-paint a sign for the game. Should have checked the weather before wasting their time. It's supposed to get into the forties by noon."

Fourth classmen were encouraged to show spirit before games. The wackier, the better. Malone asked, "You secure the victims' room?"

"Kranski arranged it with the SPs. I sent Morrissey to check out their gym lockers. The security cops are also in the process of impounding their cars."

As usual, Mother was on top of things. Malone asked her when it had started to snow.

"Around 2100. It's pretty clear the victims were dead long before then, so we can forget about any footprints belonging to the killer. Oops, you okay?" Looking back, Mother saw Kaitlin slip on an icy patch and almost fall.

"Fine," she said, continuing unsteadily. "The girls were shot, right?"

"More like executed," Mother answered.

Malone and Kaitlin looked at her.

"See for yourself," Mother said, coming to a stop. She pointed to the left, at an open area cordoned off by yellow crime scene tape and surrounded by Security cops. In the middle of the perimeter was a gnarled bush, an object poking through the base.

It was an arm.

Chapter 5

"OH, GOD . . ."

Kaitlin turned away and faced the frozen lake, unable to look more. She, Malone, and Mother had walked about ten paces from the trail, to where two bodies lay crumpled behind the large bush, several yards apart. Both victims wore Academy varsity running suits; one was a darkly complected brunette, the second, a noticeably shorter black girl. The impression was they were pretty, but it was hard to tell for sure because portions of their foreheads were missing and frozen blood obscured their faces.

"You okay?" Mother asked Kaitlin.

She nodded gamely and forced herself to take another look.

"Their names," Malone said. "Tell me their names again."

Kaitlin preempted Mother's reply and pointed to the brunette with a shaky finger. "That's Mary Zinnel, the roommate . . ." Her finger shifted. ". . . and Rachel Owen. She's the one I told you about, Malone."

"You *knew* them?" Mother said.

"I . . . yes. I only spoke to them yesterday. I finally convinced Rachel to . . . to come forward . . ." Kaitlin had to turn away again.

"Rape," Malone said to Mother. "Rachel Owen was raped several months ago and had finally decided to report it."

"Oh, hell." Mother scowled angrily. "She identify the guy? No?"

Kaitlin was shaking her head. "She wouldn't tell me. Not until we could guarantee her protection. She was afraid of him, what he might do." She struggled with her emotions. "This is my fault. If I hadn't pushed her . . ."

"No," Mother said sharply. "Don't go there."

"But I'm the one who—"

"Told her to report a crime. That's *all*."

Kaitlin nodded dully, her face still laden with guilt. Malone found her reaction curious. Obviously, his earlier assessment was mistaken; she wasn't as tough as the image she tried to convey.

He carefully squatted over Mary Zinnel, noting that she'd twisted against the bush as she'd fallen, her left elbow planting awkwardly in the ground. It was her arm they had seen.

"She was standing when she was shot," he said. "One round into the back of her head. Hollow point, judging by the damage."

"Killer wanted to make damn sure he got the job done," Mother said.

Using a pen, Malone parted Mary's hair, revealing

the scalp. "Killer probably used a handgun fired at close range; you can see the stippling." Stippling was burn marks left by gunpowder residue.

"One foot. No more than two." Mother watched Malone study the ground. "We'll have to brush away the snow to find the shell casings. Shouldn't take long." Seeing Malone was about to say something, she added, "And yeah, I got the SPs searching the Dumpsters for the weapon."

Malone nodded.

When they first worked together, he'd found Mother's habit of voicing what he was thinking annoying. But he soon realized it was just an assurance her ego needed, to prove she was more than his equal. It's one reason he'd made her the officer in charge of crime scenes; she could play the boss without interference from him, freeing him to run down leads.

Malone studied the thin layer of snow covering the body. Mother said automatically, "No melting. It's the same depth as the ground, little more than an inch."

Confirming the girls had grown completely cold before the snow started. It made sense; the victims wouldn't have jogged in the dark.

"Were they reported missing?" Malone asked, rising.

"Sergeant Boller was going to check. Hey, Boller!" She scanned the faces of the security cops, pausing at a technical sergeant standing by the edge of the lake. "You call the duty desk about a missing person?"

"No report was called in, ma'am."

Cadets who'd used up their monthly pass privileges sometimes resorted to sneaking off base. When they were discovered missing, the Air Officer Commanding often notified the Security Forces, so the cadets could be picked up once they tried to reenter.

"They were from Eighteenth Squadron," Mother said to Malone. "The AOC will know for sure. His name is Topper—"

"Tupper," Kaitlin corrected. "Major Brad Tupper. He's Army." This wasn't unusual; other services sent personnel to the Air Force Academy as part of an exchange program.

Malone asked Mother if anyone had notified Tupper of the murders.

"The Com handled it." She checked her watch. "Tupper should be at the squadron by now, waiting to talk to us. I told Kranski to swing by when he finishes questioning the fourth classmen. You want him to begin the interview or—"

"I'd better handle it. Did General Crenshaw issue a recall yet?" A cadet recall was standard procedure during an emergency.

"About an hour ago. Since it's a football weekend, the cadets would have stayed close. Most should be back pretty soon." Even if cadets signed out for the weekend, they were required to attend home football games.

Malone stepped over to study Rachel Owen, who had fallen spread-eagled on her stomach, hands splayed to the side, head tilted to the left. In contrast to her roommate, Rachel's entry wound wasn't centered on the back of her head, but was located above the left ear. Her distance from Mary, coupled with the absence of stippling and her apparent forward momentum as she fell, suggested what had happened.

"She tried to run when Mary was shot," Malone said. Mother nodded.

A grim silence followed as each pictured the killings, how they had played out.

"Varsity runners," Mother said quietly. "The killer must have known they trained along this route. Mary could have been at the wrong place at the wrong time—" She saw Malone's head shake. "I agree. They were roommates; the killer would assume Rachel told Mary who raped her. So she had to go, too."

Mother looked down the trail, the way they'd come. "He waited for them at the edge of the clearing. If he was a first or second classman, he'd have a car, but I figure he walked or jogged. Less chance of being noticed. Pulled a gun and forced them back here. Christ. Two young girls, blown away because some sick son of a bitch—"

"Three," Kaitlin said.

Mother squinted at the remark, but Malone knew what was coming.

"Three," Kaitlin repeated. "There might be three victims. It's why Rachel decided to come forward. There would be no way of hiding what happened. Eventually everyone would know."

"Know what?" Mother said.

Then her eyebrows shot up when she understood. She sighed. "Don't tell me Rachel was . . ."

"Almost certainly pregnant," Kaitlin said.

* * *

The setting in the woods resembled a postcard. Wind softly rippled through the trees, loosening a dusting of snow, which floated gently to the ground. From somewhere above, they heard the familiar whine of an Academy powered glider. Mother's face remained knitted in thought, digesting this new wrinkle.

Malone stared at Kaitlin, watching her transform before his eyes. After her statement, her body straightened and her eyes hardened until they exuded their earlier determination. Within seconds, all trace of her emotional turmoil was gone. It was as if a switch had been suddenly turned off.

And Malone wasn't sure why.

Mother was fixated on Kaitlin; she'd noticed the change, also. "Almost?" she said, responding to the qualifier in Kaitlin's remark.

"Rachel hadn't taken a pregnancy test," Kaitlin replied. "She was afraid of the result."

"So it's not definite?"

"Pretty definite. She hasn't had a period for three months. Since after the rape."

Mother eyed Malone knowingly. "I'll give the coroner a heads-up for the autopsy. If Rachel was pregnant, we'll have the bastard's DNA. Problem?" She'd read Malone's pensive expression.

"It seems pretty stupid on the killer's part. To kill Rachel when she can be linked to him."

She shrugged. "The guy was desperate to keep Rachel from charging him with rape. Besides, it's not like we can run DNA tests on all four thousand cadets."

Malone slowly nodded. "For now, we'll assume rape was the motive—"

"*Assume?*" Kaitlin was incredulous. "Of course the rape was the motive. What else could it be?"

"Kaitlin, we need to keep our options—"

"There are no other options. After Rachel was raped, the guy kept threatening her. That's why she was so scared and wouldn't trust anyone except Mary. Rachel knew what he would do if she talked, which is precisely what he did. He *murdered* her."

She folded her arms, defying him to respond.

"You through?" Malone asked quietly.

"Unless you want to make another try at protecting the Academy's reputation."

At this remark, Mother bristled. "Now just a damn minute—"

Malone said, "I'll handle this, Mother."

"No. If she thinks we would—"

"*I'll handle it.*"

Mother lapsed into a surly silence. A year earlier, she wouldn't have done so. But after numerous arguments with Malone, she'd learned to accept that she could conduct her investigations any way she wanted.

As long as she remembered he was the boss.

"Kaitlin," Malone said. "This is the last time we talk about this. Frankly, I'm tired of your innuendos— Let me finish." Kaitlin clammed up, glaring at him.

Malone edged closer, staring right at her. "Do you trust me?"

"Define trust."

"Do you believe I'd cover up a crime to protect the Academy?"

She met his gaze. "You . . . might."

Mother sputtered, clearly furious. Malone held her in check with a look.

Stepping away from Kaitlin, he said, "That's settled. I'll notify General Crenshaw."

Kaitlin said, "Notify him of what?"

"Mother, it's your case," Malone said.

He calmly turned and walked away.

"You're quitting? You can't just quit."

Malone ignored Kaitlin and kept on walking.

"Oh, for— Malone! Hold on, Malone. Will you hold on?"

Still walking.

"*Okay*, okay. No more comments. Cross my heart."

Malone slowed and faced her. Kaitlin grimaced in frustration; she knew she'd been outsmarted. Behind her, the security cops sported crooked grins while Mother contemplated Kaitlin with what could only be described as a malevolent smile.

"Trust," Malone said to Kaitlin. "I want your trust."

"Cut me some slack, huh? If you act like you're ignoring the evidence, I'm obligated to—"

"Precisely."

She frowned at him.

"Follow the evidence. As a lawyer, you should know assumptions are dangerous. Do I believe Rachel was killed by the person who raped her? Yes. But I don't *know*."

Mother nodded approvingly.

"What I do know," Malone continued, "is there's a likelihood of another killing. Even now, we could be too late."

Kaitlin visibly started at the remark. But she still looked puzzled. "Probably are too late," Mother threw out. "Killer couldn't take the chance."

Kaitlin's head swiveled between them. "What chance? What killing? What are you talking about?"

"According to you," Malone said to her, "only Rachel and Mary knew Rachel was going to come forward . . ."

"Yeah, right . . ."

"No one else?"

"I told you they wouldn't have told anyone. They were too fright—"

She stopped. She finally understood. Her eyes widened in horror. "Oh, Jesus . . . Jesus . . ."

Malone and Mother nodded solemnly.

"Rachel and Mary," Kaitlin said. "They must have told someone else. Someone whom they trusted. And that person told the killer."

"Only way he could have known," Mother said.

No one spoke. Kaitlin still appeared stunned by this realization.

Malone said to Mother, "We could get lucky. Maybe the killer hasn't had a chance to act."

"Maybe not," Mother said.

But from their grim expressions, nether appeared as if they believed it.

Taking out his cell phone, Malone asked Mother how many security cops she could spare.

"Three or four. Why?"

After he told her, Mother voiced her skepticism, saying the killer wouldn't be so stupid. But the reality was the killer might have already done something stupid; he might have killed a girl carrying his DNA.

"Come on, Kaitlin," Malone said. "We'll have to move fast. Mother, find out what's keeping the coroner and light a fire under him. I want Rachel's autopsy completed ASAP."

Malone hurried down the trail, thumbing in a number.

Chapter 6

"HEY, MALONE," BRITT DIXON HOLLERED. "ARE we cleared in yet?"

Malone was striding quickly, talking on his cell phone. He flashed a thumbs-up to the forensics technicians as he went by.

Dixon grunted sourly, "About damn time. All right, people, load 'em up."

"Wait, Malone. Come on, wait up!"

Glancing behind, he saw Kaitlin stumbling across the snow after him. "I said *wait!*"

Malone continued to the car, concentrating on the voice of the Eighteenth Squadron AOC, Major Brad Tupper. Tupper sounded completely calm, as if the brutal murders of two of his cadets was an everyday occurrence.

". . . no reason to realize they were missing," Tupper was saying. "Upperclassmen aren't required to be in their rooms during a weekend. We had no way of knowing. If we had, I assure you I'd have reported it."

"Wouldn't have done any good, Major. By then, the girls were dead."

The major was silent, taken aback by Malone's bluntness. Guess he's a little human after all, Malone thought. "Have the cadets been told what happened, Major?"

"The commandant ordered me to delay an announcement until the families are notified. The cadets suspect something is wrong because of the recall and the presence of the security policeman."

The one Agent Kranski had arranged to guard Rachel and Mary's room.

"Grab a pen, Major." Malone waited for a couple of strides. "I need a list of cadets who were close to Mary and Rachel. Include cadet and Social Security numbers. If the cadets are available, tell them I'll be coming by to question them. Don't say why. If any cadets haven't returned, I'll need their cell phone numbers." Almost every cadet had a cell phone, so they could be easily contacted when they were out of the cadet area.

"Define close. They had a lot of friends."

"People they'd share intimate secrets with."

"You mean the rape, right?"

"You know about that?" Malone said, surprised.

"Not from Rachel or Mary. The Com told me. He'd been briefed by Ms. Barlow. That all you need?"

"Two more items. Until further notice, no cadet leaves your squadron for any reason."

Tupper sounded puzzled, but resisted the urge to ask. "All right."

Malone explained his rationale anyway. Afterward, Tupper finally lost his calm demeanor and became angry. "You really think there could be another killing?"

"Not as long as the cadets remain in the squadron. You know the name of the security cop?"

"Sergeant Brayles."

"He have a key to Rachel and Mary's room?"

"I gave him the one from the master ring."

Malone told him to put Brayles on the phone. Twenty seconds later, a husky voice said, "Sergeant Brayles."

"I need a favor, Sergeant . . ."

A minute later, Brayles came back to the line. By then, Malone was sitting in the BMW, the engine running.

"The laptops are both in the room, sir."

"Could you tell if they were on?"

"Both powered off."

"Thanks, Sergeant. I'll be there in fifteen minutes."

Punching off, Malone immediately cycled through his preset phone listings for the person who could access the computers. As he did, he glanced outside.

Uh, oh.

Kaitlin was a mess.

Snow clung to her designer suit and crusted her face and hair. She stalked up to the car and flung open the passenger door. She stood there panting, her expression furious. She announced savagely, "I *tripped*."

"More like a face plant. Clean yourself off first. I just had the car detailed."

"You heard me calling, right? Asking you to slow down?"

"I was on the phone—"

"Screw you."

She deposited herself in the seat and began brushing herself off.

"Hold on. You're getting snow all over—"

She cut him a glacial look. With a sigh, Malone put the car into gear and drove away.

Having wiped off the snow onto the car's floor mat, Kaitlin inspected herself in the sunshade mirror, produced a brush from her purse, and carefully began fixing her hair. As she did, she gave Malone a sideways glance, to see if he was watching.

He was; he couldn't help it.

His gaze followed the slope of her long throat, the taper of her perfectly formed jaw, the fullness of her lips. He lingered on the brilliant green of her eyes, which contrasted with her smooth, pale skin and rich, auburn hair. It was remarkable that one woman could be so beautiful, much less two.

Malone felt a stabbing pain at the memory of Christina. Wishing she were the one beside him.

Shaking his head, he forced himself to look away. In the cell phone listing, he found the number he wanted and punched select.

"Give me a break, Malone," a sleepy female voice said, reacting to his request. "Check the calendar; it's Saturday. My daughter's been sick and I was up half the night—"

"It's important, Bonnie."

"It's always important. How about some details? Something juicy."

"Can't."

"Malone—"

"Sorry. I would if I could."

She sighed. "How important?"

"Absolutely crucial."

"You smooth talker, Malone. Okay. Give me an hour to shower and grab breakfast—"

"No time. I'll need the information now."

"This keeps getting better and better. Fine. My age, who needs beauty sleep anyway. Give me the names . . ."

After Malone passed them on, Bonnie said, "Oh, and Malone, next time you think about calling me . . ."

"Yes?"

"Don't. You, I'm starting not to like."

Malone clicked off with a smile. The BMW was rolling down Field House Drive, toward a Security Forces guard post. Similar posts monitored all the access routes into the cadet area, the most visible of the post-9/11 security enhancements. Without a proxy card, no one, not even a general officer, could gain entry unless escorted.

Malone clipped on his proxy card and Kaitlin did the same. Having reapplied her makeup to perfection, she resembled a painted porcelain doll.

The most beautiful one Malone had ever seen.

Malone felt a stirring inside him. Any other time, he would have welcomed the feeling, but now he was disgusted with himself. Kaitlin was Christina's sister; he couldn't allow himself to be attracted to her.

"Who's Bonnie?" Kaitlin said, breaking in on his thoughts.

She had a suggestive smile. It took Malone a moment to figure out what was behind it.

"You know," he said, "I don't sleep with every woman I know."

"Because they have pride and a sense of self-worth."

Brother. "I'm really not the misogynist you think I am."

"Oh? What kind of misogynist are you exactly?"

Malone decided to quit while he was behind. With the chips Kaitlin carried on both shoulders—an understandable resentment because of what happened to her sister—there was nothing he could say to alter her opinion of him. He was a womanizer and therefore morally bankrupt.

"So who is Bonnie?" Kaitlin asked again, after the guard waved them through.

He looked at her.

"I really want to know."

"Uh-huh."

"I do. You wanted information from her."

"Bonnie," he said, "is the cadet-wing systems administrator."

"Passwords?"

"Passwords."

At a three-way stop, they turned up a gradual rise toward Vandenberg Hall, the older of the Academy's two enormous six-story rectangular dormitories. The various buildings in the main cadet area—the dorms, Sijan and Vandenberg; the academic center, Fairchild Hall; the dining facility, Mitchell Hall—were arrayed in a precise square around the crest of a large hill. Because of this novel design, the Academy's terrazzo courtyard was actually four stories up, built on the hill's flattened summit.

"It really is long, isn't it?" Kaitlin murmured.

Malone's head jerked around. Bad move.

"Out of the gutter, Malone," she said. "I was talking about Vandenberg Hall."

Malone felt his face get hot. As he pulled under the dorm a minute later, Kaitlin said, "It's a sixth of a mile long, isn't it."

He chanced a reply. "Yeah."

She gave him a sardonic smile. "I'd say I made my case, wouldn't you?"

Malone was tempted to ask for an appeal, but knew it wouldn't do any good. Regardless of what he said, she wouldn't change her mind about him. For some reason, that realization disappointed him.

A lot.

Cadet Squadron Eighteenth was located on the west end of Vandenberg Hall, one story above the terrazzo courtyard, placing it on the fifth floor. The Academy's four thousand cadets were divided into thirty-six squadrons, which meant CS 18 had a complement of approximately 120. When Malone and Kaitlin emerged from the stairwell, it appeared as if the entire squadron had gathered in the hallway. Since it was the weekend, most wore civilian clothing. From their grim expressions and hushed conversations, it was apparent they had more than a suspicion that something was terribly wrong.

The muscular third classman serving as the Cadet in Charge of Quarters—essentially the squadron gofer, responsible for maintaining security and answering the phones—sat at a large desk adjacent to the stairwell, squinting at a sign-out log. Three additional logs were stacked nearby, one for each class.

Malone held out his OSI credentials and coughed.

The CQ glanced over and popped to his feet. He barked in a foghorn, "Sir, Major Tupper is expecting you."

At that pronouncement, the conversation in the hallway instantly quieted. Dozens of eyes focused on Kaitlin and Malone.

A female cadet came forward, worry evident on her face. She wore a uniform with double chevron epaulets, marking her as a second classman or junior, the same year as the two victims. "Sir, can you . . . can you tell us what happened to Mary and Rachel?"

"You'll know soon."

"At least tell us if they're okay? Please."

Malone had no desire to lie and glanced at Kaitlin, hoping she had a more palatable response. She didn't.

"You'll know soon," Kaitlin repeated gently.

At the absence of reassurance, the cadet could only nod numbly.

"Agent Malone. Sir?"

Major Brad Tupper stood by his office a few doors down, wearing a pressed green Class A service blouse. Like most AOCs, he resembled a recruiting poster: athletic build, square jaw, closely mown scalp that only hinted at hair. Unlike most, he wasn't just a pretty face but a certified stud. Below his silver master jump wings and combat infantryman's badge, he wore five rows of medals, the most notable being a silver star and a purple heart. Beside him stood a slight, baby-faced blond man wearing an off-the-rack suit that looked several sizes too big; he was the person who had called out.

As Malone and Kaitlin made their way over, the cadets wordlessly parted. "Looks excited," Kaitlin murmured to Malone—an observation of the blond man who was anxiously shifting his feet. Malone didn't read much into it; Second Lieutenant Paul Kranski was a rookie OSI agent and tended to spin up easily.

As they approached, Kranski sprang upon Malone, stumbling over his words. "The major's got something, sir. He thinks he knows. It's a cadet who—"

"Don't say it," Malone growled.

The young agent stood with his mouth open. His eyes slowly focused past Malone. The sea of cadets gazed solemnly back.

Kranski stared at his shoes, mortified. "Ah, heck, boss."

Malone patted him on the back. "No harm, no foul."

"Shall we talk inside?" Major Tupper said, holding open the door.

Chapter 7

A TYPICAL AOC'S OFFICE: A LARGE DESK SET AT the back, several chairs in front, and the prerequisite wall filled with photos and mementos of Tupper's Army career. The office's dimensions mirrored a standard cadet room for the simple reason that it had been one before being renovated. As Malone trailed Kaitlin and Kranski inside, two items of interest jumped out: First, the photos and plaques confirmed Tupper had spent multiple tours in Iraq and Afghanistan, explaining his somewhat detached manner when discussing the victims' deaths; and second, Tupper did not care for Kaitlin.

Malone reached the latter conclusion from Tupper's sour expression as Kaitlin slipped past him—a look that fell somewhere between discomfort and disgust. That brought the count to two males in the room who were resistant enough to Kaitlin's charms to be irritated with her; there wouldn't be a third.

Kranski made a head-snapping double take when he saw Kaitlin. Then he took a third look and sprouted a silly grin.

Kaitlin played up to him with a beaming smile and Kranski promptly blushed. When she introduced herself, he could only stammer a reply. Watching this scene, Tupper grimaced as if physically ill.

Moving to his desk, Tupper motioned everyone toward seats. Kaitlin and Malone accepted the offer, while Kranski remained standing. Malone watched him expectantly, but he remained transfixed by Kaitlin.

"Cadet Second Class Terry Jefferson," Tupper announced loudly, grabbing everyone's attention. "He's the person Agent Kranski was referring to."

"Right. Right," Kranski came to life at the mention of his name. "The major was telling me Cadet Jefferson and Cadet Owens were involved—" He noticed the AOC's glower. "Uh, you go right ahead, Major."

"*Thank* you."

Addressing Kaitlin and Malone, Tupper said, "Cadet Jefferson and Rachel had dated since they were three degrees. Their romance became serious and they became engaged. This past summer, Rachel broke up with Jefferson without any explanation. He took it pretty hard."

"Enough to kill her?" Malone said.

Tupper's eyes measured Malone. "I've led people in combat. You get to be a good judge of character. My instincts say that Cadet Jefferson could never hurt anyone, much less the girl he loved."

"Is that why you neglected to mention him as a suspect on the phone?" Malone asked bluntly.

Tupper hesitated. "I had . . . to clear it first."

Malone had concluded as much. "The superintendent?"

"The commandant."

"He didn't have a problem with it?"

"Quite the opposite. He said to cooperate fully."

"Reassuring," Kaitlin said dryly. She briefly contemplated Tupper. "Let me get this straight; you don't believe Jefferson murdered Rachel and Mary . . ."

"No."

"Yet you felt compelled to mention him to Agent Kranski as a potential suspect. Why?"

Tupper focused on her, absent his usual grimace. "There are additional facts I can't ignore. After Rachel broke up with him, Cadet Jefferson became extremely depressed. So much so that I was forced to send him to a psychiatrist, who prescribed medication."

"You're telling us you believe Jefferson might have been unstable enough to—"

Kaitlin broke off, staring at Kranski. He was squirming to say something.

Malone sighed. "Out with it, Kranski."

"The suicide," Kranski said excitedly. "Tell them about the suicide attempt, Major."

Kaitlin and Malone's eyebrows arched up.

"It wasn't a suicide attempt," Tupper said. "Not exactly. It was during the summer, shortly after the breakup, when Cadet Jefferson was home on leave. His mother called me; she was very upset. She'd found her son in his room; he was extremely drunk and . . ."

He trailed off, unable to finish the statement. He shook his head apologetically. "This isn't easy."

"Take your time, Major," Malone said.

Tupper nodded, obviously conflicted. As a soldier, he felt a natural loyalty to the cadets under his command. No one else in the room said anything; they just waited for him to tell them what they already knew.

Except that when Tupper finally spoke, he not only confirmed that Cadet Jefferson had a loaded gun, but he also revealed a second additional fact.

One even more damning.

Cadet Terry Jefferson ran on the Varsity cross-country team. This revelation was met with surprised reactions all around. Even Kranski hadn't been aware of this fact.

"My God," Kaitlin murmured, "Cadet Jefferson would know Rachel and Mary's running route. He would know exactly where and when to—"

"You're jumping to conclusions again," Malone cautioned. "Don't."

Her eyes flashed and Malone braced for another charge that he was protecting the Academy. Instead, she curtailed her impulse, saying, "We can settle everything by interviewing Cadet Jefferson."

"Not any time soon, I'm afraid," Tupper said.

"Oh?"

"Jefferson signed out yesterday, for the weekend. His folks have a cabin in Pagosa Springs. The family was going to have a get-together. Considering his frame of mind, I thought being with them was probably the best thing for him. The cabin doesn't have a phone and cellular reception in the mountains is sporadic. I left several messages, but whether he can check his voice mail is anybody's guess." As an afterthought, he added, "And before you ask, the answer is, yes. I spoke directly with his family—an older sister, and she confirmed the family would be at the cabin."

Kaitlin said, "Jefferson drove up there alone?"

"As far as I know, yes."

"What time did he leave?"

"He signed out at 1806."

If the girls were killed in the late afternoon, this still made Jefferson a viable suspect. Malone voiced the obvious follow-up and Tupper nodded reluctantly. Jefferson had gone on a training run before leaving.

That cinched it; they had to talk to Jefferson. Malone asked Tupper if he had given Jefferson permission to skip the football game.

"Sure. It's four hours to Pagosa Springs. Be crazy for him to drive back."

"I'll need the cabin's address."

Tupper plucked a Post-it note from the edge of his desk and passed it over. Malone said, "I'll also need contact information for Jefferson's psychiatrist." Tupper was already handing him another Post-it; the man was sharp.

Dr. (Colonel) Patricia Garber was Jefferson's psychiatrist. Tupper had jotted down her home, cell, and office numbers, the last indicating she worked at the Academy hospital. Malone handed the cabin address to Kranski, who wordlessly spun for the door. Though he looked as if he was still in puberty, Kranski was a computer whiz and could think on his feet; he would know what to do with it.

After Kranski left, Kaitlin asked Tupper two pointed questions: Did Cadet Jefferson express rage or anger over the breakup, and did he ever threaten or attempt to intimidate Rachel in any way?

"Not to my knowledge," Tupper said. "But as the AOC, I'm not privy to all the rumors. When the Com told me she might be pregnant from an alleged rape, I almost fell over. I still don't believe it. I can tell you that if Rachel was raped, Jefferson's not your guy."

Kaitlin frowned at his logic. "Excuse me?"

"I'm assuming," he said, "the rape was the motive for the murders. That *is* the theory you're working on, right? Whoever raped Rachel also killed her?"

Kaitlin hesitated.

"Yes," Malone said.

She immediately countered: "That's only one theory, Major."

"We have a second one?" Malone said mildly.

She blew him off.

Tupper said, "Then that clears Cadet Jefferson. He needed a height waiver to get into the Academy. He's five-six and weighs maybe 120 on a good day. He couldn't rape anybody, much less Rachel. She had him by a couple inches and was strong. Maxed the Physical Fitness Test every time."

"GHB or Rohypnol," Kaitlin said. "Date rape drugs."

"Won't flush," Tupper countered without a pause. "If Kaitlin was going to report the rape, it follows she had to be conscious as it had happened. Drugged or not, the first chance she had, she'd have come to me and reported it."

"Hold on," Malone said. "Are you saying you don't think she was raped?"

Tupper shrugged. "All I'm saying is she'd never have kept quiet about it."

"Can't have it both ways, Major. Either she was raped or—"

"Of course she was raped," Kaitlin said. "The reason she didn't report it was that she was threatened. Someone frightened her so badly—" She noticed Tupper's scowl. "Oh, please, Major. It happens to rape victims all the time."

"Not to Rachel. I'm telling you she wasn't afraid of anything. She was a tough kid. Grew up in the Detroit projects without a father. She wasn't someone who could be intimidated by anyone, least of all Jefferson. Don't take my word for it. Ask any of her friends. Ask them."

Game, set, and match, Malone concluded. But, of course, Kaitlin wasn't about to let Tupper get in the last word.

"Why would Rachel lie about being raped?" she demanded.

Tupper's face went blank, thrown off-balance by the question.

"You're intimating," Kaitlin went on, "that the rape never occurred because she never reported it. You also seem to have forgotten her pregnancy. If that turns out to be true . . ."

She let Tupper fill in the blanks, watching his reaction.

His mouth worked, hunting for a response. But this time she'd confronted him with conditional logic he couldn't get around. Seeing she had him on the ropes, Kaitlin hit him with a knockout punch.

"And we know the killer had a gun."

That did it. Tupper was forced to accept that someone who was borderline unstable and armed with a gun could have terrorized Rachel Owen into silence. With a grudging nod, he said, "I suppose she could have been raped."

"By Jefferson," she pressed.

Tupper reacted with his telltale grimace, but said nothing. He wasn't about to surrender completely. Watching Kaitlin in action, Malone couldn't shake the suspicion that she'd pursued the argument not so much to win it as to win it over Tupper. As a combat soldier, he represented the ultimate macho male, a species she seemed compelled to dominate.

"At any rate," Kaitlin said to Malone, "DNA will tell us if Jefferson is a good suspect."

"There's a faster way," Malone said, taking out his phone.

Since it was Saturday, Malone called Dr. (Colonel) Patricia Garber at home. A young boy answered and hollered, "Mom!"

Before Malone could finish making his request, Dr. Garber shot him down. "You're getting into patient and doctor privilege, Agent Malone. As you're aware, I'm not allowed to discuss my patients' cases."

"Even if a patient poses a danger to himself and others, Colonel?"

There was a brief pause; Malone had said the magic

words, freeing her from her Hippocratic oath. "Go on."

"It's a close-hold subject, ma'am. Until the families are notified."

"Families? There have been . . . deaths?"

"Two."

"All right," she said quietly. "Tell me what happened."

After he did, there was another predictable pause as she assimilated the horrific news. In a strained voice, she said, "You're sure about the victims' identities? It was definitely Rachel Owen and her roommate?"

"Yes, ma'am. You knew Rachel?"

"Only through Cadet Jefferson. But he spoke of her so often, I felt as if I knew her."

Taking a ragged breath, she finally told him what he wanted to know.

When Malone ended the call, Kaitlin and Tupper's somber expressions confirmed they'd overheard enough of the conversation to know what Dr. Garber had concluded.

Cadet Terry Jefferson could be a killer.

Malone said to Tupper, "It doesn't prove anything, Major. It's only her opinion."

"Yeah . . ." Tupper picked up his phone and hit the redial. He listened for several seconds, then hung up. "Jefferson's voice mail." Forcing a smile, he said to Malone, "One thing I learned in combat was you can never know what's in someone's head. People will fool you every time. Quiet guys you think will freeze at the first shot turn out to be studs, while the John Wayne types shake in their boots. Guess that's where I made my mistake. I forgot that lesson. I thought I had Jefferson pegged." His eyes settled on Kaitlin. "Looks like I was wrong and you were right."

There was no gloating. She merely nodded her acceptance of his concession; she could afford to be magnanimous in victory.

"Malone," Tupper said, his brow knitting at a thought, "you and Dr. Garber discussed Jefferson being agitated and acting jealous—"

Malone nodded.

"When was this? Recently—"

"Their session on Tuesday."

"Three days ago, huh?" Tupper was thoughtful. "Jefferson's good, I'll say that for him. Had me fooled. I ran into him ten, fifteen times since then, and never noticed anything unusual. And I was looking, believe me. If he'd ever bothered Rachel, I was going to transfer him to another squadron. But as far as I know, he never did and Rachel certainly never mentioned anything to me. Who was Jefferson supposed to be jealous of, anyway? Because I'm pretty sure Rachel wasn't dating anyone. She didn't have the time. Girl was driven. It's the reason she broke off her engagement. Marriage wouldn't fit with her goal of having a military career. She was shooting for the top, to be a general. On top of her athletic requirements, she took extra courses on military strategy and doctrine. What little free time she had left, she spent at the parachute hangar, going through free-fall training. She was something, she really was. So, did Dr. Garber tell you the name of this new guy?"

"No," Malone said. "Cadet Jefferson apparently didn't know who he was. Or if he did, he wasn't saying. What set him off was that he'd heard Rachel might have a boyfriend."

"I suppose it could be true, but I have my doubts. Like I said, I don't hear all the rumors. If Rachel was dating someone, that could mean her pregnancy—"

"There's no boyfriend," Kaitlin said flatly. "I asked her that question specifically. She was *raped*, remember?"

The men had no response; they generally agreed with her conclusion. Malone said, "Rachel's e-mails and friends can probably tell us. You got that list, Major?"

Tupper produced a single page from a lower drawer. As he held it out, Kaitlin snatched it free, tossing Malone a look of defiance. It was starting. She was sending him a message that she was ready to assert control over the case.

Tupper watched Malone with an amused smile, as if to say, *You going to take it, buddy?*

Since Malone had no desire to go another round with Kaitlin, he settled on a second option. Leaning very close to her, he began reading over her shoulder.

"You're breathing on me."

"Hard habit to break."

She tried to intimidate him with a glare. He smiled pleasantly and kept breathing. After several seconds, she gave up and thrust out the page between them. Malone exhaled deeply before sitting up. That garnered a look of disgust from Kaitlin and a grin from Tupper.

He and the major were bonding against a common enemy.

Looking at the page, Malone saw two columns, one for each victim. Five names were typed below Mary Zinnel; at least ten under Rachel Owen. "*Close* friends?" Malone said.

Tupper shrugged. "Rachel was a popular girl."

Most of the entries were accompanied by cadet and Social Security numbers—Malone could pull their cadet records if needed—and a few had cell phone numbers, those who had yet to sign in.

Malone had almost finished scanning Rachel's column when he went tense. He stared at the last two names, feeling a sickening sensation. His eyes crawled to Kaitlin, who was still reading. Any moment now, he anticipated a reaction of anger.

But when she lowered the page, her only response was to shrug and say, "Rachel was good friends with Coach Ralston and his wife, huh?"

"They were Rachel's sponsor family," Tupper said.

Malone couldn't believe it.

Chapter 8

"SOMETHING THE MATTER, MALONE?" KAITLIN asked.

Malone realized he was staring at her. "No," he lied. "Everything's fine."

"You sure? You have a strange look."

"Everything is fine. Not a problem." He gave her his sincerest smile to convince her.

Apparently it wasn't sincere enough. Glancing at the page again, she said, "You saw something. What was it?"

A rap on the door saved Malone a response. Kranski's voice: "The SPs are here, boss. How do you want to handle it?"

Malone was thinking fast. "Be out in a minute. I need to brief Major Tupper."

"On?" Tupper asked.

"We're going to search every cadet room for the murder weapon. You'll supervise the search with Agent Kranski, while Kaitlin and I interview the cadets. We'll use your office."

"Fine. But I'm not sure why you need me—"

Malone swung toward Kaitlin. "We'll start with Rachel's friends and question them in two groups. Be quicker. Round up the top half of the list; I'll brief Major Tupper on the legalities for the search."

Kaitlin hesitated; she had no desire to leave before she learned what Malone had seen. Malone tossed a conspiratorial glance in Tupper's direction. "We'll talk later."

"Count on it." She finally left the room.

"Malone," Tupper said, mystified, "this is a criminal search. I'm not sure I have the authority to supervise—"

"You don't."

"Oh?"

"I'll get someone else to handle it. Any word on when we can expect the victims' families to be notified?"

Tupper was shaking his head, thoroughly confused. "No one told me. Why the hell did you ask me to assist in the search—"

Malone went to the door and opened it a crack. Kranski was standing outside, his back to him, flanked by security cops. Past them, Malone saw Kaitlin talking with several cadets. The group slowly moved down the hallway, still in conversation. Malone called to Kranski; as he briefed him, the young agent couldn't stop grinning.

Snapping to attention, he said, "I won't let you down, sir."

"Easy, tiger. You're not charging a machine-gun nest. Just find out if Rachel Owen was seeing another guy, and if so, whether Jefferson confronted her about it. You spoke to the fourth classmen who found the bodies . . ."

"They don't know anything, sir."

"And the Pagosa Springs PD?"

"Chief Hawkins will personally drive to the Jeffersons' cabin. He'll call your cell after he gets there. He'll have to find a land line, so count on at least an hour."

"Good boy. When Bonnie gets the passwords, the laptops will be your priority. Better secure them— Not yet." Kranski had started to rush off. "Hang around and let me know when Kaitlin's out of sight."

This part Malone hadn't explained and Kranski knew better than to ask.

Malone closed the office door and made two quick calls. The first was to the Security Forces commander, telling him to provide an increased presence in the cadet area. Until they ID'd the person who had told the killer about Rachel's pregnancy, this was essential to prevent another possible murder.

"It'll take a while," the commander said. "I need to call people in."

Next Malone phoned Mother.

"I can spare Anderson," she said.

"Send Sanders, too. I want him to search the victims' rooms."

"Some reason you can't do it? Sanders is still over at the gym, checking out their lockers."

"Something's come up." Because Tupper was listening, Malone danced around the subject.

"I'll be damned," Mother said, catching on. "You going to talk to Ralston now?"

"No choice."

"I'll meet you."

Clicking off, Malone said to Tupper, "Here's the drill, Major. Agents Anderson and Sanders will oversee the weapon search and go through Rachel and Mary's room. Kranski and Kaitlin will question the cadets. Until we get word the families have been notified, the cadets will be ordered not to discuss the murders outside this room. They'll be tempted, so that's where you come in. You make sure they understand to keep their mouths shut. What I also need from you . . ."—he held Tupper in an even gaze—". . . is to forget about my phone conversation. You don't know where I'm going."

A faint smile crossed Tupper's face. "Will Ms. Barlow ask?"

"She'll do a lot more than ask."

Tupper grinned, relishing the idea of another confrontation. The man didn't learn. Malone asked Tupper what he had against Kaitlin.

"Other than the fact that she comes off like she's too good for us military lowlifes and has an agenda? You know she always waltzes in here dressed to the nines and wearing those damned gloves. Someone should tell her this isn't 1950 and she's not a movie star."

"When you say she has an agenda . . ."

"Don't take my word for it, talk to the female cadets. They've been complaining about the way she's hounded them, looking for dirt. Not just in my squadron, but all over the cadet wing. Rachel and Mary were especially bothered by her. A couple of days ago, they asked if I could get Ms. Barlow to back off. I tried. It was a short conversation. She got in my face, accusing me of interfering with her investigation. Threatened to go up the chain if I didn't stay the hell out of her way."

"Kaitlin admitted pressuring Rachel into coming forward?"

"Pressure? You don't know the half of it. She really worked on them hard, badgered the girls to come up with something, anything, she could use. You ask me, she just wore Rachel down."

"You blame Kaitlin?"

Tupper looked at Malone for a long moment. "You might not believe me, but I don't. Not entirely. I understand what's driving her. This place let her sister down. In her shoes, I'd probably do the same thing." He added, "Still doesn't make it right."

"An honest assessment, Major."

"You sound surprised."

"I am."

"It's human nature," he said, as if that explained it all.

Since Malone couldn't come right out and ask him about Ralston, he threw out a generic question. Was there anyone else besides Jefferson, anyone at all, who might have had a reason to kill Rachel Owen?

"No," Tupper said.

But the hesitation before his response was unexpected. Malone said, "You sure? Nobody else?"

This time there was no pause, but Tupper appeared uncomfortable as he repeated his denial. Before Malone could pursue the subject, Kranski rapped on the door. "Coast is clear, sir."

As he left, Malone wondered if the honest Major Tupper had just told him a lie.

Malone walked quickly down the hallway, in the direction opposite that in which Kaitlin had gone, his heels clicking on the polished tile. When he was about midway toward the opposite stairwell, he casually checked behind and was startled to see Kaitlin rounding the far corner with a group of cadets.

He swore, quickened his pace.

Thirty yards, twenty . . . He took another look.

Kaitlin's attention was on the cadets, who were filing inside the office. Malone realized he might make it. Only a few more seconds—

She glanced over, her eyes popping wide. "Malone! Where are you going?"

Malone broke into a jog.

"What the hell is this, Malone? Get back here!"

Heels chattered rapidly after him. Cadets were staring. Several sprouted grins.

"We had an agreement," Kaitlin shouted. "You promised to tell me—"

Malone ducked into the stairwell, Kaitlin continuing to holler after him. Taking the stairs three at a time, he reached the ground floor in under forty seconds; another twenty brought him to his car. As he peeled out, Kaitlin burst through the stairwell door. She pulled up and thrust up her hand as he went by, giving him the finger.

Turning down the hill, he shook his head, regretting his sloppy exit. But it wasn't as if he had a choice. Since Kaitlin apparently didn't understand the significance of Ralston, he was not about to tell her. Not until he did his homework so he could convince her Ralston was in the clear before she overreacted.

The problem was Kaitlin's connection to Senator Smith. If she told him about Ralston, the senator would use the information to smear the coach and, by extension, the Academy. The fact that there wasn't any evidence of criminality wouldn't matter; Smith's specialty was destroying reputations through suspicion and innuendo, the truth be damned.

Malone couldn't allow that to happen.

He took out his phone to call the superintendent, to let him know what he intended. But before he could punch in the number, it rang.

He checked the caller ID, concerned it might be Kaitlin. Then he remembered she didn't have his cell number.

"Running late, Mother," he said. "Be there in a minute."

"Ralston isn't here," she said. "There's no car in his space."

She was already at the Field House, where the coach had an office, overlooking the practice fields. A control freak and workaholic, Ralston had a habit of studying film even on game day, looking for any last-minute edge.

"Maybe he left for the stadium."

"Game's been postponed. And there's no answer at his home."

As Malone rolled through the four-way stop, his call waiting beeped. It was General Crenshaw, and Malone knew it was more than coincidental timing. The Field House was off to the left, and he spotted Mother's stout frame in the parking lot, standing beside her battered pickup. He honked and she looked.

"The Supe's beeping in; Kaitlin must have called him. He'll have Ralston's cell number." Malone switched over. "Sir, I was about to—"

Crenshaw cut him off. "Ms. Barlow is pretty damned upset with you, Malone."

"Sir, I had to run out on her because—"

"Explain when you get here. The important thing is she isn't with you. I want you to question someone. He'll be here in a few minutes."

"Who will, sir?"

Malone swung in beside Mother's pickup and motioned her over. In his ear, he heard Crenshaw say, "Coach Ralston. I want to know if he's a killer."

Chapter 9

"NOT MUCH OF A TURNOUT, IS IT?" MALONE remarked, turning into the near-empty parking lot adjacent to Harmon Hall.

"The press weren't told the reason for the news conference," Mother said with a shrug.

She was sitting beside him. They'd ridden over together, so he could fill her in on Cadet Jefferson. Mother made no attempt to hide her disappointment that they had a better suspect than Coach Ralston.

Walking across the parking lot, Malone picked out the press vehicles. There were three vans marked with TV station logos and a couple of sedans with press passes stuck under the windscreens. The TV stations represented Denver and Colorado Springs media only. Other than the sex scandal—now considered old news—and the football team's recent success, the Academy rarely attracted national coverage.

"Enjoy it while you can," Mother said. "By this afternoon, all hell will break loose."

Malone nodded, hoping he'd have a chance to clean

up a little and shave. Unlike civilian cops, military investigators rarely talked to the press, but in a case this big, he could easily be ordered before the cameras.

Mother was pensive, shaking her head. "I don't get it," she murmured. "I just don't get it."

"I'll bite. What?"

"General Crenshaw. What's his hurry? You'd think he'd wait until we cleared Jefferson before giftwrapping his head coach for us. Talk about the fallout if Ralston is the killer. Why would Crenshaw push this angle, throw suspicion on him, unless it was necessary. No. I don't get it."

Malone didn't either. He'd fully expected Crenshaw to be resistant to an interview with Ralston.

"Obviously," Malone said, "Crenshaw believes Ralston could have committed the murders."

"So he must know the coach and his wife sponsored Rachel Owen. But that doesn't make much sense either. Since when does a superintendent pay attention to who's sponsoring what cadet?"

"We're talking about Coach Ralston," Malone said.

She frowned at him. "You think Ralston brought Rachel to some social function, attended by Crenshaw?"

"The more likely candidate is Ralston's wife, Laura. Like me, she was a cadet in Crenshaw's squadron, back when he was an AOC. They've been close ever since, and she served as his aide at the Pentagon."

They crossed the road, stepped onto the curb. It was almost ten-thirty, and the temperature had risen significantly, softening the snow. As Malone and Mother angled toward the walkway, he watched her to see whether his remarks had tweaked her memory.

Nothing yet.

"All I know about Laura Ralston," Mother said, "is she's a light bird and runs the powered glider squadron. She's supposed to be some kind of fast burner."

"Very. She pinned on lieutenant colonel three years early."

Mother whistled. "Crenshaw pushing her?"

"Who else?"

As they came up to the stairwell, Mother still hadn't fit the pieces together. Understandable. Fourteen years was a long time and Laura had looked nothing like she did now. Opening the door, Malone reluctantly faced her, knowing he had to come clean. He said, "There's something I need to tell you about Laura Ralston. You know her. You interviewed her after Christina was raped."

"I did?" She thought for a moment. "Doesn't ring any bells."

"Tinsley," Malone said. "Laura's maiden name is Tinsley."

Precisely three seconds later, Mother's mental Roledex scored a jarring hit. "*That* Laura? Christina Barlow's roommate?"

Malone ducked through the door, hoping to avoid the fireworks.

A futile attempt. Malone hadn't made it to the stairs before Mother grabbed his arm. Turning, he saw her face flushed with anger.

"You *knew*," she said, "you knew Tinsley was married to the coach and you didn't tell me."

"I'm the OSI commander. I don't have to explain to you or anyone—"

She released her grip only to poke a stubby finger in his chest. "The hell you don't. It was my case. I lived it and breathed it. It was *mine*."

"Mother, it's not what you think. I didn't even know who she was myself until I ran into her at the club. She looks completely different now."

"When was this? If it wasn't last night, you're in trouble."

"It was last . . . month."

"*Last month*." Another poke harder than the first. "You son of a bitch. You held out on me for a month."

"I was going to tell you after I interviewed her. We haven't been able to link up. She's been TDY and—"

"The reason. I want the fucking reason you didn't tell me."

"It's personal."

Mother exhaled slowly. Of all the excuses she expected, this hadn't been on the list. She said, "Personal? You *didn't* intend to question Laura about Christina's rape?"

"Of course, but . . . there was something else I had to know."

"About?"

"My . . . relationship with Christina. How she really felt about me."

"*Relationship?*" Mother searched Malone's face. "Well, I'll be— You did. You *slept* with Christina Barlow."

"Only once."

"Give me a break. You're something, Malone. You really are. Hell, I can't say I'm surprised. You lived across the hall from her, and knowing the way you operate—"

She stopped, her brow crinkling. "Hang on. Why would you care what Christina thought about you? After all this time?"

"It's . . . important to me."

"Why? You dump women all the time and never think twice. What was so special about her?"

Malone was silent, looking uncomfortable.

Mother's eyes continued to dissect him. She said quietly, "You got me thinking, Malone, and I don't like it. I don't like it at all."

He still said nothing.

"The truth," she said. "I want the truth. You have anything to do with Christina's rape?"

"You can't be serious."

"I always wondered why you never heard anything. You lived across the hall. The rapists must have made noises—"

"If I slept with Christina, why would I rape her?"

"There's a reason you didn't tell me about Laura and wanted to talk to her behind my back. You're hiding something. I can feel it. What is it? What don't you want me to know?"

"Mother, there's nothing . . ."

"What?"

Malone knew what that tone meant. He sighed. "All right. It's a little complicated. The truth is I felt responsible for what happened to Christina. If it hadn't been for me—"

Mother squeezed him by the elbow hard. "Upstairs. Move it. Unless you want to start the interview right here."

Malone glanced past her. Through the glass doors, he saw two people start up the walkway toward them, a tall man wearing an Academy-blue blazer and a slender woman dressed in the uniform of an Air Force lieutenant colonel.

It was Coach Ralston and his wife, the former Laura Tinsley. Neither looked happy.

Mother guided Malone up the steps, her voice clipped and urgent. "This doesn't change anything. Tell me the rest of it, but make it fast. You said you felt responsible for what happened to Christina. Lord help you if you're talking about the rape."

"Let go of my arm, first."

Women had always been attracted to Malone, and Christina was no different. Academy policy prohibited fraternization between fourth-class cadets and upperclassmen, but that didn't stop Christina. From the beginning, she made it clear she wanted a relationship with Malone. He didn't reciprocate her interest; he was dating several other women from Colorado Springs and had no desire to become involved in a clandestine relationship.

But Christina persisted. She dropped by his room often, citing one pretext or another, and had a habit of suddenly showing up at the gym or the library, wherever he happened to be. While Malone was flattered by her attention, he also found her infatuation troubling. On numerous occasions, he considered telling her to stop, that nothing would ever happen between them.

But he never did.

She was the most beautiful thing he'd ever seen and the truth was, he wanted her as much as she wanted him. So he let her pursuit continue. And with each encounter, his resistance weakened.

They finally got together on a Presidents' Day weekend. She came by his room, ostensibly needing help with a math problem. As she opened her textbook, she brushed her breasts against his arm and he felt a jolt of electricity. When he looked at her, she was smiling.

"I want to fuck you," she said.

Every alarm in his head sounded, telling him to say no. Clandestine relationships at the Academy were doomed from the start. Invariably one of them would let something slip and they'd get caught.

Say no, Malone.

But she'd slowly pressed her body against his, her eyes shiny with anticipation. She licked her lips seductively and his heart pounded through his chest. She was so damned beautiful.

"When and where?" he managed.

Like most cadets, Christina had a sponsor family. Hers would be gone over the weekend and had left her the keys to their house. Malone and Christina met there the following Saturday night. Since they couldn't risk being seen together in public, she cooked him dinner and afterward, they killed off a bottle of wine.

Taking him by the hand, she led him to the bedroom. When the petting got heavy and he was almost out of control, she breathed out a remark he never saw coming.

"I'm a virgin."

Looking back, Malone realized this admission should have been a warning flag. But at the time, he was too far gone to see it for anything except the ultimate compliment. A beautiful girl had chosen him to be her first.

Over the weekend, they had sex several times, each session more intense. After the last time, as they lay spent in bed, she turned to him and made another surprising statement.

"I love you."

And her big eyes looked into his, waiting for his response.

But he couldn't lie to her, so he said nothing. She reacted with understandable hurt and as her tears fell, Malone knew what he had to do.

When they returned to the dorms, he avoided her. It was a calculated decision; he believed it would be cruel to encourage her. She didn't see it that way and constantly tried to corner him, but he always walked away. After several weeks, she got the message and quit coming by. It was at this point when he noticed she'd begun to change.

Christina became openly flirtatious with other male cadets and began dressing more provocatively, whenever she went downtown. She went to parties unescorted, and he heard stories about how she was hitting on all the guys. She followed the same pattern on the football trips she went on as a cheerleader. She developed a reputation as a tease; a girl who liked to turn guys on, but never put out. A number of cadets whom Christina flirted with reacted angrily and there was talk of teaching her a lesson.

Of course Malone realized she was doing this because of him, trying to make him jealous. He went by her room, to tell her to knock it off. Stirring passion in twenty-year-old males, even ostensibly honorable cadets, was a dangerous game; she could get hurt.

"Worse than you hurt me?" she said dully.

Malone had no response.

On his own, he did what he could to look out for her. If she was going to a party or a group outing like a ski trip or a concert, he followed. Whenever she got too crazy, he would talk to her, get her to settle down.

"You know what to do to make this stop," she said.

"I can't. I'm sorry."

"Don't wait up."

Their little game lasted less than a month. Until Christina told him to back off because she'd found someone else she was interested in. "You keep hanging around, you'll scare him off."

"Who is he?"

"An upperclassman. I really like him and I know he likes me."

"Is he a football player?"

"Why do you care?"

"I care."

"I don't believe you. Now leave me alone. Please."

Malone was still convinced this was a ploy to make

him jealous. But Christina had insisted he stay away from her, so he did. It was a decision he regretted. Two weeks later she was attacked and raped.

Mother and Malone reached the third floor. Facing him, she said, "That it? Anything else you haven't told me?"

"One. I like Laura Ralston."

"So you don't believe she knew her roommate was going to be raped?"

"I know damn well she didn't."

"This could be the reason Crenshaw is suspicious of Coach Ralston. Maybe she knows something."

"She doesn't."

"She's his *wife*."

Malone let it go.

"You were going to talk to her why? So you could soothe your conscience, make yourself feel better?"

"I don't know. I suppose so."

"You could have checked with me," Mother said with a surprising resentment. "As far as I'm concerned, you *do* bear responsibility for what happened. Christina was what, seventeen, eighteen? Young and impressionable as hell. Saw you as her knight in shining armor and what did you do? You used her to get your rocks off and tossed her aside. How did you think she was going to react? Did you even consider that?"

Malone was silent, his face miserable.

Mother's expression slowly relaxed. She sighed. "Look, maybe I came on too strong—"

"It's why I quit."

"You mean the Academy?"

"After what happened, I didn't feel I deserved . . . that I had a right to be . . ." He shook his head. "Anyway, I quit."

A smile tugged at her lips, as if she saw him in a new light. "There's hope for you yet, Malone."

They heard the Ralstons enter the stairwell below. At the sound of their footsteps on the stairs, Mother whispered to Malone, "You're convinced it's only a coincidence that Laura Ralston was gone the night of the rape and is now married to Ralston?"

"Yes."

"You sleep with Laura, too?"

Malone darkened. "Go to hell."

The footsteps were coming closer. Mother grinned and reached for the door. "Hey, I had to ask. Christina never identified the guy she was interested in—"

"No."

"One more thing. You owe me for keeping me out of the loop. *I'll* handle Ralston's questioning."

She threw open the door and they heard people talking. An obnoxious voice said loudly: "No more goddamn delays, Major. Mark Bruner isn't someone you can push around. You tell the general that unless he gives me a reason, I'm outta here."

Chapter 10

FIFTY-SOMETHING MARK BRUNER, THE FORMER anchorman who'd drunk himself down to field reporter, stood in the hallway outside the superintendent's main conference room, arms folded across his belly, his heavy face locked in a belligerent scowl aimed at Major Seth Wilson. Flanking Bruner were two young women with tight-lipped attitudes, a beak-nosed blonde and frizzy-haired redhead. A ponytailed guy wearing a cowboy hat and a female photographer with a necklace of cameras peered out from the conference room doorway.

Major Seth Wilson said, "Please, Mr. Bruner. The general will begin the news conference as soon as he can. If you'll be patient—"

"*We've been patient.* For an hour. And you still won't tell us why we're here."

The women reporters emphatically bobbed their agreement. The photographer and the cowboy stood behind them, gazing out with only mild interest.

Wilson said, "You'll be told everything as soon as it's feasible."

"When will that be?" frizzy-hair demanded.

"I don't know, ma'am."

"Twenty minutes? Thirty?"

"I don't know."

"Does the reason have anything to do with the football game being postponed? Why *was* the game postponed?"

"Ma'am, I really can't comment."

"Does it for me," Bruner said, making a motion as if washing his hands. "Willy, grab your saddle and let's ride." He hitched up his trousers and lumbered for the stairs. Reaching back, the cowboy picked up a TV camera, slung it over his shoulder, and hurried after Bruner.

"Mr. Bruner," Wilson called out. "If you'll just wait a few more—"

Bruner snorted.

"Let me express your concerns to the general. I'm sure something can be arranged."

Bruner slowed, looking back. He growled, "Five minutes."

Major Wilson took off for the superintendent's outer office, several doors down. Bruner winked slyly at the two women. "The power of the press, ladies. You just have to know which buttons to push." He frowned at Malone and Mother, who'd suddenly materialized behind him. "Who are you?"

A query generated by their civilian attire. They ignored Bruner and entered Crenshaw's spacious anteroom, finding it a swirl of activity. In the time since Malone had left, it had been turned into an impromptu command center. A long table had been brought in and was occupied by three senior sergeants and a captain, who were clicking on laptops, a lieutenant colonel looking over their shoulders. Communications technicians were also installing a bank of temporary phones along both sides of the table. Even though it was Saturday, Crenshaw's secretary, Mrs. Weaver, was at her desk, her normally cheerful smile absent as she placed a phone call. Colonel Marvin Greenley, the vice-com, paced impatiently before her.

He said, "I'll talk to them, Wanda." Taking the phone: "Colonel Greenley, Ben. Nothing yet? Check again. I don't give a damn. Maybe she slipped or had a seizure. We can't wait much longer. Call me back pronto."

Returning the phone to Mrs. Weaver, Greenley saw Major Wilson exit Crenshaw's office, the commandant of cadets and a major from Public Affairs right behind him. Wilson cut over to his desk and snatched up a phone.

"Let's go, Marv," the Com said to Greenley. "Boss gave the green light for the news conference."

"What about Mrs. Owen, sir?"

"We'll withhold the victims' names until we contact her. We'll also request the press hold the story until we give them the okay."

"Good luck," Greenley grunted, falling into step behind the Com and the Public Affairs major.

"Larry," the Com said, pausing to address the lieutenant colonel at the long table, "how much longer until you're ready?"

"Thirty minutes, sir. And I have three more people

coming in. We'll work twelve-hour shifts to handle the calls."

"Good, good."

Malone and Mother were waiting by the hallway door. Striding up to them, the Com said, "Go on in. General Crenshaw wants to talk to you before the Ralstons arrive."

"They're right behind us, sir," Malone replied.

He and Mother walked toward Crenshaw's office. The door was open and through the plate glass window at the back, they glimpsed the general standing on his balcony. He turned, noticing them.

Filing past Mrs. Weaver, Mother said to her, "There's a problem locating Mrs. Owen?"

"Her car's in the garage, but no one seems to know where she's gone."

"She has a garage?"

Mrs. Weaver seemed puzzled by her question. "Sure. She lives here in the Springs. The casualty notification team has been outside her house since eight this morning. The neighbors think she might have gone for a walk. She walks almost every morning, rain or shine."

Mother glanced at Malone. "Didn't you say Rachel grew up in a Detroit project?"

"According to Major Tupper." Malone checked his watch. "Some walk. Over two and a half hours."

"Get in here," General Crenshaw ordered.

"Coach Ralston," Mrs. Weaver said pleasantly, "it'll be just a few minutes. If you and Lieutenant Colonel Ralston will have a—"

Malone shut the door and he and Mother went over to General Crenshaw, who was sliding into his armchair behind his desk.

"Sit," he grunted.

They did.

Seeing the general up close, Malone was shocked by his appearance. In the past two hours, he'd appeared to age at least five years. His normally smooth face radiated deepening lines, and large bags were visible under his eyes. Clearly, the murders were getting to him, a realization Malone found disturbing.

A combat fighter pilot who'd flown hundreds of missions over Kosovo and Iraq, Crenshaw had earned a reputation as someone immune to pressure. From Malone's history with the man, he found this assessment to be true. After Christina's rape and the subsequent finger pointing, Crenshaw kept his cool. Later, when confronted by Senator Smith's blistering personal attacks and the death of his wife, Crenshaw never displayed any public anger or emotional pain.

Yet now, after all he'd been through, his carefully crafted psychological barrier had suddenly begun to fail. It didn't make sense, or maybe it did.

Breaking point, Malone concluded sadly.

"Mother," Crenshaw said, focusing on her with irritation, "you weren't part of the deal."

"Sir, Agent Malone thought it would be better if I questioned Coach Ralston."

"This was Malone's idea?"

"I'm more familiar with the Barlow case, sir."

"Crap." But he tempered it with a tolerant expression. "You want in because you believe there could be a connection between Christina's case and the murders."

"And you don't, sir?"

He conceded her point with a reluctant smile. "You win, Mother. You handle the questioning." Nodding to the corner door leading to his private briefing room, he said, "It'll take place in there. Coach Ralston resents being questioned, but I've convinced him it's in his best interests to cooperate. He made two requests: he doesn't want me included, and he wants his wife present. Go ahead, Mother." She'd bent forward to say something.

"We can't compel him to answer questions, sir."

"Does it matter?"

Mother shook her head. If Ralston clammed up, they would wonder why.

"Now," Crenshaw said, shifting to Malone, "Cadet Jefferson. The Com told me Major Tupper mentioned him as a possible suspect. How strong a candidate is he?"

"On paper, he looks good, sir."

Malone relayed the key points. Afterward, Crenshaw was thoughtful. " 'On paper,' " he said, "implies you aren't sold on Jefferson."

"For a couple of reasons . . ."

"Such as?"

". . . why he would kill the girls on the Academy grounds. Especially in a location he was known to be familiar with and at a time when there's every expectation he would be in the vicinity."

"Which he was, since he was out running."

"Yes, sir. With his connection to Rachel, Jefferson had to know he was pointing the finger at himself."

"The logical conclusion is he knew Rachel was going to name him as the rapist, so he had no choice— Why not?"

Malone continued to shake his head. "If Jefferson couldn't kill without hope of getting away with it, why go through with it at all? So she accuses him of rape, so what? No rape kit was ever done; there's no serological or forensic evidence to implicate him, and no witnesses to the act, as far as we know. Even if the baby turns out to be his, that still wouldn't prove rape because they'd had a relationship for two years. Hell, they were engaged. No, sir. I don't buy it. Jefferson could easily have beaten the charge by doing nothing. Now he's looking at the death penalty."

"Anything to the jealousy angle you mentioned?"

"We're checking, but Major Tupper doesn't think Rachel had a boyfriend. Besides, if Jefferson did act out of jealousy, that precludes rape as a motive."

"Not from where I sit, Malone. Jefferson could have believed Rachel was seeing someone else, raped her out of anger or spite, then later decided to kill her."

Crenshaw was a three-star and Malone wasn't about to argue with him. But Mother held no such reservation. She announced, "Unlikely, sir. You're overcomplicating Jefferson's motive. It's certainly plausible he killed Rachel solely because she jilted him and never intended to get away with it. He'd contemplated suicide at least once; he might have decided that if he was going to die, she would, too."

"Crime of passion," Crenshaw murmured.

Mother nodded.

Malone checked his watch, feeling a growing sense of foreboding. Still almost forty minutes until the police chief estimated he'd be at the Jefferson family cabin.

Crenshaw said to Mother, "And the rape still fits your scenario?"

"Sure. After raping Rachel, Jefferson waved the gun in her face and convinced her he was crazy enough to kill her if she talked." Reacting to Malone's skepticism, she said, "Strong women get intimidated all the time."

"You wouldn't."

"What's that supposed to mean?"

From her tone, Malone knew he was in trouble. "Nothing. It's an observation."

"You think I'm too pushy? That it?"

"Of course not."

"Uh-huh." She folded her arms, glowering at him.

Crenshaw slowly shook his head. Mother's thin skin was well known; a result of having to put up with a career of snide remarks as she struggled to succeed in a male-dominated world.

"Getting back to the rape," Malone said. "I'm still bothered that Rachel never reported it. If she had, we'd have questioned Jefferson, searched his room and car, and found the gun. End of threat. Rachel was a smart girl; she'd know that's how things would have played out."

"So you don't believe Jefferson could have frightened her enough to keep her mouth shut?" Crenshaw asked.

Malone shrugged. "Major Tupper had his doubts."

A brief pause as they digested this possibility. Crenshaw said, "Then we have a problem, Malone. Rachel Owen kept quiet for a reason. Why, if she *wasn't* intimidated by Jefferson?"

Malone knew the response Crenshaw was seeking; it's why they'd been summoned. Before Malone could reply, Mother beat him to the punch line.

"She was raped by someone else," she said. "Someone with influence and power."

His suspicion validated, Crenshaw grimly reached for his intercom, to request the Academy's head football coach and his wife be sent in.

"General," Mother said, "there's something I'd like to clear up first. Why are you pursuing this now?"

Mother's tone was casual, indicating she'd only asked this to satisfy her curiosity. But instead of answering, General Crenshaw visibly tensed, his finger poised over the intercom. For fully two seconds, he didn't move.

Malone watched Mother, knowing she wouldn't let it go.

Of course Crenshaw realized his reaction was a mistake. He cleared his face to neutral, hoping to convince Mother that her question hadn't bothered him. He enhanced his act with a mild, "Mmm, doing what exactly?"

"The interview with Ralston, sir."

"We just discussed this. Coach Ralston is a suspect."

"We have a more viable suspect, sir. I'm wondering why you want us to question the coach before we've determined Cadet Jefferson's culpability."

"I'm being hasty; is that it?"

"Not from our position . . ." She looked at Malone. "But from yours. Frankly, it's in your best interest that suspicion not fall on your head coach unnecessarily."

Her implication sparked resentment in Crenshaw's eyes. He said irritably, "Go ahead and say it, Mother. Ask me if I have additional evidence implicating Coach Ralston."

Mother complied with a blunt: "Do you, sir?"

"Do *you* have reason to believe I have evidence?"

Crenshaw was trying to turn the tables on her. It was becoming a game of cat and mouse. Mother knew he was holding back information, and he knew she knew. But as a three-star, Crenshaw also realized there wasn't much Mother could do about it.

He misjudged Mother.

"Lieutenant Colonel Laura Ralston, sir," she said suddenly. "We know she mentioned something that incriminated her husband."

He stared at her. "How could you possibly know—"

Crenshaw stopped when he saw Mother's smile. He grimaced in disgust, knowing he'd just made another mistake. He peered at Malone. "She's good."

"Yes, sir."

Crenshaw weighed his response and still seemed reluctant to admit what he knew. Finally, he began, "When I was at the Pentagon, Laura . . . Lieutenant Colonel Ralston . . . served as my aide. This was before she was married, and she was totally dedicated to me. She was around so much that she became, well, a member of the family. Lucille and I didn't have children, and when she died, Lieutenant Colonel Ralston was a big reason I got through it. Maybe the only reason. So it was out of my obligation to her, my affection for her, that I went against my better judgment and agreed to wait."

Mother said, "For?"

"The night before last, she called and said she had reason to believe her husband was involved in Christina's rape. She'd found something incriminating. She wouldn't tell me what the item was. She was understandably distraught and wondered if she was doing the right thing, coming to me. She asked me . . . begged me to sit on it until she could confront her husband. For her own peace of mind, she wanted to be certain he was guilty."

Mother looked smugly at Malone—her way of saying I told you so.

Malone shrugged. He wasn't going to convict Ralston before seeing the evidence. "How long were you willing to wait, General?" Mother asked Crenshaw.

"Monday. I said I'd give her the weekend before notifying you. The murders obviously changed the timeline. You know the Ralstons sponsored Rachel?"

Malone and Mother nodded. He asked the general why Rachel had a sponsor if her mother lived in town.

"Mrs. Owen only moved out a few months ago. By then, Rachel had developed a relationship with Lieutenant Colonel Ralston. Privileges were also part of it. Since the Ralstons live at the Academy, Laura didn't need to use off-base passes to visit." Crenshaw paused, his voice becoming softly reflective. "I knew Rachel fairly well. When Coach Ralston was out of town, Laura and I often had dinner together. Rachel sometimes came along. The girl impressed me. She was bright and ambitious. She wanted to be a warrior, lead people in combat. She said she was going to be a general. A black woman general. Where she came from, her background, that was something. And she would have made it. Jesus, she and Mary Zinnel were so young. Kids entrusted to my care. When I think about that, how some bastard murdered them . . ." He abruptly turned away, blinking rapidly.

Seeing Crenshaw display such raw emotion was another first for Malone. But it seemed like a day when the general was going through a lot of firsts in his life.

No one said anything for a while. Crenshaw gazed out of the picture window overlooking his balcony, lost in his private thoughts. Malone noticed that Mother seemed in no hurry to resume the questioning. She had her game face on, preparing for her interview with Coach Ralston.

After coughing politely to get Crenshaw's attention, Malone asked him if he'd discussed the murders with Lieutenant Colonel Ralston.

"Right after I notified her husband."

"And her reaction, sir?"

"What you'd expect. Horror and shock." He added, "She was adamant her husband couldn't possibly be the killer, if that's what you're asking."

It was. "Yet she believed he could be a rapist?"

"Yes."

"And even after you told her about the murders, she

still wouldn't tell you what incriminating evidence she'd found?"

"You're not dealing with logic here, Malone. You're dealing with a woman who deeply loves her husband. With the murders, it's even more difficult for her to come forward. But she will. Laura was very fond of Rachel, almost like a big sister. She'd never cover for Ralston, if she believed he was the killer. You ask me, that's the reason she's accompanying him here. To see for herself if there is evidence of his guilt."

"There isn't any yet, sir," Malone said. "Nothing beyond coincidence and suspicion."

"It could be enough," Mother said. "It all depends on what Laura Ralston found."

Malone nodded; she was the weak link they had to exploit. And since he was the one who knew her . . .

"Laura's mine, Mother," he said.

"But you like her." As if it were a crime.

"We'll talk to the Ralstons now, General," Malone said.

Chapter 11

Opposites attract.

One look at the Ralstons and that conclusion immediately came to mind. He was six-three, blond, and ruggedly handsome, and at thirty-five, still possessed the solid frame of the All-American quarterback he once was. In contrast, his wife was petite and darkly complected, with pointed features that could never be considered pretty. As a cadet, Laura had rarely showed much interest in her appearance, but that had changed. Her makeup was skillfully applied and her once-curly black hair was now a rich auburn, cut stylishly back off her ears. But the most significant alteration in her appearance was her nose; it had been trimmed down to fit her small face.

As Malone and Mother stood, Mrs. Weaver ushered the couple inside. Mother nodded, recognizing Laura now.

The couple's expressions were subdued, as if resigned to being questioned. Malone read that as a positive sign . . . until Mrs. Weaver slipped from the room.

The instant she left, Coach Ralston swung toward Malone and Mother, focusing on the former. He demanded, "This your goddamn idea? You put the general up to it?"

During Malone's tenure as a cadet, they'd been casual acquaintances. After Christina Barlow's rape, Malone had confronted Ralston and the two almost came to blows.

Malone puffed up to his full height and looked down the two inches to Ralston. "I wish I could take credit, John."

"Fuck you."

Laura Ralston said, "John, I told you not to—"

"It was *my* decision," Crenshaw said, rising from behind his desk.

There was a tense silence. Laura and Malone were looking at each other. She dropped her eyes, as if embarrassed. Ralston faced Crenshaw, his voice like ice. "General, I suggest you reconsider."

Crenshaw's jaw knotted. "Coach, we've had this discussion. Unless you cooperate, I'll be forced to suspend you, pending a formal—"

"Hell, you won't suspend me," Ralston said arrogantly. "You can't."

"Going over my head won't do you any good. I've spoken to the Chief and he won't intervene. In fact, he's authorized me—"

Ralston cut him off again. "You know why you won't suspend me? It's in *your* interest to reconsider, General."

And he looked at Crenshaw in a particularly knowing way.

Initially, Crenshaw seemed confused by the unstated message. Then his eyes widened and he looked accusingly at Laura Ralston. She had a stricken expression, mouthing the words, *It wasn't me.*

"Well, General?" Ralston said.

Crenshaw took a deep breath, as if to gather himself. When he spoke, his voice was low and menacing. "Coach, if you don't submit to questioning, you are suspended. It's your choice. Either way, I don't give a damn." He calmly sat down, his gaze never leaving Ralston.

Coach Ralston appeared genuinely surprised by the general's response. His eyes darted around the room, as if uncertain what he should do. Laura Ralston took him by the arm and drew him to a corner. They spoke in hushed, terse tones. Soon they began arguing, their voices growing heated.

"Do it, John. Do it for me."

"Why the hell should I? I'm innocent."

"To clear your name. It's the only way."

They went back and forth. Ultimately, Laura prevailed and Ralston threw up his hands in resignation. "All right. I'll do it. Let's get this damn thing over with."

"This way," Mother said.

Her eyes were shiny with anticipation. She'd waited fourteen years for this.

Eleven.

That was the number of cadets Christina Barlow had initially identified as ones who could have been involved in her rape. In addition to fulfilling the criterion of being football players, the eleven had two other things in common: Christina had played varying degrees of kiss and giggle with them, and they'd all reacted angrily when she wouldn't seal the deal by jumping in the sack with them.

Of the eleven, Mother had focused on five candidates as the most likely—the ones who crashed at the same house in Colorado Springs, after being at a party. In her estimation, their alibis were the weakest; they'd mutually supported one another. Also, the team's star, leader, and Academy golden-boy Cadet First Class John Ralston—the one person whom Christina most believed was responsible for her rape—was among that group. When Mother learned from witnesses that Ralston had been heard saying, "That cock-teasing bitch Christina needs to be taught a lesson," she became convinced Christina's suspicions were correct.

But she couldn't come close to proving it because Ralston had a trump card.

There were *five* suspects and only three rapists.

It was the one obstacle Mother couldn't get around. After numerous interviews with the five cadets, it seemed inconceivable that the two who were innocent would continue to hold out and risk a prison term simply to protect their friends.

As the months passed, Mother's fellow agents began to doubt the players' guilt. So did the Academy brass and ultimately the OSI's commanding general.

"Listen," her supervisor finally said to her. "The guy Ralston's a star and knows people. Generals, colonels, the Association of Grads, you name it and they're all giving me heat for harassing him. So either you find the evidence to put him away or move on to someone else."

But there was nobody else, so Mother was forced to suspend the investigation. A week later, she received a phone call. The voice was muffled, but she knew who it was.

"Can't win 'em all," the voice said cheerfully.

"Better take something for that cold, Cadet Ralston," Mother said.

Watching Malone, General Crenshaw knew what was coming. Moments after the agent followed the others into the briefing room, he reappeared and began walking purposefully toward Crenshaw.

"Can't let it go," Crenshaw said, as Malone stopped before him.

"No, sir. Coach Ralston said it was in your interests he not be suspended. Why?"

"He's mistaken."

"He sounded confident."

"He's mistaken."

"Sir, if there's something he has on you . . ."

"Then you'll soon know."

Crenshaw's dismissive tone made it clear the discussion was over. Still, Malone was unwilling to leave. Twice he attempted to speak, but held back. Unlike Mother, he had to work up his courage to confront Crenshaw.

"Let's have it, Malone," Crenshaw finally ordered, after Malone's third attempt.

Malone began awkwardly, "Sir, we've had . . . disagreements in the past. But none of that matters. You can trust me to be discreet. I have no . . . animosity toward you. In fact, it's just the opposite. I know you're the reason the Air Force let me back in."

Crenshaw frowned, completely confused.

"Your recommendation, sir. Cadet Olson saw it on your desk. Told me about it a few years ago."

The general finally remembered. After Malone had separated from the Academy, Crenshaw had written a routine evaluation for his file, concluding that Malone possessed the potential to be a good officer.

Smiling faintly at Malone's offer, Crenshaw said, "You figure I did you a favor and you'll do me one."

"If I can. But I have to know what I'm dealing with, sir."

"Nothing." Crenshaw held Malone in an even gaze to convince him. "Ralston has nothing on me."

"All right, sir. Just wanted to be sure." But as Malone backed away, his troubled expression belied his words.

"Malone—"

Malone paused, waiting.

Crenshaw's eyes narrowed into a flat stare. "You should know that I regret my assessment. You're not a good officer and never will be."

A damning indictment, but Malone's expression never changed.

"I agree, sir," he said calmly. "But I am a good cop. Let's hope you didn't make a mistake in not confiding in me." With a respectful nod, he continued to the briefing room.

*   *   *

Crenshaw couldn't bring himself to confide in Malone. Not yet. Not until he knew whether Coach Ralston was bluffing. Because if that egotistical bastard really did know . . .

Crenshaw slowly shook his head. In the end, he supposed it didn't matter. Events were closing in on him, and with two murders on his watch, his career was finished. The best he could hope for was retirement and years spent growing old alone. It wasn't the outcome he'd ever envisioned, but then he'd never planned on Lucille dying of cancer.

And he had certainly never planned on Rachel.

He looked at the silver-framed picture of his wife, sitting on the corner of the desk. He could almost feel the accusation in Lucille's eyes.

"Forgive me, honey," he murmured.

He slipped the photo into a drawer, feeling ashamed.

Chapter 12

MALONE AND MOTHER BRACKETED THE ENDS OF the short, rectangular conference table, Coach Ralston and his wife sitting between them, along one side. Subtlety had never been Mother's strong suit, and she intended to pepper the coach with nonstop questions, hoping he'd let something slip. Once she wrapped up, Malone would start in on Laura Ralston.

All the while trying to forget she was a friend.

Mother took out her notepad and Malone did the same. When Mother clicked her pen, Laura Ralston tensed at the sound, while her husband gazed back arrogantly.

Mother began: "Do you have any knowledge of the murders, Coach Ralston?"

"Of course not."

"Where were you yesterday afternoon, between 1500 and 1800?"

"Is that when the girls were killed?"

"Answer the question, please."

"In my office until a little before 1600. We had a

walk-through practice until 1700. After that, I went back to my office to tweak the game plan."

"Witnesses?"

"Get real. There must have been a hundred people who will swear—"

"*After* practice? When you returned to your office?"

Ralston hesitated. "The staff had gone home. Coach Skarstedt came by around 1815 or so. Could have been earlier. I wasn't looking at the clock."

"So you were alone for approximately an hour?"

"Oh, for chrissakes. I was in my office *working*. I didn't kill those girls."

"I never said you did, Coach."

"Like hell. This is personal. Admit it. You and Malone want me to be guilty because—"

"Shut up, John," Laura Ralston said.

"No. This is bullshit. I told you we shouldn't have—"

"Shut *up*."

The couple traded glares. Laura Ralston hadn't become a military pilot and lieutenant colonel by being a wallflower. She kept her eyes riveted on her husband until he backed away. "Fucking bullshit," he grumbled.

Mother asked him if he knew either of the victims.

"You know damn well I do," he said sourly. "We sponsored Rachel Owen."

"So she spent time at your home?"

"Sure. Not as much as before her mother moved to town."

"Did she ever stay over while your wife was away?"

Ralston shot forward at the inference. "That finishes it. I'm not going to stand for this."

Mother said, "Does that mean she did stay with—"

Ralston spun to his wife. "I'm going to tell them. I have to."

"Don't, John. I'm asking you—"

"I'm your husband. You want them to pin this thing on me?"

"Of course not, but—"

He thumped his chest hard. "Look, *you* promised to keep quiet, not me."

Mother prompted, "Quiet about?"

"Rachel," Ralston said. "She used to sign out to spend the weekend at our house, but would usually disappear as soon as she got there. Twice she was gone the entire night. This was before her mother moved here. Anyway, I asked Rachel where she was going, but she would never tell. Laura would back her up, say it was okay. But it wasn't okay. When she was with us, she was our responsibility—"

Laura Ralston said, "John, don't do this. Please."

But Ralston talked right over her, becoming even more animated. "Anyway, a couple of weeks ago, I happened to hear Rachel on the phone. She was telling someone she would be by later that night. After she hung up, I asked her who she was talking to, but as usual, she wouldn't tell me. So when she left, I hit the redial and bingo, a man picks up. It really knocked me for a loop. You'll never guess in a million years who—"

Laura Ralston suddenly grabbed him hard by the shoulder, to prevent him from saying the name. It was too late. By then, Ralston had already revealed the name.

"General Crenshaw," he said, grinning. "It was General Crenshaw. You believe that shit?"

"You son of a bitch," Laura Ralston said.

Malone and Mother remained completely calm at the pronouncement. Coach Ralston's grin faded into a quizzical frown. "Hell, you knew. You fucking knew."

"We suspected . . . something," Mother said.

"It's not what you think," Laura Ralston said, sounding miserable.

"What *do* we think?" Mother asked her.

"Same as me," Ralston answered. "The general's a widower. Probably got lonely and—"

"You're sick," his wife said. "You're really sick."

"*Me?* You knew they were getting together. Shacking up."

Mother asked, "Did you ever notify Mrs. Owen of your suspicions?"

"I wanted to about a hundred times, but Laura talked me out of it." He stared at her disgustedly.

She said, "Because it's not true. The general would never—"

"They spent *nights* together. What would you call it?"

She stared at her husband with something approaching hate.

Now, Malone thought, glancing up from writing. They had to go after Laura now, when she was more likely to talk.

But they needed her alone.

He caught Mother's eye across the table. She nodded; she understood the situation.

Now that Ralston had revealed Crenshaw's name, he became noticeably more relaxed. He stretched back in his chair, no longer in a hurry to carry out his threat to go. That changed precisely three questions later.

"Coach Ralston," Mother said to him, "are you aware Rachel might have been pregnant?"

"General Crenshaw mentioned it. We had no idea." His wife supported his claim with a head shake.

Making a note, Mother tossed out casually, "So, was it you, Coach?"

"Sorry?"

"You," Mother repeated, her tone hardening. "I'm asking if you're the one who raped her and fathered her baby."

The coach almost came out of his chair. "Oh, for crying out—" He angrily thumbed at the door. "Talk to General Crenshaw. He's the one who spent nights with her."

Laura Ralston sat there with an anguished expression, murmuring, "It's not true, it's not true."

"We will," Mother replied to Ralston.

"I'll friggin' bet," he grunted. "Just because he's a general, you assume he can't possibly—"

"We assume nothing."

Ralston snorted derisively. Mother asked him again if he had raped Rachel Owen. "I need a yes or—"

"You people are unbelievable. No. *No.*"

"Will you take a lie detector test?"

He actually hesitated as if considering it. Then he flashed Mother a cocky smile. "Nice try, but I don't think that would be wise. You know how unreliable lie detectors are."

"John," his wife said, "if you're innocent, why don't you—"

"*If?* You think I could be guilty."

She was silent, avoiding his gaze.

"Hell, you do. You actually think I'm capable of murder."

Laura's lower lip quivered. She bit it, saying nothing.

"One last question, Coach. To tie up a loose end . . ."

Ralston swung to Mother, his eyes suspicious.

"For the record," she asked, "did you participate in the rape of Cadet Christina Barlow?"

This time there was no angry outburst or caustic comment from Ralston. He had known this question was eventually coming. With a disgusted grimace, he stood and addressed his wife. "We're done. Let's go, Laura."

She didn't move.

"We'd like you to stay, Laura," Malone said, weighing in. "We only have a few questions."

Ralston said, "She's got nothing to say."

Malone and Mother looked expectantly at Laura. Ralston said, "Laura, let's go."

She flinched when he laid a hand on her shoulder. But she didn't resist as he helped her to her feet.

"It won't take long, Laura," Malone persisted. "Only a few minutes."

Laura shook her head. "No. It's . . . better if I go."

Malone felt a sinking sensation as Ralston led her to the door. He said suddenly, "Laura, is General Crenshaw a rapist?"

She spun around. "He isn't. You know he isn't."

"Did he sleep with Rachel?"

Anger and disappointment flashed in her eyes. "How could you possibly think—"

"Then what was he doing with her?"

A silence.

"Laura, please. Help me understand why . . ."

"You'll have to ask him."

"I did. He wouldn't tell me."

She hesitated, torn. Malone recalled Crenshaw's words about Laura: *She became a member of the family.*

No choice. He had to ratchet up the pressure. He said, "General Crenshaw mentioned your phone conversation . . ."

He let the statement float toward her, watching her reaction.

But there wasn't any to speak of. Her self-control was remarkable. Instead of appearing alarmed by the remark, she seemed only mildly puzzled.

"Phone call? What phone call?"

"The one on Thursday. You called the general at home."

Ralston said, "What's so important about this call?"

Laura frowned. "I may have called Thursday. I really don't remember. If I did, it couldn't have been important."

She came across as completely truthful. Malone didn't understand it. "Are you denying you called him?"

"It's hard to keep track. I call him several times a week." She shrugged.

"C'mon, honey, we've wasted enough time," Ralston

said. "I've got a coaches' meeting to plan this afternoon's practice."

Malone said, "You're having practice today?"

"Damn straight. We got Notre Dame next week.
And baby, that's a game we're going to win."

Seemingly on impulse, Laura suddenly thrust her
hand out to Malone "It is good to see you, Malone.
Sometime, when this is over, we need to get together."

In the adversarial setting, her words and the gesture
seemed inappropriate. As they shook, Ralston moved to
the door, saying, "Feel free to tell Crenshaw I didn't
cooperate. He hasn't got the balls to suspend me. Not
unless he wants to explain to the press why he was
meeting Rachel on the sly. Hell, I'm tempted to tell the
reporters anyway, on my way out." He winked at
Mother. "Like I said, you can't win 'em all."

"Two words, Coach," Mother said quietly. "The first
is pregnant . . ."

Ralston frowned.

". . . and the second is DNA." Her mouth spread into
a predatory smile. "We'll call you to arrange a sample."

He went pale, his bravado gone. Yanking open the
door, he took his wife by the arm and hurried out.

"Prick," Mother said.

Chapter 13

THE RALSTONS STRODE PAST GENERAL CRENSHAW, who was seated at his desk, talking on the phone. The coach regained his composure enough to throw the general a scowl, but Crenshaw didn't appear to notice. Moments later, the front door closed with a bang, Ralston's final gesture to communicate his annoyance.

Crenshaw was doing more listening than talking. Mother had twisted in her chair and was watching him. "Malone," she said uneasily, "you and I need to talk about a few what-ifs."

"Like . . ."

Her eyes remained on Crenshaw. "I know you like the general. Admire him and all. But what if Ralston's right? What if the general lied about the phone call from Laura Ralston to implicate the coach?"

"You're reaching."

"Am I?" She shifted, staring at him across the table. "I don't like this any more than you do, but Rachel Owen was rumored to have a new boyfriend. What if it was General Crenshaw? Crazier things have happened.

Rachel's black, came from a tough background. So did the general. Maybe he felt an obligation to mentor her, help shape her future. But somewhere along the way, they became attracted to each other. Maybe she saw him as a father figure and—"

"Boyfriends don't usually rape."

"So she lied about the rape to cover for sleeping with him. That's not the point. What is the point is that powerful men fall for young women all the time. And if Crenshaw got her pregnant, he had a helluva motive to— I say something funny?"

Malone had an enigmatic smile. "What have I always said about jumping to conclusions?"

"Give that line a rest, Malone." She jerked her head at Crenshaw. "If we prove he lied about the phone call, he becomes a prime suspect— Yeah, yeah, I see it. So?" Malone was holding up a small piece of paper.

"Read it."

Leaning over, he passed the paper to her. It was heavily wrinkled, as if it had been tightly balled up. Mother squinted at the single sentence written on it.

MY OFFICE 1700.

Mother nodded her understanding. "The handshake with Laura?"

"Yeah. I almost dropped the damn thing." Still smiling.

"You're pissing me off."

"I'm trying to."

She sighed. "Listen, Laura clears the general, fine. But you heard the way General Crenshaw talked about

Rachel. He felt some connection to her. Until we know what it was, he's a person of interest. Okay?"

"Sure." Malone stood and threw up a mock salute.

Mother shook her head and pushed her bulk up from the table. "That means we have to keep Crenshaw out of the loop. Don't mention Laura Ralston's denial of the phone call or her note. We'll also need to determine where Crenshaw was at the time of—"

"Mother," Malone said, "I'm a cop, too. I think I know what questions to ask."

"You sure you're up to it?"

"And I wouldn't be because . . ."

"No reason other than it takes balls. Because if he doesn't have an alibi, you're going to have to ask him to provide a DNA sample and take a lie detector test. And Crenshaw will absolutely *love* that. If I were you, I'd call the hospital."

"Why?"

" 'Cause you're about to get ripped a brand new asshole. Have fun." She slapped the note to his chest harder than necessary and went into the office.

Crenshaw was cradling the phone as they walked up. "The president of your fan club, Malone," he announced dryly. "Ms. Barlow learned something from the cadets, for your ears only. She wants you to swing by ASAP." Scowling, he added, "I don't expect any more calls from her. You understand?"

"I'll give her my cell number, sir. But as to her demands that I be replaced—"

"Relax. She's cooled off. Never mentioned the subject."

"Oh?"

"Of course, when you tell her about Coach Ralston, all bets are off. Personally, I wouldn't worry. Her credibility will take a hit if she demands you be tossed after she requested you. So, how'd it go with Ralston?"

But Malone was still trying to understand something Crenshaw had first said. "We should *tell* Kaitlin about Coach Ralston, sir?"

"She'll find out about him eventually. I don't see how you can avoid it. You?"

Malone didn't have to look at Mother to know what she was thinking. But she was mistaken: The general wasn't purposely trying to implicate Ralston; he was only being pragmatic.

"Sir," Malone said, "I could stall Kaitlin, tell her I was running down a lead—"

"The SECDEF promised *total* cooperation. The Air Force can't take any more heat from Senator Smith. Better to tell her about Ralston now and deal with any repercussions."

"Sir, the press will play it up. The Academy will be crucified for hiring a coach who—"

"You're preaching to the choir, Malone. If it was my call, Ralston would never have gotten the job. But in the Academy's defense, no one brought up Christina's rape because no one in a position of power recalled much about it. Unlike us, they wouldn't have known the details. And even if they had, it wouldn't have been much of a factor. There was never direct evidence implicating Ralston, and you can't condemn someone on suspicion. Not someone like him, anyway. The only

Academy grad in the last thirty years to be named an All-American. Helluva standard, huh?" He sounded disgusted.

Malone couldn't let the subject go. "Sir, initially you didn't want Kaitlin to know about Ralston. Why the change now?"

"Easy. She'd overreact, make a judgment based on emotion. And I was looking for an unbiased assessment about Ralston's culpability." He squinted at Malone. "So, what's your determination? Could he be the killer?"

"He's a suspect, sir," Malone said cautiously. "How solid, we don't know. Laura never told us what she found . . ."

Crenshaw nodded, as if he had anticipated this.

"But the coach doesn't appear to have an alibi and wouldn't submit to a lie detector test . . ."

More nods from Crenshaw.

". . . which reminds me, sir. You mind telling me where you were yesterday afternoon?"

The general bobbed twice more before Malone's smoothly worded request registered. "You want *my* alibi?"

"It's routine for anyone who knew the victim, sir."

So much for being smooth. The general began a slow burn.

Mother eased to the side, out of the line of fire. This was what she'd been referring to earlier, the general's temper. He rarely lost it, but when he did, he often exploded in a spectacular display of—

Abruptly, Crenshaw's expression relaxed. As he

rocked back in his chair, the tension left him. "One question," he said to Malone, "and I want a straight answer. No bullshit . . ."

"No, sir."

"Am I a suspect?"

"No, sir."

He blinked. "Then what's this crap about—"

"Technically, you're a person of interest, sir."

"Meaning," he said slowly, "I could become a suspect."

"Yes, sir."

Crenshaw's left eyelid twitched. Another dent in his psychological armor. "When?"

Malone realized he'd switched gears. "Yesterday between 1500 and 1800, sir."

Crenshaw pressed the intercom and asked for Major Wilson. "He's down the hall, sir," Mrs. Weaver's voice replied.

"Agents Malone and Hubbard need to look at my schedule."

"I'll notify him, sir."

Crenshaw's gaze cycled between Mother and Malone. "Major Wilson has the exact times. I was in the office or in meetings most of the afternoon. At least a dozen people will swear to that, including Mrs. Weaver and the Com. At around 1630, I went to the Field House for my daily workout. It lasted about an hour, including the shower. I was back here a little before 1800. Went home around 1930."

"Any witnesses at the Field House, sir?"

"Major Wilson accompanied me. We saw a number

of cadets who will remember us. None that I knew, but Major Wilson might be able to identify them. Now if there's nothing else . . ."

Crenshaw didn't care if there was. He rose and walked over to the door, leading to the balcony.

"One thing, sir," Malone said quickly. "Once Mrs. Owen has been notified, we'll be making an announcement through the cadet command post, asking for witnesses who might have seen anything."

Crenshaw pushed open the door, looking at him. "I'll call ahead to tell them you're coming." His eyes narrowed. "You understand the repercussions if you mention your suspicions concerning me to Ms. Barlow . . ."

"We won't say anything, sir," Malone said. Mother shook her head.

The general continued to contemplate Malone. "It appears," he said, "that I should have accepted your offer."

Their eyes met. Malone said, "It's not too late, sir."

"Malone . . . Malone . . ." The general shook his head, sounding disappointed. "You still don't get it, do you?"

"Sir?"

"It's why you won't make a good officer. You lack character. By now you should understand ethics aren't situational. They can't be compromised for personal consideration."

Yet another criticism. As before, Malone let it slide off him. The reality was the general wasn't telling Malone anything he hadn't told himself.

"Implying," Malone replied, "that I should forget you're the superintendent and ask you straight out what your relationship was with Rachel Owen, sir?"

"That's a start," Crenshaw said quietly.

"All right, sir. I'd like to know what your—"

The general stepped onto the balcony, pulling the door closed behind him. He leaned against the railing and gazed out over the cadet area. Someone must have waved, because he waved back.

"Well?" Mother said.

Malone sighed, knowing what she wanted. "He's all yours, Mother. You called it; I can't go after him." He eyed her, adding, "But it's not for the reason you think. I'm not intimidated by him."

No *I-told-you-so* this time. Instead, she said bluntly, "And this offer . . ."

"It was nothing. I was just trying to get him to confide in me."

She appeared unconvinced, but refrained from comment. Gesturing at Crenshaw, she said, "Explain something to me, Malone. You put him on some kind of pedestal, practically worship the guy. Always have. But it's pretty clear the feeling isn't mutual. I'm not sure the man even likes you."

"And you'd like to know why?"

She nodded. "It can't be just because he was your AOC. Hell, you quit."

"It is partly. I didn't have many male role models growing up. My grandfather did what he could, but he wasn't around much."

"You saying Crenshaw was a father figure? Come on."

"Let's just say he was the man I wanted to be, but never could."

Mother's expression softened. She didn't seem to know what to say. "Jesus, Malone, just when I think I got you pegged . . ." She shook her head. "But dammit, this is a murder investigation. If he was anyone else, we'd question him now. We can't make allowances for rank."

"No . . ."

She watched him. "It means that much to you, huh?"

"I don't want to embarrass him unnecessarily."

She turned and looked at Crenshaw. "Screw it. He's not going anywhere. Let's check out his alibi first. And Malone . . ."

"I know. I owe you. Thanks, Mother."

As they left the room, General Crenshaw remained on the balcony, gazing out across the Academy. A modern-day emperor watching over his subjects. But soon those subjects would be taken from him.

"It's a shame," Malone murmured. "He doesn't deserve this."

"As long as he isn't a killer."

Mother at her pragmatic best.

Chapter 14

THE ACTIVITY IN THE ANTEROOM HAD DIED AWAY. The calm before the storm.

The Com and Colonel Greenley were still absent, overseeing the press conference. Mrs. Weaver was over by a cabinet, sipping coffee as she filed papers. The communications technicians had finished installing the phones and were gone. Two more senior NCOs had arrived, which made it a total of six people seated at the table, three to a side. The lieutenant colonel circled the group, passing out folders.

"Restrict your comments to the talking paper," he said. "It shouldn't be difficult. The parents are concerned about their children's welfare and once you confirm they are safe and there's no danger—"

A phone rang. The people at the table looked to the receivers before them.

It was Mrs. Weaver's. She stepped over to her desk and picked up.

Mother said, "I've seen enough, Major."

"Print it, Seth," Malone said.

She and Malone stood over Major Seth Wilson, peering at his computer screen. General Crenshaw's schedule was right there in blue and white, confirming the general indeed had an alibi for the killings. Upon viewing this, Malone had felt a palpable sense of relief.

Then he'd asked Wilson if he'd been with Crenshaw during the hour they were at the gym.

"Hold on," Wilson had said, finally understanding their interest. "You don't think the general could have anything to do— Ow!" He grabbed his neck and glared up at Mother. "What'd you do that for?"

She'd pinched his neck. "You talk too much, Major."

"What's that supposed to—"

He fell silent. He'd noticed the people at the table were watching him. Wilson wasn't the brightest bulb in the room, but he was smart enough to realize what would happen if it got out Crenshaw was being investigated.

"Answer the question, Seth," Malone said.

"Uh, no. We each do our own thing. I like to lift weights. I'm not a big aerobic guy, like the general— I say something?" He'd reacted to Mother's grimace and Malone's sudden, almost angry head shake.

Malone said, "By aerobic?"

"The general's a runner," Wilson said. "Took it up a few months ago. He runs almost every day."

Malone swore.

The office printer was located behind Mrs. Weaver's desk. When it stopped humming, Malone went over to retrieve Crenshaw's schedule. Mrs. Weaver, still on the phone, waved him off. She slid into her chair, simultaneously plucking the page free and saying into the mouthpiece, "The commandant and Colonel Greenley are in the news conference, Lieutenant Colonel Culpepper. It will be another ten or fifteen minutes at least. The superintendent? If this concerns Ms. Owen, I'm sure he'll want to . . . What was that?"

She smiled at Malone, offering up the page. As he reached for it, the paper began to tremble in her hand. Her face grew ashen, her eyes widening in horror.

She dropped the phone, bolted from her chair, and rushed into Crenshaw's office.

Pocketing his cell phone, Lieutenant Colonel (Dr.) Benjamin Culpepper, a psychologist trained in grief counseling, twisted around in the passenger seat of the Air Force staff car, facing the two officers seated behind him. "Colonel Greenley wants us to check out the house again."

The other officers also wore the rank of lieutenant colonel and neither appeared particularly thrilled at the news. One was the senior chaplain from the Academy chapel; the second, a medical doctor assigned to the base hospital. The three men were members of the casualty notification team. The fourth person in the car was the driver, a young female airman.

The driver immediately opened her door. The doctor and chaplain shook their heads and reluctantly followed her lead.

"Tell you what," Culpepper said. "You all can hang loose. I'll look in the windows to keep Colonel Greenley happy. Back in a minute."

"I'm tired of sitting, sir," the airman said.

"Suit yourself," Culpepper said, climbing out.

The doctor and the chaplain remained in the car, while the airman and Culpepper walked up the snow-covered driveway, following a trail of footprints toward the modest home. Most of the prints were theirs, but not all. And it was those that had initially lent credence to the neighbor's suggestion that Mrs. Owen had gone on her morning walk.

As they approached the house, the dog inside began to bark.

"What kind is he, sir?" the airman asked.

"Don't know. He's in one of the bedrooms. We'll split up. Be quicker."

Waving her to the back, he continued toward the front stoop. Three minutes later, Culpepper had finished peeking into the living-room and kitchen windows. As before, there was nothing to see.

When he returned to the driveway, he didn't see the airman, but could hear the dog barking intensely. He went around to the rear, passing through the gate of the fenced backyard. The airman was kneeling by the patio door, peering through a rubber dog flap. She spoke in soothing tones, the dog continuing to bark.

Walking up, Culpepper said, "You're wasting your time. My guess is he's locked in the bedroom."

"He isn't, sir. I just saw him in the hall. He's a poodle. There he is again. He's running up to—"

She broke off, staring. The dog was barking feverishly, right on the other side of the door.

The airman suddenly pulled back, looking fearfully at Culpepper.

"What?" he said. "Something wrong?"

"The dog is all . . . red."

A Colorado Springs patrol car responded within minutes to Lieutenant Colonel Culpepper's 911 call. After the two officers went through the drill of ringing the bell and shouting out to the occupant, they kicked in the front door. They went in with guns drawn and methodically searched the house. The last room they checked was the master bedroom located at the very back, and that's where they found her.

Protected by a small poodle standing in a tacky pool of blood, barking at them.

During the short ride from Harmon Hall to the Field House, Mother and Malone never said a word. They couldn't. They were still trying to come to grips with the curve that General Crenshaw had thrown at them.

Mrs. Lola Owen, Rachel's mother, had been murdered.

As they pulled up to Mother's truck, she murmured, "One shot to the head. Execution style. Same MO, same killer."

"Same motive, too. Mrs. Owen was killed for the same reason as Mary Zinnel; she must have known who raped Rachel."

"So," she said, eyeing him, "you now think she might have been raped after all."

"Hell, I don't know. Everything's so damned . . . unclear." He shook his head. "But it's the only thing that makes any sense."

"Three suspects," Mother said. "We have three prime suspects, including Crenshaw. Coach Ralston might've been able to intimidate Rachel into keeping quiet, but we know Crenshaw could have. No one would have believed her if she'd accused the superintendent of rape."

She anticipated a rebuttal, but there was nothing Malone could say in Crenshaw's defense. Overcome by lust and desire, even a seemingly moral man could be driven to do immoral things.

"It'll take me a couple more hours," Mother said. "Keep me posted. " She got out and went over to her pickup. After dropping by the cadet command post to make the announcement seeking witnesses, she'd return to Jack's Valley and finish processing the crime scene. In the meantime, Malone would drive into Colorado Springs, learn what he could about Lola Owen's murder.

But first he had an en route stop and a call to make.

The importance of Rachel Owen's e-mails was growing. In those, she would have shared her most intimate thoughts with people who were close to her, including her mother.

And if they got lucky . . .

Driving off, he phoned Bonnie, the cadet systems administrator. "Great minds think alike, Malone. I was about to give you a shout. I'm in the office and just retrieved the passwords."

"Give me a sec."

Malone balanced the notepad on the steering column. "Okay, go."

Bonnie gave him Mary Zinnel's password first: girl-pilot12. Typical.

"And Rachel Owen's?"

"It's a funny one. She must have a thing for a parachutist."

"A parachutist?"

"Listen." She read off the letters one by one, to make sure Malone understood: "I-l-u-v-p-a-r-a-m-a-n," she said.

As he wrote, Malone recalled what Major Tupper had said about Rachel: *What little free time she had left, she spent at the parachute hangar, going through free-fall training.*

Malone felt a twinge of excitement. Passwords were highly personal, and the odds that Rachel would fabricate this one—

"Yo, Malone. I know you're there. I can hear you breathing."

"I appreciate this, Bonnie. I owe you one."

"One? Try about ten. I was thinking about dinner at Sparza's. A nice bottle of wine, candlelight. No kids."

"Bonnie . . ."

"Yeah, yeah. You love me for my mind. Hey, it's your loss. You can't count on me waiting forever. Husband number three is out there somewhere."

He had to smile. "Tell you what, maybe I'll give you a call in a couple of weeks."

"That'll be the day. But if you're ever in the market

for a mature woman with intelligence and her own health plan . . ."

"You'll be first on my list."

"You're such a liar."

She was laughing as she hung up. In contrast, Malone clicked off with a troubled expression. He stared at Rachel's password before slowly tucking the notepad in his jacket.

Who the hell was paraman?

As Malone tossed around this new wrinkle, his mind felt dull and slow. Part of it was the lack of sleep and the remnants of a hangover, but mostly it was because things were coming in too fast. The parachutist, if he existed, couldn't be Ralston or Crenshaw, since they weren't qualified. That left the only other player in the game—Cadet Jefferson. Could he be a jumper, perhaps a member of the Academy's Wings of Blue parachute team?

Unlikely. Major Tupper would have mentioned it. Besides, cadets involved in varsity sports don't have time to parachute full time.

So they were looking for someone else. A fourth person.

Another possible suspect.

Damn.

Turning into the parking area under Vandenberg Hall, Malone felt the beginnings of another headache. It immediately became worse because of the phone call he received moments later.

"Agent Malone," a gruff voice said, "someone's wasting your goddamn time and mine."

Chapter 15

MALONE PARKED BESIDE A SECURITY FORCES SUV—the extra security he'd arranged. As the phone hissed, he tried to place the name on the caller ID. Someone named Green.

The man said, "Agent Malone?"

Malone finally realized who it must be and retrieved a name from his memory. "Chief Hawkins?"

"Yeah, and I'm not a happy camper. Damn near froze my ass off. It's snowing like hell up here and I got stuck twice. Listen, I don't mind helping you out— Can you hold on?"

Someone in the background spoke to him—a woman. Chief Hawkins said, "Coffee would be fine, Karalyn. Black." To Malone: "Anyway, it was a waste of time."

"Cadet Jefferson wasn't at the cabin?"

"*No one* was there. Place was locked up tight; no tracks in the snow. I'm calling from Karalyn Green's. She's the closest neighbor, about a half-mile away. Karalyn's pretty sure no one's been to the Jefferson cabin for several months. You ask me, I'd find out who told you the Jeffersons would be here. Because they sure as hell ain't."

"I'll do that, Chief. Sorry to put you out. Listen, I hate to ask, but if the Jeffersons do show up—"

"Karalyn will keep an eye out and call me."

"Thanks again, Chief."

Leaving his car, Malone recalled more of Major Tupper's words: "*And before you ask, the answer is, yes. I spoke directly with his family—an older sister, and she confirmed the family would be at the cabin.*"

There were two possible explanations, neither good. Now the question was whether Major Tupper was familiar with the voice of Jefferson's sister.

Swallowing two more packets of aspirin, Malone went up the stairs to find out.

A loud squelch reverberated over the cadet area loudspeakers, reminiscent of a scene from M*A*S*H. Only instead of Radar O'Reilly's familiar falsetto, a deep male voice came on: "Attention in the area, attention in the area. All cadets are reminded to assemble in their SARs by 1200 hours. I repeat, 1200 hours. Command post out."

Malone checked his watch, confirmed it was the ten-minutes-to-go call. With the discovery of Mrs. Owen's body, the cadet wing would finally be told they'd lost two of their own. He continued up the stairs, cadets streaming past him. The squadron assembly rooms were located adjacent to the stairwells, on the terrazzo level.

At the fifth-floor landing, Malone squeezed past

exiting bodies and entered Cadet Squadron Eighteen. Unlike before, it was almost empty. Down a cross hallway from the CQ desk, he saw Agent Doug Anderson appear from a room, trailed by two security cops. Anderson noticed Malone, read his boss's quizzical gaze, and shook his head.

No weapon had been found yet.

The muscular CQ was no longer on duty. The new guy was about half his size, sported a flat-top haircut, and wore a silver Commandant's List wreath on his left breast pocket, indicating he was near the top of his class militarily. He stood in a brace, nervously eyeing Malone. Malone tried to relax him with a smile, but the brace only became more rigid.

"Don't hurt yourself, son."

"Sir?"

"Never mind." Malone glanced at his nametag. "Major Tupper in his office, Cadet Wallace?"

"Sir, no, sir—the cops . . . I mean the OSI agents are in there, sir."

Three sirs in one sentence. This guy was going to make general. "He down in the SAR?"

"Sir, no, sir. Sir, he went over to Twentieth Squadron, to talk to Major Schiller, sir."

Four this time. Malone said, "There's an agent searching Cadet Owen's room—" Wallace nodded hard enough to snap his neck. "Have the agent and Major Tupper meet me in the major's office."

"Sir, yes, sir."

Wallace took off in a sprint. Watching him tear down the hall, Malone had to shake his head. When he'd been a cadet, he specialized in being sarcastic to the Patton wannabes like Wallace, those who played the spit-and-polish soldier game and internalized arcane notions like duty and honor and chivalry. To Malone, it had all been tiresome propaganda and he wasn't about to fall for it.

It was only after Malone left the Academy, at a time when he felt rudderless and uncertain of his future, that he finally appreciated the underlying value of the very concepts he'd criticized. Cadets came to the Academy as blank slates and needed a standard to measure themselves against, and more important, something bigger than themselves to believe in. Even though he was too jaded and, frankly, too self-serving to become a complete convert, this realization energized him with a sense of purpose. While he could never change what had happened to Christina, Malone decided there was at least one way for him to make amends.

"You'll never make a good officer," Crenshaw had told him.

But the general had missed the point. Malone never had a desire to be a "good" officer or even a fair one, certainly not by Crenshaw's standards. He wanted only to be able to look into the mirror someday without feeling the guilt, because he'd tried to live a life that was worth a damn. And maybe, just maybe, make up for the mistakes of his past.

Malone slowed, approaching Tupper's office. The door was partially open, snippets of conversation floating out. Not wanting to disturb a cadet interview, Malone peeked inside and saw Kranski and Kaitlin huddled together. No one else was in the room and they were speaking in earnest tones. Kranski, sounding embarrassed, said, "I never went on a date in high school, Kaitlin. And I only went on two while I was a cadet here. Two dates in four years. It sucked. The guys made fun of me."

Malone almost gagged.

"I can't believe that, Paul," Kaitlin replied sincerely. "You're a very attractive young man."

Kranski stared at her. "You mean it?"

She took his hand in hers, smiling. "Of course. You're quite good-looking. You just lack confidence. What you need to do is be more assertive—"

Malone couldn't take it anymore and stepped inside. Kranski took one look, jerked his hand from Kaitlin, and jumped up with a guilty expression.

"Jeez, you surprised me, sir. Kaitlin and I . . . I mean Ms. Barlow and I . . . we finished the interviews. We didn't learn much except for a lead on Rachel Owen's boyfriend. Actually, it's kinda confusing 'cause, well, I mean if it's Jefferson, why would—"

He was all over the place. Malone told him to slow down and take a deep breath. The agent did, inhaling loud enough for them to hear.

"I'll brief Agent Malone, Paul," Kaitlin said. "Leave us for a few minutes. I need to talk to him alone."

Back to being formal, Malone noted. Not a good sign.

Kranski appeared relieved at the suggestion. His eyes darted to Malone, who was blocking the door. "Uh, sir . . ."

But instead of moving, Malone asked Kranski if the two laptops sitting on a corner of Tupper's desk belonged to the victims.

"Yes, sir."

"Be back in ten minutes. I've got the passwords and want you to go through the e-mails."

Another bob. Kranski shifted his feet anxiously. Malone finally put him out of his misery and moved aside. Ducking past, Kranski practically ran from the room. Malone shut the door and faced Kaitlin.

"He's afraid of you," she said.

As if that were a bad thing. Malone noticed she still wore gloves.

"Ten minutes," Kaitlin went on coldly, "isn't enough time for what I have to say."

"It will have to be. We're leaving."

"After your stunt, I'm not going anywhere with you."

"You will."

"Try again. I'm thinking about calling Senator Smith and asking him to have you replaced."

"You won't." This time Malone threw in a confident smile. An instant later, he regretted it.

Kaitlin's face flushed a bright red, matching her lipstick. She jumped from her chair and set upon him in a rush of pent-up anger, the words flying from her mouth. Crenshaw had been mistaken; she hadn't cooled off, not by a long shot.

"You son of a bitch. You promised to cooperate. *Cooperate*. But the first chance you had, you took off, left me out in the cold. I want to know what you're hiding and why the hell you think—"

"Kaitlin. Keep it down. The cadets might hear—"

"Screw the cadets and *screw you.*"

She continued to rail at him, completely incensed. Malone calmly took it all in, waiting his chance. When she finally paused for a breath, he got in a short statement, only four words.

"Rachel's mother was murdered," he said.

Kaitlin reacted as if she'd been slapped and said nothing more as he explained.

A soft tap on the door. "Come in," Malone said, hoping it was Tupper.

Instead, a slender, bookish man wearing black-framed glasses poked his head inside. His tentative expression indicated he'd caught at least some of Kaitlin's rage. "You wanted me, boss?"

Next to Malone and Mother, Senior Master Sergeant Rob Sanders was the most competent agent in the unit. Painstakingly methodical, Sanders checked everything about a hundred times, which was the reason Malone had wanted him to search the victims' room. If there was anything there, Sanders would find it.

"Any luck, Rob?" Malone asked.

"No, and I'm almost done." His eyes narrowed through the lenses. "But I got a month's pay that says someone cleaned out the room. You know how a lot of cadets stick their letters and cards on the bulletin boards above their desks . . ."

"Right, sure."

"The girls' boards were empty, but I could see pin-holes. Pins were also scattered on the floor, like someone in a hurry pulled away whatever was stuck to the boards. But the kicker is Mary Zinnel's diary. It's missing. Major Tupper and another cadet swore she kept one. Had a blue cover—"

Malone pivoted and walked over to the laptops on the desk. Kaitlin joined him, as did Sanders. A Post-it note was stuck to each computer, indicating which was whose.

Kaitlin said, "Malone, you think . . ."

"The letters and diary were taken for a reason."

Quickly donning latex gloves, Malone picked up Mary Zinnel's laptop and passed it to Sanders, who already had on gloves. "Power it up, Rob." Opening Rachel's, Malone did the same. Both computers booted up normally.

"Password?" Sanders said.

After telling him, Malone typed in Rachel's password, got the Desktop display, and clicked on Outlook Express. As the Inbox screen came up, he heard Sanders swear softly. Moments later, Malone understood why.

The layout of Rachel's Inbox page was normal, but under the From and To headings, there was only gibberish. Random patterns of nonsensical symbols and letters.

"Machine language," Malone murmured.

"A randomizer program to scramble the data," Sanders said. "Our killer's been a busy boy."

Both men clicked to Sent Messages. More random symbols. Closing the laptop, Malone said to Sanders, "Rachel Owen's mother was also murdered—"

"Ah, hell—"

"Kaitlin and I are going there now, so you're in charge. When you finish with Rachel and Mary's room, start in on Cadet Jefferson's. Also send Kranski over to the computer center. I want those e-mails ASAP."

"E-mails?" Kaitlin asked, surprised. "You think he can retrieve them from the server?"

"I know he can," Malone said.

"Outlook Express allows you to delete e-mails off a server. We do that all the time in the senator's office, to prevent anyone from seeing confidential information. It seems to me that whoever was smart enough to destroy the e-mail data would have— Oh, come on. Of course, they would."

Malone's and Sanders's expressions remained skeptical. Sanders said, "The Academy has its own servers, ma'am. Even if Outlook Express tried to remove the e-mails, the security systems would have prevented it."

Kaitlin said, "Couldn't someone who knew what they were doing figure out a way to bypass the Academy's computer security?"

"Not likely. A new system was installed after 9/11. The person would have to be a real computer whiz."

"Which is what he was, I'm afraid," a voice said.

Turning, they saw Major Tupper standing behind them. They hadn't heard him come in. Picking up on his grim expression, Malone put two and two together. He said, "Major, are you telling us—"

"Cadet Jefferson's a computer science major," Tupper said. "The top student in his class."

Chapter 16

AT TUPPER'S STATEMENT, KAITLIN FLASHED Malone her patented superior look. It was similar to Mother's I-told-you-so glance, only more patronizing.

He said to her, "You knew Jefferson was a comp sci major, didn't you?"

"Rachel told me." Her eyes shifted between Malone and Sanders. "But you two were so damned sure the e-mails would be on the server." She sounded sarcastic and amused.

"He still might not be able to pull it off," Sanders tossed back.

"Don't bet on it," Tupper said. "Jefferson knows more about computers than his instructors. For the past year, they've assigned him advanced projects to work on his own."

Sanders and Malone scowled. Sanders said, "I'll send Kranksi to the comp center now. Find out the bad news."

"Take the laptops. Maybe Kranski or someone at the center can retrieve some of the data."

"Rog." He grabbed the computers and left.

"I can give you five minutes," Tupper said to Malone. "I've got to brief the cadets. Still not sure what I'm going to tell them."

Malone asked him if he'd gotten the word on Mrs. Owen.

He got quiet, nodding. "Only met her a couple of times, since she moved out here. But she was a good woman. Sweet-natured. So damn proud of her daughter. In combat, people die and you understand why. But this is . . . insane. And to think that Jefferson might be responsible, that he'd actually be capable of killing three people." He shook his head. "I don't believe it. I simply can't."

Malone was about to completely ruin his day with the bad news about the cabin, but Tupper abruptly resumed speaking. His voice had a disjointed quality, as if he was trying to work things out. "The e-mails . . . if the ones on the servers are destroyed . . . I suppose . . . I suppose it has to be Jefferson. No one else . . . he's the only one who could . . . And the diary. Jefferson knew Mary kept a diary. He must have slipped into their room after the murders . . . before he signed out. Or . . . or maybe he left and came back—"

"Anyone with a proxy card could have taken the diary," Kaitlin said, suddenly speaking up.

Tupper slow-blinked her.

"Kaitlin," Malone pointed out, "only a cadet could have removed it without being noticed."

"Have you *seen* the girls' room?"

Malone hesitated.

"That's what I thought. It's around the opposite corner of the squadron, next to a stairwell. Anyone could slip in without being seen. Especially in the evening when everyone is studying, or after taps. I stopped by only yesterday, and no one noticed me."

Malone and Tupper stared at her. Malone said, "You were here yesterday *evening*?"

"Yeah. Around 8:00 P.M."

"Did you go into the room?"

"Sure. The door was unlocked. I waited for about ten minutes, then left." She shrugged.

"The computers? Where were they?"

"On the desks."

"Did you notice if anything was on their bulletin boards?"

"They were cluttered with stuff, as usual. Major Tupper can tell you. Rachel had a thing for Far Side cards." She flashed a bemused smile. "My, my. All these questions. Does this somehow make me a suspect, Mr. Policeman?"

Christ. She's acting like this is a joke. He demanded, "Why didn't you tell me this earlier?"

"Maybe I would have," she said coolly, "if you'd hung around."

Her gaze cut through him. He sighed; there was nothing he could say.

Tupper coughed. "Look, I've got to run—"

Malone quickly related his conversation with Chief Hawkins. The major gazed at Malone as if he didn't understand. Kaitlin, on the other hand, appeared completely unsurprised.

"What do you mean no one was at the cabin?" Tupper said. "That's impossible. The family should be there. I spoke to Sandra Jefferson. Why would she lie to me?"

"Had you spoken to her before?"

"Well, no, but what does that have to do—" Tupper looked sick. "Oh, *hell* . . ."

He rushed over to his desk and bent over his computer. Grabbing for the mouse, he knocked over a mug, spilling coffee everywhere. "Shit, *shit.*" He tried to pick up the mug, but it slipped from his grasp. "Fuck!" He grabbed the mug, slammed it to the desk, and clicked furiously on the mouse.

Malone and Kaitlin eyed each other. Combat veteran or not, the major was losing it.

Leaning close to Malone, Kaitlin murmured, "I'll tell you what Kranski and I learned about the boyfriend on one condition. No more games. I want you to tell me why you ran off. And I want the truth."

As she spoke, her breath caressed his ear. He instantly became aware of . . . her. And as he breathed in the familiarity of her perfume, he found himself transported into the past. Remembering Christina, that day in his room.

I want to fuck you.

Malone felt a sudden excitement, which disgusted him. What the hell was wrong with him? Christina was dead; he shouldn't be reacting this way. Yet being with Kaitlin continually reminded him—

"Well, Malone?"

He faced her, managing to sound calm. "I could simply ask Kranski."

"You really want to go down that road?"

He didn't hesitate. "You know I don't."

She relaxed with a smile; it was a nice smile. She said, "I'll even go first. Rachel denied having a boyfriend to me, but that obviously wasn't the case. She told at least two friends about him, so it follows that Jefferson also must have known about him. As to who told him, no one will say. The cadets we interviewed swore it wasn't them. They didn't even know who the guy was; Rachel was careful never to identify him by name. All she said was—"

"Jefferson has one sister," Tupper announced. "Sandra is two years older. She lives in Durango."

Malone said, "You have her phone—"

Tupper was already placing the call. As he did, he offered Malone the receiver.

"You talk to her," Malone said. "You're the AOC. If she didn't make the call, I don't want to alarm her or the family just yet."

Tupper nodded. Into the phone: "Sandra Jefferson, this is Major Brad Tupper from the Academy . . . Right, his AOC. I apologize for calling, but we're trying to reach your brother." After telling her about the cabin and the conversation he'd supposedly had with her, Tupper listened for several seconds. He shook his head at Malone, mouthing, "It wasn't her."

Malone began scribbling questions on his notepad.

"He's older," Kaitlin said.

Malone looked up from writing.

"Rachel's boyfriend is quite a bit older." She punctuated the remark with a suggestive look. As the inference settled in, it was all Malone could do not to react. He asked casually, "Were Rachel's friends aware she might be pregnant?"

"No."

Still fixated on him with an unblinking stare. Another message, Malone decided.

She knew.

Does Sandra know who her brother might have gotten to impersonate her?

Was her brother interested in any girls? Close friends? Romantically?

Does she have any idea where her brother might have gone?

Could she attempt to contact her brother and have him call Major Tupper?

These were Malone's questions. As Tupper asked Sandra Jefferson the first three, he relayed her responses by shaking his head. After the fourth question, he nodded to Malone and Kaitlin, then thanked Sandra and hung up.

"She hasn't spoken to her brother in weeks," he said, "and the family definitely had no plans to be at the cabin. Couldn't. The parents are vacationing in Mexico."

"Time," Kaitlin concluded. "Cadet Jefferson arranged the ruse to buy time to get away. You think there could be another reason? Like what, for instance?" She'd noticed Malone's furrowed brow.

"Hmm. No, no. I'm just wondering why he's trying to get away at all. It doesn't fit our profile of him. His state of mind."

"The suicidal part?"

Malone nodded.

"By your logic," she said, "it wouldn't make sense for him to kill Mrs. Owen."

"It doesn't."

They were quiet, mulling this over.

"Hold on," Tupper said to Malone, "are you saying you *don't* think Jefferson is the killer?"

"We won't know anything until we talk to him. I'll need a description."

"Black male, five-six, 130 pounds, no distinguishing marks."

"You have a photo we can e-mail?"

"All the cadet yearbook photos are in the computer."

"Print me a copy. I also need his cell number and make of car."

Tupper clicked his mouse and the printer under his desk whirred. Jotting the number on a Post-it, he passed it and the disk to Malone, saying, "His car is a 2005 Mustang. Black. Don't know the plate."

"Call Security Forces and get it. Advise them to have the gate guards watch for him."

As Tupper made the call, he gave Malone the photo of Jefferson. It was a head shot, depicting a clean-cut young black man sporting a toothy grin.

"Doesn't look much like a killer," Kaitlin observed.

Neither did Jeffrey Dahmer, Malone thought.

After contacting the Colorado State Police on his cell, Malone requested an APB on Jefferson, got their e-mail address, and had Tupper transmit the cadet's photo. The entire time, Kaitlin continued to stare at him with a curiously confident expression. Even if she knew about Coach Ralston, Malone wasn't particularly concerned. Despite her revelation about the older boyfriend, she wouldn't be able to make a case against Ralston, certainly not one that was a slam dunk.

Unless she could somehow get past the card Malone had up his sleeve.

"You have reached the voice mail for Terry Jefferson," the mechanically precise female voice said. "Press one now to leave a message, or wait until . . ."

Malone thumbed one.

He was alone in the office; Kaitlin had left to use the restroom and Tupper was down in the SAR, briefing his cadets. At the chime, Malone identified himself and in a nonthreatening tone, asked Jefferson to contact him. As Malone saw it, the cadet's reaction was crucial. If Jefferson did phone back, it was possible that he was simply an unstable kid who had disappeared for personal reasons unrelated to the murders. And if he didn't call . . .

Malone shook his head. Even with evidence lining up against Jefferson, he couldn't accept the cadet's apparent guilt. Not completely.

There were too many inconsistencies that couldn't be explained. Moments earlier, Malone had finished a conversation with Dr. Patricia Garber, who confirmed his suspicion that Jefferson, once having murdered Rachel and Mary, would not attempt to escape.

"He'd kill himself. I'd be surprised if he hasn't already done so."

"You're sure, Doctor?"

"Psychiatry isn't an exact science, Agent Malone. But yes, I'm fairly certain you'll find him dead somewhere."

"Then he'd have no reason to kill Mrs. Owen?"

"Not unless he blamed Mrs. Owen for his breakup with Rachel. I can assure you, that's not the case."

"Did Cadet Jefferson have a close woman friend, possibly a civilian?"

"Other than his family . . ."

"Yes."

"His world was Rachel. He wasn't interested in other women." She hesitated.

"Yes?"

"It may be nothing. But he was wearing cologne the last time we met. Way too much, as a matter of fact."

"Excuse me?"

Then Malone understood. "It was unusual for him to wear cologne?"

"He never did, which is probably why he used too much. Usually, when a man starts wearing cologne, there's only one reason."

"A woman. Thank you, Doctor."

Before ending the conversation, she added one final remark. "I told you Cadet Jefferson was emotionally incapable of the murders and I still believe it. Until last week, he was making real progress. It was only after he learned Rachel had a boyfriend when he began to regress. To me, the timing is troubling. To build the kind of rage that would lead him to kill would take an extended period of time. In my judgment, that suggests there was a catalyst, something that pushed him over the edge."

"Rachel's pregnancy?"

"Possibly. Something."

Malone had filed the word *catalyst* in his mental Rolodex, right beside another nagging question.

Who was the woman who pretended to be Sandra Jefferson?

Was she a cadet or a civilian? Could she be the person who had tipped Jefferson off about the existence of Rachel's boyfriend and her possible pregnancy? If she did, could she have known about his intentions beforehand, perhaps been involved in the killings?

So many questions; too many.

With a frustrated sigh, Malone stepped from the office into the hall. Except for the CQ, Cadet Wallace, it was a ghost town. From somewhere, he heard drawers slamming open and closed—the search. He walked away from Wallace, toward the stairwell he'd used for his earlier escape from Kaitlin. He continued around the corner, to where he remembered seeing the women's restroom. Leaning against the wall, he was puzzled to hear angry conversation. The voices were muffled, but he occasionally recognized Kaitlin's voice.

Within moments, she emerged, looking agitated. She spat, "That sick bitch—"

She stopped, startled to see Malone.

He pushed upright. "The bitch?"

She hesitated. "Someone from Senator Smith's office."

"You were on the phone?" Malone asked, surprised.

"With her royal highness Marcy Dyers, the senator's chief of staff. Marcy is one controlling bitch."

"Why? What'd she say?"

But Kaitlin blew past him, walking quickly toward the stairwell. Following after her, Malone appeared perplexed. As they left the squadron, he still didn't see anyone emerge from the restroom.

Chapter 17

MALONE AND KAITLIN STARTED DOWN THE stairs. She still appeared tense, angry. She said, "It's your turn. Tell me why you ran out of here."

"I need you to promise me something first."

"That," she snapped, "wasn't part of our agreement."

"Relax. Investigations are supposed to be confidential. All I want is your word you won't share this with anyone until we have evidence."

"Define evidence."

"I don't want your boss Senator Smith smearing anyone without proof."

"Fine."

This was too easy. "I mean it."

"Unlike you, I *keep* my word."

"You going to keep throwing that in my face?"

She just looked at him. He took it as a yes.

"Coach Ralston," he said, and waited.

Her expression turned quizzical. "What about him?"

"Come on. You really don't know?"

"Know what?"

"Who's holding out on who? The way you were looking at me earlier. When you told me about the older boyfriend—"

"You're imagining things."

They passed the terrazzo level and continued to the third floor. "Your sister never mentioned him?"

She was getting irritated. "Why would she—"

Her head gave a little jerk. "Oh, Jesus. Are you saying Coach Ralston . . ."

"Yes."

Malone rapidly filled her in on everything—Mother's suspicions about Ralston, the conversation with General Crenshaw, the interview with the coach and his wife, the supposedly incriminating item Laura Ralston had found—he told her all of it, leaving nothing back.

Except, of course, the part about Crenshaw and Rachel Owen.

When he finished, Kaitlin smoldered with anger, but when she spoke, the bitterness in her voice was controlled. "What the Academy did to my sister was bad enough, but this is completely indefensible. How could they hire someone like him to be the head coach? Someone who was involved in a rape and could be a murderer. It's beyond comprehension; it's criminal. There's no other word for it."

She continued to vilify the Academy and its leadership. Malone tried to keep from responding. But Kaitlin was citing assumptions as fact and viewing everything with 20/20 hindsight. As they exited onto the ground floor and started toward his car, Malone had had enough and said, "Cut it out."

She looked at him in surprise.

"You're holding the Academy to an unrealistic standard. There was no evidence of Ralston's guilt. None. Without it, you can't expect—"

"*Laura Ralston found something.*"

"Fourteen years after the fact. And if it does implicate Ralston, he'll be prosecuted. General Crenshaw will see to it and so will Mother and I. But first, let's make damn sure he is guilty— Don't give me that look. Right now, everything points to Jefferson. You know damn well it does."

They came to the car and she pivoted to him. Her voice was patronizing and moralistic. "What I know," she said, "is the Academy hired a potential rapist who might be a killer. For that, there is no excuse. When this is over, I can promise you Senator Smith and his colleagues will demand answers, as will the public and the press. I have every confidence the American people will judge this place for what it is, an institution run by misogynists who routinely foster a climate of hate against women. In the future, Agent Malone . . ." She emphasized his name as if it were something you stepped in ". . . I doubt you'll admit you attended school here."

Even for a lawyer it was quite a speech, and Malone realized it was time to play his ace in the hole. He set her up with: "So you're convinced the coach is Rachel's boyfriend?"

"You bet I am and so are you. The cadets said it was an older man— What's this for?"

Malone was holding out his notepad, pointing to

Rachel's password. Kaitlin reread the letters twice. Then a third time.

When she glanced up, she still seemed confused. "This suggests she was involved with a parachutist. But aren't they all cadets?"

"The jump team cadre are enlisted and officers. Most are in their late twenties and early thirties."

Kaitlin visibly deflated. More than anything, she wanted the killer to be Ralston, the man whom she now believed was responsible for her sister's rape. "Congratulations, Malone. You must be relieved."

"Kaitlin, it's not a matter of—"

She abruptly turned away and went over to the passenger door. Malone sighed, shaking his head. This was something else she was going to keep throwing in his face.

As they got into the car, Mother's voice came over the Academy's loudspeakers. "Attention in the cadet area. This is Agent Hubbard of the OSI. If anyone was in the vicinity of Dead Man's Lake yesterday afternoon or has any information concerning the deaths of—"

Malone shut the door and started the car. Driving off, he knew he should ignore Kaitlin's insinuation, but he couldn't.

"What you said wasn't fair," he said quietly. "My job is to find the killer, whoever it is."

A silence. She was slumped forward, staring at her hands.

He added, "I'd think you'd want that, too."

Again no response. Malone was about to give up when he finally caught the hint of a nod.

"The rape," she said with feeling. "At least we'll get him for the rape."

"I wouldn't get your hopes up just yet."

Kaitlin became tense, staring at him.

"Chill," he said. "I don't want you to be disappointed if the evidence Laura Ralston found isn't as incriminating as she believes."

She slowly relaxed. "You had me worried. For a moment, it sounded as if you didn't believe Ralston was a rapist." She frowned, glancing around. "Where are we going? Aren't we heading downtown to see Mrs. Owen's body?"

"Not yet," Malone said.

Mrs. Lola Owen lived in an older neighborhood northwest of Rockrimmon Drive, twenty minutes south of the Academy. By the time Malone exited off I-25, he'd made two calls—the first to update Mother on Jefferson; the second to confirm whether the Ninety-eighth Flying Training Squadron, the unit responsible for parachute training, was jumping this afternoon—and had listened to most of an Alan Jackson CD.

"You *like* country music?" Kaitlin asked, when he first put it in.

"I enjoy watching NASCAR, too."

She made no attempt to hide her disgust.

He grinned. "Didn't watch much NASCAR while you were at Harvard, huh?"

"Please."

"You should. The races are pretty exciting. There's a

new driver named Bobby Baker who's really coming up in the points standing—"

She looked out the window—an anticipated reaction, and not only because she possessed the innate superiority of a northeastern aristocrat.

Since they'd left the Academy, Kaitlin had made it clear she had no interest in conversation. Initially, Malone had assumed she was still down because Ralston might get a pass on the murders. But now he was thinking it must be the phone call.

They stopped at the Subway by the visitor center to grab lunch. Kaitlin's cellular rang just as she sat down with her salad. One glance at her caller ID and she was up from the table, hurrying outside to take it. She paced constantly as she spoke, pausing every few steps to make angry, stabbing gestures. Returning to the table, she looked at least as upset as when Malone saw her outside the restroom.

"The chief of staff again?" Malone managed, between bites of a turkey sub.

"I don't want to talk about it."

"Why? What does she want you to do?"

"I don't want to talk about it."

"Kaitlin—"

She promptly rose from the table with her salad untouched, tossed it in the trash, and went outside to make a call. This time, she appeared noticeably more relaxed. She didn't pace and once even smiled.

She was still talking five minutes later, when Malone left the restaurant. Spotting him, she hurriedly clicked off.

"You know," he said to her, "a guy could get a complex."

She didn't say anything then, and had said little since.

Malone came down the exit ramp and stopped at a red light. He debated whether to allow Kaitlin to continue with the silent treatment, but a couple of questions bugged him.

Turning off the CD, he said, "I think your sister told you she suspected Ralston."

The hum of the heater was the only response.

"Kaitlin . . ."

"I'm a liar?" Her voice was like ice.

"I didn't say that."

"How?"

"What do you mean how?"

"How?" she repeated. "Christina suffered a massive breakdown after the rape. How was she supposed to tell me?"

"You expect me to believe that she never once mentioned her suspicions—"

"She couldn't talk about the rape. Whenever she tried, she'd withdraw into a shell, become almost catatonic. For days afterward, conversation was out and so was everything else. She spent almost two years in the hospital, trying to recover emotionally from what those bastards did to her."

"But she must have improved enough to—"

"I'm telling you we never had a chance to talk. I was at school when she was released from the hospital. It was during finals of my last year as an undergraduate and I couldn't get away. I'd done an internship with Senator Smith. He was going to arrange a scholarship to law school, if I graduated in the top 10 percent—" She broke off as she realized she was making excuses. "As soon as I finished my exams, I met Christina in the cabin our father left us when he passed away. It's up in the Cascades, in Washington State. Our parents were divorced, and we never saw our mother. It's similar to your situation, Malone. Only our mother was the one who never gave a damn about us. She never visited Christina while she was in the hospital. Not once. So it was just the two of us. We were going to spend a week together. Sisters again." Kaitlin smiled to herself at the memory. The light turned green and Malone stepped on the gas.

Kaitlin resumed talking with longer pauses; the process was becoming increasingly painful for her. "Christina was still very fragile. She had these compulsions and the doctor said if she displayed them . . . I shouldn't discuss the rape. We spent the first few days talking about the good memories. Our father, our childhood . . . growing up as twins . . . We talked about everything except . . . you know . . . the rape. But it was only a matter of time. We both knew she had to talk about it . . . to get it behind her. But Jesus, it was hard for her . . . she was still afraid . . . had this . . . fear. For the longest time, it didn't make any sense, but then she told me about the calls she'd get. Every few months or so. Was she telling the truth? I don't know. The staff had their doubts. Christina often woke up in the middle of the night, screaming that the rapists were in her room. Of course it was a nightmare, but she believed it."

The calls surprised Malone. He'd never heard about them. He said, "The rapists threatened her?"

But Kaitlin continued speaking, as if she hadn't heard him. "The cabin was good for her. Peaceful, you know. Christina became more relaxed and I could tell she was getting ready to open up. Before she could, we had the accident. The goddamn, stupid accident. A storm came up while we were out for a drive up to Hurricane Ridge. It's a place she always loved . . . we loved. There was gravel on the road and it was raining so hard and . . . I never saw . . . never had a chance to . . ." She closed her eyes tight, reliving the moment. Her voice began to tremble. "Christ, it all happened so fast. I was thrown clear . . . somehow . . . and there was a fire and . . . and when it was over, she was dead. Gone."

Her eyes suddenly opened and Malone saw they were wet. She said, "So you see, I couldn't have known about Ralston. I never knew. But now I want to know everything; I have to know. Do you understand?"

Malone nodded.

Neither of them spoke for a while. At the next street, Malone turned into a sprawling subdivision, built in the eighties tech boom. He began, "I don't have a right to ask. But those gloves you wear . . ."

Her head went back and forth, as if she wasn't going to tell him. But slowly, almost painfully, she removed a glove and held up her hand.

He saw the scars. Horrible burn scars that covered her fingers and much of her palm.

"The other hand looks even worse," she said softly.

"I'm sorry," Malone said.

She nodded, put the glove back on. "I tried to pull her from the car. But the flames. The flames and Christina . . . she was screaming for me to help her . . ."

She couldn't go on. She choked up, her tears beginning to flow. Malone passed her a handkerchief and tried to think of something appropriate to say. But what could one say to someone carrying her burden?

There was gravel on the road . . . I never saw—

In that unfinished statement, Malone realized what fueled Kaitlin's hate was an overwhelming sense of guilt. Because she'd been behind the wheel of the car that killed her twin sister.

Malone made a left onto a quiet street and pulled over. "Take your time. Let me know when you're ready to face them."

"Face who?" Kaitlin asked dully, dabbing her eyes and smearing her mascara.

He pointed to a house at the end of the cul-de-sac.

Chapter 18

THIS TIME ALL THE MAJOR NETWORKS AND SEV-
eral minor ones were represented.

Satellite trucks painted with familiar logos rimmed
two-thirds of the cul-de-sac. The remaining third was
occupied by an assortment of official-looking vehicles,
including an armada of police cruisers and an AF staff
car, arrayed on either side of a single-story home.
Across the street, two burly cops set out a line of red
cones, shouting and gesturing to several dozen jostling
reporters, ordering them back. Farther down, television crews were setting up cameras, and in nearby
yards, somber neighbors watched the scene.

"I'm ready," Kaitlin said.

As usual, she'd reapplied her makeup with seamless
perfection. In the rearview mirror, Malone saw an
approaching car and decided to wait. He was really
using it for an excuse. He hadn't asked her his second
question, concerned he would appear insecure and
needy.

But if anyone understood guilt, it was Kaitlin.

"Listen," he said, "I'm not sure how to put this. But Christina and I had a history . . ." She nodded; of course she'd known. "It's important to me to know whether she . . . blamed me for what happened."

"She didn't," Kaitlin said with conviction. "She would never blame you. At the cabin, you're all she ever talked about."

A knot welled up inside Malone's chest. Loss, regret, and relief, all rolled into one. Before he knew it, he was saying, "I cared for her. I really did. After I left the Academy, I tried to visit her at the hospital. But the nurse told me Christina didn't want to see me. So for all these years, I wondered . . ."

"She wanted to see you, believe me. But she was afraid of your reaction, what you would think."

"What *I* would think?"

A sadness came to Kaitlin. "Those compulsions. She developed this . . . belief that her looks were responsible for the rape. She did things to herself, to make sure it would never happen again. It's why they kept her in the hospital so long. She wouldn't stop. They couldn't get her to stop."

"What kind of things? Did she disfigure herself?"

"It doesn't matter. She'd want you to remember her the way she was. Will you do that?"

Malone swallowed away the marble in his throat. "I'll always remember her. I'd have done anything to change what happened to her. I want you to know that."

"I do. So does Christina." She patted his arm.

The car rolled past and Malone followed it to Mrs. Owen's home.

*   *   *

Two houses down, the car turned into a driveway. Malone continued ahead, parking behind a police cruiser, thirty yards from the Owen home. As he and Kaitlin stepped onto the sidewalk, he asked her about the calls Christina received, the ones that made her afraid.

"They came from one of the rapists. The leader. He kept his voice disguised and would say sick, disgusting things. He liked to torment her by describing details about her rape. He'd get real excited and she could tell he was getting off."

"Why didn't she hang up on him?"

"She never said, but I think she was hoping he'd make a slip, say something that would give her a clue to his identity."

"How did she know he was the leader? Did he tell her?"

"Unh-unh. He had this name he used."

"Name?"

Before Kaitlin could explain, reporters began shouting to them. Several tried to come forward, but the cops kept them back. Cameras began clicking nonstop.

"They act as if they know you," Kaitlin said.

"Don't see how," Malone said, worming on latex gloves.

They were almost to the house. A belligerent voice sang out, "That's him. That's the guy. Twenty bucks he's a military cop. You *are* a military cop, right, buddy?"

"He's a cop, all right," a woman answered.

Malone knew who they were even before he looked. There, standing behind the cones, was the former anchorman Mark Bruner and one of the female reporters from Harmon Hall. The cowboy was squeezed between them, his TV camera focused on Malone.

The flurry of questions intensified. The woman's nasal voice cut through the shouts. "C'mon, mister, give us a break. Three murders is big news. Who was killed first, Mrs. Owen, or her daughter Rachel? What about the second girl, Mary Zinnel? Why was she killed? You think it was the same killer?"

The press had obviously figured out the murders of Rachel and Mrs. Owen were related, probably because of their last names—a deduction further reinforced by the presence of the shiny blue AF staff car.

Malone and Kaitlin turned up the driveway, the questions following. Several uniforms were stringing crime scene tape between the trees. On the snow-crusted yard, a detective was interviewing three AF lieutenant colonels and an airman. Malone didn't recognize anyone on the casualty notification team, so he merely nodded his acknowledgment. The detective said to him, "You the guy from the OSI?"

"Yeah." Malone clipped his credentials to his jacket pocket and started over.

The detective waved him on. "Lieutenant Canola is waiting for you inside."

A trail of footprints led up the driveway. Because the temperature was climbing, they wouldn't last more than an hour. Malone asked the detective if they should avoid them.

"It's probably too damn late." He scowled at the AF contingent.

Bad move.

The three light birds bristled. "Now just a damned minute, Detective," the tallest one barked. "We had no way of knowing—"

"Hey, hey, Colonel Culpepper. I'm not accusing you of anything."

"The hell you aren't. You just implied it was our fault we walked on those footprints."

"Colonel, I never actually said—"

"I've got half a mind to report you. Who's your supervisor?"

"Colonel, there's no need to talk to him. I'll apologize."

"His supervisor is Lieutenant Tom Canola," Malone said.

The detective glared at him. Malone shrugged it off. Air Force officers had to stick together.

Ducking under the tape, he and Kaitlin headed out across the lawn toward the house. She said, "The killer's luck is holding."

He nodded. She was talking about the footprints. He prompted, "You were going to tell me the name the caller used . . ."

"Right. It came from the masks they wore when they raped her. When the guy called, he'd always start off by identifying himself as . . ."

At that instant, Malone knew. "Mickey Mouse," he said.

Malone's surprise gave way to annoyance. "Why didn't you tell me this before, Kaitlin?"

She shrugged. "I thought you knew."

"We didn't. No one ever told the OSI."

"You're wrong. I know Christina talked to somebody in the OSI. Man, you look pretty upset about this."

He was. What she'd told him made no sense. He knew the case file word for word and there was no mention—

And then he remembered what Kaitlin had said about the doctors. Their skepticism.

He took out his phone to check.

"Am I missing something?" Kaitlin asked. "What's the big deal about the bastard threatening her?"

Mother picked up almost immediately. Their conversation lasted less than a minute.

Hanging up, Malone said, "The agent who replaced Mother was the one who actually spoke to Christina . . ."

"And?"

"The agent never made a report because there were no calls. None that matched the ones Christina says she received. The police checked the phone records."

She shrugged. "So she imagined the calls? So what? It doesn't change the fact that the son of a bitch raped her."

Point taken.

Chapter 19

A SHORT STAIRCASE LED TO A SMALL PORCH SUR-rounded by a railing that needed paint. The front door was closed, a female cop standing guard. After giving Malone's credentials a once-over, she opened the door and ushered them inside.

A realtor would call the room off the foyer a great room, but the description was charitable. It was essentially a box, roughly fifteen feet square, with a tiny fireplace and a couple of plain wood-framed windows. The opposite wall was lined with photographs, and through an arched doorway, a dining room was visible; past it, the entry into the kitchen. Two technicians dusted for prints, while a graying criminalist squatted on the beige carpet, a photographer hovering nearby. The criminalist was placing numbered markers beside dark, rust-colored stains. He was up to 52. The markers continued down a hallway, which led to the rear of the house.

"The dog's bloody prints?" Kaitlin murmured to Malone.

A given. The stains were too numerous to be anything else.

Malone took note of the spartan furnishings. Other than a cheap floral couch, a couple of inexpensive vinyl recliners, and an end table with a lamp, there was nothing else in the room except for the TV, sitting on a stand against the wall. It was on, tuned to CNN, the sound turned off. Malone was curious to note that everything appeared completely pristine; no scuff marks or worn patches.

"New," Kaitlin said. "Everything looks new."

"They are," the criminalist grunted, rising stiffly off the carpet. "The sofa over there still has the tag. Delivered last month. Same thing with the stuff in the bedroom. All the furniture's fresh off the shelf." He squinted at Malone's credentials. "Air Force OSI, huh? I'm a Navy man myself. Three years and that was plenty. The lieutenant's down the hall. Last room at the end. Stay to the left side and try not to knock over any markers. My back's killing me as it is. Okay, Artie. One more time." As the photographer snapped pictures, the criminalist glanced at the TV. "Hey, Ronnie, turn up the volume. It looks like they picked up the story."

Pat Dryke, CNN's midday commentator, was at her anchor desk, talking soundlessly. A scrolling banner at the bottom of the screen read: Two cadets murdered at the Air Force Academy. Third murder possibly linked.

One of the fingerprint techs turned up the volume. But Pat was actually discussing a recent bombing in Iraq. The criminalist shrugged. "Leave it up. They'll get to it pretty soon."

Malone said to him, "Mrs. Owen only moved out here a few months ago."

A nod of understanding. "Right. Must have sold all her old stuff beforehand. Makes sense."

But as Malone followed Kaitlin into the hall, he realized it didn't make sense. He said to her, "Rachel and her mother grew up in the Detroit projects . . ."

"So you're wondering how Mrs. Owen could afford to move out here? Buy this house and new furniture?"

"Aren't you?"

They hugged the left side of the hall, avoiding the markers. Kaitlin said, "Can't help you. I asked Rachel once, but all she said was her mom came into money. You think her windfall could have something to do with— Malone?"

She frowned, looking back.

Malone had stopped to look at one of the larger photographs lining the walls. The image depicted an attractive woman in her late thirties, standing with an arm around a smiling girl who looked about seventeen. As he stared at the image, his pulse began to race. His eyes darted to the other photographs. In those, the girl was always there, at varying ages, either alone or with another woman, one who appeared significantly older, in her forties and fifties.

Malone never saw the woman in the first picture again and more important, never saw a man. Any man.

"That's Rachel," Kaitlin said suddenly, walking up to him.

Malone nodded, his eyes returning to the first photo.

A lot of years had passed, and he could be mistaken. He wanted to be mistaken.

As he unhooked the picture, Malone worked to keep his face neutral. "I need a photo of Rachel to show around," he said.

Kaitlin stepped away, accepting. From the room at the end of the hall, they heard a man talking. He suddenly swore. Malone recognized the voice; it was Lieutenant Tom Canola. Canola was demanding to talk to the chief of police. Something about a decision only the chief could make.

Malone looked at the picture in his hand, wondering if there were others. Ones that showed a man with this woman.

He had a bad feeling as he continued down the hall.

A massive, ponderous man with a slicked-back mane of black hair and sleepy eyes, Lieutenant Tom Canola looked more like a made-for-TV wise guy than the precisely competent homicide cop he'd been for twenty-two years. Levelheaded and pragmatic, Canola rarely swore or smoked unless under stress. As he spoke into a cell phone, he was on the brink of engaging in both practices.

"*Dammit*, Joyce, you're not hearing me," Canola said, waving an unlit cigarette like a baton. "I don't give a shit whose wedding the chief is attending. You send a car to the church and tell him to call me. No. Not the deputy chief or Captain Morgan. They don't have the authority. Yeah, yeah, I'll take the heat."

Pocketing his phone, he jammed the cigarette into his mouth with a scowl. "Fuck."

"Hi, Tom," Malone said.

Lieutenant Canola slowly turned. Four other faces also looked over: a white-jacketed coroner's assistant, a matronly woman detective clutching a file, and two criminalists who were unpacking their cases. As in the great room, the master's furnishings were few and apparently new: a queen-sized bed minus a headboard, a night stand with a framed photo of Rachel in her cadet uniform, an oak dresser topped by a vase of silk flowers, a large bookshelf, filled mostly with paperbacks. The master bath was at the back, the door partially open, someone visible inside.

Since they were casual acquaintances, Malone expected Canola to at least acknowledge his greeting, maybe offer a perfunctory handshake. But the big homicide cop never moved. Neither did anyone else. Everyone just stood there, gazing at Malone and Kaitlin somberly.

As the seconds passed, a tension filled the room. Kaitlin shook her head, as if puzzled by it.

Malone wasn't. He knew exactly what was worrying the cops.

His concern was whether Canola would give him the time to check things out. Probably, if Mother sweet-talked Canola into it. They had a history together, going back to her first Academy tour. Now the question was what to do about Kaitlin. Could she be trusted not to call Senator Smith with news this big?

Recalling the frenzied press outside, he had his answer.

Canola finally eased out a reluctant, "Hello, Malone." After a beat, he added, "I spoke to Mother."

"Fine, Tom." For a moment, Malone was curious why Tom felt compelled to tell him this. Then he understood. Tom was letting Malone know that Mother had warned him about—

Kaitlin coughed suggestively.

Taking the hint, Malone began introducing her. Before he had finished, Canola was shaking his head apologetically. He said, "I'm sorry, Ms. Barlow, I'm afraid you'll have to leave. City policy prohibits civilians at active crime scenes." His manner firm, his tone polite.

Not that Kaitlin even noticed.

She regarded him in complete disbelief. "Leave? I'm *authorized* to be here, Lieutenant. I have an arrangement with the Air Force. Tell him, Malone."

"She's right, Tom," Malone said, playing along. "General Crenshaw and Senator Smith agreed to—"

Canola brushed past him, practically shouldering him out of the way, a less-than-subtle way of telling Malone to shut up.

So Malone shut up.

Canola repeated his statement about the department's policy. Kaitlin said she didn't give a damn what the policy was. She had an *agreement*. They went back and forth. She said, "You don't seem to realize who I am, Lieutenant. The Secretary of Defense authorized me to investigate this case *personally*."

"Do you have a badge?" Canola asked mildly.

"Of course not—"

"I'm sorry, ma'am. No one mentioned you. I'm expecting a call from the chief. I'll ask him about you.

Now if you don't mind . . ." He placed a hand on her shoulder, guiding her to the door.

She jerked away from him, livid. "Malone, are you just going to let this happen? *Are you?*"

"It's Tom's jurisdiction. There's nothing I can do." Malone offered her his car keys, his tone sympathetic. "Wait in the car. I'll try to clear this misunderstanding up."

She was defiant, making no move to go. Canola sighed. "Grace . . ."

The woman cop set the folder on the bed and came over. She was several inches shorter than Kaitlin's six feet, but had her by twenty pounds. Glaring at her, Kaitlin snatched the keys from Malone and left in a huff, the woman cop trailing.

Canola sighed unhappily. "She's one hot-looking woman. I hate pissing off hot-looking women. Tell Mother this is another one she owes me."

"I will, Tom."

"By the way, you look like hell."

"It's a new look I'm going for. Grunge."

"I mean it. You gotta start taking better care of yourself."

"I'm trying to quit smoking."

"You smoke?"

"Not since I was sixteen."

Canola chewed on his cigarette. "Hysterical. You're breaking me up." He noticed the photo Malone was holding. "Something I should know about?"

"You already might."

But when he showed Canola the photo, the detective's face was blank. That told Malone they'd found a different connection. An Asian woman wearing a county coroner's jacket suddenly materialized from the bathroom, carrying a leather case. "I'm done, Lieutenant," she said briskly. "Time of death, between 2100 and 2300. The ME will narrow the window after the autopsy. Once your people finish processing the hall, we'll remove the body." She looked at Malone. "OSI, right? Agent Morgan?"

"Malone."

"Dr. Tullia started your two autopsies. Results should be available after three."

"Thank you."

She and her assistant left.

Canola nodded Malone's attention to the bathroom. "Take a look and we'll talk."

"I'd rather talk now, Tom."

"Better take a look first."

Malone got the message. There was something Canola wanted him to see.

He went over to the bathroom to view the body.

Chapter 20

SHE LAY CRUMPLED ON HER SIDE ON THE TILED floor, her head resting in a large pool of coagulated blood, her left arm dangling in the open commode. The bullet had struck her above the left eye, entering with a dime-size hole and emerging in a grisly spray of bone, brain, and blood that had textured a two-foot circle on a tiled wall. She appeared to be in her sixties, a bone-thin woman with a worn face that suggested a life filled with hard work and little hope. She had died wearing what appeared to be her Sunday best; a gold-buttoned red suit and matching shoes.

Malone leaned down to study her face. Even in death, he could tell it was her.

Mrs. Lola Owen, the woman in most of the pictures.

Tiny bits of blue cloth matted to her entry wound. Malone looked around and spotted a large blue bath towel wadded in a corner. Carefully avoiding the blood, he picked the towel up and saw the burned hole the bullet had made.

Leaving the bathroom, Malone found Canola waiting for him by the bed, the cigarette still clinging to his mouth. "We'll go out back. I need a smoke."

On the way out, Canola retrieved the file from the bed.

Canola wedged the file under his armpit, lit up the cigarette, and inhaled gratefully. They were standing on the covered patio, beside the door with the dog flap.

Squinting at Malone through the smoke, he said, "Pick up anything about Mrs. Owen?"

"She's dead."

"Since when you become such a smart-ass, Malone?"

"I've been taking a night course."

Not even the suggestion of a smile. It wasn't that funny.

"Sorry, Tom. I'm a little punchy. I didn't get much sleep last night."

"Don't come crying to me. I got four kids. So, how about it?"

"I noticed her clothes and the towel."

A nod. "Anything else?"

"Any signs of forced entry?"

"No."

"All doors and windows were locked?"

"Like a drum."

"Anything in the kitchen indicating she entertained a guest last night? Dirty dishes or—"

"A full pot of cold coffee. Two cups were also on the counter, clean."

Malone nodded slowly. "She met someone here last night, someone she dressed up and made coffee for.

They might have gone out to dinner beforehand—" Canola shook off the suggestion; Malone agreed. The killer probably wouldn't risk being seen in public with Mrs. Owen. "Anyway," he said, "we know the shooter arrived sometime after 2100 and killed Mrs. Owen before she had a chance to serve the coffee. House have a basement?"

"No."

"That's why he killed her in the bathroom. He chose a windowless room to muffle the shot. That's also why he used the towel." Malone watched Canola take a massive hit of smoke. "The towel wouldn't have silenced the sound much. Neighbors hear the shot?"

"We just started the interviews."

Malone gave him a long look. "The use of the towel suggests an amateur, someone who doesn't know guns."

Canola puffed thoughtfully. "Like this cadet Mother mentioned? Jefferson?"

"Maybe."

"Don't cadets have firearms training?"

"Enough to scare themselves. They're Air Force cadets, not Army."

"And Mrs. Owen would dress up for Jefferson because . . ."

"Who knows? He was once engaged to her daughter. Maybe Mrs. Owen still felt an affection toward him, or maybe Jefferson arrived on a pretext of taking her out to a late dinner. Another possibility is she dressed up for someone else and Jefferson happened to show up . . ." Malone trailed off; he was grasping at straws. "Pretty thin. It doesn't figure she'd dress up for Jefferson."

"No," Canola said, eyeing him, "which means you've got a big problem."

You, not *we.* Canola *had* found another connection.

The big detective fired his cigarette into the snowy yard before addressing Malone. "Mrs. Owen was a hotel maid in Detroit for thirty years. I checked her closet. Her clothes were what you'd expect, bargain-store variety. Except for that suit. It was the nicest thing she owned. She'd only have worn it for someone special. Real special." He paused for effect, adding, "Then there's this." Slipping the file from under his arm, he removed a sheaf of legal-looking documents and passed them to Malone.

"The loan contract for the house," he said. "Look at the last page. The signatures."

Malone flipped to it and saw the cursive scrawl of Lola T. Owen. And below it, a second signature.

Neal D. Crenshaw, it read.

"There's more," Canola said.

A lot more.

Canola produced an uncashed check dated only days earlier, made out to Lola Owen for three thousand dollars, from Neal Crenshaw. Then came a series of bank statements showing monthly deposits of three thousand dollars to Mrs. Owen's account. Canola had also contacted the stores that had supplied Mrs. Owen's new furniture. All her purchases had been charged to Crenshaw's credit card.

The picture Canola painted was damning and suggested two possibilities: either the general was being blackmailed by Mrs. Owen or he was paying her out of a sense of obligation for an indiscretion.

"According to Mother," Canola said, "Crenshaw had a shot at a fourth star. That means he had a helluva motive to keep Mrs. Owen and her daughter quiet. A guy in his position couldn't afford to have it get out that he'd had an illegitimate kid. Money could also have been part of it. Generals aren't exactly rich. He could have gotten tired of handing out three grand every month, not to mention the house and furniture and Lord knows what else . . ."

Malone wasn't really listening. He was staring at the photo from the hall. He shook his head, knowing he was missing something obvious. Instead of her, it should be—

"What?" Canola said. "You don't buy it, Malone? Come on. What else could it be? Crenshaw was paying Mrs. Owen because they did the dirty deed and the dead girl Rachel was his kid. She has to be his kid. Why else—"

"Son of a bitch," Malone said suddenly.

Canola frowned.

Malone looked up from the photo, his face flushed with excitement. "That's it, Tom. That has to be it. There's no other reason."

"Reason for what? What are you talking about?"

"Crenshaw? Are there any photographs of General Crenshaw in the house?"

"No, which is what you'd expect. The relationship was supposed to be a secret, remember?"

"How about the woman in here?" Malone thrust out the picture.

Canola studied it. "I'm not sure. She might be in a couple of photos in the living room. Where you going?"

Malone was striding through the kitchen door. He crossed over to the great room, and in less than thirty seconds, spotted the same woman in two more photos, always with her arm around Rachel.

"Dammit, Malone, who the hell is she?" Canola demanded.

Malone was about to tell him when he noticed the crime scene techs watching. He whispered his response. "Jesus," Canola said. "You sure?"

"No. I only met her a couple of times when I was a cadet. If we find Rachel's birth certificate—"

Canola pivoted and went down the hall. Malone followed him into the first bedroom. It was set up as a rudimentary office, with a card table serving as a desk, a computer on top of it. A metal file cabinet stood against the wall, two of the three drawers open.

They found the birth certificate tucked in a folder titled Rachel's Papers. As Canola and Malone looked it over, they saw the father's name wasn't listed. This wasn't unexpected for out-of-wedlock births. What was unexpected was what they read in the block marked Mother. Instead of Lola Owen, another name was printed.

Lucille T. Johnson.

"The first name of Crenshaw's dead wife?" Canola asked.

"Lucille."

Malone and Canola spent another ten minutes sifting through every file. No adoption papers turned up, but they discovered a safe deposit key from a bank in Detroit. "We'll arrange for a court order to have it checked," Canola said.

"Fine." Malone sat down in front of the computer and powered it up.

Watching him, Canola said, "I told Mother I'd talk to the chief. Get him to agree to keep Crenshaw's name from the press as long as we can. Won't be easy with a story this big. You'll be lucky to get twenty-four hours."

"Thanks, Tom." Malone clicked on the mouse.

"You know this still doesn't clear the general. So Rachel was his wife's kid and not his. The general was paying Mrs. Owen, which means we can't rule out blackmail. I was in the Army and know how the military works. It'd be embarrassing as hell for Crenshaw, if it got out that his wife got knocked up and put her kid up for adoption."

"The general didn't kill anyone, Tom."

"Hey, I'd love to forget about him and move on. But who the hell did Mrs. Owen get all dolled up for if it *wasn't* Crenshaw? What's so funny?"

Malone was smiling at the computer screen. "We can forget about Crenshaw. Odds are Jefferson was here last night." He pointed. "See those e-mails."

Canola bent forward, frowning. "What e-mails? I just see a lot of garbage."

"Precisely."

Reaching for his cell phone, he quickly explained.

Mrs. Weaver, General Crenshaw's secretary, sounded close to tears. When Malone asked her what was wrong, she didn't reply. In the background, voices hummed and phones rang constantly. The response from worried parents was in full swing.

Malone said tentatively, "Mrs. Weaver . . ."

She blew her nose. "It's the general. It's not his fault what happened. It isn't."

That's when Malone knew. He said, "He's been relieved?"

"It's more than that. Senator Smith is all over the news, accusing him of negligence. Criminal negligence. He's demanding the general be court-martialed. It's not fair. The general is a good and decent man. He had no control over what happened. It's not fair."

"Where is the general now?"

"Gone. Went home. The commandant is temporarily in charge. You should have seen the look on General Crenshaw's face. It was as if someone died. I . . . we're worried about him."

So was Malone. He'd seen the cracks in the general's armor and realized this could push him over the edge. "Is anyone with him now?"

"He insisted he wanted to be alone. Major Wilson drove him home. I tried to call Lieutenant Colonel Ralston at the airfield, but she's flying."

The superintendent resided at Carlton House, a stately mansion donated by the Carlton family, who had once owned the Academy land. The residence was located on the east end of the Pine Valley housing area. Malone asked for Crenshaw's home number. After Mrs. Weaver passed it on, he told her not to worry, that the general had handled a lot of disappointments in his life and he would get past this. Her only response was a sniffle; she knew he was just talking.

Malone's impulse was to give the general time to accept this kind of professional devastation before questioning him. But when he voiced this suggestion, Tom Canola shot it down with a terse: "Not a chance, buddy boy. You call him or I will."

It was an elegant study lined with shelves full of books, most with military-oriented topics. Because the drapes were drawn, the room sat in semidarkness, the only light a glowing computer monitor on the mahogany desk. As per custom, one wall was reserved exclusively for plaques and photographs, highlighting the general's remarkable career.

In the small sitting area near the door, the lone figure of General Crenshaw sat rigidly in a wingback chair, eyes closed, his breathing deep and regular. When the ringing of the phone shattered the quiet, he never so much as flinched. He could have been asleep except for the glass of bourbon balanced in his hand.

The answering machine on the desk came on, followed by: "General, it's Agent Malone. I know you're there, sir. I need to speak with you. Please pick up."

The general's eyes cracked open. He sipped from his glass, listening.

"Sir, I heard about what happened. I'm sorry." Malone paused. "Sir, I know your wife was Rachel's mother."

Crenshaw took another swallow, larger than the first. The answering machine hissed.

"Sir, I'll contact you later this afternoon or evening. We need to talk."

A click.

Silence.

The general continued to sip. On the coffee table before him were three objects: a framed photograph identical to the one Malone had taken from Lola Owen's hallway wall; a single sheet of paper; a triangular leather case embossed with his initials.

The general finished his drink, staring at the photo. His face was a mask, devoid of all emotion. In reality, he was in turmoil, but not because he'd been forced to relinquish his command in disgrace. Rather, he was conflicted by what was on the paper, an e-mail he'd just printed.

His eyes went to a gleaming silver plaque on his wall, a quotation from General Robert E. Lee. It was too dark for him to read the engraved words, not that it mattered. He knew them by heart.

Duty, then is the sublimest word in our language.

Do your duty in all things.

You cannot do more.

You should never wish to do less.

The general shook his head, knowing where his duty lay. His wife, Lucille, had entrusted Rachel to his care and he'd failed to protect her. All that was left was to regain his honor . . . if he could.

He set his glass down and unzipped the case.

And removed a shiny black nine-millimeter pistol.

Chapter 21

"ASAP," Canola said, following Malone into the hallway. "Call me ASAP after you question the general."

"He wasn't here last night, Tom."

"Then he better have an alibi."

"If the general was here, why didn't he take the pictures of his wife? Why leave them for us to find?"

"He was in a hurry or got spooked. Or maybe he thought it would look suspicious if someone noticed the pictures were missing."

Malone felt himself getting angry. But Tom was just doing his job, considering all suspects equally. They entered the living room. The graying criminalist and the two fingerprint technicians were crowded in front of the TV. As Malone and Canola continued to the front door, the men looked over, their expressions grim.

"All right, boys," Canola said, noticing. "Let's have it. What's the problem now?"

In response, the criminalist turned up the volume and Malone's name blared out from the TV.

*   *   *

With Senator Smith's image frozen over her shoulder, CNN anchor Pat Dryke said, "The senator has raised serious questions about Agent Nathan Malone, who is heading the investigation into the cadets' murders. In a statement, Senator Smith, citing a source close to the case, alleges that Agent Malone, a former cadet, is more concerned with protecting the Air Force Academy's reputation than apprehending the murderer of the two women cadets. Whether Malone is operating on his own or with the approval of his superiors, Senator Smith has yet to determine. He is appalled the Air Force would entrust an officer with Malone's questionable record to oversee such a high-visibility investigation. According to Smith, Agent Malone is, and I quote"—Pat consulted a sheet of paper—"'a marginal officer with a well-documented history of unprofessional conduct.'"

"Sweet Jesus," Canola murmured.

Malone nodded dumbly. He held his breath, waiting for the revelation that he'd been picked up for a DWI.

It never came.

After scanning the page, Pat Dryke looked into the camera and said, "In a press conference scheduled for tonight in Colorado Springs, the senator will detail his concerns about Agent Malone and the Academy leadership. There are unsubstantiated reports that he will request the FBI intervene in the murder investigation of the two cadets."

The screen changed to footage of Malone and Kaitlin walking up the sidewalk to Mrs. Owen's home.

In a voice-over, Pat continued, "Thirty minutes ago, Agent Malone arrived at the home of Mrs. Lola Owen, whose daughter, Rachel, was one of the murdered cadets. Mrs. Owen was also murdered and the appearance of Agent Malone indicates the deaths are linked, though the authorities have yet to say so publicly."

Malone's image was replaced by a still photo of the Air Force Academy.

"The charges Senator Smith makes against Agent Malone and the Air Force Academy leadership are extremely serious. CNN has just learned that General Crenshaw, the Academy superintendent, has been relieved. Whether this is a result of the senator's allegations is anyone's guess, but the timing is suggestive. In fairness, we must remind you that Senator Smith has a history of flamboyantly attacking the Air Force Academy for what he's often termed a 'boys-will-be-boys mentality,' which led to a rash of rape and sexual harassment accusations. While the senator has been criticized for politically exploiting this issue, there's no denying that his efforts have forced the military academies to change their policies concerning female cadets."

A rapid slide show of photos: West Point, Annapolis, the Air Force Academy. Then Pat again, her expression grave. "Three women are dead, including two cadets at one of the country's premier military institutions. Is it possible that the Air Force would knowingly engage in a conspiracy to shield the killer, if it protected their interests? A reasonable person would conclude no. The military is an honorable profession, filled with honorable people. At the present, young men and women are dying on the battlefields of Iraq and Afghanistan." She shook her head. "Still, we can't ignore the concerns of a United States senator or the troubling questions he's raised. We also can't ignore the fact that someone at the Air Force Academy is in all likelihood a multiple murderer."

A prolonged, ominous silence. Then a Pepsi commercial came on.

"Turn that fucking thing off," Canola said.

Malone stepped away from the TV, feeling numb. No one spoke. Malone was aware of the four faces staring at him. All were sympathetic.

"Don't let it get to you," Canola said quietly. "Smith's only doing this to make himself look like a hero before the election. His whipping boy Crenshaw is out of the picture and you're an easy target. He's going after you to keep his name in the papers."

Malone understood all this, as well as something else. He now knew why he'd been chosen for the case.

Canola was right; he made an easy target. With Malone's track record, the senator had a perfect patsy to—

Malone's phone rang. Canola shot him a questioning look. Malone glanced at the caller ID: U.S. Air Force, it said generically. But the number confirmed the caller's identity.

He nodded at Canola.

"This is a load of bullshit," the detective growled. "Smith throws about a bunch of lies and everyone runs scared. It's not right. You want, I'll talk to them. Tell them you're a good cop."

Malone smiled tightly to let Canola know he appreciated the offer. But it was pointless and they both knew it.

"Hello, General," he said into the phone.

"You catch the CNN report, Malone?" the commandant of cadets asked. With Crenshaw gone, he was temporarily in charge of the Academy.

"Yes, sir."

Malone waited for the axe to fall.

But instead of telling him he was fired, the Com said, "I just got off the horn with the SECDEF and the chief of staff. It was a case of pick your poison, but so far they've decided to stick with you."

"Sir?"

Reacting to Malone's surprise, the Com said, "The SECDEF is worried about the precedent your removal would set. He relieved General Crenshaw as a preemptive measure, knowing that bastard Smith was going to make an example of him. In hindsight, he realizes that was a mistake. You can't give in to a guy like Smith; it only encourages him. He won't back off, no matter what we do."

"Sir, the senator mentioned the FBI—"

The Com snorted. "He's dreaming. There's no way SECDEF will turn over the investigation to the FBI. It would be an admission there was validity to Smith's charges. Frankly, that's what tipped the scale in your favor. We pull you from the case and Smith will be dancing on his soapbox, claiming it's proof you were engaged in a cover-up. That's what I meant by picking your poison. Either way we go, we're going to lose the PR war. The SECDEF doesn't really give a damn. He knows the only way to deflect Smith's accusations is to wrap up this case and fast." He lowered his voice ominously. "No matter where it goes, Malone. You understand what I'm saying. No matter where."

The words sank in and Malone felt sickened. "Sir, there's something you should know. It's about General Crenshaw."

"Go on."

After Malone laid out what they'd learned, the Com sighed heavily. "You know, he always looked out for Rachel. I knew there was a connection between them. But if he was her stepfather, he'd have no reason to kill her."

"Sir, it's possible the general was being blackmailed."

"Forget it. The general is no killer."

"Sir, he was paying Mrs. Owen large sums—"

"And I'm telling you General Crenshaw wouldn't kill for money. He doesn't give a damn about money. Ask anybody."

"Yes, sir."

"Now, how long will the CSPD sit on it?"

"Lieutenant Canola said maybe twenty-four hours."

"I'll call Chief Haney, get him to commit to that." He fell silent, thinking.

"Sir, Senator Smith has a press conference scheduled tonight."

"Right. At 2100 hours at the Broadmoor Hotel."

"He's sure to bring out my letters of reprimand and the DWI—"

"*Alleged* DWI. Sure, he might press to test the issue, but you got picked up on base. And I can promise you we're not giving him your Breathalyzer results without a court order."

"Even so, sir, once he brings it up—"

"Relax. There's a chance we can convince Smith to back off you completely. It depends if he wants to engage in a little political suicide."

"Sir?"

"You can thank General Crenshaw. He's been burned by Smith so many times, he finally installed a recording system in his office, to cover himself. Smith's chief of staff, Marcy Dyers, is in town, setting up the press conference. The SECDEF gave me the green light to play a little hardball. I'll be leaving in a few minutes to meet with her. If Smith keeps shooting his mouth off, I'm going to tell her we'll release the tape to the media. On it, he accuses us of a cover-up even before the investigation got started. It'll also give us cover, since we agreed to include Ms. Barlow in the investigation from the beginning. Smith's a smart guy; he'll know he'd look like the horse's ass he is unless he cuts a deal. The bigger problem is Ms. Barlow. You do realize she's the unnamed source who gave Smith the dirt on you . . ."

"Yes, sir."

"For now, we're stuck with her, so do what you can to keep her out of the loop. Especially about Crenshaw. This doesn't change what I told you earlier. This is your investigation; you run it any way you want, follow any leads. Anyone gives you grief, call me. Just find the damned killer. Oh, and one more thing . . ."

"Yes, sir."

"I can't stop you from checking out General Crenshaw. But I need you to clear him by the time the shit hits the fan."

"I'll try, sir."

The Com had already hung up.

The four men in the room grinned, watching Malone put away his phone. They'd caught enough of the conversation to know the verdict. "I'll be damned," Tom Canola said, chuckling. "The brass has more sense than I gave them credit for. You're still alive and kicking, huh?"

"So far."

Canola's grin faded. "Guess I jumped the gun. You don't look happy for a guy that got a reprieve."

An understatement. Malone's face was knotted in a grim scowl. He said, "Kaitlin Barlow and I had an agreement. She flat-out lied to me."

"What'd you expect? She works for Smith. It's her job to find dirt."

"She set me up, Tom. She humiliated me. It's not right."

"Right? Right and wrong has nothing to do with it. This is *politics.*"

Malone shook his head in disgust and headed for the door.

"Think before you do something stupid," Canola called out after him. "You piss her off, you'll only make things worse."

Malone kept walking.

"Oh, hell—" Canola hurried after him. "Wait up. I'm coming with you."

Malone swung around. "I can handle her, Tom."

"That's what I'm afraid of. Another stiff I don't need."

"Tom . . ."

"You'll thank me. Believe me." He prodded Malone out the door.

As the men stepped out onto the porch, Malone stopped so abruptly that Canola bumped into him. "Now what's the problem?" Canola said in annoyance.

"There."

Malone pointed toward the street. Canola stared quizzically. "What am I looking for?"

"My BMW."

"I don't see a BMW."

"You should."

Canola's eyes grew wide. Then he began to laugh and laugh.

Chapter 22

MALONE LIVED IN A RENOVATED BARN ON SEVEN wooded acres, minutes north of the Academy reservation. He'd chosen the place because it had space to house his toys and, more important, offered seclusion. Molded by his father's abandonment, he'd grown up mistrustful of relationships and now found himself preferring a solitary lifestyle. It wasn't that he had aspirations to be a monk or disliked people, far from it.

It was a defense mechanism. If he didn't let anyone get too close, they couldn't disappoint him.

"Malone," Mother had once philosophized over a beer, "you can't live your life that way. You can't treat every woman like a one-night stand, pushing them away just because you're afraid of being hurt. That's frankly paranoid and a little nuts."

Malone supposed it was, but the one time he'd let down his guard, he'd been rejected. Afterwards, he'd been hurt and angry. In the intervening years, whenever he developed feelings for someone, the memory of that incident always pulled him back. It was the reality of his life and he'd come to accept it.

"Tell me, Malone," Mother had asked, "do you have *any* close friends? Anyone you confide in?"

"I hung out with some guys in high school."

"That's not what I asked; I want to know if you're close to anyone now."

"Guess not."

"You're pretty fucked up, Malone," Mother had concluded.

If she only knew . . .

It was a little before two-thirty when the patrol car dropped Malone off in front of his barn. During the twenty-minute ride, his anger toward Kaitlin dropped below the homicidal level. He kept going back to that moment in the car, when they'd discussed Christina's time in the hospital, and the tragedy of her short life. The connection he and Kaitlin had shared was real. She hadn't been putting on an act; he knew she hadn't.

And yet . . .

And yet her desire for revenge had won out. He'd been a fool to expect anything less. It was the singular purpose that drove her, overriding everything else. He'd been a means to an end. If he had to be sacrificed and his reputation smeared, that was okay.

As long as she got her revenge.

Malone shook his head, telling himself to drop the matter. Even if he spoke to her, confronted her, what did he expect her to say? What could she say?

Drop it, Malone.

But as he walked around to the side door that served

as the main entrance, he found himself pressing the send button on his cell phone. As with the two previous attempts, he didn't anticipate anyone to answer.

But this time she did. Or at least someone did.

He heard breathing. He waited, but the person didn't speak.

"Kaitlin, it's me, Malone. I'm calling about the CNN newscast, but I'm sure you know that. I want an explanation. You owe me that much."

The breathing continued.

"You want to play games, no problem. You're good, lady. All that stuff about having me assigned to the case because I helped Christina was crap. You set me up and I fell for it. You wanted me so Senator Smith could attack my record, question my integrity—"

"It . . . wasn't . . . me."

He was surprised she'd spoken. Her voice was a dull monotone and sounded like a record played at too slow a speed. Something was wrong. "Kaitlin, you okay?"

"It wasn't . . . me. She . . . forced me."

"Who forced you? Smith's chief of staff? Marcy—"

She sounded suddenly frightened. "She's . . . coming. She'll be angry. I have . . . to go. I'm sorry, Malone."

"Kaitlin—"

Dead silence; she was gone. Malone hit the redial, but she never picked up. Keying the alarm code by the side door, he tried to decide whether Kaitlin had been drunk, drugged, or putting on another act. Whatever the answer was, he was certain of one thing.

Kaitlin was a troubled woman.

*　　　*　　　*

The barn's interior was cavernous, the walls all gleaming oak rising thirty feet to enormous beamed ceilings. The front third was dominated by a stained concrete floor where a cherry-red H-2 Hummer and a ski boat sat parked, the remaining space an open living area decorated in a starkly modern style, a large loft jutting above it.

Malone grabbed the H-2's keys off a hook, then checked his watch. Enough time.

Weaving through the chrome and glass furnishings, he took spiral aluminum stairs to the loft, where his bedroom was located. His answering machine blinked eleven messages, double the norm. He pressed play and began to undress. "Agent Malone, this is Rob Garland with the *Rocky Mountain News*. I was wondering if you cared to comment on Senator Smith's allegations—"

"Kiss my ass, Rob."

Malone deleted the message and eight others from reporters. The ninth was from a salesperson and the tenth was from a woman he'd promised to call. And the last—

He tensed.

It was a voice from his past: "Malone, Richard. Dan and I heard the news about the killings and all the stuff about you. We're wondering if, you know, there is anything to worry about. I live in Florida now. I'm the president of my dad's company. I finally grew up. Married a wonderful woman and we've got two girls. Life's good, Malone. After all this time, I don't need any problems. Hell, we were kids. Call me, Malone." Richard left a number.

Malone stood there, staring at the answering machine for a long time.

Finally, he went into the shower and stood under the hot water for a long time. But no matter how hard he scrubbed, he still felt unclean.

He was toweling off when his cell rang. It was Mother. She rarely sounded excited but did so now.

"Jesus, where you been? I've been calling for the last five, ten minutes. It was the damnedest thing. The Academy computer security must be better than we figured. Kranski was at the computer center and located some of Rachel's e-mails. But as he was watching the screen, he saw the e-mails were in the process of being erased. He tried to prevent it, but couldn't. He ran a trace and realized the delete commands were coming from an internal—"

"Slow down. What are you talking about?"

"Jefferson," she said. "Jefferson was at the computer center."

Malone flew around the room, throwing on a fresh suit and jamming items into his pockets. As he did, Mother gave him the rest of it.

The terminal Kranski traced was located in a room several doors down. By the time Kranski arrived, no one was there. Kranski knew he couldn't have missed the person by more than a minute or two, so he ran down the stairs to the parking garage and saw a car driving off.

"Only it wasn't Jefferson's black Mustang, it was a red Taurus," Mother said. "So Kranski almost passed on following it. But since it was the only car that left, he figured the driver had to be the person on the computer. Good thing, too. Kranski was afraid to get too close, but could tell the driver was a black guy. He managed to get the tag number. Colorado plates. The CSPD is running them now."

"Kranski still tailing the car?"

"No. The driver just drove for a couple minutes and parked. I'm on my way there now."

"Hang on. You mean he's still on base?"

She sounded almost giddy. "Damn right. He's making this easy for us. He's sitting in front of Lawrence Paul. You believe it?"

Malone almost couldn't. Lawrence Paul was a rustic lodge located on the wooded hillside behind the cadet area. It was used only sporadically, for squadron functions. More significantly, the only access was a single gravel road.

Jefferson, it seemed, was cornered.

A realization which puzzled Malone. Once Jefferson had successfully sneaked into the computer center and deleted Rachel's e-mails, the logical thing would have been for him to run. Get away from the Academy as fast as he could. That he hadn't—

And then Malone remembered Dr. Patricia Garber's assessment. It all made perfect sense. Lawrence Paul was a wonderfully scenic setting, quiet and isolated.

The perfect place to gather your nerve.

"Go slow," Malone said to Mother. "We don't want to spook Jefferson. My guess is he went up there to—"

"Blow his brains out. Relax, I'm way ahead of you. Kranski's parked out of sight behind the trees and the SPs have orders to only block the road. Unless Jefferson tries to leave, he won't even know we're—" Her call waiting beeped. "Give me a sec. That should be the CSPD."

By the time Malone cinched on his shoulder holster, Mother was back.

"Bingo," she said. "The Taurus is registered to Larry Jefferson from Durango. Age forty-seven. Father or uncle?"

"Probably father. Jefferson's parents live in Durango and are on vacation. I'll be there in fifteen minutes."

Malone hurried down the stairs, praying it could be this easy. But at the back of his mind he kept asking himself why Jefferson would go to the trouble of destroying the e-mails before killing himself. There was no purpose. Not unless . . .

Starting the Hummer, Malone shook his head. The answer was obvious.

Someone else was mentioned in the e-mails.

Malone drove his Hummer like a wild man, wheeling the big machine in and out of traffic and riding the horn. Once he passed through the Academy North Gate, he stuck his portable flasher on the roof and kicked the speed up to eighty.

The gravel road to Lawrence Paul was located almost directly opposite the Visitors' Center. Even though the lodge was less than a mile up the steep slopes of Rampart Range, it was completely hidden behind a dense layer of pines.

Cresting a long hill, Malone spotted the SP roadblock, Mother's pickup, and two other cars belonging to his agents. He came on the brakes hard and lumbered to a squealing stop. Jumping from the vehicle, he read everyone's anxious expressions and knew something must have happened.

"Is it Jefferson?" he asked, jogging up to Mother, who was standing with Rob Sanders and Doug Anderson. "Did you hear a shot?"

She gestured uncertainly up the hill with her cell phone. "It's Kranski. He's not answering his phone."

"When was the last time you talked to him?"

"Maybe ten minutes," Rob Sanders replied. "He called me. From where he was parked, he didn't have a view of Jefferson. Kranski wanted to take a look, make sure Jefferson was still in his car. I told him no, to sit tight."

No one said anything, but they were all thinking the same thing.

Kranski hadn't sat tight.

"He's probably okay," Anderson said. "We'd have heard a shot. He could be stuck somewhere, afraid to move."

Everyone looked up the road. It was almost fifty degrees and the snow was almost completely melted, the gravel shiny in the early afternoon light.

Malone said, "There a guard on the footpath?" He was referring to the trail that cadets often used to walk up to Lawrence Paul.

Mother glanced northward, where the road dipped out of sight. The path was a quarter-mile away, across from the cross street leading to Harmon Hall. "I sent an SP to guard it."

Malone contemplated the trees. They were still and silent. "Try him again, Mother."

When she got no answer, Malone unholstered his weapon and the other agents did the same. To Mother, Malone said, "Jefferson will hear a car. You'd better stay here. It's a steep walk."

"Like hell."

The four agents started up the hill.

Chapter 23

AFTER A QUARTER-MILE, THEY WERE ALL BREATH-ing heavily. Mother was gasping in lungfuls of air, but Malone knew better than to ask her to turn back. The road curved before them, the lodge still hidden.

They came to a flat section. Looking down, they had a dramatic panorama of the Academy, the silver spires of the chapel gleaming in the light. Anderson and Sanders were walking several yards ahead. Rounding a bend, the men stopped.

"I see it," Sanders said softly.

Malone and Mother came forward. In the shadows, they saw a blue Jeep Cherokee parked alongside the narrow road. Kranski's.

"Damn," Mother said.

Even from a distance of thirty yards, they could tell it was empty.

They cautiously moved toward it, scanning the woods, guns raised. They glimpsed flashes of brown through the trees up ahead. After another dozen steps, they could make out the lodge clearly.

Anderson whispered, "A red car. You see it?"

"Yeah. It's the Taurus."

The Taurus was sitting in the parking area, directly in front of the lodge. It didn't look as if anyone was inside, but they were too far away to be sure.

"Watch it," Malone said.

"Rog."

Anderson and Sanders trained their guns on the Taurus while Mother and Malone inspected the Cherokee. The doors were unlocked, the windows rolled up. A briefcase lay on the passenger seat, Kranski's cell phone beside it, the cord plugged into the lighter receptacle. An empty coffee cup sat in the holder, a candy bar wrapper stuffed inside.

Mother picked up the cell phone, looking at Malone. "Explains why he didn't answer."

They stepped away, gently closing the doors. Mother studied the ground and shook her head. There was no way to detect footprints on the gravel.

"C'mon," she said.

Three minutes later, they crouched at the edge of the tree line and peered into the clearing.

"No Jefferson," Mother said.

They were close enough to confirm the Taurus was empty. They remained for another minute, scanning the area, ears straining. But the lodge was dark and silent.

"Where the hell are they?" Anderson asked.

"Rob, Doug, check the grounds. Mother . . ."

Malone and Mother walked toward the lodge, a

sprawling structure built to resemble a log cabin. Circling it, they focused on the doors and windows. Nothing was forced or broken. They came to a walk-in refrigeration unit attached to the left side of the building. As they started by it, they noticed a glistening wetness on the gravel. It could have been water except for the color.

Red.

There was a larger patch of wetness to their right. A trail led to the refrigeration unit. Mother pointed her gun at it as Malone moved forward. He unlatched the metal door and slowly creaked it open.

They were just lying there.

"Anderson! Sanders! Get over here!"

Kranski and Jefferson were heaped on top of each other. Their chests were matted with blood and at first, it appeared they'd been shot. But no one had heard gunfire. Malone peered closer and saw narrow entry wounds. "Stabbed," Malone said.

"Blood's still oozing. Couldn't have happened more than a few minutes ago."

Malone nodded, staring at the faces of the two young men. He felt something swell up inside him: hatred. Stepping back, he squinted down the road, which continued by the lodge for a hundred yards before narrowing into the footpath. "You stay here, Mother," he ordered. "I'm going after the bastard. Call the SPs. Warn them the killer might be on the way down. I want roadblocks placed on every access to the perimeter road."

No argument from Mother; she knew she wouldn't be able to keep up. As she took out her phone, Anderson and Sanders ran up. "Boss, what's the matter? Did you find—"

Anderson broke off with a stricken look. "Oh, Christ."

The men stared at the bodies in horror. "*Dammit*," Sanders said. "I told the kid to sit tight. I told him not to be a hero."

"Follow me," Malone said. "Move. *Move.*"

He ran toward the footpath, the two agents trailing. Walking leisurely, they could reach the main road in five or six minutes. They made it in less than four, arriving as two Security Forces vehicles squealed to a stop.

The doors flew open and four SPs popped out, crouching behind their doors, handguns drawn. Moments later, a master sergeant stepped away from his vehicle, lowering his weapon. He was staring toward the front of the third vehicle, at something on the ground.

"It's okay, people. You can relax."

His eyes locked on those of Malone, who was coming toward him. The master sergeant shook his head grimly, confirming what Malone suspected.

Another body.

Malone recognized the dead cop.

It was the technical sergeant who'd been guarding the entrance to Jack's Valley this morning. As with Jefferson and Kranski, he'd been killed with a knife. Unlike them, his wound was to the throat, a single slash mark delivered with such force that he'd almost been decapitated. Two SPs who were little more than kids had to turn away.

"The cop's gun," Anderson murmured. "It's still in his holster."

"Kranski's was, too," Sanders said. "You notice? He was still wearing his weapon."

Both agents looked uneasily at Malone. He nodded. Neither Kranski nor the dead SP had pulled their pistols because their killer was someone beyond suspicion.

Like a head coach or a general.

"Cadet Jefferson," Sanders said quietly. "He must have been in on the murders of Rachel and Mary."

"And Rachel's mother," Malone added.

Anderson said, "Whoever was working with Jefferson must have planned to meet him at the lodge. Saw us standing by the road, put two and two together, and went up to kill Jefferson before he could talk." He frowned at Malone's pensive head shake. "You don't think so, sir?"

"Depends, Doug." Malone glanced at the dead SP. Mist steamed from the grisly wound to his throat. "How long after you showed at the road until he was in position here?"

"Couldn't have been more than six, seven minutes," Anderson said.

"Plenty of time for the killer to go up the path before the cop got here, boss," Sanders added.

Malone nodded. The timing had bothered him, since the dead cop had been slashed as the killer escaped. He was also troubled by the killer's relationship to Jefferson. It had obviously been close enough to become a partner in murder.

Following this thread, Malone asked Sanders if he'd found anything during his search of Jefferson's room.

"Zip. Jefferson cleaned out his desk and took his laptop. I talked to his roommate, but all he could tell me was that Jefferson was a strange guy. Kept everything to himself."

"Agent Malone," the SP master sergeant called out. "The south end of the road by Douglas Valley is secure."

"Thank you, Sergeant."

The radios in the Security Forces' vehicles were chattering nonstop. One by one, units reported securing the remaining access points. After the last call, Malone checked his watch. Almost eight minutes to seal off the perimeter road. Add in the killer's five-minute head start and he could easily be beyond the six-mile loop they'd closed off.

And that wasn't the only problem. Since the Academy was closed to visitors and the cadets were restricted to the cadet area, traffic on the road was nonexistent. In the time they'd been standing there, only a single car had driven past. The chances of a witness to the cop's killing were somewhere between slim and none.

Malone swore under his breath. His men reacted with somber nods, mirroring his frustration. Even though they realized the killer was still somewhere on the reservation, they didn't have much hope of finding him. Thousands of people lived and worked at the

Academy. Searching every vehicle and person would be impossible.

But at least they were down to two prime suspects now, excluding the unknown parachutist. And if they got lucky, they could reduce that number by one.

Malone made a call, praying it would be answered.

"You have reached the residence of Lieutenant General Crenshaw . . ."

At the beep, Malone informed the general about the new murders and told him to pick up. "Sir," he said with an edge to his voice, "if you don't answer, I'll have to consider you the lead suspect," a not-so-veiled threat normally guaranteed to generate a response.

Only this time, it didn't.

"Sir, how many more people have to die before you'll talk to me?"

Silence.

Malone angrily clicked off; the general had forced his hand. He took a moment to gauge his priorities. In addition to processing the latest murder sites and conducting searches, they had to identify the parachutist and make the 5:00 P.M. meeting with Laura Ralston. All with a complement of eleven agents, which wasn't close to being enough.

He couldn't afford to wait on Laura. To focus his investigation, he had to find out precisely what she knew. Not only about the item she'd found, but what she could tell him about Crenshaw. After all, the general described her as a member of the family.

But when he called the ninety-fourth Flying Training Squadron, the glider squadron she commanded, a major confirmed he was too late; Laura had just departed on a training flight with a cadet.

"When do you expect her to land?"

"Between 1645 and 1700."

After leaving a message for Laura that he would be by at 1700, Malone addressed his men. "Doug, get over to Carlton House now. If the general is there, check his cars. I want to know if an engine is warm. If he's gone, have base housing send out someone with a key. When the detail working the Zinnel/Owen crime scene wraps up—"

"Should be done by now," Anderson said. "Mother said they were buttoning up when Kranski called her."

That freed up four agents, excluding Mother. It was a start. "Who'd Mother leave in charge? Randy Martinez?"

"Yeah . . ."

"Tell Randy to split his people into two search teams. One for Ralston's home and one for General Crenshaw's. I'll get you more help, Doug, but it will be a while. Rob, you run the show here. Call the detachment commanders at Pete Field, Buckley, and Schriever and have them send out all available agents. Whoever you don't need, assign to Rob." In the civilian world, they'd need to obtain search warrants first. But since both men resided on a military reservation, niceties like the Fourth Amendment didn't apply.

The SPs appeared stunned when they realized the homes of General Crenshaw and Coach Ralston would be searched. Malone didn't give a damn. He was through playing with kid gloves. If he'd treated them like typical murder suspects from the beginning, searched their homes and placed them under surveillance, maybe Kranski and the cop and that misguided kid Jefferson would still be alive.

Sanders got on his cell to get the ball rolling. By then, Anderson had commandeered a security cop's SUV and was speeding off. Malone made another call, knowing it was a waste of time. Since he didn't have the number, he went through the base operator. When the Ralston home answering machine came on, he hung up. The workaholic coach would be at his office, less than five minutes from where they were standing. In twenty minutes, he could have slipped away, killed three people, and been back at his desk looking at game film.

Convenient.

In rapid succession, Malone made three more calls, the first to the Colorado Springs PD, requesting technicians to process a triple murder. "Jesus," was all the stunned forensics supervisor could say. Next he phoned Tom Canola, to give him a heads-up.

"What kind of psycho are we dealing with, Malone? Who kills six people to cover up a relationship with a twenty-year-old girl?"

As if Malone had an answer.

His third call was to the commandant of cadets. He thumbed in the Com's cell number, knowing he was meeting with Smith's chief of staff. The sounds of traffic confirmed the Com was still en route.

When Malone told him about the murders, the Com reacted with the expected shock. A series of *f* words followed as Malone detailed his plan for targeting the two key suspects. The Com said, "Malone, this is *insane*. I know General Crenshaw. He wouldn't kill anybody." As before, there was no such defense of Coach Ralston.

"General Crenshaw will talk to you," the Com went on. "I'm sure it's a misunderstanding." Away from the phone: "Marv, call the supe. Tell him I need to talk to him. He probably won't answer, so you'll have to— Never mind, I'll do it. Give me your phone."

Moments later, Malone heard the Com's increasingly desperate voice, first asking then begging Crenshaw to answer.

But the general never did.

"Malone," the Com said, back on the line. "Your men on the way to search his house?"

"Yes, sir. Along with Coach Ralston's."

"Marv, turn around, we're heading back. Notify Ms. Dyers we'll reschedule." To Malone, "Tell your people I'm on the way."

"Sir, there's a chance General Crenshaw isn't home."

"He's home, dammit. Where the hell else could he be?"

Precisely the question that worried Malone . . . and the Com. Though neither would say it, they were fearful of another reason why General Crenshaw wasn't answering his phone. One that had nothing to do with the murders and even seemed likely, in light of the circumstances.

Had the general reached his breaking point?

Two more calls.

After notifying Agent Doug Anderson that the Com

was en route, Malone contacted Mother to give her the bad news about the dead cop.

"Yeah, I heard over the net when the SPs picked me up. I'm in my truck now. Be down in a minute."

Malone glanced up the hill. Seconds later, Mother's pickup came into view. But instead of continuing toward him, it lurched to a sudden stop on the crest of the hill.

It began backing up.

"Uh, Mother . . ."

"Change of plans, Malone. Grab a ride and get up here fast."

"Why?"

"How many people you know drive a green Jag?"

"A green—"

Malone gripped the phone hard. "Is it him? Can you tell?"

"Oh, yeah, it's him, all right. I'm looking right at the son of a bitch."

Chapter 24

THERE WERE FOUR CARS AT THE ROADBLOCK. The green Jag XKE was the second in line, waiting behind a van being searched. As Malone drove up, Mother was escorting a very animated Coach Ralston off to the side of the road. From his gestures and grimaces, it was clear the coach was one unhappy man.

The master sergeant pulled the SUV onto the shoulder. Malone was out the door before it came to a complete stop. The SPs finished searching the van and waved it past. One cop shouted to Malone, "Sir, we'll need to move the Jag."

"The keys inside?"

"No, sir."

"Have the cars drive around."

When Malone strolled up, Ralston was swearing at Mother. "*Goddammit, this is ridiculous. I'm telling you I don't know anything about any murders.*"

"Then what are you doing here?"

"*I'm the football coach.*"

"I thought you had practice this afternoon."

"Not until 1530."

"It's fifteen-twenty now. You'd have to hurry to make practice, Coach."

"I had an errand—" His head jerked to Malone in surprise. "You still hanging around? After what Smith said about you, I figured you'd be hiding out somewhere. Afraid to show your face." He laughed meanly.

"Sorry to disappoint you, John."

"Me, I'm not disappointed. Smith's just getting started. The radio says he's got a big press conference planned tonight. I can't wait to hear what else he has to say about you. 'Marginal and unprofessional.' Isn't that what he called you?"

Malone kept his cool. He knew Ralston was trying to get a rise out of him.

"You're way out of line, Coach," Mother growled.

"Hey, if you saw the CNN report—"

"I heard about it."

"Then you know what Smith said about him was true." Ralston stared insolently at Malone. "It is true, isn't it, Malone? You *are* a marginal and unprofessional officer."

Malone's expression never changed.

But Ralston's comments were pissing Mother off. She got right into Ralston's face. "Listen, asshole, I knew you as a cadet, remember. If anyone is a marginal and unprofessional—"

"It's okay, Mother," Malone said.

"The hell it is. He's the last one who should be accusing anyone of anything."

"You're letting him get to you. Don't."

She sullenly backed away, glowering at Ralston.

"Mother asked you a question, John," Malone said. "What are you doing here?"

A shrug. "I was running an errand."

"What errand?"

"We *had* this conversation. I'm done talking to you."

"It's a simple question," Mother shot back. "Just tell us what you're doing here."

"None of your damn business. I'm not saying shit without a lawyer." He turned and started toward his car. Malone stepped in front of him. Ralston attempted to skirt around him, but Malone grabbed his arm.

Ralston slowly faced Malone. He puffed up his thick frame, to make sure Malone noticed. "Let-me-go."

Malone kept holding him. Ralston tried to twist his arm free and seemed genuinely surprised when he was unable to do so. Malone gave him a little smile and released his grip.

He said, "You're wrong about me, John. I don't think you raped Christina."

Ralston squinted suspiciously. He gave a bitter laugh. "Nice try, Malone. But it won't work."

"It's true. I don't believe you're a rapist."

"You're a liar."

Malone shrugged.

Mother came over, her eyes locked on Malone questioningly. "One more time, Coach," she said to Ralston. "What were you doing here?"

"You deaf? I'm not talking. The way I see it, you got two choices: either arrest me or get the fuck out of my way."

Without waiting for a response, Ralston once again headed for his car.

"John," Malone called after him. "You're forgetting a third option."

He spun. "Like what?"

Malone's eyes dropped to the coach's shoes. After several seconds, he looked up with a pleasant smile and held out his hand. "We'll need your car keys."

Before getting into the Jag, Malone inspected the rug on the driver's side. Dry, with no noticeable streaks of dirt or mud. And unlike Malone's shoes, which were badly scuffed from the rocky footpath, Ralston's loafers were unmarked. Same thing with the coach's clothes and hands. No smudges or discolorations; certainly nothing that would suggest bloodstains.

And there should be.

Three people had been stabbed to death. When arteries are ruptured, they spurt like geysers. It would be almost impossible for the killer not to have gotten blood on himself, somewhere.

Sliding behind the wheel, Malone shook his head. Were they wrong about Ralston?

Making a tight one-eighty, Malone cut across to the gravel road leading to Lawrence Paul, parking between his Hummer and Mother's pickup. Mother and the SP master sergeant were already there, searching Ralston. The sergeant patted the coach down while Mother went through the pockets of Ralston's blue blazer, removing items. The drivers in the remaining two cars had recognized the coach and were watching the scene, mesmerized.

For someone with an ego the size of Ralston's, it was too much. His face was very red and he sputtered continually, saying things like, "I'm going to sue every last one of you for harassment, you hear me? When I get through, you won't have a pot to piss in. You can't do this to me. For chrissakes, I'm the head football coach of a top-ten team."

And so on.

Ignoring him, Mother placed the items on the hood of her pickup. A comb, a BlackBerry planner, car keys, a cell phone . . .

Popping the Jag's trunk latch, Malone told the master sergeant to inspect it. As the man did so, Malone carefully ran his eyes over the interior of the car. The leather seats and dash gleamed. He checked the shift lever, steering wheel, door handle—things Ralston had to touch. Nothing. And there wouldn't have been much time to clean up.

Nuts.

He opened the glove compartment and began rummaging—

Mother said suddenly, "Hold it right there, Coach."

"No. You have no right to look at that."

"The hell I don't. This is a military installation. Get back. *Get back*."

The sound of a scuffle. The master sergeant hollered, "Hey, get off her!"

Mother shrieked, "*Malone!*"

By then, Malone was scrambling from the car. He banged his knee on the door. Swore. Ralston was wrestling with Mother, bearhugging her back, trying to wrench something from her hands. The sergeant joined in, trying to pull Ralston off her. It was futile; the guy was about half his size. The three of them grunted and turned like a rugby scrum. Mother was jackknifed forward, desperately clinging to the object for all she was worth. She screamed, "Get him off me! For God's sake, Malone, get him off me!" She kicked Ralston in the shin. He yelped, but kept fighting with her. She bit him on the hand and he said savagely, "You *bitch.*"

Malone came up behind Ralston and shouted, "Let her go, John."

"Fuck you, asshole."

Malone jammed his gun against the back of Ralston's neck. "Let her go."

Ralston looked back with a slightly crazed smile. "Fuck you. You haven't got the balls."

He was right; Malone didn't. The cops at the road-block ran over, but didn't seem to know what to do. The bizarre dance continued. The master sergeant tumbled to the ground, landing hard. He tried to rise, got accidentally kneed in the head by Ralston, and fell again. Mother roared, "Malone, don't just stand there. *Do something!*"

Flipping his pistol around, Malone lowered it, circling, waiting for an opening. When it came, he swung up hard. The blow caught Ralston in the groin and he collapsed in a howl of pain.

Mother coughed. "Jesus, he's crazy. The son of a bitch is crazy."

When she turned toward Malone, he finally saw

what she was holding. He was expecting the BlackBerry planner, but it wasn't.

It was the cell phone.

Ralston rolled on the ground, moaning, clutching his groin. Everyone stood around, looking down at him. A female cop turned away with an embarrassed expression. The master sergeant slumped against the Jag, spent from his effort. After a minute, Mother's breathing rate slowed to the point where Malone wasn't worried she'd have a coronary. "Any time you're ready," he said.

She nodded vaguely, attempting to smooth her hair, which was a mass of tangles. A rare display of vanity for a woman who never wore makeup. She gave up, realizing it was pointless.

"A voice mail?" she asked.

"Probably."

She selected the icon from the menu and held up the phone, so Malone could hear. Nine messages, one new. He said, "It will be an old one."

But the service played them in sequence, beginning with the most recent. The first message was from a sports reporter, confirming an upcoming interview. The second and third were from Ralston's wife, Laura, saying they needed to talk. The fourth . . .

When the last message ended, Mother lowered the phone, perplexed. Nothing they'd heard was remotely suggestive or suspicious.

Malone said, "Try the caller ID memory."

She tapped the button, cycling through the numbers.

She stopped on the fourth one. "We got him," she murmured.

They were staring at a local number and a time. And just below, a familiar name: Jefferson, Terry.

"It's not the way it looks," Ralston called out. "I can explain."

Mother and Malone turned. The coach was sitting up, his face no longer etched in pain. In a wavering voice that suggested panic, he said, "I didn't kill Jefferson. He called, wanting to meet me."

"Why?" Mother asked.

Instead of replying, Ralston glanced to the SPs circled around him and the people watching from the cars. He dropped his eyes, humiliated. He struggled to his feet in an attempt to recover what little dignity he had left.

"I didn't kill Jefferson. I never even saw him. I swear to you."

"Start talking, John," Malone said. "You'll have to convince us."

Lowering his voice as if worried someone would overhear, Ralston attempted to do so.

Chapter 25

RALSTON HAD AGREED TO MEET JEFFERSON FOR one reason: evidence.

Jefferson said he had evidence that proved who murdered Rachel and Mary. He didn't let on what the evidence was or identify the person it implicated. He only told Ralston to meet him at Lawrence Paul and he would turn the evidence over to him.

"By the time I arrived, your people were already here. I couldn't have driven up to Lawrence Paul, even if I wanted to."

The key word was "driven."

Ralston squinted at Malone and Mother for a sign they believed him. They gazed back with practiced indifference. Mother said, "And Jefferson called you instead of us or the SPs because . . ."

"You won't like it."

"Try me."

"Jefferson was afraid. He knew you were looking for him, thinking he might be the killer. He said he was being set up and couldn't trust anyone in the chain of command because the killer was someone high up." Ralston paused, eyeing her. "Very high."

His inference was clear, though Mother voiced it anyway. "In other words, General Crenshaw."

"That's how I took it. Sure."

He flashed a smile as he said it. Not smart. Mother tossed Malone a skeptical glance.

"Oh, for crying out—" Ralston threw up his hands. "I guess Senator Smith was right. You're trying to cover this thing up."

"You know better than that," Mother snapped.

"The hell I do. I *told* you Crenshaw had a thing for Rachel, but you blew me off. He's a three-star, so he couldn't possibly be a killer. Now Jefferson practically accuses him by name and you still don't—"

"He didn't," Malone said, cutting him off. "He never told you the killer was Crenshaw. Why didn't he, John?"

Ralston hesitated. "Well, because . . . I'm sure Jefferson was concerned over . . ."

That was as far as he got.

"And why," Malone pressed, "didn't he tell you *what* the evidence was? Why play it cute and insist you come here first? *Why didn't he tell you what he had?*"

This time Ralston gazed back sourly, not even attempting an answer.

"The thing is, John," Malone said, "you haven't told us anything. For all we know, Jefferson was lying to you or you're lying to us."

"Now listen, you—"

"I don't want to hear it, John. What I want is the truth: Why did Jefferson call you?"

"Huh? I just explained that he wanted to turn over—"

"Why you *specifically?* Jefferson must have known you."

Ralston was already nodding. "Right, right. He did. Jefferson used to come over to the house, when he and Rachel were engaged. He called me because he knew he could trust me."

Malone had figured as much. "So after Jefferson called you, you drove right over?"

"Yeah. Like I told you."

Malone caught a sharp look from Mother; he understood. This had to be a lie because of the timing. "What time did you get here, John?"

"Somewhere between 3:05 and 3:10."

"According to your cell phone, Jefferson called you at 2:52. Your office is only five minutes away—"

"I was on my way to the airfield. Laura had a few minutes between flights and wanted to talk."

Laura Ralston's messages. Malone asked Ralston precisely where he was when Jefferson called.

"A little past Falcon Stadium. Almost to Community Center Drive."

No hesitation before answering; he was either being truthful or was a practiced liar. "When you arrived and saw the cops, you didn't leave right away."

"I wondered what was going on, so I asked one of the SPs. When he told me about the murders, I knew I had to get out of here."

Malone didn't bother to ask him why; the reason was obvious. He glanced over to Mother, to see if she had any other questions. She did; she wanted to know which cop Ralston had spoken to. When he pointed out a husky staff sergeant working the roadblock, she went over to talk to him. Malone and Ralston stood in an uncomfortable silence.

"So," Ralston said, "you finally going after General Crenshaw?"

"We'll see, John."

"You'll *see?*" Ralston's face darkened. "You don't believe a damn thing I said, do you? You think I'm making all of this up? Admit it."

"Cool it, John."

"No. I see where this is going. This is all personal with you. You've had it in for me for years."

"John—"

"You'd love to haul me in, embarrass the hell out of me, maybe get me fired. Well, forget it. I didn't kill anybody."

"Then you have nothing to worry about."

Ralston snorted. "With you running this case, give me a break. I knew it was bullshit when you said you didn't believe I raped Christina. That's what this is all about. Christina."

Ralston was becoming increasingly confrontational, and Malone had no desire to get into an argument. He turned away, focusing on Mother. She was talking with the husky cop, who was peering at his watch.

"Here's a news flash, buddy boy," Ralston said. "I didn't rape Christina. I wasn't anywhere near the Academy that night. Four other people swore to that fact. But that wasn't good enough for you. For the longest time, I never understood why you got it in your head that I was one of the rapists. I wasn't the only football player Christina had hit on. Why me, Malone? *Why accuse me?*"

A reference to their long-ago confrontation, which had almost led to blows. Malone eased out a breath, but said nothing.

"You know what I think?" Ralston said. "I think maybe the rape had nothing to do with it. I think you were jealous. So, am I right? Were you jealous, Malone?"

Malone's jaw knotted. Still he remained silent.

"What happened, Malone? Someone tell you Christina really had the hots for me? It's true. At first, I thought she was pulling her usual come-on bullshit, but she wasn't. She was definitely interested. I mean *interested.* Me, I couldn't wait to do her. She was one hot number—"

Something finally snapped in Malone. He spun, his hands balling into fists. He was furious, his face twisted into an unrecognizable snarl. He roared, "You're a goddamn liar, John. Not another fucking word or so help me I will arrest you."

Ralston was stunned by Malone's raw anger. He stood with his mouth open, uncertain what to do. When he attempted to speak, Malone took a menacing step toward him. Ralston flinched, rattled by the gesture. He slowly backed away, as if he realized he'd finally gone too far.

Malone continued to glare at him, defying him to respond. But Ralston wisely remained silent; he wouldn't even look at Malone.

Malone pivoted and stalked over to the Jag. SPs who'd witnessed his eruption watched nervously, not that Malone noticed. All he could think about was finding something that would give him a reason to arrest that lying son of a bitch.

"Now *that*," Mother said, coming over to the Jag, "was impressive. Mr. Cool finally lost his temper. All I can say is it was about time. Want to tell me what the dirtbag said that finally got to you?"

"Nothing. Forget it." Malone was wedged into the Jag, searching behind the seats with a flashlight borrowed from an SP.

"*Nothing*? For a second there, I thought you were going to take a swing at him."

"He talks too much."

"He always talks too much. So what was it? What'd he say? He make another smart-ass remark about us being part of a cover-up?"

Turning, Malone saw her standing over him, Ralston's jacket slung over her shoulder. She shrugged. "Your choice, Malone. You either tell me, or I ask him."

She smiled sweetly.

He sighed and backed out of the car, clicking off the flashlight. "He brought up something from your report. When you interviewed him, Ralston said he had no reason to rape Christina because she was interested in a relationship with him. At the time, you concluded Ralston was lying, making up the story to take the heat off himself."

Mother thoughtfully placed the jacket on the hood.

"And that pissed you off why? Because you think it might be true?"

"I don't know. I suppose it's possible."

"C'mon, Malone. *Cadet* Ralston was one of the main people who badmouthed her. Called her a tease and a slut."

"Right, but that could have been before he realized she *was* interested in him."

"Malone . . ." Mother shook her head. "Malone . . ."

"What?" he said, with a trace of irritation.

"You. Where's this coming from? He's been dogging you. Just now you were mad enough to punch out the jerk. As long as I've known you, you've never made a secret of how much you hated the guy—"

"*Hate*'s a little strong."

"*Hate*. We both hated him. Yet all of a sudden you're defending him. You also told him you didn't think he raped Christina. I figured that was only a line to get him to talk. But now I'm starting to wonder about you again." She held Malone in a steady gaze. "I'm starting to wonder about a lot of things."

This was another topic he'd wanted to avoid, but it was obvious she wasn't going to let him. He sighed. "Look, it's just that I think there's room for doubt. We never understood why those cadets supported Ralston's alibi, risked prison—"

"Old news. You know something. What?"

When he didn't answer, she didn't press him. She just stood there with her hands on her hips.

He took a deep breath, let it out. She kept looking at him. Waiting.

To hell with it . . .

And he told her the one thing he'd neglected to mention earlier—that Christina had asked him to back off because she was interested in someone else.

Mother was dumbfounded by this news. Then her face frosted over when she realized he'd again withheld crucial information from her.

"What the hell is the matter with you, Malone? First, you don't tell me Laura married Ralston. Okay, that I could live with, maybe understand. But *this*, this could exonerate Ralston for the rape. You should have told me this before. Why the hell didn't you?"

"I thought Christina made the story up, to make me jealous. It wasn't until I spoke with Ralston that I realized—"

"You *read* Ralston's statement in the report. You *knew* it could be true." She leaned close, her voice harsh and demanding. "Cut the crap and level with me. *Now.*"

"I didn't want to believe—"

"The truth, dammit."

"I'm *telling* you the truth. I never believed there was someone else because I didn't *want* to believe it. I cared for Christina a great deal and if I admitted . . . allowed myself to admit that she'd found—" He shook his head. "Look, it never occurred to me that she would choose someone over me. It just didn't."

He looked at Ralston. The coach was nervously watching Malone and Mother. Apparently, Malone's blowup had convinced him he might actually be arrested.

"Anyway," Malone said to Mother, "that's the reason I didn't tell you. I liked Christina too much to admit she'd rejected me."

Mother no longer appeared irritated. She sighed. "You're a piece of work, Malone. You figured she was so hung up on you, she couldn't possibly be interested in someone else. Talk about an ego."

"That wasn't it at all. It was something else entirely."

"Oh?" She weighed his remark for a moment. "You telling me you were in *love* with Christina?"

This was something Malone had never admitted, even to himself. "I don't know. Maybe."

"But you broke off the relationship . . ."

"Yes."

"And regretted it?"

"Yes."

"You know it could have been true. Christina denied being interested in Ralston, but she did admit flirting with him more than the others." She studied Malone for a long moment. "You must have known that, Malone. Other cadets did. Is that why you disliked Ralston so much? Because you were jealous?"

Malone looked increasingly uncomfortable. "Listen, can we talk about something else?"

"Just tell me. Were you jealous?"

Malone noticed the beginnings of a smile. She was enjoying making him squirm. "I don't know. Maybe."

"Maybe?"

He was getting annoyed. "I told you I didn't want to believe she liked someone else."

"Bullshit," she said, grinning now. "You were jealous.

Admit it. You dumped Christina, but she turned the tables on you. She made *you* jealous."

"Fine. You stay here and have fun at my expense. Me, I'm going back up to the lodge. The killer was in a rush and there's a chance he slipped up, left something for us to find." He turned and walked toward his Hummer.

"C'mon, Malone. I didn't know you were so thin-skinned."

He ignored her.

"Aren't you forgetting something?"

"Like what?" he snapped.

Then he remembered.

Chapter 26

WHAT TO DO ABOUT RALSTON? THEY NEEDED more than his presence here to arrest him.

When Malone asked, Mother confirmed that Ralston's story checked out. The husky cop remembered the coach arriving a little after 3:00 P.M. This fact coupled with the absence of blood on Ralston's clothing or in his car made it unlikely that he could be the killer.

But according to Mother, it didn't make it impossible.

Pointing in the direction of Harmon Hall, she said, "If Ralston lied about driving past the stadium when Jefferson phoned, he could have gotten here before the cops arrived. Parked by Harmon and walked up. From where the cops were, they wouldn't have seen him coming or going. And if he had planned to stab Jefferson, he probably brought stuff to clean up any blood." She shrugged, facing Malone. "We check the public trash cans by Harmon, we might find some rags or paper towels; he had to toss them somewhere. We'll also need to question everyone in the superintendent's office; if

Ralston parked there, someone will remember the Jag. A car like his, people notice."

Malone brought up the agents from the other units who were coming to assist. Once they arrived, he'd have Sanders send someone over to Harmon. Malone also mentioned another possible explanation for Ralston's apparent cleanliness.

"An accomplice?" Mother said. "Jefferson *was* the accomplice. He's the one who destroyed Rachel's e-mails."

"I'm talking about a third person working with Ralston. Someone who committed the murders instead of him."

"If that were the case, why would Ralston risk showing up here? Drive up in a car that everyone would recognize and make himself even more of a suspect?"

"I don't know. What I do know is that it makes no sense for Jefferson to have phoned Ralston, if Ralston wasn't involved. Jefferson certainly wasn't going to identify the real killer to him. Why would he? He was working with the killer."

Mother's brow knitted. Malone had thrown her a curve she hadn't considered. "It's . . . confusing."

"Very. There's no rational explanation for that call unless Ralston was—"

A sudden thought popped into Malone's head. One even more implausible except for one thing; it fit. He began, "Don't say anything until you hear me out . . ."

"Go."

"A frame-up."

Mother slowly leaned against the Jag. "I'm listening."

After Malone explained, Mother said cautiously, "You know this sounds a little crazy . . ."

"Only a little."

"You're saying Jefferson called Ralston to lure him here, so Ralston would be implicated in the murders. If true, that would mean Jefferson had no knowledge of the purpose behind the call; he had no idea he would be the victim."

"Right."

She closed her eyes, continuing to voice her thoughts. "So the killer was already in place, when Jefferson drove up. Since that person was planning a murder, it follows he walked up the path instead of using a car. Less conspicuous. At some point, this person . . . this killer met up with Jefferson. Used some pretext to lure him behind the lodge, to the area by the refrigeration unit . . ." She paused, visualizing the precise sequence of events. "Kranski. They weren't expecting Kranski to show up. The killer must have killed him first, while Jefferson was still alive. If not, Kranski would have seen the body and pulled his gun. But the kid never did. He just walked over to them. And the bastard jumped him, shoved a knife into . . ."

Mother never finished the statement. She swallowed hard in unanticipated emotion. Kranski had been one of theirs, a member of their family. "I liked him. The kid was a screwup, but I liked him."

"We all did."

Mother shook her head sadly, lost in her thoughts. She sounded suddenly angry. "I want the son of a bitch. I don't care how long it takes or what we have to do, I want him."

"We'll get him."

Looking over at Ralston, she said, "It's only a theory. Personally, I think it's iffy as hell. Jefferson could have called him for a reason that had nothing to do with a frame-up. And Laura Ralston said she found evidence implicating him in Christina's rape. You ask me, we should question her now—"

"Can't." Malone told her why.

"You tell Kranski that Ralston was a suspect? No? Then that's why Kranski wasn't alarmed. He'd never think the head football coach could be a killer. You know, I meant to check—"

She snatched up Ralston's jacket and dug out his BlackBerry planner. Malone peered over her shoulder, watching as she went through Ralston's monthly schedule. There were several meetings with Crenshaw, but none with anyone else that raised red flags.

She shook her head, disappointed.

"We can't hold Ralston," Malone said. "I've ordered his house searched as well as General Crenshaw's. We'll impound his car and have him turn over the rest of his clothing. If the lab finds blood, we'll pick him up."

Mother reluctantly nodded, her eyes drifting to Ralston. "He know?"

"Not yet."

"He'll be one pissed-off camper." She sounded pleased at the prospect.

"Something else might piss him off even more. It's after three. The results should be in by now."

He reached for his cellular, but Mother was already going for hers. Seconds into the conversation with the coroner, she grinned wickedly.

The security police master sergeant listened to Mother's instructions with little enthusiasm. He rubbed a reddening welt on his chin, saying, "Ma'am, if he tries something again, I won't be able to—"

"What's your weapon for, Sergeant?"

"Ma'am?"

"If he resists, blow his ass away." She was only half-kidding.

"Yes, ma'am." The master sergeant gloomily shuffled off.

Mother winked at Malone. "Let's have some fun."

As they went over to Ralston, her mood was upbeat. She walked with a spring in her step and couldn't resist smiling. She was looking forward to breaking the news to Ralston, watching him sweat.

When Mother informed Ralston he could go, the coach started to smile. Then Mother told him they would be impounding his car.

"I see," Ralston said.

That was it. No howls of protest or antagonistic comments.

"We've also begun searching your house, Coach. I'll have to ask you to turn over the clothes you're wearing."

A slight tension around his jaw, but you had to look

to see it. Ralston was working hard to behave. "Surely, you don't want me to undress here."

"Don't tempt me." She pointed him to the master sergeant, waiting by his SUV. "He'll give you a ride. You can turn over the items to him."

More jaw tightening. Ralston took a deep breath, reining in his irritation. "Practice has started. I have a change of clothing in my office."

"Tell the sergeant."

Ralston turned to go.

"Oh, Coach, there's one more thing—"

He swung around cautiously.

"It's about Rachel Owen. We thought you might be interested . . ."

"What about her?"

Mother waited several beats, setting him up.

Then announced: "She was two months pregnant."

At the instant Mother made the statement, Malone was fixated on Ralston. He was searching for an indication of panic or fear. A sudden grimace or eye twitch, perhaps a nervous swallow.

Something.

But the coach's self-control was exceptional. He didn't so much as blink. Not even when Mother turned up the heat by informing him they would arrange for him to turn over a blood sample at the hospital tomorrow.

"I'll cooperate fully," he said. "I have nothing to hide."

He calmly went over to the SUV and climbed inside. Watching it drive away, Mother shook her head.

"Fuck," she said.

Which was precisely Malone's response only moments later. As he and Mother went over to his Hummer to return to Lawrence Paul, Agent Doug Anderson called to report he'd arrived at General Crenshaw's house. Doug also told Malone they had a problem. A big one.

"Oh, Christ," Malone said. "Don't tell me he committed suicide."

"I don't know, sir."

"What do you mean, you don't know?"

At his response, Malone wasn't sure if he should be relieved or pissed off. He settled for the latter and swore.

"General Crenshaw's *gone?*" Mother said.

As she and Malone stood beside the Hummer, a Security Forces SUV roared up, dropped off a stack of red cones, and continued up the road to Lawrence Paul. In the distance, the sound of sirens signaled the approach of more cavalry. The radios the SPs wore continued to chatter incessantly. Someone at a checkpoint nervously requested assistance from a supervisor to deal with a colonel who was irate over being delayed—

Malone said to Mother, "One of the general's cars is also gone. The black Lincoln."

"Anyone call the gates?"

"Anderson did. The guards don't recall seeing the general. But they were only checking the people entering."

"Damn. *Damn.*" Mother began pacing the length of the Humvee. She appeared even more upset by this development than Malone and he knew why.

"Tom Canola," he said. "He called you recently . . ."

"Three times. Tom's a talker. The last time we spoke was right after you left him. He told me about Smith's smear job and how Kaitlin sold you out. He also said she took off in your car and left you high and dry. You know where she went?"

"Probably to brief her handler."

"Handler?"

He told her about Smith's chief of staff, Marcy Dyers, who was in town.

"Well, all I can say is good riddance. Kaitlin was trouble from the start. The longer she stays out of our hair, the better."

Malone no longer felt a similar resentment toward Kaitlin. He'd been thinking a lot about his phone conversation with her and had decided the fear in her voice was real. But that conclusion only confused him more.

Kaitlin was the one who intimidated people. Her statuesque physique coupled with her striking beauty and arrogantly uncompromising persona made her more than a little off-putting. She wasn't the type to be frightened of anyone or anything.

But she apparently was. It didn't figure. Neither did her oddly stilted speech. She wasn't a boozer or a druggie. Not this girl.

"So what is it?" Malone muttered.

"Huh?" Mother said. "You say something?"

After he told her, she gave a dismissive laugh. "It's an act, believe me. She knows you're pissed at her; she's trying to gain sympathy. That's all."

"I don't think . . ."

"I'm right about this, believe me. I've been around enough walking Barbie dolls to know. Girls who look like her use men because they can. Don't think you're any different. She already screwed you over once. She's just looking for a chance to do it again. Don't fall for it. Keep your little soldier zipped up and your mind off of her tits and ass."

"That's not it at all."

"Oh, please. You slept with her sister. You tell me you're not fantasizing about sleeping with her, also?"

Malone was silent. If he tried denying it, Mother would know he was lying.

"Yeah. That's what I thought. Forget about Kaitlin Barlow. We've got bigger problems, like what to do about Crenshaw." Shaking her head, she resumed pacing. "The first time Tom called, he mentioned Mrs. Owen was dressed up all nice and pretty when she was killed, possibly because she met Crenshaw last night. I never believed there was anything to it, which is why I asked him to put a lid on it. When Tom called again and told me Rachel was Crenshaw's stepdaughter, I was convinced I was right; the general couldn't be a killer."

"And now . . ."

"Hell, I don't know what to think. Not anymore. For the past hour, Crenshaw was supposed to be home alone, licking his wounds. The same scenario we laid out for Ralston could apply to him. And if Crenshaw is the killer, it supports your theory about the frame-up and explains why Kranski never went for his gun." She looked at him. "You understand I'm not saying I necessarily swallow that Ralston is being framed . . ."

"Noted."

"We have to remember that the general was out running at the time the girls were killed. Toss in his connection to Rachel, and he's got even more of a motive to find someone for us to pin this on."

She came to a stop, waiting for Malone's response.

But he couldn't bring himself to agree with her assessment. Not yet. He said, "Suspicion and coincidence. That's all we have. We have nothing tangible."

"Big surprise. We're dealing with a killer who is smart, doesn't make mistakes."

"That's just it. He already made one. Rachel's fetus will give us his DNA."

"*If* we find a match and *if* the baby's father is the killer."

"You don't believe he is?"

She sighed. "I told you I don't know what to think anymore. My gut tells me the killer wouldn't make that kind of mistake. He takes risks, big risks, kills five people in broad daylight, but no one even gets a look at him. How? He sure as hell isn't a ghost. The only thing I can come up with is that every move he makes is . . . I don't know . . . scripted. This guy thinks through everything about a hundred times before— I say something? What'd I say?"

Malone had flinched as if startled. He said, "I wonder."

"Wonder what? Malone?"

He suddenly sprang to life, motioning Mother to get into the Humvee. "Get in. You're right about this guy. He's a thinker, a planner. Call Sanders. Tell him to leave one SP to guard the dead cop's body and bring everyone else to the lodge. If it's there, it won't take us long to find it. He *wants* us to find it." Hurrying to the driver's door, he called out to two security cops who were placing red cones across the gravel road. He told them to move the cones out of the way and follow him.

"Find what?" Mother asked him. "What are you talking about?"

"Get in. I'll explain on the way."

Chapter 27

CHANCE.

If the killer was intent on framing Ralston, Malone concluded, he wouldn't have left anything to chance. Once he murdered Kranski and Jefferson, he would have left something behind to implicate the coach. Something to remove any doubt about his guilt.

The search team consisted of the three OSI agents and five security cops. After Malone voiced his suspicions, he was met with blank stares. "Boss," Rob Sanders said. "Are you saying if we find something tying Ralston to the killing, it means he's really innocent?"

"It means he might be innocent, Rob."

"So he could still be the killer and just happened to drop something incriminating. Something that wasn't planted."

"Right."

"That's what I don't get, sir. How can we tell whether something was planted or not?"

"We probably can't yet."

Sanders and the security cops looked even more confused. "Look," Malone said, "let's cross that bridge when we come to it."

While Mother and Malone checked out Jefferson's car and inspected the two corpses, Sanders and the cops started at the refrigeration unit and moved down the road toward the footpath, searching overlapping five-yard sections. Since it was winter, the undergrowth was sparse and they worked quickly. After twenty minutes, the group was well down the trail and had come up empty, unless you counted beer cans. The only item of interest was something they *hadn't* found.

Jefferson's cell phone. It hadn't been on his body or in his car.

"You do realize," Mother said, joining Malone on the footpath, "it shouldn't be this hard."

"No." If the killer had left something, they should have found it by now. "Let's give it a few more minutes."

"It's almost 1600."

He looked at her, wondering why she should care.

She shrugged. "The parachute squadron buttons up in an hour. We need to head over to the airfield now, if we want to talk to the cadre."

Another of Malone's priority items he hadn't had time for. "You go. I'll be over later. If Laura lands early—"

"I'll call."

Mother left and the search continued. After another ten minutes, Malone knew they were wasting their time. He didn't understand it. He'd been so certain—

"Sir," a voice called out. "I see something."

Malone looked down the trail. A young cop was staring into the brush. "Hang on," Sanders ordered. "Don't touch anything." Sanders was only yards from the cop and rushed over. Everyone else did, also.

Reaching into the brush, Sanders rose, clutching a hand-sized object. From a distance it appeared to be a small radio, but as Malone got closer, he realized it was a cell phone.

One that was shattered and broken, as if by great force.

Sanders held out the phone to Malone butt-first, so the small label stuck to the bottom was visible. Even though the name was smeared with mud, they could still read it clearly.

Jefferson, it said.

Cadets often marked their phones, to avoid confusion. Malone and Sanders stared at the label, trying to understand.

Sanders sighed. "I give up, boss. If this is what the killer wanted us to find, why destroy it? Why make it harder for us to figure out who called Jefferson?"

Malone shook his head. "It could be he really wanted to destroy the cell phone."

"Wouldn't it have been easier to keep it and toss it where it wouldn't be found?"

"It'd be tough to explain if he were caught."

"But why take the phone in the first place? We pull Jefferson's phone records, we'll know who he called."

"Maybe that's the reason, Rob."

"Reason?"

"Time. The killer could have been trying to buy time."

"We're only talking a few hours, sir. That doesn't make sense to me."

But Malone realized maybe it did. He asked Sanders if anyone had requested a copy of Jefferson's phone records.

"No one's had a chance. It's been pretty hectic."

"Do it now."

As Sanders phoned in the request, Malone moved away from the circle of cops, trying to decide why it would be important for the killer to buy a few hours. Only one explanation jumped out: The killer needed the time to escape.

And since General Crenshaw was missing . . .

Malone felt the sickening sensation return. Up to this moment, he hadn't wanted to believe, wouldn't allow himself to believe that someone like Crenshaw could—

"Uh, sir," an SP said. "Your phone is ringing."

On the other end of the line was Randy Martinez, one of the agents assisting Doug Anderson in the search of the homes. Martinez sounded out of breath and an instant later, it became apparent why.

"We found it, sir. Jesus, we found it."

Relief.

Listening to Martinez's account, Malone initially felt an overwhelming sense of relief. But the more he learned, the more he realized his reaction was premature. This find didn't dispel the frame-up theory.

Not by a long shot.

After clarifying several points, Malone ended his conversation. Sanders and the cops were moving down the hill, resuming their search. Glancing back at Malone, Sanders said, "Phone company says it'll be about an hour. They'll fax Jefferson's phone records to the office. I told the duty officer to watch for them."

"You can quit searching now, Rob. We were looking in the wrong place."

"The wrong place?"

"Randy Martinez found a forty-five automatic in Ralston's bedroom."

At that statement, the SP's eyes snapped wide, but Sanders just stood there with a mystified expression. "His bedroom?"

"Actually, it was in Coach Ralston's closet."

Sanders came up the hill toward him, frowning. "We sure it's the murder weapon, sir?"

"As much as we can be without ballistics. The gun was recently fired and five rounds are missing from the clip."

He nodded, doing the math. Two rounds each for the girls and one for Mrs. Owen. "Prints?"

"Wiped clean."

Another nod. If Ralston was the killer, the gun might or might not have been wiped clean; if it was planted, it certainly would be. "You could be right about a frame job, boss. But it would have to be someone with access to the house, someone who—"

A third, more pronounced nod when the answer came to him. Malone knew it would; it was obvious.

"Rachel Owen," Sanders said.

"Yes," Malone said.

"She was sponsored by the Ralstons, stayed over all the time. She probably had a key."

"Yes. And you searched her room . . ."

Sanders was already thinking, trying to remember. "Only one set. Car and room keys. I found them in her roommate Mary's desk. I remembered wondering where Rachel's car keys were."

"You also searched the girls' gym lockers?"

"No keys. And nothing was found on their bodies." He shook his head. "Hell, that's how the killer did it. He used Rachel's keys."

"But why frame Ralston? Why not someone else Rachel was close to? A cadet or maybe one of Rachel's coaches or instructors?"

Sanders backed off from a reply. He realized he'd only be guessing.

Malone retraced his steps up the path, to ask the one person who might know.

Malone was in turmoil.

For a long time, he sat in the Hummer, hand on the ignition, staring blankly out the window. Over and over, he told himself he was doing the only thing he could, that he was a cop and had a duty to uncover the truth. Still, his personal feelings held him back. By pursuing the theory that Ralston—a man he despised—was being framed, he was building the case against Crenshaw, someone he admired.

The irony of the situation was heightened by Crenshaw's own words to Malone.

You're not a good officer, Malone . . . you lack character.

In the end, that's what it came down to—Malone's

character. Did he possess the character to do the right thing?

The frame-up theory was far-fetched; even Mother said so. As the head of the OSI, he had the power to disregard it and focus on the evidence. With the discovery of the probable murder weapon, no one would fault him if he arrested Ralston. They certainly wouldn't if Laura really possessed information tying Ralston to Christina's rape.

But of course Malone would question himself.

General Crenshaw had called it: Malone wasn't a man of character. With his past, who could be? Since as far back as Malone could remember, his mother and grandfather had plied him with money and gifts, hoping to make up for his father's absence. It didn't work. Malone grew up spoiled and undisciplined, engaging in a lifestyle he would later regret. People with his background don't develop character because there's no reason to do so. What they do develop, however, is an appreciation for the limits of their conscience; the precise boundary that even they aren't able to cross.

At the top of Malone's list of parameters was letting a killer go free.

He checked the clock on the dash: 4:20. Ralston would be at the practice field for at least another hour.

Malone started the car.

Who would want to frame you for murder, Coach?

A single question. That was all Malone intended to ask Ralston, but he never got the chance.

At the bottom of the hill, the red cones again lined

the road. Rolling down his window, Malone ordered a cop to remove them. As the man hurried forward to do so, a transmission crackled over his radio. A tinny voice was talking about a break-in reported by a woman—

Malone had been in the middle of a yawn when he sat up fast. But the woman's name wasn't repeated. His first thought was he'd heard the name incorrectly. That it was someone else.

"Sergeant," he called out to the cop, "that radio call about a break-in . . ."

"Yes, sir. At the TLFs." TLFs are transient living facilities, where visiting personnel often stayed.

Malone said, "You catch the name of the person who called it in?"

The cop's face went blank. He relayed Malone's question to a nearby group of SPs. A female technical sergeant had the answer. Malone hadn't heard the name incorrectly.

Someone had broken into Kaitlin's TLF.

"Is she hurt?" Malone demanded. "Do you know?"

The tech sergeant had to get on the radio to ask. "She's fine, sir."

Malone eased back in his seat, surprised to realize he was trembling. He tried to convince himself he was overreacting. The Academy averaged a couple of break-ins a year. That could be all this was, a simple burglary.

But he knew better.

He motioned the cops out of the way and punched the gas. The TLFs were in the Douglas Valley housing area. It'd take seven minutes to get there and another couple to find Kaitlin. Call it nine minutes until he could ask her why the killer would go after her. Because as with everything else about this case, he didn't have an answer. Neither did Mother, when he called her.

But she gave him an earful over what he planned to do about the discovery of the gun. "You're outta your fucking mind, Malone," she said.

Their conversation deteriorated from there. Mother wasn't shouting, but she was coming close. In self-defense, Malone held the phone away from his ear.

"Malone," Mother said, "the gun might not be a plant."

"It's a plant. Someone's trying to frame Ralston."

"So we ignore the gun? Oh, Senator Smith's going to love that. He'll have half the country singing cover-up. Hell, I'd be singing cover-up. You *can't* ignore it."

"We'll keep a lid on it until we can determine who the real killer is."

"That could take weeks or months. What if you're wrong? What if Ralston is the killer?"

"He's not."

"There you go again. What's he got on you?"

"Nothing. He's not the killer."

"Malone, we had this talk. If you're holding out again—"

"*He's being framed.*"

A pause. When Mother spoke, her voice was resigned but had a hard edge. "Does the Com know about the gun?"

"Probably. He was going to General Crenshaw's house."

"I'll call him now. Talk to him."

"Mother—"

"Shut up and listen. The brass won't let you ignore the gun; they can't. If you try, they'll yank you off the case so fast it will make your head spin. If ballistics comes up with a match, we arrest Ralston. End of story. If he's innocent, that's too fucking bad. Like it or not, Smith's calling the shots here. The Air Force can't afford to piss him off and neither can you. So sit tight and let me handle this. Okay?"

Malone hesitated. He told himself to do the right thing, tell Mother no, it wasn't okay.

Just tell her no.

"Yeah," he heard himself say. "Okay."

He expected her to hang up. Instead, she said quietly, "I went through this on Christina's rape. I knew Ralston was a rapist, but they made me back off. It sucks, doesn't it?"

"It sucks," Malone said.

Ending the call, Malone felt ashamed. This had been a test of character, a crucial one.

He'd failed.

A block past the Douglas Valley Elementary School, Malone spotted the TLFs—a series of identical two-bedroom duplexes lining a U-shaped street. He found it surprising that Kaitlin would stay in one because he assumed someone with a Harvard pedigree would prefer a ritzy downtown hotel. But as a government employee visiting the Academy on official business, she was certainly authorized to slum it.

Turning onto the street, Malone didn't bother to check addresses. A Security Forces SUV and his BMW were parked in front of the third duplex on the right. The front door was open and Malone didn't see anyone standing outside. He parked out front and hurried up the walkway.

He entered a combination kitchen and living area, furnished in typical wood-veneer chic. Nothing appeared disturbed except for the sliding glass door at the back. It stood open, a jagged hole the size of a fist in it. The room was empty, but Malone heard voices coming from the hallway to his left. He went down it, following the sound into the farthest of the two bedrooms.

He took one step inside and stopped in his tracks.

This was no simple burglary.

Chapter 28

Chaos.

No other word fit the scene. It resembled the aftermath of a tornado. Clothing was literally scattered everywhere. The mattress rested half on the bed frame, the sheets and bedspread torn off it and thrown in a corner. The closet doors were open, expensive leather suitcases lying on the floor, the linings cut out. The dresser drawers were piled in a heap, their contents—mostly undergarments and papers—strewn nearby.

"Some mess, huh, sir," a deep voice said.

Malone nodded vaguely at the two security cops who were standing near the foot of the bed, a barrel-chested staff sergeant and a reed-thin airman with a complexion problem. Kaitlin was over by the window, watching Malone. If she was under the influence of booze or drugs, she gave no sign; she certainly didn't appear frightened. Her eyes were clear and chillingly resolute, her lips pursed in a tight line. She met his gaze evenly, making no move to acknowledge his arrival.

Translation: She was pissed off.

"You okay?" Malone asked her.

"I'm fine. I wasn't here when this happened."

"You're lucky. In the past hour, there've been three more murders, including Agent Kranksi."

"The sergeant told me. I understand Cadet Jefferson and an officer were also killed."

Malone nodded.

She got quiet, the chill thawing from her eyes. "Poor Kranski. I still can't believe it. We talked quite a bit, waiting for you. He was such a sweet young man. Vulnerable. All he wanted was advice on how to find a nice girl—" She hugged herself, her voice turning bitter. "Senseless. So many damned senseless deaths. When is it going to stop? When?"

Malone didn't offer an answer. She didn't really expect one.

The sergeant gave a little cough, looking worried. "Sir, you think it could have been the killer who did this?"

Before Malone could reply, Kaitlin said, "That's highly unlikely, Sergeant."

"You don't think it was the killer?" Malone asked her, surprised.

"I'm certain it wasn't him."

Malone frowned, puzzled by her conviction.

"Well," the sergeant said, relaxing, "maybe it's like we first figured. Sir, you probably noticed the hole in the sliding glass door . . ."

"Yes," Malone said.

"Airman Broderick here . . ." The sergeant nodded to the two-striper. ". . . found a big rock on the patio that the intruder probably used to smash the glass. That made us think it was someone who happened by. It being a weekend and all, we figured it could be high-school kids looking for a thrill or easy money." He paused, taking in the room. "But I got to tell you it don't look like some kid did this. Ms. Barlow says nothing is missing . . ."

"There isn't," Kaitlin said. "Certainly nothing of value."

Malone asked, "No jewelry or money? What about your laptop?"

"This is the only jewelry I brought," she said, indicating her diamond earrings. "My laptop is in my car. Parked over at Harmon."

"You didn't leave any money here?"

"Everything was in my purse, which I had with me." She indicated the handbag at her feet.

"Any idea when the break-in might have occurred?"

"Uh-uh. I've been gone since this morning."

Which meant either of the two main suspects had had a chance to come here.

"Ain't much to go on," the sergeant said to Malone. "But from the way this place is torn up, it's pretty clear our boy was looking for something specific."

"If he was," Kaitlin said, "I don't know what it was. But then again, I'm not the person you should ask."

"Ma'am?"

"Ask him, Sergeant. I'm certain he knows."

And Kaitlin looked at Malone in a blatantly accusing way.

*　　*　　*

The two security cops frowned at her, as did Malone. At first, they all thought Kaitlin must be joking. But her eyes were fixed on Malone with no suggestion of a smile.

It wasn't a joke.

Malone felt his temper rise. This was the last straw. It wasn't enough that Kaitlin had fed Senator Smith the ammunition so the bastard could declare open season on him. Now she was insinuating he might be the person who—

And then it came to him, why she was doing this.

"Excuse us, Sergeant," Malone said.

"Oh, yes, sir. Absolutely." The cop hitched his belt over his ample stomach, moving toward the door. "We need to check the place out anyway, make sure nothing is missing. The duplex next door is empty, but we'll ask around at the others. See if anyone saw the guy."

"Please."

"Let's go, Broderick."

But after the sergeant left, Airman Broderick didn't move. He was staring down at something on the other side of the bed. Glancing up with an embarrassed smile, he hurried from the room.

The bed blocked Malone's view and he came around for a look. In a flash, Kaitlin lunged forward, practically knocking him out of the way. In one motion, she snatched the object from the floor and stuck it in her jacket pocket. Malone was incredulous. He ordered her to turn it over.

"No."

"The person who came here was searching for something. If that's evidence—"

"It's not. It's personal."

"Kaitlin, this isn't a discussion. I need to determine whether—"

"No."

They stood there, trading glares. Kaitlin's gloved hands were on her hips, her manner defiant. She was completely transformed from the disjointed, fearful woman on the phone. Malone had wanted to believe her apology to him had been sincere, that she'd been intimidated into selling him out. But the woman he was looking at now couldn't be intimidated.

Ever.

Malone felt a pang of disappointment. Another lie. He was tempted to haul her to the detachment, have a female agent strip-search her. But that would only antagonize Senator Smith even more and he wasn't ready to be tossed from the case quite yet.

Besides, there was an easier way to find out what she'd picked up. Kaitlin obviously knew this, suggesting her I-got-a-secret routine was a show, an attempt to push his buttons, get him to do something that might further embarrass himself and the Academy.

He gave her a flat smile. "Nice try, Kaitlin, but it won't work."

"What won't work?" Her expression innocent.

"Quit playing head games, huh? We need to figure out what the guy was looking for."

"What were *you* looking for, Agent Malone?"

"Stop it. I'm trying to be serious here."

"That makes two of us."

She was determined to jerk his chain. If he was going

to get anywhere, he had to show her he wasn't screwing around. He had to go at her hard, treat her like an uncooperative suspect. Easier said than done. Whenever he looked at her, he'd get a flashback to Christina. Crazy, but that's the effect she had on him, the power to recall a memory that haunted him.

Get past it, Malone. Christina's dead. That's never going to change.

They could hear cabinets opening and closing as the cops checked out the kitchen. Malone reached back and shut the door. Kaitlin watched him with a confident smile. She knew what was coming and didn't give a damn. As a lawyer, she could certainly handle a round of twenty questions with a military cop.

Malone took a breath and began.

Chapter 29

"You really believe I'm the intruder?" Malone demanded.

"Yes." Sounding amused.

"Why?"

"You're the bright detective. You figure it out."

"You think I tore up your place to get back at you?"

Patronizing now: "Men have such tempers when they're ridiculed."

"Answer the fucking question."

"My, my. Aren't we forceful?"

"Kaitlin—"

"You tell me. Did you?"

"You know damn well I didn't. I didn't even know you were staying in the TLFs."

"It wasn't a secret. You could have found out."

"I'm telling you I didn't come here. Ask Mother. I drove here right after she called me. Before that—"

"She *works* for you. You think I'd take her word for it."

"It is the truth. This is ridiculous. You're ridiculous."

She grinned, enjoying his irritation. At least she was

making this easy for Malone. He didn't have to try to get ticked off at her, he was already there. He gestured angrily around the room. "You know who did this. We both know who did it. It had to be the killer."

"Why? I'm no threat to him."

"Obviously, he thinks you are."

"C'mon, Malone. I'm only *observing*. You're the one in charge of the case. You're the one who's gathering the evidence, questioning everyone. You're the one who is the direct threat—"

"*He came here.*"

His pent-up frustration made her pause, but only for a moment. She shook her head. "He'd have no reason. I have nothing related to the case here."

"You must have taken notes of your interview with Rachel Owen."

"In the briefcase in my car . . ." She immediately corrected herself. ". . . your car. The audiotapes I made are there, too. But there's nothing in them. Certainly nothing indicating who the baby's father was."

"*Think.* Did Rachel Owen give you something, anything, that might indicate his identity?"

"She wouldn't. If she didn't reveal him to her cadet friends, why would she tell me?"

Logic he couldn't deny. Not that it meant anything. Kaitlin was a rarity, someone who could lie with absolute sincerity.

He rubbed his face hard. He'd taken a shot and come up empty. "All right. Fine."

"You don't believe me?"

"I said fine."

"I'm telling you the truth."

"You must be very proud."

"You don't think much of me, do you?"

Malone didn't want to go there. He ignored her, checking the time. The talk with Coach Ralston would have to wait. He had to leave for the airfield to meet with—

"Malone . . ."

When he glanced up, Kaitlin was smiling at him. Only this one was more than friendly. "Listen," she said, "if I was wrong about you . . ."

"You were."

"Maybe it was just some crazy kid after all. Someone who was hyped on drugs."

"Maybe."

"I suppose it could also have been the killer. He might believe Rachel Owen gave me something. But she didn't."

Malone nodded.

The smile turned shy, almost schoolgirlish. She glided toward him, gazing up into his eyes. "I guess what I'm trying to say is I'm sorry. You probably don't believe this, but I never wanted to turn over your file to Senator Smith. I even tried to talk him out of using it. But he kept pressuring me. He and Marcy both did. You don't know Marcy; she's . . . *relentless*. Anyway, I'm sorry, Malone. I really am. I know what you did for my sister, how you helped her. Besides, I like you. I like you . . . a lot."

The remark caught Malone off guard. He stared at her, uncertain how to react. Slowly, provocatively, she moved toward him, her smile becoming kittenish, seductive.

Alarms went off in Malone's head. He remembered what Mother had said about Kaitlin, how she used men. He knew Kaitlin was using him now, playing up to him to get something she wanted. He knew she was lying to him. No one had forced her to turn over his record; she had done it on her own. He knew all this.

And he didn't care.

He was overcome with a desire to touch her, caress the perfection of that face. A face from his past.

"So," Kaitlin said huskily, "do you believe me? That I'm sorry."

Her big eyes held his, drawing him in. Malone swallowed hard, nodded.

"I'm glad. So glad . . ."

She pressed her body against him, her face turning up, inviting his. Her arms circled his shoulders, her lips glistening. He found himself bending toward them. She smelled faintly of soap; it excited him. Their lips touched—

Kaitlin suddenly stepped back. "I can't. We can't do this."

Malone looked at her in disbelief.

"I'm sorry. It's not right."

Again. Malone couldn't believe he'd let her sucker him again. He felt embarrassed and angry. He said nastily, "What the hell is it with you? This some kind of ego thing for you? You get off on proving you can turn a guy on—"

"Is that what you think?" She appeared shocked. "No, no. It's not that at all. I like you. I wanted you to kiss me. But it wouldn't be right. It just wouldn't."

"Why the hell not?"

Kaitlin started to reply, then suddenly stiffened. She focused on a wall, staring intently at something. But there was nothing there. A faraway look appeared in her eyes and after several seconds, her mouth curled into a kind of grimace. She shook her head, paused, and shook it again. Finally a slow, reluctant nod.

Malone was mystified, watching her. If he didn't know better, he'd swear she was responding to—

She abruptly moved back and picked up her purse. In a brusque tone, she said, "I'm sorry, Malone, it wouldn't work. I gave in to an impulse. I am attracted to you, but it's better if we keep this professional."

"Hang on. If you like me—"

"I know what you meant to Christina. It would be too awkward."

"Christina? Wait a minute. You mean because Christina and I dated—"

"You were her first love. The first person she slept with."

"You can't be serious. We only got together for a weekend."

"It doesn't matter. She was in love with you."

"Then why did she tell me she was interested in someone else? There were stories about her and Coach—"

He clammed up, realizing he shouldn't have brought this up. Kaitlin's face became a mask. She said, "That was Christina's mistake. John Ralston was a star football player. A big man on campus. She believed if you thought he was interested in her, you'd come back."

"She must have liked him. I told her I wanted to get back together. She said no."

"Of course she did. You hurt her. She had to be sure about you. That you wouldn't do it again."

So it was true; Christina had been trying to make him jealous. And it had worked. He had been jealous.

Malone shook his head. He'd been such a fool.

"Please," Kaitlin said, "I don't want to discuss this again. There's no point. We can't get involved; it's as simple as that. Now, didn't you tell me you planned to meet with Laura Ralston at five? We should be leaving." She hesitated. "Unless you have a problem with me accompanying you?"

He just looked at her. They both knew it didn't matter if he did.

Her expression softened. "I am sorry about this, Malone. I truly am. I do like you." She squeezed his arm affectionately, then hurried from the room.

Watching her go, Malone wasn't sure he understood her rationale or ever would. But then he wasn't a twin who blamed herself for her sister's death. He was only a former lover doing precisely the same thing.

Leaving the bedroom, Malone called Mother to give her a heads-up that Kaitlin was coming with him. Instead of screwing herself to the ceiling, Mother said, "Doesn't matter. The Com got the word from the SECDEF that she's to be kept on the investigation. Apparently, another bucket of shit's about to hit the fan. More senators are climbing onto Smith's bandwagon and the brass is running scared. Can't blame them . . ."

"No."

"We also got our marching orders on what to do if

Ballistics matches Ralston's gun to the murder weapon or Laura implicates him in the rape. We arrest the son of a bitch."

Malone entered the living area and slowly circled toward the front door. He didn't reply.

"Earth to Malone."

"I heard you."

"Aw, Christ. Not this again. You understand that's a direct order. From the SECDEF."

"Yes."

"You *do* intend to obey it, right?"

"Maybe."

"You crazy? What'll it prove? They'll just can your ass and find someone else."

"Mother, it's premature. We haven't cleared General Crenshaw or identified the parachutist. If it turns out either of them—"

"*Now* you think Crenshaw could be a killer?"

"No, but—"

"I've talked to three of the parachute cadre. A civilian contractor and two senior NCOs. They all say none of the staff showed Rachel any unusual interest."

"There's a connection; there has to be."

"If there isn't? What if that password was some kind of inside joke? Or what if Rachel came up with it because she thought one of the jump masters was a hunk? It's what twenty-year-old girls do, Malone; they get silly crushes the way they change their hairstyles."

"They're cadets. Their hairstyles don't change."

"Stop being a smart-ass. You going to arrest Ralston or not?"

"I haven't decided."

"Sir," a voice said suddenly, "we found this outside."

The security cop sergeant had just entered through the front door. He pulled up, waving a square piece of white cardboard.

"Look," Mother said wearily to Malone. "You want to fall on your sword for a scumbag like Ralston, be my guest. But spare me the song and dance about how you plan on quitting the Air Force anyway. If you did, you'd have been gone long ago. Admit it. You like the service for the same reason I do. It's all you've got."

Again Malone said nothing.

She sighed. "You're making me old. Be at Laura Ralston's office in fifteen minutes. Let's be clear on one thing: maybe you're right about Ralston being framed, but that may not matter. If Laura has evidence her husband was involved in Christina's rape, you better slap some cuffs on him, or I will." She clicked off before he could respond.

Malone shook his head at the dial tone. Events were closing in on him. No matter what he did, his hand would be forced.

"Uh, sir." The sergeant eyed him with concern. "You okay? You don't look so good."

"I'm fine, Sergeant." He attempted a smile, but couldn't quite manage it. "What's that you've got there?"

When the sergeant held up the cardboard, Malone realized it was actually a lid to a box, a pretty pink label attached to it.

Diana's Custom Wigs, it said.

Chapter 30

"Ms. Barlow says it's not hers, sir," the sergeant said. "Guess it couldn't be the thief that dropped it. Thought I'd check with you before tossing it."

Malone almost told him to toss it. Then he read the small print at the bottom of the label; the store was located in Denver

Which was where Senator Smith had his main office.

Coincidence? But if Kaitlin did have a wig stolen, why not tell them? Vanity? And why would the killer have taken her wig in the first place?

"Where did you find it, precisely, Sergeant?"

"In the driveway, under the BMW. That's why I thought maybe someone had taken it from here."

Valid. "Any other women staying in the TLFs?"

"Haven't seen any. Most of the places aren't occupied." The sergeant shrugged.

"Log it into the equipment room for now, Sergeant. Airman Broderick around?"

"Knocking on the last couple of doors, sir. So far, no

luck. We talked to a couple of majors and a full bull colonel; they didn't see anything."

"Earlier Broderick noticed something . . ."

"Right." The sergeant grinned. "Don't worry, sir. I ordered the kid to keep it under his hat. It'd only cause him grief if Ms. Barlow heard he was shooting off his mouth. Besides, it's none of our business."

"What did Airman Broderick see exactly?"

He seemed surprised. "I thought you knew, sir."

"I don't."

He peeked behind to make sure Kaitlin had gone. "It was a condom packet, sir."

Malone tried not to react. "I see. When you say a packet . . ."

"Torn open. No rubber inside."

"Thank you, Sergeant." Malone handed him his card. "If you do locate a witness, call me immediately. And you're right to caution Airman Broderick not to mention the condom packet to anyone."

"Yes, sir. Guess she must have hooked up with someone from the base. Wonder who the lucky guy was?"

"No clue, Sergeant."

But as Malone went down the hall, he was wondering the very same thing.

Kaitlin was waiting for Malone on the curb. From her tight-lipped expression, he could tell that she knew he knew. As he approached, she tensed slightly, seeming to anticipate a remark. But Malone never said a word to her. The sergeant had been right; her sex life wasn't his concern. Why should he care if she had screwed her brains out last night? She wasn't anything special to him.

But the hollowness in his chest suggested otherwise.

She asked, "Which car?"

The Hummer partially blocked the BMW, sitting in the driveway. "The Hummer," he said.

Kaitlin seemed on the verge of saying something. When she remained silent, Malone shrugged and got into the Hummer. Before joining him, Kaitlin retrieved her briefcase from the BMW. She returned his car keys, careful to avoid his eyes. As they drove off, she stared out the window.

The silence felt like a wall between them. After several minutes, Malone was surprised to see it was getting to her. The signs were subtle at first: a nervous tapping of a gloved finger on a tooth, a fidgeting of her hands. Then came the constant shifting in her seat and the furtive peeks in his direction. It was killing her. She wanted him to say something.

But he kept his eyes straight ahead.

They turned south onto Stadium Boulevard. In the fading afternoon light, they could see the airfield tower in the distance, the speck of a plane coming in for a landing. Among the perks of being an Air Force Academy cadet was the opportunity to jump out of airplanes as well as fly them. Assuming, of course, you considered launching your body into a three-thousand-foot free fall a perk.

Malone was massaging his tired eyes when he noticed Kaitlin had changed tactics; she was now staring at him. A minute passed, then two. She continued to fixate on him, attempting to unsettle him enough to get him to break the silence.

Malone hummed to himself, a picture of disinterest.

They drove another mile. Kaitlin couldn't take it any longer.

"*Jesus*," she said in exasperation. "Aren't you even going to ask?"

Malone looked over mildly. "Excuse me?"

"He was just a casual friend. He needed a place to stay and . . ." She shook her head disgustedly. "Anyway, we had too much to drink. It wasn't something I planned; it just happened. Shit happens. He didn't mean anything to me."

Malone concentrated on driving. It was easier to take if he didn't look at her.

"Dammit," she said, "say *something*."

"Why?"

"I don't make a habit of hopping in the sack with guys I barely know. I'm not a slut."

He shrugged. "I never said you were."

"Ah, but that's what you were thinking. You, of all people. How many women have you slept with, Malone? Fifty? A hundred?"

"Kaitlin, you don't owe me an explanation. It's not as if we're involved."

"That's what I'm trying to tell you. I wish we could be."

His head snapped around to her. In her eyes, Malone detected a desperate quality that suggested she was being sincere. Or maybe he just wanted her to be.

"We still can," he said cautiously. "If you really want to."

She hesitated, considering the invitation. She shook her head, sounding bitter. "What I *want* doesn't matter. It hasn't mattered for years."

Malone's eyebrows crawled up. "What you *want* doesn't matter?"

"Forget it. It's not important. The bottom line is, we can't have a relationship."

"Kaitlin, it's your life, not Christina's. I understand your guilt, but her death was an accident. You have to realize you can't martyr yourself—"

"We have too much history, Malone."

"History? My history is with your sister, not you."

She smiled sadly. "Poor Malone. You don't understand."

"Then tell me," he said irritably. "What the hell am I supposed to—"

Kaitlin held up a finger. Her cell was ringing.

She answered it, listened briefly, and said, "You're sure? Yes, I understand. I'll take care of it." Clicking off, she shook her head unhappily.

"Anything I should know about?"

"No."

"That your office?"

"Yes."

"Was it Marcy Dyers, the chief of staff?"

She cut him a hard look. He got the message. She wasn't going to tell him.

"Well, how about it?" he asked, returning to their earlier topic. "You going to tell me what I need to understand?"

"Believe me, I'd like to. I really would. But it's not my call."

"Not your call?"

She gazed out the window, saying nothing further.

On most Air Force bases, the flight line consisted of dozens of large hangars and support installations. At the Academy's small airfield, two long rectangular buildings served those same functions. The buildings were home to the Ninety-fourth Flying Training Squadron, the glider unit commanded by Laura Ralston, and the Ninety-eighth FTS, the parachute training squadron.

Entering the Ninety-fourth FTS through an end door, Kaitlin and Malone found themselves in a gleaming hangar area containing two squat, single-propeller airplanes with inordinately long wings. A bearded civilian mechanic was working on one.

"This way," Malone said, leading Kaitlin to a door on the opposite side.

"The planes look funny," she said.

"They're gliders."

"They have engines."

"Saves having to be towed. After the pilot climbs to altitude, he kills the engine and glides."

The beard squinted at them suspiciously. Malone flashed his OSI ID and the squint disappeared. The hangar doors were open and they could see several powered gliders on the ramp, being refueled. Farther down, the aircraft they'd seen land was taxiing their way.

"Did my sister fly these?" Kaitlin asked.

"She wasn't here long enough."

She smiled wistfully, recalling a private memory. "Christina came here to be a pilot. Did you know that?"

"Yes."

"She wanted to fly ever since she was a little girl. We used to lie in bed talking about how she was going to be . . ." She swallowed hard, the smile fading. "But she'll never be anything. Ever."

Watching her, Malone realized he'd been mistaken. He'd assumed the reason Kaitlin couldn't get past her sister's death was that the memories wouldn't let her go. But that wasn't it at all.

Kaitlin *wanted* to remember.

They came to the door and as Malone opened it, Kaitlin said, "Wait, there's something we should clear up."

Her tone told Malone this wasn't something he was going to like. "Okay."

"My feelings toward you don't change anything. Despite what you think, I'm here to ensure justice is served. If you interfere, I will take action against you."

"Report me to your boss and have him take more potshots?"

"Malone, this isn't easy for me."

"You didn't have much trouble sacrificing me before."

Her face darkened. "Now listen—"

"You listen. I'm tired of your insinuations. You know damn well I'd never cover up for a killer."

"I know what I was told," she snapped.

"Which is . . ."

"The phone call I received. Marcy told me that the Secretary of Defense had phoned Senator Smith to keep him abreast of the investigation . . ."

"Good for the senator."

"This isn't a joking matter."

"I'm not laughing."

"Imagine my surprise," she announced cuttingly, "when I learned the possible murder weapon was found at Coach Ralston's home and he was near the scene of the last murders."

Malone's bravado instantly disappeared. There was nothing he could say, so he didn't even try. Stepping aside, he ushered her through the door.

"After you, Ms. Barlow."

Chapter 31

A HALLWAY LED INTO AN OPEN OFFICE SPACE containing a half-dozen partitioned desks. At two of them, instructors debriefed cadets on their flights, talking animatedly with their hands in the usual pilot sign language. Malone and Kaitlin crossed to the private offices at the back. A closed door on the right said Commander 94th FTS. Mother's height-challenged bulk was standing outside.

Uh-oh, Malone thought.

As they walked up, Mother's eyes coldly dissected Kaitlin, her way of politely telling Kaitlin to go to hell.

Kaitlin obviously got the message and said with a disarming smile, "You're mistaken about me, Mother."

Mother wasn't about to kiss and make up. She fended off the smile with a not-so-polite "fuck you" look.

Kaitlin bristled. In a harshly dismissive tone, she said, "If you'd done your job, none of this would be necessary. *You* are the one responsible for what occurred. *Your* incompetence allowed a rapist to go free."

She stuck her hands on her hips, daring Mother to respond.

Mother was silent, measuring Kaitlin with a flat stare. She breathed, "My incompetence?"

"You heard me."

A tense moment followed. Mother smiled as if amused, the pulsing veins in her neck indicating otherwise. Malone knew what was coming and decided to let it play out, teach Kaitlin a lesson.

He heard a sound behind him.

At that instant, Mother torched off in a dramatic fashion, unleashing a torrent of words. "Where the hell do you get off criticizing me? *Me?* You're not even a cop, lady. I was investigating crimes when you were in *diapers*. Yet you have the nerve to accuse me of incompetence. By God, you have a lot of unmitigated gall." She moved toward Kaitlin, stabbing emphatically with a stubby finger. "*You're* the one who is incompetent. *You're* the one who has disrupted the case. *You're* the one who has fabricated conspiracies and cover-ups and Lord knows what else—"

The dance began. It was almost comical. Kaitlin was overwhelmed by the verbal barrage and tried to backpedal from it. But there was nowhere to go. She was already against the wall. She slid along it, trying to escape. Mother followed after her, her voice shaking with the outrage of the truly wronged. In the main office, the instructors and cadets were rising to their feet, watching the show. A muscular sergeant had entered the room and was staring slack-jawed.

Malone sighed. It was time.

He had to call out to Mother twice before she acknowledged him. Her face was flushed, her eyes were wild; she had Kaitlin on the ropes and smelled blood. He said sharply, "That's enough, Mother."

"No. She's been a pain in the ass from the beginning. I want to make sure she doesn't—"

"*Enough.*"

She spun angrily to Malone. He pointed her to the door marked Commander. It stood open, two figures in green flight suits peering out. One was Laura Ralston, the other, a young female cadet. Both had wide-eyed expressions of disbelief.

Mother's face slowly relaxed. She calmly stepped back from Kaitlin.

"Jesus *Christ*," Kaitlin said, hurriedly moving away from her. "You're crazy. You're a crazy woman."

Mother shrugged unapologetically. For a long moment, no one spoke.

"I take it you're finished," Laura Ralston finally said to her.

Mother nodded.

"You can leave now, Cadet Markel," Laura Ralston told the cadet.

The cadet hesitated, nervously eyeing Mother.

"It's okay," Malone told her. "She won't bite."

The cadet looked unconvinced. She darted past the desks and out the exit opposite the hangar.

"All right," Laura Ralston said. "Let's get this over with."

Kaitlin hadn't learned her lesson. Following Laura Ralston into the office, she made a point of shooting Mother an icy stare.

Mother smiled back. Under her breath: "Bitch."

Malone said, "Behave, Mother."

"Well, she is."

"Uh, ma'am?"

They glanced over as the muscular sergeant hesitantly approached Mother. "I was told you wanted this." He nervously handed her a thin file.

"Right. Thanks, Sergeant." To Malone: "Parachute cadre roster. Four of the seven jump masters weren't around today."

Like with the cadet, the sergeant couldn't get away from Mother fast enough. Within seconds, he'd crossed the room and was gone. Mother winked at Malone. "Nice to see I haven't lost my touch."

"Except you didn't succeed in intimidating Kaitlin."

"No, but she'll watch her mouth from now on. If not . . ." She smiled at the thought.

"Be nice. I mean it."

"You know me, Malone."

Precisely the problem. They filed into the office.

"Looks like they know each other," Mother whispered.

Malone nodded, closing the door.

Laura was at her desk, Kaitlin seated across from her. They were discussing Christina with a familiarity suggesting they were at least casual acquaintances. It wasn't surprising; Laura had once been Christina's roommate and closest friend.

As Malone and Mother eased onto a short sofa near the door, she said dryly, "That's a little much."

From what was on display, it was apparent Laura

Ralston loved only two things: airplanes and her husband, not necessarily in that order. The photographs of military aircraft far outnumbered the single image of Coach John Ralston, but that was the one you noticed. You couldn't help it; it made you stop and stare.

It was a portrait hanging over her desk. It depicted a younger Ralston, wearing his football uniform, the current football schedule mounted below it. The painting wasn't overly large, perhaps three feet by five. Still, for anyone seeing it for the first time, it came across as inappropriate, especially for an office.

But then they weren't Laura Ralston, a woman who obviously loved her husband.

Or did she?

Watching Laura, Malone was confused. For someone about to implicate her husband in a rape, her composure was extraordinary. She seemed calm and completely at ease. In fact, on several occasions, she even smiled. From the way she was acting, she could have been discussing a variety of inconsequential topics, from movies to the weather to a favorite restaurant.

But she wasn't.

After reminiscing about Christina, Laura began setting the stage for what she was about to reveal. She was telling Kaitlin that she was glad she was here, that she should be here. She expressed her sorrow for everything that happened and reminded Kaitlin that Christina had been her best friend and that she never would have done anything to harm her memory. Her only excuse was that she'd loved her husband and had wanted to believe him. If she'd known the truth, she never would have married him. She was trying to make up for her mistake and asked Kaitlin to please forgive her.

Laura said all this in a straightforward manner, as if this wasn't any big deal. As she waited for Kaitlin's response, she again managed a smile that didn't appear forced.

"Denial," Mother concluded softly.

"Of course I forgive you, Laura," Kaitlin said. "It's not your fault; you didn't know."

"But I know now," Laura said. "I found this."

From a lower drawer, she produced a small paper sack and casually dumped out the contents on her desk. Mother drew in a sharp breath; Malone stared, unable to speak.

"My God . . ." Kaitlin said.

They were looking at a piece of rubber molded into an image. One of the most famous images in the world.

Mickey Mouse.

Chapter 32

A VENT HISSED SOFTLY AS THE HEATING UNIT kicked in. From the outer office came a smattering of laughter as if someone had told a joke. But inside the office, no one was smiling. Laura calmly sat in her chair, waiting for everyone to recover from their shock. Kaitlin came to life first, saying, "I know how difficult this must have been. This couldn't have been easy for you."

"It will be harder on John. He'll find prison unbearable." Laura spoke in an emotionless monotone. Stating a fact.

"Where did you find it, Colonel?" Mother asked, nodding at the mask.

"Between the mattress and box spring, when I was changing the sheets on the bed."

"This was Thursday?"

"Yes. In the evening. John wasn't home."

"So he doesn't know you've found it?"

"Not to my knowledge." She shrugged. "It was only two days ago. He probably doesn't realize it's missing."

Mother hesitated, her tone softening. "There's something you should know, Colonel. Earlier we searched your home . . ."

"And found a handgun." Reacting to Mother's surprise, she added, "The Com left me a message. I called him as soon as I landed. He told me about the gun and the other murders, and John's upcoming arrest." She flashed a tight, brief smile. "He wanted me to be . . . prepared."

"Don't you find it a little strange, Laura?" Malone asked.

Laura's brow wrinkled. "Strange?"

"That your husband suddenly hides an incriminating piece of evidence he's kept for years, in a place where you're sure to stumble across it."

She sighed. "I wondered about that, believe me. But I decided he must have had to move the mask from its original hiding place."

"Sure," Mother said. "He put it under the mattress temporarily. Until he could find someplace more secure."

"But why keep it at all?" Malone asked. "Frankly, that's stupid as hell, and Coach Ralston isn't a stupid man."

"You know why, Malone," Mother said. "It was a trophy. He wanted to relive his rape of Christina."

"That's typical of serial rapists and murderers. He wasn't either."

"Malone," Kaitlin said, her voice rising in warning. "Don't go there. We talked about this."

"Save it, Kaitlin," he countered irritably. "I'm not about to sit by if I think someone's being framed. I won't do it."

"Framed?" Laura said, sitting up. "You think someone might be framing him?" For the first time she was displaying concern over the fate of her husband.

"Don't listen to him, Laura," Kaitlin said. To Malone: "Just stop it. You have no evidence anyone's framing him. Stop it."

"I hate to say it, but I've got to agree with Kaitlin," Mother said. "You got nothing, Malone. You're wishing for something that's not there."

Laura was perched on the edge of her seat, staring at Malone. "Is there evidence? Is there?"

"See what you've done?" Kaitlin said. "You're giving her hope. Stop it."

Malone weighed his answer, gazing into Laura's anxious eyes.

"The truth," Mother said to him. "She deserves the truth."

Malone reluctantly shook his head. "There's no direct evidence, Laura . . ."

Her face sagged.

"But Rachel Owen's missing keys are suggestive. I assume she had a key to your home . . ."

A vague nod.

". . . which leaves open the possibility that the killer stole them, planted the gun and mask—"

Mother cut him off. "Not the mask. That was found *before* Rachel was murdered."

Malone felt his frustration toward her growing. Over a decade earlier, she had been convinced of Ralston's guilt, and she still was. He said, "The killer might have stolen the keys several days earlier."

"Without Rachel noticing? Come on. You're talking about a key chain with her car and room keys. Believe me, she'd have noticed and reported it."

"But she didn't," Kaitlin said. "If she had, Major Tupper or one of her friends would have mentioned it."

She glanced at Mother knowingly and got a nod in return. Their animosity was forgotten in the face of a common enemy.

Malone didn't press the issue. No matter what he said, they wouldn't be convinced. Laura watched him, the hope fading from her eyes. "So all you have is a suspicion that someone is framing my husband?"

"I'm afraid so."

Her face withdrew into its defensive shell. Once again, Laura was creating an emotional barrier to protect herself against the inevitable. She asked Malone if he had anything else incriminating her husband.

"Laura, I'd rather not go into—"

"I'm his wife. I have a right to know."

Emphatic nods from Kaitlin and Mother. Big surprise.

So Malone told Laura that Ralston had been found in the vicinity of the murders at Lawrence Paul. She listened without the slightest sign of emotion. It was creepy how she could do that, just turn off her feelings.

Taking a deep breath, she concluded, "It appears as if he is guilty."

A curious remark from a wife. Even Mother and Kaitlin were puzzled by it.

"You don't believe that, Laura," Malone said.

"Don't I?" She shook her head. "Maybe I do. When I married John, I knew about the rape, that he was a suspect. Of course I never wanted to believe it. But that was before I knew him, really knew him. He only cares about one thing, his career. I don't matter, people don't matter. I wanted kids, but he didn't. He said they would interfere. With him, it's all ambition and his coaching career. And if that was ever threatened, if he ever thought he would lose it . . . I know he's capable of . . ."

She trailed off, staring off into space. Her eyes told you what she was thinking. Because of the pain they contained.

A lot of pain.

Mother gave Malone a look and he nodded. They stood to leave and Kaitlin followed suit. Malone said gently, "Laura . . ."

She blinked, dully focusing on him.

He came forward, picking up the mask and sack from her desk. "We're going to arrest him now. If you'd like to accompany us . . ."

"No. He'll be . . . angry. He'll know I was the one who turned him in."

Everyone gazed at her sympathetically.

"Can I . . . ask you something?" Laura asked Malone hesitantly.

"Anything."

"Since you don't believe John is guilty . . ."

"I don't."

"I assume you've been ordered to arrest him."

"Yes."

"Who gave the order? The Com?"

"He can't," Mother answered. "Technically he's not in our chain of command."

298 PATRICK A. DAVIS

"It's not important, Laura," Malone said. "What is important is to remember that John will be given a fair trial."

"The Secretary of Defense," Kaitlin volunteered.

Laura nodded, unsurprised. As a former Pentagon staffer, she knew how the military hierarchy worked. In a case this big, the arrest order for someone as prominent as her husband would come from the top.

"A fair trial when the Secretary of Defense believes you're guilty," she said to Malone. "That would be a first. He'll be lucky if he doesn't get the death penalty."

Her voice was simultaneously bitter and resigned. Malone had no reply. By definition, court-martials were independent proceedings free of external pressures. But in a widely publicized case with the military's reputation at stake, the reality was that the board members sitting in judgment would know the verdict expected of them.

"We'll call when he's in custody," Malone said.

Laura inhaled deeply, nodded.

"I'm sorry, Laura."

"Thank you."

As they left, she was staring at the picture of her husband, her face again an emotionless shell. But as before, her eyes communicated her true feelings, this time with tears.

Malone softly closed the door.

Malone didn't get it.

As they retraced their steps through the hangar and out the building, he was mystified by Kaitlin's reaction.

She was on the verge of getting her pound of flesh and bringing her sister's rapist to justice. She should have been upbeat, smiling from ear to ear.

Instead she was grimacing, looking more agitated than vindicated.

They turned left down the sidewalk toward the parking area. Kaitlin's grimace deepened. "Okay," Malone finally said to her. "What gives? You seem upset."

"I am. I never expected to like Laura, but I do. She doesn't deserve this."

Mother glanced up from the folder containing the parachute cadre roster she'd been scanning. She said, "You *didn't* expect to like Laura?"

"I met her for the first time last week. We had dinner. I wanted to hate her because she'd married Ralston. How could she do it, knowing he was a suspect in my sister's rape? But she really loved him and believed he wasn't involved. In some respects, she's also a victim of that bastard. She's worked so damned hard to get where she is. But her life and career are destroyed. It's not right."

Mother resumed looking at the folder without comment. "I don't know about Laura's life," Malone said, "but her career is certainly over."

"Maybe not," Mother said.

Malone and Kaitlin looked left. But Mother was no longer beside them. Turning, they saw her standing behind them, the folder open in her hands. She stared right at Malone. "You were right after all."

"Right?" Kaitlin said. "Right about what?"

But Malone knew. He stepped over to Mother and

snatched up the folder. "Last line," she said. "He's not part of the cadre; he's an advisor."

Malone's eyes flew down the page. He blinked, jarred. He read the name twice and a third time.

"Yeah," Mother said. "I never saw it coming either."

Malone realized he should have. He'd been in the office, seen the pictures. It was right there before him the whole time, but he hadn't been paying attention.

"*Dammit.*"

"What?" Kaitlin said. "What are you getting so worked up over?"

He gave her the folder. She peered at it and did a double-take. "Why, it's—"

"Major Bradley Tupper," Malone growled.

Chapter 33

THE SECDEF'S ORDER NOTWITHSTANDING, MA-
lone knew what he had to do. Speaking quickly, he said,
"This changes everything. Mother, call Tupper and tell
him we want to talk to him now. Then notify the Com
to pass it up the chain that we're not arresting Ralston."

No argument from Mother. Not this time. As she
took out her phone, Malone swung around to Kaitlin.
She still appeared dazed. "Major Tupper," she said, "was
an Army parachutist, right?"

"Yeah. Eighty-second Airborne."

Her mouth opened and slowly closed. As much as
she wanted the killer to be Ralston, she knew this was a
revelation they couldn't ignore.

Tupper fit the key elements for the suspect they'd
been looking for: an older man with a close relationship
to Rachel who was a parachutist. Add in his tours in
Iraq and Afghanistan and his guilt seemed like a slam
dunk. Unless someone was psychotic or at least a borderline sociopath, he couldn't kill six people.

But a soldier who'd seen combat could.

Mother said into the phone, "Academy information? I'd like the home number of Major Bradley—"

"Stay here," Malone said to Kaitlin. "I'll be back in a minute." He pivoted and headed down the sidewalk.

"Wait," Kaitlin said. "Where are you going?"

"The hell you think?"

Laura.

Malone still saw the image of Laura, the tears rolling down her cheek. All he could think about was telling her that things would be okay. It wasn't her husband; he probably wasn't a killer.

But when he tried the door leading from the hangar into the pilot offices, it was locked. He banged on it, calling out.

"The pilots are gone, mister," a voice from behind said.

Malone turned as the bearded mechanic came through the big hangar doors, wiping his hands with a greasy rag. Malone said, "Lieutenant Colonel Ralston was in her office a few minutes earlier. I noticed her car is still outside."

The man ambled up, pocketing the rag. "Right. She should be back in a half-hour or so."

"A half-hour? Where is she now?"

He pointed toward the ramp. They were looking into the setting sun and Malone had to squint. "All I see is an airplane taxiing."

"That's her."

"She's going on a flight *now?*"

"You got it."

"Was it scheduled?"

"You kidding? Tower shut down ten minutes ago. The field's supposed to be closed. But when the boss lady says she wants to fly, who's going to argue?" He went over to the powered glider he had been working on earlier. "Still, it makes you kinda wonder, you know. We never fly this late."

"You don't?"

"On account of it'll be getting dark soon. Gliders don't fly at night." Retrieving pliers from a tool box, he gave a little shrug. "But hey, she must have a reason. She was in one big hurry, I can tell you. Didn't even do a preflight. And that's not her. She's always real careful. But she just cranked up the engine without even bothering to check—"

Malone wasn't listening to him anymore. He was staring at the taxiing airplane, thinking about what the mechanic had already said. Trying to put it all together.

The tower's closed.

She was in a hell of a hurry.

Didn't even do a preflight.

The pieces started to fit. But the picture they formed was blurred, obscured by the absence of logic. What Malone was considering was ludicrous. Even if Ralston asked her, begged her, Laura would never do something this rash. Then again . . .

He recalled the portrait in Laura's office. If she loved him enough to hang that—

The sudden whine of the engine as the glider went to full power. Malone ran from the hangar, watching as it rolled down the runway. He'd know in a moment. If the plane remained in the pattern or headed south, there was nothing to worry about.

But if it turned northwest . . .

The long wings flexed and the glider climbed steeply into the air. Malone squinted, trying to follow it as it turned. It rolled out, the waning sunlight glinting off the wings. He watched until he was sure.

Northwest.

A sinking sensation gripped him. He tried to stay calm. Think, Malone. *Think.*

One possibility.

He spun, shouting to the mechanic.

"A radio?" the man said, as Malone ran up. "Sure. There's radios in the tower, but it's closed—"

"In here," Malone said, gesturing around the hangar. "There must be a radio around."

"In the pilot offices."

"Who has a key?"

"Only the pilots."

"There's what, two more doors to the building—"

"They'll be locked. They're always locked when the offices are empty."

Malone swore.

The mechanic seemed puzzled by his reaction. "What's the big hurry, Mister? You can't wait to talk to her when she lands?"

Malone jabbed a thumb at a powered glider. "That has a radio, right? How long to power it up?"

"Flip a switch. But you're probably wasting your time.

Reception won't be too good on account of the antenna."

"Antenna?"

"Line-of-sight reception. That's why the antenna is attached to the bottom, so you can talk to the ground from the air. Don't work too good the other way around." He shrugged. "Anyway, it'd be better to try a plane out on the ramp."

"I'll need a headset."

As Malone walked out onto the ramp, the mechanic detoured over to a metal locker. He joined Malone at one of the powered gliders, opened the canopy, plugged in the headset, and powered up the radio. He said, "You know the frequency?"

"No."

"We'll try guard. The emergency frequency. She should be monitoring it."

Malone donned the headset and keyed the mike. "Laura, this is Malone. Everything is okay. We believe John is innocent and there's another suspect. I repeat, we believe John is innocent and there is another suspect."

He waited. The headset hissed.

He tried twice more. Same result. The mechanic watched him with astonishment. Malone thrust the headset at him. "Keep trying. Say exactly what I did. If you make contact, call me." He handed him his card.

"Son of a bitch," the mechanic said slowly. "You're investigating the murders of those two cadets. You think Coach Ralston might have—"

Malone interrupted him. "This is confidential. You say a word about this to anyone, I mean anyone, and I'll haul you in for obstruction."

His face went blank beneath the beard. "I don't know what you're talking about, sir."

The man caught on quick.

Striding away, Malone clung to the notion that Laura really had gone on a little joy ride to clear her head. Forget about her problems and Ralston's arrest. But if so, that still didn't explain the one question he couldn't get around. Why was she flying to the cadet area now?

Why?

He broke into a run.

"I think I see her," Kaitlin said excitedly, peering through the windscreen. "Yeah. It's definitely her."

She was sitting beside Malone in the passenger seat of the Hummer. Mother was in back, rattling off instructions to the security cops on a cell phone. They were speeding down Stadium Drive toward the cadet area. Malone felt a spark of hope realizing Laura hadn't made her move. He leaned down, staring up. It was almost dusk and he couldn't pick her out in the haze. "I don't see her. What's she doing?"

"Kind of circling."

"Over where? Can you tell?"

"I think she's over the athletic fields."

Malone cut her a look. Kaitlin sighed, reading the message it contained. "Okay, maybe you're on to something."

"Maybe?"

"I won't believe it until I see it. You're talking about Laura Ralston. She's a lieutenant colonel in the Air Force and an Academy grad, which means she's someone who plays by the rules. There's no way she'll land on the grass and pick up her husband in some kind of wild escape attempt."

"Not even to save him from a death sentence?"

"Not even then. She's too rational. Besides, where could they possibly go?"

"So she's flying over the athletic fields because . . ."

Malone trailed off, waiting. But Kaitlin had no reply because there was no other plausible explanation for Laura Ralston's actions.

None.

Traffic was light and they blew by a van like it wasn't moving. The turn for the Parade Loop was coming up and Malone tapped the brakes. In the backseat, Mother clicked off her phone and announced, "The SPs are responding. Should be there anytime."

Malone asked, "Is practice still going on?"

"Probably. That's why Laura's circling. She's waiting until it's over."

"Why didn't Coach Ralston end it?" Kaitlin asked. "You'd think he would if he knew what she was going to do."

Malone and Mother shared a glance. This had been bugging them also.

They squealed around the turn onto Parade Loop. A minute later, they sped onto Cadet Drive. Ahead, they could see a nest of security police SUVs parked out front of the Field House. Swinging into the parking area, they lurched to a screeching stop and everyone bailed out. Jogging across the asphalt, they spotted Captain Dave Sapper, the Security Forces operations officer, standing by the concrete steps leading down to the varsity practice field. Captain Sapper hollered, "The coach is still here, Agent Malone. You want my men to move in?"

"We'll handle it, Dave."

They ran over to him as he relayed the order. The stairs descended fifty feet and a dozen cops had stopped midway down, waiting. On the field below, the team was running a play. A lone figure stood on a tower, bellowing out harsh criticism through a megaphone. It was Ralston.

"Uh, oh," Kaitlin said. "Looks like she's going for it."

They all watched the powered glider nose downward, begin its descent. Malone's eyes darted to the man on the tower. Ralston was still addressing his players, seemingly oblivious to the plane above him.

Something was wrong. Malone could feel it. Surely Ralston had to know his wife was about to—

"Oh, no. No . . ."

This strangled cry came from Mother. When Malone looked up, his blood went cold.

He'd been wrong. The powered glider wasn't coming in for a landing. It couldn't be.

Because it was pointed almost straight down at the ground.

Murmurs of surprise from the security cops. "My God," Kaitlin said. "She can't be doing this. She can't."

But the terrifying reality of what they were seeing played out before their eyes. They watched as the plane continued downward, rapidly picking up speed. They saw the angle shift slightly, as Laura corrected her heading. An instant later, it became clear what she intended. A chorus of alarm rose up from the cops.

"That pilot's crazy. He's flying straight into the ground."

"It's got to be a stunt, Sarge."

"A malfunction. There must be a malfunction."

"Pull up. For God's sake, pull up, Laura!"

The last remark came from Malone. He tore down the steps, continuing to shout up at the sky. A useless, desperate act since Laura couldn't hear him.

He watched the plane close on its target. Seconds out.

Oh, God—

By now, the players had become aware of the plane and were looking up. Then the panic set in and they began to scatter. Malone ran out onto the field, hollering out Ralston's name at the top of his lungs. But the coach was already staring skyward. He stood transfixed, as if unable to comprehend what he was seeing. Then he frantically reached for the ladder and tried to scramble down. But by then, his fate was sealed.

Halfway down, Ralston looked up as if he knew.

When the impact happened, Malone was less than thirty yards away. At that fractional instant, time slowed, each image shuttering across his mind's eye like a sixteen-millimeter movie that was out of synch. He saw the plane strike the tower and explode in a ball of flame. He saw Ralston's frozen image on the ladder, a split second before he was engulfed in the fiery ball. He saw a piece of the wing fly toward him, knifing past his head by inches. He felt a searing heat and the sensation of being thrown on his back. It was almost a pleasant feeling, the rush of air reminding him of a roller coaster. Then came the pain as he struck his head and the world went black.

Chapter 34

SOMEWHERE IN THE FOG, MALONE HEARD PEO-
ple screaming and shouting. He cracked open his eyes
and struggled to his feet. His head throbbed and he
could taste the salty wetness of blood.

The tower was all burning, mangled metal, flames
shooting twenty feet into the air. The stench of avia-
tion fuel was everywhere, the sky filling with smoke.
Malone staggered back, his eyes stinging. He inhaled
the acrid air and coughed violently.

The players!

He blinked furiously, trying to survey the field. Much
of it was afire from the fuel. The smoldering tail of the
plane lay crumpled beside the tower, bits of debris
slowly raining down all around it. Players and coaches
were running toward the opposite end, desperately trying to get away. Malone moved forward through the
smoke, coughing and gagging.

More shouts, this time from behind. He turned. Two
cops were running up, more on their heels.

Malone yelled hoarsely, "Check the area. Make sure
no one is hurt."

"Yes, sir." They ran past, skirting the fire, Malone jogging after them. Once the cops cleared the burning tower, they fanned out, looking up and down the field.

"I don't see anyone, sir," one cop hollered.

More negative shouts from reinforcements followed. Malone felt the tension fade from him. In the horror of the moment, this was something he could grasp, a small victory.

Laura Ralston had done what she had to do without killing an innocent.

Turning back, he saw Kaitlin and Mother hurrying toward him. He took a few steps in their direction, felt something soft under his foot, and quickly stepped back.

He recoiled.

A blackened hand lay there, sheared at the wrist. It still had on a wedding ring, a woman's ring.

Malone felt a stinging sense of remorse. If only he could have gotten through on the radio. If he could only have spoken to Laura, told her.

"Malone," Mother hollered out. "You all right?"

"I'm fine," he called back.

Which was a damn lie.

"It's your decision, sir," the paramedic said, "but you might have a concussion. That's an ugly bruise. You should go to the hospital for observation."

"No," Malone said.

"Sir, at least have your lip checked out. It might need stitches."

"It doesn't. It stopped bleeding."

Malone was sitting on the bottom step of the practice bleachers, the paramedic standing over him. The field lights were on bright and Malone could see the man's exasperation clearly.

"Sir, people die from concussions all the time. They're nothing to fool with."

"If that happens, I promise I'll come to the hospital." Malone flashed a smile.

The paramedic wasn't amused. Muttering, he snatched up his medical bag and headed toward a line of ambulances, which had arrived in force. Only Malone had been injured, explaining the paramedic's irritation.

He'd been spring-loaded to treat *someone*.

Hunched forward, Malone stared at the skeletal remains of the tower as the fire crews foamed the last of the flames. In the forty minutes since the crash, the players and coaches had been cleared out, replaced by an assortment of security cops, emergency response crews, and Academy brass. By the concrete stairs, Mother and Kaitlin were briefing the Com and his staff on what had transpired. As OSI commander, it was Malone's responsibility to talk with the heavy hitters. But his adrenaline rush had long since petered out, leaving him physically and emotionally spent. He just wanted to sit here in the quiet, be alone with his thoughts. And think what might have been.

Malone wasn't a religious man. But as he gazed out at the destruction, he found himself murmuring a prayer for Laura and John Ralston. When he finished, he was surprised to find his eyes were moist.

But then Laura had been a friend.

He watched the group by the stairs. The Com was simultaneously talking into his cell phone as he listened to Mother. No mystery who was on the receiving end of the play-by-play.

Malone pictured the SECDEF's face when he got the news that the wife of the Academy's head football coach had dramatically taken out herself and her husband for what could turn out to be no reason. If that proved the case, heads would roll, maybe even Malone's. Mother had been right; he would miss the military. But the truth was, he deserved to be fired. He should have seen the clues, but he hadn't.

And two more innocent people had died.

Malone's jaw tightened. While much of what had happened was his fault, two others also shared the blame. The first was that grandstanding son of a bitch Senator Smith, whose lies and distortions had pressured the military into calling for Ralston's arrest prematurely. Then there was the homicidal maniac who started all this because he'd knocked a girl up. More than anything, Malone wanted to confront the bastard and make him talk.

But that would have to wait. Major Tupper lived on base and when he hadn't answered his phone, Mother had dispatched Anderson, to see if he could find out when Tupper would return. According to neighbors, Tupper's son had a birthday tomorrow and the major had taken the family skiing. He wouldn't be back until the following night.

So they had to wait.

Unlike Malone, Mother thought that was a good thing. Tupper wouldn't crack easily, and another day allowed them to prepare for their interview. Maybe uncover evidence of his relationship with Rachel.

"We're going to have to rattle his cage," Mother said. "Put him on the defensive from the git-go."

It occurred to Malone there was another way to do precisely that. Calling the number Mother had given him, he said into the answering machine, "This is Agent Malone, Major. I know about Rachel."

Short and sweet, and Tupper would stay up all night wondering. Malone was smiling to himself as he hung up. The smile faded when the Com called to him and held up his cellular.

Reluctantly, Malone walked over to find out what the Secretary of Defense wanted.

The group clustered around Malone as the Com handed him the phone. Malone backed away. The group followed, led by the Com. After several yards Malone gave in and stopped. Nothing like a little privacy when you're about to talk to one of the most powerful men in the world. He began, "Mr. Secretary—"

That was as far as Malone got before the SECDEF interrupted him. His voice sounded just like it did on TV—a high-pitched southern twang bolstered by a heavy dose of sarcasm. "You're sure you've got the right man *this time*, Agent Malone?"

"No, sir."

"*What?*"

"DNA will confirm if Major Tupper fathered Rachel Owen's baby, Mr. Secretary. We still need to prove he actually killed her and the other victims."

"How sure are you he's the killer?"

"He fits the profile."

"That's not good enough."

"Sir, I can't give you a better answer until I interview him. If he declines a lie detector test, I'll be more confident he's the killer."

"When will that be?"

"Monday." Malone explained the problem.

"You can't have Tupper picked up tonight?" the SECDEF demanded.

"Two problems, sir. First, we don't know where he went skiing, and we haven't been able to get through on his cell phone—"

"Christ."

"And second, we don't have the evidence to support a civilian arrest warrant, sir."

A silence. The SECDEF wasn't happy. "For crying out loud, you're telling me there's a chance he might not be the guy."

Malone was tempted to go with his gut. But Air Force majors who overstated something to the SECDEF didn't grow up to be lieutenant colonels. "Yes, sir."

"No more fuck-ups, Malone," he growled. "The military is looking like a horse's ass over this thing. You make an arrest, Tupper better be the guy. You dot every *i* and cross every *t*, *twice*. You understand me?"

If he was crazy, Malone might have reminded the secretary that he was the one who caved into pressure and gave the conditional order for Ralston's arrest. But crazy Malone wasn't.

"I understand, sir."

A click. Malone handed the phone back to the Com. Mother and Kaitlin caught his eye. They looked as beat as he was. "So what do you plan to do now?" the Com asked Malone.

"Nothing, sir."

He frowned. So did his entire staff. "It's only 1840 hours," the Com said.

Malone didn't know what he expected him to do, and he was way past caring.

"General," he said wearily, "I almost got killed tonight."

And he walked away.

Of course Kaitlin drove a Mercedes.

It was parked in the first row of the near-empty lot outside Harmon Hall. Pulling up to it, Malone resisted the urge to bring up her comments about his BMW. Now wasn't the time.

She picked up her briefcase, looking at him. "Can I talk to you for a minute?"

"Sure."

As they got out, Malone noticed Mother in the back-seat rolling her eyes. While she and Kaitlin had settled upon a working truce, Mother wasn't about to forgive and forget. "Remember what I told you, Malone," she whispered.

"About?"

"Tits and ass. Keep your mind off her tits and ass."

"Give it a rest, Mother."

Shaking his head, Malone closed the door and followed Kaitlin to the curb several yards away. It was a cold, clear night with only the hint of a breeze. Kaitlin stared out at the cadet area, looming quiet and dark below the chapel wall.

"You love this place, don't you?" she asked.

"I . . . appreciate it." He added, "I didn't always."

"Christina loved it," she said softly, "at first."

A pointed qualifier. Malone passed on a reply.

Kaitlin was pensive, in no hurry to voice what was on her mind. They continued to gaze in silence. A group of cadets walked toward Arnold Hall, the social center, laughing and joking. From one of the corner cadet rooms, someone turned up a stereo and the pulsing beat of rap music floated toward them. Kaitlin murmured, "It seems . . . I don't know . . . almost sacrilegious."

Malone felt the same way. But the music and the laughter were stark reminders that even after all the deaths and turmoil, life went on. "You wanted to talk?" he said.

She faced him hesitantly. "I want you to know I'm sorry about Laura. I'm sorry about . . . everything." Under the soft glow of the moonlight, her eyes were vulnerable and sad.

"We all are," he said, because it was the thing to say.

"What she did was the ultimate act of love, wasn't it? Laura loved him too much to watch him get arrested and sent to prison."

"Something like that."

She was silent, thinking about that. "I never thought it was possible, that a person could love someone that much."

He held her big eyes in his. He said gently, "We all can, if we try."

Kaitlin abruptly stepped away from him, shaking her head. Not the reaction he anticipated. She sounded angry. "Malone, don't *do* this. We can't get involved."

"Why not?"

"I *told* you."

"So I went out with your sister? That's no reason."

"Malone . . ."

"It isn't."

The sound of a door opening. Looking over, they saw Mother emerge from the back of the Hummer. "Captain Sapper called," she said. "He can spare a couple of men. They'll meet you in twenty minutes."

"Thank you," Malone said.

She climbed into the passenger seat, closing the door harder than necessary. Her way of telling Malone what she thought of his tête-à-tête.

"Malone," Kaitlin said with feeling, "don't make this harder than it is. Please. We have different lives. In a month, I'm transferring to Washington, D.C. It will never work."

"Just have dinner with me tonight. If you still feel the same way—"

"I can't. I'm leaving immediately for the airport, to pick up the senator. He's returning from Washington and wants me to brief him before his press conference. It's scheduled for nine."

Malone felt a wave of disgust. "He's actually going to continue his vendetta against the Academy, after all that's happened? That's sick."

She sighed. "I'll do what I can to tone down his rhet-
oric. I'll tell him he was wrong about you, that you're a
good cop who was only doing his job."

"And the Academy leadership?"

She hesitated. "I know what you want me to say, but
I can't. I can never forgive what happened to my sister.
The institution still has a lot to answer for, concerning
women."

Malone grudgingly accepted her response. It was the
only one she had the capacity to give. "So this is good-
bye? You're not staying around for the big finish?"

"It's for the best. Knowing my investigation con-
tributed to so many deaths . . ." She shook her head.
"No. Someone else will have to finish the sexual harassment inquiry. I can't stay here. Not anymore. Good-
bye, Malone." She held out her gloved hand.

An awkwardly formal gesture considering their feelings for each other. "Good-bye, Kaitlin," Malone said,
taking her hand.

They stared at each other, reluctant to let go. Finally
Kaitlin released her grip, picked up her briefcase, and
walked toward her car.

"If it's okay," he called out, "I'd like to call you."

No reply. She got into her car and drove away without looking back. Not even once.

This really was good-bye.

Chapter 35

"I'D SAY THAT WENT WELL," MOTHER ANNOUNCED cheerfully, as Malone got in behind the wheel.

"I don't want to discuss it."

"So don't. I'll do the talking."

When it came to Malone's love life, Mother regarded herself as something of an amateur Dr. Phil, albeit a harshly judgmental version.

"Mother, I'm not in the mood." He tossed her a sour look, to convince her.

No dice. She promptly threw back, "How does it feel being shot down in flames? 'Cause that's sure the way it sounded to me."

"Sounded?"

He looked to the windows; they were all down. "Mother, that was a *private* conversation."

"Can I help what I overhear?"

He motored up the windows, glaring at her. She grinned, pleased with herself. Shaking his head, Malone started the car and drove from the lot. "So?" she pressed. "How does it feel being shot down again? Must be something about those Barlow girls."

"Mother, lay off."

"Not a chance. You deserve it."

A dig Malone understood only too well. He flipped on the radio and turned it up loud.

She immediately clicked it off.

"Mother—"

"Ego take a little hit? Hmm?"

Malone hunkered over the wheel. Mother watched him with amusement. "Why fight it, Malone?" she said lightly. "You know we're going to talk about it eventually. It's a big event. It's only happened twice, right?"

She was laying it on thick. He continued to ignore her, not that it did any good.

She said, "The king of one-night stands gets a taste of his own medicine. He went down in flames. I gotta give Kaitlin credit. She had enough pride not to be another notch on your bedpost. Or maybe she's paying you back for what you did to her sister. Either way, good for her."

Let it go, Malone.

But he couldn't. "You're wrong," he said quietly.

She seemed surprised he'd spoken. "About?"

"Kaitlin." He glanced over. "She wasn't like the others. I really liked her."

"Her tits and—"

"Don't say it. I mean it."

"This is Mother you're talking to, Malone. Your idea of a long-term commitment is what, maybe a month? You were hung up on Christina because you never had a chance to get tired of her. But you would have. Same thing with Kaitlin."

"That's not true."

"Oh, no? Remember that blond lieutenant you were dating a couple months back? You were crazy about her also. For chrissakes, you even met her parents. What'd that last? Two weeks? Three? You broke her heart, too. Face it, you're just like Kaitlin only the other way around. You use women. Don't turn away from me. You need to hear this. You say you want to change, but you can't. Not until you get over your fear of relationships and rejection and the other hang-ups you've got because of your father. And we both know that won't happen until you get some professional help." She gave him a hard look, scolding him as if he were a child. "You're a thirty-four-year-old military officer, not some oversexed college kid. You're probably hurting now because she turned you down, but so what? It's not the end of the world. Get counseling and learn to deal with it."

He smiled at her.

"Great," she said. "I don't even know why I bother. It's a damned joke to you."

"It's not that. I just realized I might be okay."

"Take it from me," she said with conviction. "You're not."

"Will you listen to me? Kaitlin turned me down and I think I'm okay with it."

"You *think*?"

Malone shared her skepticism. He analyzed his feelings to be absolutely certain. But the absence of anger and hurt led him to only one conclusion. "I'm really okay," he said again.

"Why this miraculous change now?" Mother countered.

Malone had an answer. Eight people had died, two of them friends. He'd also come within seconds of dying himself. By comparison, a bruised ego didn't seem to matter much. It just didn't.

"Maybe you're growing up, Malone," Mother said. "Maybe you finally realize what's important."

"Maybe."

"This is only a start. People don't shed their baggage this quickly. You're weird about relationships. You really are. Do me a favor and get counseling."

"I'll look into it."

"Promise?"

"Cross my heart."

He sounded completely sincere and Mother nodded as if she believed him. In reality, it was a game they were playing.

Because they both knew Malone was lying through his teeth.

By the time Malone dropped Mother off at the airfield to retrieve her truck and drove over to Kaitlin's TLF, it was after seven-thirty. The two cops Captain Sapper had sent to drive his BMW were waiting for him. Kaitlin's Mercedes wasn't anywhere to be seen; she'd cleared out in a hurry. Malone felt both disappointed and relieved.

One good-bye was enough.

He parked behind the cops, who were leaning against their SUV. Both were young, barely twenty: a blond guy who looked surfer-cool and a slender Hispanic kid with a mustache and a cocky walk. Not

---

the low-testosterone candidates he was hoping for, and Malone revised his plan.

He got out of the Hummer as they came over.

"Who's driving and who's following?" he asked.

"I won the toss," the surfer said, eyeing the BMW with a predatory smile. "That's one hot car, sir. How fast you been in it?"

"Fast enough. Here." Malone passed him the keys and waved him inside the Hummer.

The surfer frowned at Malone, taken aback. "You mean I'm driving *this*?"

Malone nodded.

His face fell. His buddy grinned. The surfer said, "But Captain Sapper told us—"

"A misunderstanding. Twenty bucks help?"

He handed them each a twenty-dollar bill. From the look the surfer gave him, fifty bucks wouldn't have made a difference.

"Follow me," Malone said.

"Yes, sir," the surfer said gloomily.

His buddy was laughing as he went over to the SUV.

Malone got into the BMW and cranked the engine. As he checked behind to back out of the driveway, he immediately faced front with a puzzled expression. He'd grasped the steering wheel, rubbing away some kind of residue. Under the glow of the nearby streetlight, he noticed dark flecks stuck to his fingers.

He touched the wheel again. The substance covered only a small section on the back side. Still, he felt irritated. He always kept his vehicles immaculate.

Flipping on the map light, he reached for the

Kleenex box in the backseat. As he started to wipe his hand, he froze. He began to tremble as he stared at his palm.

Oh, Christ—

He frantically focused the light at the steering wheel and leaned forward, straining to see. The black leather made it difficult to tell. He ran Kleenex over a portion of the residue and held it under the light. Against the white, there was no mistaking what the flecks were. What they had to be.

And there could be more.

He shone the light around the interior. No discolorations jumped out. Not that it mattered. The obvious stuff would have been cleaned up.

Malone slumped back, realizing he was panting. He wanted to be wrong. He had to be wrong.

But if he wasn't—

As he stared at the Kleenex, the acceptance finally came. Of what he was looking at and what it meant.

One by one, the pieces slowly came together, creating an image that was no longer obscured. Things that had been unclear came into focus. Not every detail, but enough. Once again, he had ignored the first rule of criminal investigations—his own rule—and had seized upon the obvious. But that was precisely what the killer had intended. Mother had called it; they'd been actors in a precisely written script with the killer directing them every step of the way. And he'd been the star, uncovering the clues he'd been meant to find.

He shook his head. It had been lies. All of it.

But now he knew the truth. He *knew*.

Malone carefully pocketed the Kleenex and massaged his eyes. He was tired and his head ached and his lip throbbed. He wasn't up to dealing with this now. He fought the impulse to go home, grab a shower, and crawl into bed. Just for a few hours.

But he was a cop with a job to do. One who'd been used and played for a fool.

He waited for the anger to come, but it never did.

Because deep down, he knew who was ultimately responsible for what had happened. And that person would never face justice.

A sharp rap on the window. The surfer stood there, gazing down quizzically. Malone unfolded from the car, handing him the BMW keys. "Change of plans. I want you to have this car impounded for processing."

"*Your* car, sir?"

"Right. Stay here until the wrecker arrives. You got my Humvee keys? Thanks. Sorry for the mix-up." Walking away, Malone was already calling Mother's home number. She lived only minutes from the base.

Except there was no answer. He tried her cell and she finally picked up. She sounded tense and preoccupied.

"I know who the killer is," he said.

When he revealed the name, there was no shocked gasp on the other end. Only silence.

"Mother, you hear what I said?"

"I heard. It's impossible."

"Impossible?"

"Take it from me. Kaitlin can't possibly be the killer."

*   *   *

The finality of Mother's statement threw Malone. He said, "Mother, it has to be Kaitlin. I found blood residue in my BMW. She was driving it when—"

"It's not Kaitlin," she repeated.

"C'mon. No one else drove my car."

"Look, this is too confusing to explain over the phone. I don't really have all the details myself. How long until you can get here?"

"Get here? Where's here?"

"The superintendent's house. I'm with the general now. He contacted me right after you dropped me off. We just arrived and are waiting for a call."

"Crenshaw? You're with General Crenshaw?" Malone was completely lost. Why was Crenshaw involving himself?

"Yeah. He's been a busy boy. He's the one who broke into Kaitlin's TLF."

"He *what*?"

"That's how come we know the killer isn't Kaitlin. Because of what he found." A phone rang in the background. Away from the mouthpiece, Mother said, "That's him, sir? Be right there." To Malone: "I got to go. This could be the confirmation. I want to listen in."

"Confirmation? What confirmation? What did General Crenshaw find—"

He was talking to himself.

Chapter 36

A SEEMINGLY LITTLE THING, BUT IT SPOKE VOL-
umes.

He was the head of the OSI, and yet General
Crenshaw had called Mother instead of him. That fact
and the unstated message it contained about Malone's
character weighed upon him. But not as much as
Mother's pronouncement of Kaitlin's innocence.

How could he be wrong again? How?

During the drive to General Crenshaw's, his tired
mind cycled through everything again. When he finished, his determination was the same.

Everything pointed to Kaitlin.

The murders began a week after she arrived.

She had a motive for framing Ralston, a man she
believed had raped her sister.

From her conversations with Rachel Owen and
Mary Zinnel, she would know about Rachel's pregnancy, the rumors of her older lover, and the existence
of a jealous former boyfriend.

She had access to the squadron, which allowed her

to steal Rachel's keys and plant the gun and mask.

Then there was her sudden disappearance from the home of Rachel Owen's mother, coinciding with the murders at Lawrence Paul.

And the reactions of Agent Kranski and the cop by the road, who never displayed alarm because it never occurred to them that a beautiful woman could be a killer.

And the torn condom packet in Kaitlin's room, suggesting how an unstable kid like Cadet Jefferson could be enticed into participating in murders.

And Mrs. Owen, who would be impressed enough by a Senate investigator to put on her Sunday-best clothes.

And finally the kicker: the blood in his car.

The evidence was all there.

Kaitlin was the killer. She had to be the killer.

But apparently she wasn't.

Nuts.

The search team was packing up to leave General Crenshaw's mansion. A knot of agents were gathered on the wraparound porch, most from the nearby OSI detachments who had responded to his call for assistance.

As Malone went up the front steps, Rob Sanders came over to him. "Mother told us to shut down. Says she's cleared General Crenshaw."

"Anyone still at Coach Ralston's house?"

"No, sir. They finished up about an hour ago. Didn't turn up anything but the gun. Helluva thing, huh? His wife killing them both like that."

Malone nodded. "Mother and the general?"

"His study upstairs. Second door on the right." He waved a tired arm at the other agents. "Mother said it's your call, sir. Our asses are dragging. If you don't need us, we were going to head on home."

"Keep two men. I have another job for you."

A slow blink. Not the response he expected. "Oh? What?" Sanders was less than enthused.

"It won't take long, Rob. Maybe an hour."

After Malone told him what he wanted, Sanders was dumbfounded, as were the other agents who'd overheard. "I'll be damned," was all Sanders could manage.

Malone passed him the tissue flecked with blood and entered the house.

"Here, Malone."

He paused in the second-floor hallway by the stairwell and peered into a bedroom. Mother was sitting on the bed, listening to a phone. She cupped it, saying, "We'll be done in a minute. The doctor's almost through."

"What doctor?"

But she was again concentrating on the phone conversation.

Malone continued down the hall. The double mahogany doors to Crenshaw's study were open and he saw the general at his desk, also on the phone.

"Thank you, Doctor," the general said, motioning Malone inside. "You've verified my suspicions. Yes, yes, I understand you can't be certain. I agree, it is a shocking turn of events, if true. Thank you again, Doctor."

The general cradled the phone, watching Malone approach. In the past six hours, another remarkable transformation to his appearance had occurred. The cracks in his emotional facade had disappeared, replaced by a coldly determined expression Malone knew only too well.

The general was back and he was pissed.

"I'm glad you're here, Malone." He sounded as if he meant it.

Malone knew he was being tossed a bone, but the general had that right. After all, Malone had disappointed him before. He said, "You said something just now about confirming suspicions . . ."

"To Dr. Landow, the chief psychiatrist of the Clearwater Sanitarium."

"It's where Christina Barlow was institutionalized," Mother said, coming into the study.

Malone nodded; he knew this.

General Crenshaw said to him, "Mother says you believe Kaitlin is the killer."

"Yes, sir. I understand you don't."

"I did initially, because of this." He passed Malone a paper from his desk.

Glancing down to read it, Malone paused at the salutation. It said simply, "Dad." He looked up.

"It's an e-mail from Rachel, written yesterday," the general said.

"But you weren't her father, sir," Malone said.

He didn't reply, his expression uncomfortable. "Malone needs to know the truth, sir," Mother prompted.

Crenshaw slowly nodded. "Sit down."

Malone and Mother both did, taking chairs across from the general.

"No, I'm not Rachel's father. A cousin raped Lucille when she was fifteen." He studied Malone, watching his reaction.

Malone managed to keep his surprise in check.

The general resumed speaking in a more hesitant tone, as if the process of recalling was painful for him. He said, "It was a source of great . . . shame for Lucille and her family. Her own cousin . . . a boy she'd grown up with, was almost like a brother . . . raped and impregnated her. How disgusting is that? Of course, the family wanted her to get an abortion. But Lucille couldn't bring herself to do it . . . kill her own child. And she knew she couldn't raise it. Not if she wanted to make something of her life. The baby . . . Rachel . . . was adopted by Mrs. Owen, a neighbor. When Lucille and I got married, Rachel was almost seven . . . living in the projects. It was no kind of environment for a child to grow up in and Mrs. Owen agreed. She is . . . was . . . a good woman. So Lucille and I talked about Rachel coming to live with us. But . . . that's all it was . . . talk. We'd both worked so hard to make it. Lucille was worried for my career. How could we explain Rachel's sudden appearance? Even if . . . even if we made up a story, it wouldn't have worked. Kids . . . you know how they are. Rachel would have said things . . . things the other children would wonder about. And their parents. I'm not talking about the rape, but the rest of it. The projects . . . her life there . . . Mrs. Owen. People would ask questions . . . ones we couldn't answer. So . . . we sent money instead. Enough for Mrs. Owen to send Rachel to a private school and keep her clothed and fed. Lucille and I convinced ourselves that was enough. That we were doing the right thing. But of course, we weren't. Everyone has choices in life and we made ours. You don't become a general if your wife is raped by a relative. You just . . . don't. So . . . we made a choice based upon . . . selfishness. And it worked out. Lucille and I got what we wanted. I made general. We only had to abandon Rachel to do it. Some trade-off, huh?"

He fell silent, staring at Lucille's photo on his desk, the guilt heavy in his eyes.

Mother elbowed Malone. He understood and said, "General, we don't need to go into this any more—"

"No," Crenshaw said, interrupting him. "I've kept this secret too long. Lucille and I denied ourselves a daughter until it was almost too late. Rachel and Lucille only had a year to get to know each other before Lucille passed away. But I was luckier. I had almost three. And make no mistake. Rachel and I made up for lost time. She had a capacity for forgiveness we never deserved. She became a daughter to us . . . to me. The only one I'll ever have the privilege—"

He almost lost it. He inhaled raggedly, struggling to control his emotions. It was uncomfortable witnessing his private pain and Mother and Malone looked discreetly away.

For fully thirty seconds, no one spoke. General Crenshaw sat in his chair, chin to his chest, eyes fixed on the picture of his wife. Slowly looking up, he said, "I apologize, Malone."

"Sir?"

"I was a hypocrite. I held you to a standard I couldn't meet."

Another reference to character. "We're all human, sir," Malone said.

"That's a cop-out and you know it."

"Maybe. But it's also a fact of life. Everyone has skeletons in their past. Things they regret doing and wish they could change. You're no different . . ." Malone hesitated. "And neither am I."

General Crenshaw gave Malone a long look. "Mind answering a question?"

"No, sir."

"If anyone has a right to judge me harshly, it should be you. Yet you're giving me a pass. Why?"

It took Malone a moment. "My father. He also walked out on me."

"Which is what I did to Rachel. You should be disgusted with me."

"There's a difference, sir. You came back."

Crenshaw didn't seem to know what to say. His eyes dropped to the e-mail and he sounded suddenly embarrassed. "Look it over and we'll talk."

Malone began to read.

Chapter 37

Dad,

I don't know how to tell you this, so I'm just going to say it. I got involved in a relationship with a married man. Don't ask me who he is, it really doesn't matter. What does matter is I shouldn't have done it. Call it a schoolgirl crush or anything you want. He was someone I admired and it just happened. It certainly wasn't anything I planned. If I had, I wouldn't be in the predicament I find myself in. It's the reason I've decided to tell you. Eventually, you're going to find out anyway.

Dad, I'm in the same situation Mother was in when she had me. Yes, I am pregnant. And yes, I'm sure. I've done the test twice; there's no mistake. No, I haven't told the father. He'd want to do the right thing, though I'm not sure what that is exactly. He has children and the last thing I want is to destroy his career and marriage. In case you haven't guessed where this is all going, Dad, I've decided to keep the baby. Talk about the ultimate irony, huh? I guess I am my mother's daughter.

This means I will have to leave the Academy and

for that I'm truly sorry. But in my heart, I know it's the right decision, the only decision. If Mother had ended her pregnancy, I wouldn't be here. Once I have the baby, I promise you I'll find some way to finish college. I know how disappointed you must be in me, but I can assure you that's not half as disappointed as I am in myself.

To save you any embarrassment, I was hoping to resign from the Academy and slip away without anybody knowing the reason. But that won't happen now.

Mary talked me into confiding in the Senate investigator, Ms. Barlow. Ms. Barlow and Mary had hit it off and Mary said she was a wonderful person and we could trust her. Looking back now, that seems like such a naively stupid decision, but you have to understand my frame of mind. I was agonizing over whether to keep the baby and wasn't thinking clearly. And here was this opportunity to talk to an older, professional woman who seemed so nice and understanding. What finally convinced me to confide in her was when she told us about her sister, who'd been a cadet and had been raped. Because of that, Ms. Barlow said she was on a mission to help female cadets. Particularly ones who'd gotten into trouble, like me. She was so sincere that I believed and trusted her. Was that ever a mistake.

It turned out she only wanted to use me to make a case against the Academy. She knows the father is someone stationed here. When I wouldn't identify him, she got very angry. For the past week, she's constantly hounded me to reveal his name. A couple of days ago, she threatened me with a subpoena to testify before her panel. That scared me, but I still wouldn't tell her. That's when she started to act really crazy. She's been following me around the campus and keeps telling me that if I don't cooperate, I'll be sorry. This afternoon, when I came back to my room, I could tell it had been searched. I don't think it's the first time. I'd lost my keys for a day and they suddenly reappeared. Someone saw my old boyfriend Terry Jefferson leaving my room, but when I confronted him, he denied he'd even been there. Later, I found out Ms. Barlow had been talking to him quite a bit.

I'm not sure how far Ms. Barlow will go to get me to cooperate. But she scares me. I mean she really scares me. She has hate, Dad. A lot of hate. Could you talk to her, please? Tell her I don't want to testify and want to be left alone?

There's more bad news, I'm afraid. I don't think she knows of our relationship, but Terry Jefferson always suspected you and I had a connection and he might have said something. I'm sorry about all the trouble I'm causing you. Someday, I'll make it up to you. You won't always be ashamed of me.

I promise.

I love you, Dad.

Your daughter,
Rachel

When Malone looked up from reading, Crenshaw said, "Mother says you think Major Tupper is the father."

"He's the likely candidate, sir."

The general's jaw hardened, then almost immediately relaxed. While Tupper might have violated his ethical responsibilities by bedding Rachel, he hadn't killed her. Crenshaw wordlessly held out his hand and Malone passed him back the e-mail. The general gazed at it reverentially.

"Ashamed of her," he said. "I could never be ashamed of her. She's the one who should have been ashamed of me."

A wrenching remark.

Slipping the e-mail into a folder, Lieutenant General Crenshaw wiped at his eyes.

Crenshaw was acting precisely like what he purported to be, a father who had lost a daughter. But despite his anguish, he knew he had a job to do.

Focusing on Malone, his grim determination returned. "Now you know why I searched Kaitlin Barlow's room."

"Instead of coming to us, sir?" Malone had to ask.

"I considered it. But it was a lose/lose proposition. You couldn't officially search Kaitlin's room without the blessing of the SECDEF. With only this e-mail to go on, he'd never give it. And even on the off-chance he did, you'd be in a tough position. You'd damn well better find something incriminating or there would be hell to pay. That bastard Smith would use his bully pulpit to accuse us of trying to discredit Kaitlin and indirectly himself, as part of a cover-up. No, no. My way was better. It ensured plausible deniability for the military, if nothing was found."

Malone couldn't counter his logic. He said, "And you found . . ."

"Mother."

She went over to a file cabinet, retrieving a box sitting on top of it. She returned, placing the box on the desk before Malone.

Peering inside, Malone frowned, realizing it was empty. "It's a box for a wig," Mother said.

She and Crenshaw were peering at him expectantly. Obviously, Malone was missing something. He shrugged. "Okay, I give up."

The general said, "This doesn't mean anything to you?"

"No, other than we found the lid in the driveway. You must have dropped it, sir."

Mother said to Malone, "Didn't you tell me you visited Christina when she was hospitalized?"

"Once. But she didn't want to see me."

"That explains it," Crenshaw said to Mother. To Malone: "As her AOC, I visited Christina at the hospital on two occasions. That's why I understood the significance of the wig. Because of her appearance and what doctors told me about her compulsions."

Malone said, "Her compulsions, sir? What are you specifically referring—"

It suddenly came to him in a rush. His conversation with Kaitlin and her words:

She got this belief that her looks were responsible for the rape.

She did things to herself, to make sure it would never happen again.

She wouldn't stop. They couldn't get her to stop.

And Mother's statement only minutes earlier: *Take it from me. Kaitlin can't possibly be the killer.*

Malone's mouth turned to sand and he had to swallow to speak. "Hair," he said dully. "Christina pulled out her hair. And if Kaitlin is wearing a wig . . ."

"She's really Christina," Mother concluded.

Chapter 38

FROM SOMEWHERE OUT FRONT, THEY HEARD THE sound of cars starting up. The search team slowly drove off, one by one, the rumble of their engines fading into the night. In the ensuing silence, Malone continued to sit slumped in his chair, lost in his thoughts. General Crenshaw and Mother patiently waited, knowing he needed time to accept the viability of what he'd just learned. Decide whether it could really be true.

Closing his eyes, Malone pictured the accident, where it all began. He saw the car with Christina and Kaitlin driving down a winding mountain road at night. A storm has come up; it's raining heavily, the wind howling. The car is going too fast for the conditions. Rounding a turn, it suddenly loses control, bursts through a guard rail, and tumbles end over end, down a steep ravine. Christina, in the driver's seat, is ejected and thrown clear. The car slams into rocks or trees and explodes into flames. Kaitlin is still alive, trapped in the wreckage and screaming. Christina, miraculously unin-jured, stumbles down the muddy ravine in a desperate attempt to save her sister. By the time she reaches the car, it is engulfed in fire. Her sister is still screaming. Christina claws at the burning doors until her hands are blistered and raw. But it's no use.

They won't open. They just won't open.

The screaming seems to last forever. Finally, mercifully, it stops.

Christina drifts away from the inferno and collapses to the muddy ground, sobbing. Her sister is dead and it's her fault.

Because of the storm, it's hours until she is rescued. At some point, in the middle of her horror and grief and guilt, an idea occurs to her.

Her *twin* is dead.

A twin who hasn't been raped and institutionalized. A twin with a future and a job with a senator.

A twin with a *life*.

And she wonders . . .

She looks at her burned hands and slowly nods to herself. It *is* possible.

Malone felt himself nodding. Maybe that wasn't precisely the way everything played out, but he knew it was close.

Unless . . .

Conclusions. He had made a mistake earlier, jumping to conclusions. He forced himself to consider alternatives. Particularly ones that might explain inconsistencies he had yet to understand.

Moments later, he got a hit.

Then a second.

Malone opened his eyes and threw out a question to

Crenshaw and Mother: Could *both* women have survived the accident?

No, Crenshaw said firmly. He'd checked. A female's body was recovered from the accident. A body burned beyond recognition.

That seemed to cinch it. Kaitlin had to be Christina. The question was how to prove her identity. As Malone saw it, there was only one way to do it quickly.

"Prints?" Mother said, shaking her head at his suggestion. "They won't do any good, Malone. It's how Christina pulled off the switch. Her hands are covered with scar tissue. She can't be printed."

But Crenshaw was nodding; he knew what Malone meant. Malone said to him, "The hospital will have records . . ."

Crenshaw snatched up the phone.

Things moved rapidly.

General Crenshaw might have been relieved from his command, but this was the military and he was still a three-star. The base hospital promised to immediately fax out the response to his request, no questions asked. As they waited, Crenshaw explained how he wanted to handle the arrest. Malone and Mother responded by saying his proposal was too risky. Then the general reminded them of something they hadn't considered. This was the post-9/11 era, and security would be enhanced.

While this convinced Mother to sign on, Malone was still reluctant to agree. It went against normal protocol for the apprehension of a dangerous suspect.

"What," Mother said, when he brought up his reservations, "you're suddenly following the rules now? Give me a break."

"Malone," Crenshaw said. "Senator Smith has been using the Academy as a punching bag. Now we have a chance to fight back, show the world what kind of immoral son of a bitch we've been dealing with."

His tone had an undercurrent of desperation. Crenshaw wanted this more than anything, though not for the reasons he cited. This was a personal vendetta; the general wanted revenge.

Malone couldn't blame him. He felt the same way.

"All right, sir."

After that they divided up the required phone calls, because you didn't arrest a Senate investigator—especially in a politically charged climate—without approval and, more important, irrefutable evidence of guilt.

The general attended to the first concern while Mother and Malone addressed the second.

Rob Sanders confirmed he had arrived at Malone's BMW and was preparing to spray the interior with Luminol, to reveal additional blood Kaitlin might have wiped away. Luminol was a quick-acting catalyst and Sanders would have a preliminary indication soon. The OSI duty officer would scrounge up a print kit and meet them at Kaitlin's TLF. The DO also answered a crucial question about Jefferson's phone records, explaining why the killer felt compelled to destroy the cadet's cell phone.

"Yes, sir," the DO said to Malone. "I'm looking at the

phone company faxes now. There was a call from Cadet Jefferson to Ms. Barlow's cell number. At 1412 today."

Approximately the time Kaitlin took off in his car. "Only one?" Malone said.

"Yes, sir. There are several from pay phones over the past few days."

Kaitlin must have told Jefferson not to call her on his phone. That he'd gone against procedure this afternoon was due to panic.

After leaving the computer center, Jefferson had spotted Kranski tailing him.

The hospital's faxes came in while Mother was on her cellular to Lieutenant Tom Canola. It wasn't only that she wanted to keep Tom informed on the break in the case; they needed him. As military investigators, they had to wade through a sea of jurisdictional red tape before arresting a civilian. Tom Canola didn't have that problem.

Punching off, Mother said to Malone, "Tom will mobilize his people and give the judge a heads-up. He says we better be right about Kaitlin or he'll be busted back to traffic duty."

Malone said, "Rob will find more blood in the car."

"But on the chance he doesn't—"

"Relax, he will."

The amount of blood was critical. A trace might not convince a judge to sign a warrant.

Mother and Malone turned their attention to Crenshaw, who was still on the phone. He'd worked his way up the chain of command and from the way he was grimacing, it was apparent this final conversation

PATRICK A. DAVIS

wasn't going well. Crenshaw said, "Sir, I'm with the lead investigators now. Yes, sir, I agree with their findings. Sir, I understand your concerns over the constant shifting of the suspects. But the blood Agent Malone discovered leaves no question as to— Hold on, sir."

He held out the phone to Malone. "The SECDEF wants to talk to you."

Twice in one night. Malone made a face, taking the phone. "Agent Malone, Mr. Secretary."

If anything, the SECDEF's sarcasm was even more pronounced than before. He said, "You seem to change your mind a great deal, Malone."

"Sir, I told you Major Tupper might not be the killer."

"But you intimated he was."

"If I did—"

"If?"

The SECDEF wanted an admission. Malone reluctantly complied, saying, "I was wrong, Mr. Secretary. Major Tupper isn't the killer."

"You seem to be wrong a helluva lot."

"Sir, in my business there are no guaran—"

"Save it, Malone. I want an excuse, I'll ask for it."

"Yes, sir."

"You're certain you're not wrong this time? You have *no* doubts?"

"No, sir."

"You understand the consequences if you blow this?"

"Yes, sir. I'll be looking for another job."

"We'll *both* be looking for jobs. Senator Smith spent the day on the Hill, gathering support. At the top of his agenda is to get me replaced. You understand where I'm coming from, Malone?"

"Completely, sir."

A pause. Malone could tell the SECDEF was torn by the political realities of his decision. And if he surrendered to his concerns and ordered them to hold off . . .

To hell with him.

"Sir," Malone said suddenly, "Kaitlin Barlow is a multiple murderer and could kill again. That's not an opinion, but a fact. Whether you approve her arrest, I frankly don't care. I intend to arrange for the civilian authorities to apprehend her tonight."

Another pause, this time because of Malone's brazenness. Mother and General Crenshaw stared at Malone as if he'd lost his mind. The general sprang from his chair, sputtering, "Dammit, you can't say that to—"

Over the phone, Malone heard a chuckle.

"You got balls, Malone," the SECDEF said. "I'll say that for you. Hell, I'd love to see Senator Smith's face when you arrest Ms. Barlow. His own damned investigator. Something tells me his chances for reelection just went down the crapper."

"If the timing works out, sir."

"Timing?"

This was what General Crenshaw had proposed. After Malone detailed their intentions, the SECDEF sounded almost giddy. "Jesus, this will be good. Dramatic as hell. Tell the general he missed his calling. The man should be in politics. Call me as soon as you determine whether you can pull it off."

"Yes, sir."

The SECDEF was chuckling again as he ended the call.

"Well?" Crenshaw demanded, as Malone cradled the phone. "What'd he say? Did he relieve you?"

Malone hesitated, trying to recall. But the SECDEF had been careful not to say the actual words. "We're okay, sir. He pretty much approved the arrest."

"Pretty much? What the hell's that supposed to mean?"

"He's covering his ass, sir."

It was another ten minutes before they were ready to leave for Kaitlin's TLF. General Crenshaw insisted on changing into his Class A uniform, with the pretty rows of fruit salad on his chest and the six stars glittering on his shoulders. It wasn't something he opted for out of vanity, but rather for the effect his appearance would create, assuming he had the opportunity.

Before leaving the office, Crenshaw removed a small packet from his wall safe and slipped it into his jacket pocket. This was perhaps the most crucial element of his plan. As a soldier, he was only too aware that the objective of war was the destruction of the enemy, and that's precisely what he intended to do. Not simply embarrass Senator Smith, but destroy him.

"Payback," Mother concluded, "is a bitch."

As they went downstairs, Agent Rob Sanders got back to Malone. His awed voice confirmed his findings even before he said the words.

"We sprayed the Luminol and I just flipped on the ultraviolet light, boss. You should see it. Jesus."

The Shattered Blue Line 349

"There's more blood?" Malone asked, stopping in the entryway. "How much? Enough?"

"I'll say. The door, the knob, the carpet. Shit, your car is practically *glowing*."

That was it. They had their evidence. Evidence that was irrefutable and couldn't be explained away. Ending the call, Malone answered Mother's and Crenshaw's questioning gazes with a nod. They reacted with visible relief. Malone knew he should feel similarly, but instead was gripped with a profound emptiness. It wasn't only that he'd hoped for a miracle, some indication that Kaitlin wasn't a killer. Rather, it was sadness over a memory, one that had been a part of him for years and was finally gone.

Reading his face, Mother said softly, "You okay?"

"It could be worse," he said.

"Worse?"

"If it turns out she is Christina."

Chapter 39

THE OSI DUTY OFFICER MET THEM AT KAITLIN'S TLF with the print kit and a key. Within minutes, they found what they wanted on the shiny tile of the bathroom floor.

Kaitlin's footprints.

During in-processing, an Air Force cadet's footprints were taken, because most would become pilots and in the event they were involved in a fatal plane crash, their feet encased in boots had the best odds of surviving. Since Mother had never been a cadet, she wasn't familiar with this procedure.

"We got lucky," General Crenshaw remarked from the bathroom doorway. "If the maid had mopped the floor this morning, the prints would be gone."

The outlines of Kaitlin's prints were visible on clear tape. As Malone transferred the tape to white placards, he said, "It wasn't luck. I knew they'd be here."

Curious squints gazed back at him.

"Soap," Malone said. "Kaitlin smelled of soap this afternoon."

Nods of understanding. Malone found it ironic that the reason he remembered the soapy scent was because of something else that *hadn't* been there. The smell of perfume.

Which meant Kaitlin had showered recently.

On the tiny dining table, they compared the prints on the placards to the ones in the faxes. The general didn't know exactly what he was looking for, but Mother did.

Under a magnifying glass, she analyzed the images, frowned, and analyzed them some more. Leaning over, Malone said quietly, "You're reading them right, Mother."

She looked at him, puzzled. "Then I don't get it."

"Get what?" Crenshaw said. "What's the problem?"

"No problem, sir," Malone said. "I thought this might happen."

"You expected *this?*" Mother said. "Come on. How?"

He shrugged. "Little peculiarities about Kaitlin I noticed. Things that didn't fit her personality. For instance, she sounded genuinely frightened of someone over the phone. I assumed the person was Smith's chief of staff, but realized Kaitlin wouldn't be afraid of her. Later, I overheard a conversation while she was in the squadron restroom—"

"The punch line," Mother said impatiently. "Get to the punch line. What does any of this have to do with the footprints?"

"Everything. Kaitlin was afraid of the person belonging to the footprints."

"Huh?" she said. "That makes no sense."

"Malone," Crenshaw said. "What you're saying is impossible."

"*Almost* impossible, General."

Following Malone's account, Mother and Crenshaw cycled between pensive head shakes and deep frowns, struggling to grasp what he'd told them. The duty officer, unfamiliar with the case, watched with the same confused expression he'd worn from the beginning.

"Guilt," Crenshaw concluded. "This is more about guilt than revenge."

"It looks that way, sir," Malone said.

Mother sighed. "This case hasn't made any sense from the beginning; why should it be any different now? I'm not sure how much more of this craziness I can take."

Appropriate words, Malone thought.

Pressing the redial on her cell phone, she added, "Well, at least we know who we're dealing with. The how and the why someone else can sort out later. Between you and me and the fencepost, I'm not sure I'll ever understand—" Into the phone: "Tom? Mother. You got a judge lined up? Good boy. We need to move fast. The blood evidence is a lock and I got a name for that warrant. You sitting down, 'cause you're about to be knocked for a loop . . ."

"I'll take this to the car, sir," the DO said, picking up a large plastic garbage bag.

Malone nodded. "Seal the room after we leave. I want a forensic team in here first thing in the morning."

"Yes, sir."

The bag contained the second piece of evidence they'd collected—the sheets and pillowcases Kaitlin had used last night. On them, they'd detected stains that were probably semen. DNA testing would prove conclusively whether Cadet Jefferson was Kaitlin's lover, not that there was much doubt. The sheets reeked of cheap cologne, precisely the kind a cadet would wear.

It wasn't something I planned; it just happened.

Shit happens.

And the most telling remark: *He didn't mean anything to me.*

For once, Malone realized Kaitlin had told him the truth. Jefferson didn't mean anything to her.

Not a damned thing.

"Everything's set," Mother said, putting her phone away. "Time's a-wasting. Let's roll."

"Now?" Crenshaw asked.

"Please," Malone said.

On their way out, Crenshaw told the SECDEF the arrest would be made within the hour.

The hotel.

That's what the five-star Broadmoor Hotel was often called by locals, and deservedly so. It was a majestic old-world-style pink stucco structure built adjacent to a picturesque lake and fronted by beautiful gardens and sprawling grounds. For close to a century, the Broadmoor had specialized in catering to anybody who was anybody or thought they were anybody, which was the main reason Senator Smith felt compelled to hold his press conference here. A guy with his ego couldn't have it anywhere else.

Malone rolled up the hill to the main entrance, General Crenshaw beside him, Mother tucked in the back. In a lower parking area, they saw an army of press vans and satellite trucks. The sheer size of the media turnout confirmed that Senator Smith intended to exploit the murders for his own publicity, an eventuality Crenshaw had counted on.

"Perfect," he murmured.

No black-and-white police cruisers or uniformed officers could be seen, but that was expected. Tom Canola wouldn't tip their hand until they were ready.

"Waiting committee, two o'clock," Mother said.

A group of three stood by the valet parking stand. One was the matronly detective Grace, who had been at Mrs. Owen's home earlier. Beside her, a serious-faced black man whom Malone vaguely recognized as another homicide cop. A slick-looking guy in a white tux stood off to the side, engaged in an anxious two-step.

As Malone pulled up to the stand, a valet started toward his door. The slick guy called out and the valet hit the brakes, retreating.

Malone, Mother, and General Crenshaw got out of the Hummer and headed over to the cops. A young couple in evening clothes noticed Crenshaw and stopped to watch him. So did a group of businessmen coming down the steps. One guy who sounded half in the bag sang out, "America is behind the military all the way, General. Give those terrorists hell."

"We'll try, sir," Crenshaw said politely.

"Kill 'em all. That's the only way to deal with them. Kill the bastards and send them to hell."

"I'll remember that, sir."

The drunk threw up a sloppy wave. His companions shook their heads, sober enough to be embarrassed. By now, everyone in the vicinity was looking at Crenshaw. With a number of bases in the area, Colorado Springs was a military town and several people flashed thumbs-up gestures of support. Malone sighed. Nothing like a conspicuous entrance.

"General Crenshaw," the slick guy said, surprised. "You're involved in this affair?" He wore a shiny silver name tag identifying him as Saul Eduardo, the hotel manager.

"It seems so, Saul," Crenshaw said.

The two cops were puzzled by their familiarity, but Malone and Mother weren't. Each year, the Academy held several key functions at the Broadmoor.

Saul grimaced and started to speak. Grace cut him short with an icy, "Not here, Mr. Eduardo. We'll talk inside."

She and her partner led everyone up the steps and into a gilded lobby straight out of Victorian England. Saul kept shooting Crenshaw glances and shaking his perfectly blow-dried head. At a bay window with a view of the entrance, the group came to a stop and Grace introduced herself and her partner, Ray. As everyone started shaking hands, Saul Eduardo said, "I want to discuss my concerns."

Grace said, "In a minute, Mr. Eduardo."

"This is the Broadmoor," he said excitedly. "Patrons aren't arrested on our premises. It just isn't done. I insist you reconsider. Surely, this isn't necessary to do here."

His eyes darted over the circle of faces, demanding a response. Ray said wearily, "Mr. Eduardo, we went through this—"

"You're apprehending someone at Senator Smith's press conference. *The senator's press conference*. No, no. I simply can't allow it. I have the hotel's reputation to consider. General, you must have some influence in this matter."

He flashed Crenshaw a dazzling smile.

"I understand your predicament, Saul," General Crenshaw said.

His smile broadened, revealing gleaming caps. "Ah . . ."

"But I'm afraid it's necessary for the police to do this now. Unless you want to accept the responsibility . . ."

"Why, yes. I'll gladly assume—"

". . . for delaying the apprehension of a murder suspect."

Saul's mouth hung open. Obviously, he hadn't known this part of it. "Murder?"

Crenshaw nodded solemnly.

"My God . . ." Saul fingered his bow tie, paused, and fingered it some more. "No, no. Of course not. I couldn't accept responsibility. Is this person dangerous? Will the guests or staff be in danger?"

"We're after a *murderer*," Mother said.

Saul looked at her. "Excuse me?"

"The police have everything under control, Saul," General Crenshaw said smoothly. "There is no danger to anyone. None."

Saul didn't appear convinced. "Mr. Levin will have to be told. He might know some way to keep it out of the papers. This is extremely unfortunate. Most unfortunate."

He hurried away.

The detectives shook their heads, watching him go. "Everything ready?" Malone asked them.

"Almost," Grace said. "We're waiting for Lieutenant Canola to arrive with the warrant. To get our people into the press conference, we had to tip our hand to the senator's security. They'll keep their mouths shut. They're private and won't risk an obstruction count. As I understand it, we'll make the formal arrest, but you'll take the lead in making the charge."

"Yes," Malone said.

Grace and her partner measured Crenshaw, curious about his presence. But they weren't about to ask.

"Better tell them," her partner Ray said to her.

Mother said, "Tell us what?"

"We don't want to rain on your parade," Grace said, "but Ray and I think it might be a good idea to hold off on the arrest until after the press conference."

Mother said, "Because . . ."

Ray said, "The senator's staff doesn't pass through security."

"So Kaitlin could be armed," Mother said, voicing the obvious.

"She isn't," Crenshaw concluded flatly. "She believes

she's won. She'd have no reason to bring a weapon here."

But the two detectives' concerned expressions matched Mother's and Malone's. Kaitlin had killed six people. This was a risk they couldn't take.

"There's no need to change anything," Crenshaw insisted, scowling at the group. "Kaitlin Barlow isn't armed."

The two detectives averted their eyes; they had no desire to go toe to toe with a three-star general. Mother, of course, couldn't care less. "I'm sorry, General. But it's too dangerous to go as planned."

"She's right, sir," Malone said.

"No," Crenshaw said. "Too much is riding on this. We don't wait; we make the arrest now." His tone blunt, commanding. A general giving an order.

Mother shook it off, saying, "It's not your decision, sir."

Her voice was softly apologetic. But that didn't lessen the impact of her words on Crenshaw. He regarded her with astonishment. Generals were accustomed to being obeyed. Always. "Mother, I'm giving you a direct order to proceed—"

"And I'm *telling* you it's not your decision, sir. I'm sorry, but it isn't."

They traded glares. Mother stuck out her jaw, sending the message that she wasn't about to back down. Crenshaw upped the ante, clenching his teeth. He growled, "Mother, if you don't do what the hell I ask—"

He broke off, realizing Malone was shaking his head at him. So were Grace and Ray.

And finally Mother.

"I'm sorry, sir," she said.

Crenshaw gazed at their faces. Slowly, he nodded his acceptance, his anger fading. The harsh reality of Mother's statements had sunk in; it wasn't his decision. Not any longer. He was a general who no longer had a command.

"You're right, Mother," Crenshaw said. "You're absolutely right. I overstepped my authority."

He forced a smile, acting as if this wasn't any big deal. But there was no denying the humiliation in his eyes. "If you'll excuse me . . ."

He moved past them, walking away slowly at first, then with a more determined stride.

"Sir," Mother said, "mind telling us where you are going?"

No response. The general angled past the entrance and headed for a long hallway at the back of the lobby.

"Shit," Mother said.

"Yes," Malone said.

Crenshaw was heading for Senator Smith's press conference.

Chapter 40

THE GENERAL CONTINUED WALKING AWAY FROM them. Watching him, Malone said to Mother, "We can't prevent him from going in . . ."

"No."

"And chances are Kaitlin isn't armed. The risk would be minimal."

"Right."

"Besides, it's not like we have much choice."

She looked at him. "You trying to convince me or yourself?"

"General," Malone called out, "it's okay. We do it your way."

Crenshaw turned and smiled.

Neither Mother nor Malone was upset that Crenshaw had forced their hand; they both understood his need to play a role in the arrest. Once again, it came down to the theme running through this case—guilt and atonement. Crenshaw had abandoned Rachel and, once he'd found her, had been unable to protect her from harm. Unless he was able to redeem himself, achieve a measure of atonement by punishing those he held responsible, his guilt—a parent's guilt—would slowly press down upon him. This burden, coupled with the death of his wife and the humiliating end of his career, had the potential to crush him completely.

Did Malone think that might really occur? No.

But he wasn't about to pile more emotional rocks upon him. He wasn't.

"It's better this way," Malone said, as he and Mother watched Crenshaw walk back over to them. "Better for the general. Better for the Academy."

"It's not a done deal yet."

She was looking out the window at a car coming up the drive. As it passed by, they could clearly see the driver.

It was Tom Canola, arriving with the warrant.

Tom Canola didn't have sirens or lights going; he was still playing it low-key. He swung in behind Malone's Hummer, jumped from the car, and rushed up the front steps. Grace and Ray immediately started toward the entrance to meet him.

Crenshaw joined Mother and Malone. "Everything will work out. You'll see."

"Let's hope so, sir," Malone said.

Crenshaw frowned at something in Malone's voice. "There a problem?"

"We'll know in a minute, sir," Malone said.

Canola had entered the hotel and was talking with his detectives. He appeared surprised at something they said. "Hey, Mother," he called out, glaring at her. "I just got the word about Ms. Barlow. What's the story about you deciding not to wait?"

The three detectives hurried over.

"Now, we have a problem, General," Malone said. "Canola will never go for it. Might even prevent you from interfering."

"He can try," Crenshaw said ominously.

"Easy, General," Mother said. "I can convince him."

This was one of life's mysteries. For some reason, Canola always seemed to do what Mother said. "Mind telling me what you've got on him?" Malone asked her.

She shrugged. "Time."

"Time?"

"Twenty-five years ago we were both young."

It took Malone and Crenshaw a moment. They stared at her.

She actually blushed.

"I'm making the decision," Tom said, walking up. "We're holding off. Pick her up outside when she walks to her car." He sternly eyed Crenshaw. "General, I need you to keep out of this. I mean it."

"Now listen, Lieutenant—"

"Tom," Mother said, moving forward quickly and taking him by the elbow, "let's go over here. Grace, Ray, give us a minute." She led Canola to a corner, away from the detectives.

"It'll be okay, General," Malone said to Crenshaw. "She'll talk him into it."

Just then, Canola suddenly jerked away from Mother and threw up his hands. "You outta your mind? No way."

"You sure?" Crenshaw asked dubiously.

"Watch," Malone said.

It took almost five minutes. Twice Canola tried to walk away, but Mother pulled him back. Finally she looked over to Malone and Crenshaw and nodded.

"I'll be damned," Crenshaw said.

The Utah Room was located on the west end of the Broadmoor, in a wing reserved for conference rooms. The hallway outside was cluttered with an assortment of television paraphernalia and a knot of technicians. Malone couldn't pick out the plainclothes cops he knew were present because most wore jeans and no one wore a badge. Identifying the senator's security detail was another matter.

There were two of them, guarding the closed double doors to the conference room—no-necked linebacker types sporting identical blue blazers with suggestive bulges under their armpits. When the police entourage got within twenty yards, Malone said, "We'll wait here, Tom. We don't want to spring the general on anyone yet."

As the detectives continued, Malone, Mother, and Crenshaw hung out by another conference room. Spotting the approaching cops, one of the security men stepped out to meet them. After a brief conversation, he and Canola walked to the end of the hall, Grace and Ray remaining behind. Rounding a corner, the two men disappeared for several minutes. When they reappeared, Tom gave an exaggerated nod.

"Our cue," Malone said.

Crenshaw led the way, Mother and Malone following. As with the general's entrance outside, more stares greeted him. Several of the media technicians began chattering excitedly; they'd recognized him, but then they should. In Colorado, the Academy was a big deal, and Crenshaw had been in the papers enough.

"What's he doing here?" a blond woman wearing a headset said. "I thought the general and the senator didn't get along."

"They don't," a lanky guy replied. "Better give Bryce a heads-up. Something could be going down."

The woman spoke into her mike. Several other techs who'd been listening in went for cell phones. Neither Malone, Mother, or the general displayed the least bit of concern. By the time the reporters inside the room could react, the show would have begun.

Tom Canola waited for them at the end of the hallway, the security man having returned to his post. "This way," Canola said, turning down an intersecting corridor. "There's another entrance. More private."

After ten paces and a hard right, they came to another man in a blue blazer, standing by a door. "We'll take it from here," Canola told him.

The man nodded and headed back the way they'd come.

"Your show," Canola said to Malone. "Give me time to get in place. When the general makes his move, my people will make theirs." He looked at Crenshaw. "Mother says Ms. Barlow won't spook if she sees you."

"She won't," Crenshaw replied. "She'll assume I'm here to confront the senator."

"You better hope that's the case, sir. 'Cause if she does figure things out and this blows up, it'll get crazy in there. You could be on your own. You understand, sir?"

"Completely, Lieutenant."

"I'm hanging it out big-time, General. This is against department policy."

"I appreciate it, Lieutenant."

"Yeah, well . . ." Canola shook his head unhappily and turned to go. Scowling at Mother, he said, "This is the last time, you hear me. The last fucking time."

He walked away, muttering.

"What?" Mother said, aware that Malone was grinning at her.

"Hmm. Oh, I was just thinking you must have been something twenty-five years ago."

"I was. Guys hit on me all the time."

"Uh-huh."

"You don't think so?"

"Did I say anything?"

"Kiss my ass, Malone. I'd like to see what you look like when you're my age."

"Stop it," Crenshaw ordered. "We have a job to do."

Mother continued to glower at Malone. One thing about her, she could dish it out, but couldn't take it.

Malone concentrated on his watch. "Okay, General," he said, a minute later.

As he and Mother took out their pistols, Crenshaw opened the door.

Chapter 41

THE VOICE OF SENATOR SMITH BOOMED OUT, pontificating as only he could.

". . . charges that I've been too harsh on the military and, in particular, the Air Force Academy. But I think I've been vindicated by the terrible events of this evening. As you know, Coach Ralston and his wife died tragically in an apparent murder/suicide. What you don't know is they were unfairly targeted in a botched investigation, one so thoroughly inept that it has led to at least six additional deaths. In the past twenty-four hours, eight people have died on the Academy grounds. *Eight.* Three were cadets and all but one of the victims was murdered. It's unconscionable. How in God's name could Academy authorities allow this bloodbath to happen? They knew they had a killer loose on the reservation. Yet they were unable or unwilling to take the necessary steps to protect their personnel. And yes, you can quote me. I said *unwilling*. Many of you are familiar with my panel's lead investigator, Ms. Kaitlin Barlow, standing behind me. She was my personal observer during the investigation into the murders. She will confirm my allegations that the military investigators led by Major Malone—a former cadet, I might add—were operating under an agenda to protect the Academy leadership. Some of you might find this revelation shocking, but I, for one, do not. It's a pattern the Academy bureaucracy has displayed since the first harassment allegation came to light last year. Since then, the Academy leadership has yet to discipline a single perpetrator. In point of fact, they haven't even charged anyone. They say it's from a lack of evidence. If you believe that, you're probably a former O. J. Simpson juror or—"

Smatterings of laughter interrupted Smith. Mother whispered to Malone, "So much for Kaitlin speaking up for you."

Malone could only nod. Another lie among many.

Since Kaitlin might put two and two together if she spotted them, he and Mother remained off to the side, out of sight. They kept waiting for Crenshaw to enter the room, but he never did. He stood perhaps a foot back from the doorway and continued to listen. As he did, his jaw muscles slowly flexed into ropes.

Reacting to Mother's impatient scowl, Malone said, "Any time, General."

"Not yet."

"Isn't Tom in place, sir?"

"Someone cracked the other door."

"Then what's the holdup, General?"

Silence.

Malone and Mother traded a cryptic glance. Easing

back, Malone risked a peek. The meeting room was jammed, every seat taken, television cameras lining the back wall. Even though Crenshaw blocked much of his view, Malone caught a glimpse of Senator Smith at the podium. Appearances can be deceiving and they certainly were in his case. A diminutive, bookish man with a trademark shock of unruly white hair, he looked more like a college professor or an accountant than the ruthlessly calculating politician he was. Malone had wondered why the senator hadn't noticed the general, but soon understood. Smith was talking directly into the television cameras, oblivious to anything else. He was a senator running for reelection.

Behind Smith, Malone could make out a severe, graying woman whom he took to be his chief of staff, Marcy Dyers. Kaitlin was beside her, looking stunning as usual. Even now, Malone found it impossible to hate her. But that would come eventually if he was mistaken about her motives. And if not—

He caught his breath. Kaitlin had suddenly looked to the door. He ducked, his heart pounding. "What?" Mother asked.

Malone told her. She swore. "If she saw you—"

"She didn't," Crenshaw said. "She's amused by my presence. She's saying something to the other woman. The reporters have also noticed me. It won't be long."

"Long for what, General?" Malone said. "What are you waiting for?"

Again the general didn't reply. Smith was still talking passionately, ". . . make no mistake about those harassment allegations, people. They *happened*. Impressionable female cadets, your daughters and mine, were systematically preyed upon by a culture and institution that has yet to be held accountable. As the people of the great state of Colorado know, I have long championed women's issues and was the first senator to bring this sordid affair to light. I intend to see justice served and mark my words, it will be. I'm gratified to report that many of my Senate colleagues share my view. Currently, my committee is crafting legislation that will compel the military and the Academy—"

He fell silent.

There was a long pause. A murmur rose up from the audience.

Then Smith: "What's *he* doing here? Who invited *him?*"

A woman answered, her response too faint to understand.

Smith: "I don't give a damn how it will look. I don't want to talk to him. Get him the hell out of here, Marcy."

This time Marcy Dyer's response was audible. She said, "Yes, Senator. Sir, your microphone is still on. I suggest you—"

"You listening? I want him *gone.*"

Crenshaw finally stepped through the door.

Instant turmoil.

The TV cameras swung around to Crenshaw and flashes popped off at a dizzying rate. From the back of the room, reporters and cameramen rushed forward to shove a microphone or a lens into Crenshaw's face.

Those who'd been sitting rose, calling out questions, seemingly all at once.

"General, what's your response to the senator's charges of a cover-up? Is there a sexist mind-set at the Academy?"

"General, did the military botch the investigation into the cadets' deaths?"

"Is the killer still at large?"

"What's your reaction to being relieved of command?"

And so on.

Malone and Mother peered into the room. They were shielded by the frenetic activity, and there was little risk of being seen. Reporters crowded around Crenshaw as he walked. He calmly pushed through, ignoring them. The graying lady, Marcy Dyers, confronted him midway to the podium and said loudly, "General, I must insist you leave—"

Crenshaw continued past her. She wheeled around to follow, but was swallowed up by the reporters. Smith got into the act, saying into the microphone, "General, I'm telling you to leave. We have nothing to discuss. Your presence is disruptive and I want you to go."

But Crenshaw kept coming, his eyes fixed on Smith in an intimidating stare. The senator swallowed nervously, looking to the opposite door, the one that was ajar. "Security!" he called out. "Get in here and remove this man!"

The door never opened.

Crenshaw was no more than ten feet away from Smith now. The senator became increasingly agitated.

"Security? Did you hear me? Get in here and remove—
Who the hell are you? Let her go."

A man and woman had roughly accosted Kaitlin. As
Smith's shrill voice reverberated over the speakers,
everyone in the room stopped and looked.

The two plainclothes police officers each had Kaitlin
by an arm. She made no attempt to resist as the woman
quickly patted her down. "We're police, Senator," the
man said to Smith. "We have a warrant for Ms. Barlow's
arrest."

At this statement, the room hushed completely.
Smith was incredulous. "*What?* You're arresting her?
This is absurd. This woman is a trusted member of my
staff. Release her."

"They can't do that, Senator," Crenshaw said. "She's
being arrested for murder."

Smith swung around to him. "You're behind this. I
was right about you. You're an embarrassment to your
uniform. You overstepped your authority, General.
You'll pay for this, so help me."

"We have proof she committed the killings at the
Academy, Senator. Ask Lieutenant Canola of the
Colorado Springs police. He'll confirm what I'm
saying."

"I sure will, Senator," Canola called out.

He and his detectives had entered the room, accompanied by the security men and two more plainclothes
officers. As the cops continued to the podium, the security personnel detached themselves and hovered by the
door. By now, Malone and Mother were also moving
forward. "Senator," Canola said, waving a thick enve-

lope, "I've got the warrant here. We have more than enough probable cause to arrest Ms. Barlow."

All eyes turned to Kaitlin. She was dazed, unable to comprehend what was happening. The woman cop took out cuffs and twisted one of Kaitlin's arms behind her back. Smith appeared on the verge of a coronary, realizing the cameras were all trained on Kaitlin for a front-page photo he couldn't allow.

He screamed at the cop, "Don't you dare handcuff her. Not in here."

She hesitated. "Senator, she's being arrested—"

"You do and you'll walk a beat for the rest of your life."

The cop looked nervously to Canola. He nodded and she backed off.

"Lieutenant," Smith snarled at him, "that warrant is based on fabricated evidence. General Crenshaw is behind this. He orchestrated this stunt to deflect suspicion from himself and embarrass me."

"Those are serious allegations, Senator," Crenshaw said. "You're accusing me of murder and falsely incriminating Ms. Barlow."

"You bet I am, General," Smith flung back. "Do you *deny* you're a suspect?"

Crenshaw paused.

Smith grinned; he thought he had Crenshaw.

"Tell you what, Senator," Crenshaw said, looking out at the reporters, "suppose we debate the issue and let them decide whom the evidence implicates. If everyone will have a seat, we'll get started."

The crowd began returning to their chairs. Smith's

grin faded; Crenshaw was too confident. "What is this?" he demanded suspiciously. "What are you up to, General?"

"The truth, Senator. Only the truth."

"I don't know what kind of game you're playing. But I assure you I have no intention of taking part in your theatrics."

"No?"

"This is *my* press conference, General. You have no right to be here. And I'm telling you to leave."

"Apparently," Crenshaw said, smiling at the audience, "the senator isn't a proponent of free speech. For months, he's criticized the Academy's policies, attacked my credibility, and accused us of knowingly covering up various crimes, including rape. Now he's gone so far as to imply I'm a murderer and still won't allow me the courtesy of a rebuttal. I don't know about you, but it seems to me the senator is the one who is covering things up."

"The general's got you there, Senator," a reporter called out. "You can't have it both ways." "Let him talk, Senator," another said. A chorus of voices rose up in support.

Smith's face turned bright red. He sputtered angrily, "This press conference is over. Everyone is to go immediately. Did you hear me? You're all to leave."

But no one was paying attention to him. The reporters continued to take their seats. "Sit down, Senator," Crenshaw said. "You'll want to hear what I have to say. It's for your own good. I don't think you want to be caught in more lies."

"Lies?" Smith said. "You saying *I'm* a liar? By God, you're going to regret— What's this for?" His voice like ice.

Crenshaw had thrust out a packet to him.

"A tape. I taped your calls to me, Senator."

"You *what?*"

"What's on the tape, General?" a reporter asked.

"Derogatory comments that show the senator's bias. He made a series of threats against the Academy as an institution and me as its superintendent—"

Smith spoke into the microphone. "Don't listen to him. He's the one who's lying."

"The tape," Crenshaw said. "Just listen to the tape and decide who's telling the truth."

Smith fell silent. He had no response to the tape and he knew it. He looked at Crenshaw with hate and muttered, "You son of a bitch."

Behind him, Marcy Dyers squeaked, "Senator, the microphone—"

A reporter said, "Can we quote you on that, Senator?" Laughter erupted. Someone else said, "We just got our headline, fellas." More laughter.

Laughter directed at Smith. He couldn't take it.

Snorting and spitting furiously, he spun toward Marcy Dyers. "Call the district attorney. I want a meeting tonight. Also get the names and badge numbers of every policeman involved." He glared at Canola, standing no more than ten feet away. "I intend to sue every one of them for false arrest, starting with the lieutenant. We'll see how long these trumped-up accusations will last." He took Kaitlin by the hand and said, "Don't worry. This is a pure fabrication and I'll prove it. Once I confer with the DA, you'll be released and we'll get to the bottom of . . ."

Up to now, Kaitlin had been completely passive. She hadn't said a word in her own defense, and as she listened to Smith, her only response was to nod docilely.

So everyone was relaxed. The cops were no longer gripping Kaitlin tightly. Canola and his detectives had holstered their pistols, as had Mother. Their complacency was understandable; Kaitlin was in custody and had been checked for weapons. Unarmed, what could she possibly do against a roomful of police?

The female cop screamed.

Chapter 42

IT WAS A SUDDEN, FEROCIOUS MOVEMENT.

One instant Kaitlin had been passively listening to Smith. A split second later, she jerked away from him, violently twisted out of the male cop's grip, and stomped on the woman detective's instep. As the cop cried out, Kaitlin spun toward her, snared the pistol from beneath her coat, and wrenched it free. Realizing what was happening, the woman frantically clawed at Kaitlin. A flat crack and she fell back, a reddening stain over her right breast. The male cop shouted, "Oh, shit. Oh, fuck." He attempted to wrestle Kaitlin to the ground. But at six feet, she was as tall as he was and shoved him back hard. The cop stumbled, fumbling for his gun. Too late. Kaitlin shot him in the head and he toppled in a mist of blood and brain. A lady sitting near the front row covered her face and screamed.

By now other people were shouting and the room was in chaos. At the first shot, the audience reacted with confusion. At the second, they sprang from their chairs and rushed for the exits. A few chose to remain and ducked low, out of the line of fire. They were trampled by those bent on escape.

Taken by surprise, the police wasted several crucial seconds pulling their weapons. Before they could fire at Kaitlin, she'd swung Smith around, using him as a shield, the pistol against his head. Moving quickly back, she pulled him with her, keeping everyone in sight—the Colorado cops, security, and Mother and Malone to her front, and Crenshaw and Marcy Dyers on her right. On the floor, the female officer was moaning with her eyes closed. Her partner lay crumpled several feet away, a grisly hole in the back of his scalp.

"My God, Kaitlin," the senator said, staring at the carnage in horror. "You shot them. Why? What possible reason could you—"

"Shut up, Senator."

"It's true? You killed those cadets—"

She twisted his collar hard. "I said *shut up*."

The senator tried to breathe and gagged. She loosened her grip and he coughed uncontrollably. The room had emptied except for a handful of reporters and cameramen crouching at the back. Kaitlin looked into the TV cameras and smiled grimly.

Canola said, "Ms. Barlow, you can't get away. Let the senator go and put down the gun."

She gazed at him with contempt. "You have ten seconds, Lieutenant. Drop your weapons or I shoot the senator."

Smith said, "For chrissakes, do what she says."

Canola shook his head. "No deals, Ms. Barlow. You're surrounded. It's over. Let the senator go."

"Seven seconds," Kaitlin said coolly.

"Ms. Barlow—"

"I'm not bluffing, Lieutenant."

"I can't agree—"

"Six, five, four . . ."

As she counted down, she jammed the gun barrel against Smith's temple hard enough to make him yelp. "Jesus," he shrieked, "she means it. *Put down your guns.*"

But Canola and his officers made no move to disarm.

"I'm sorry, Senator," Kaitlin said. She sounded genuinely sad.

Smith's knees buckled. "No. I beg you not to—"

"*Christina, don't!*"

Kaitlin visibly started. Then she went still, frowning, as if confused by what she'd heard.

"Don't do it, Christina. You've won. What's the point now?"

She slowly faced Malone. "Christina. You called me Christina."

"Yes." He still had his gun on her, but she didn't seem concerned. Maybe she didn't think he'd really shoot.

"Then you know," Kaitlin said. "You understand why I had to do this."

"I think so."

"They raped me, Malone. They destroyed my life. The Academy and the military didn't care. No one ever paid. There was no *justice.*"

She spat out the last word bitterly. Out of the corner of his eye, Malone caught movement. He was confused by it. He said to Kaitlin, "The Academy tried to find who raped you. I know you don't believe—"

"Like *hell.*" She glared furiously at Mother. "You knew it was Ralston. Every cadet knew it was him. He hit on me, became enraged when I wouldn't sleep with him. But you never punished him. Why? *Why?*"

Her eyes had a wild glint. Mother made the smart decision and said simply, "I'm sorry, Christina."

"Fourteen years. I waited fourteen years for justice. But you know what they did. What *you* did."

Kaitlin swung around to confront Crenshaw. "You made him the head football coach. The bastard who raped me. I knew then he'd never be punished. You didn't *want* to punish him."

Like Mother, Crenshaw made the decision not to antagonize her. He stood with his arms folded, saying nothing.

"The Academy was wrong," Malone said. "But that doesn't justify what you did. You killed so many people. Innocent people who—"

She laughed harshly. "Malone, you still don't see it. You don't understand at all."

"Understand what?"

"You. You're to blame, not me. I needed justice and you needed proof Ralston was a rapist. So I did what I had to do. I *gave* you the proof."

Malone caught movement again. This time he understood. Mother tensed; she noticed it, too. Kaitlin's attention was on Malone, and he realized he had to keep it there. "Christina," he said, pointing to the wounded cop, "that officer will die if she doesn't get medical help. I'd like to take her outside, where paramedics can treat her." He slowly bent, placing his gun on the floor.

"You crazy?" Canola said.

"You going to let her die, Tom?"

Canola didn't reply. Malone began moving forward.

"Stop, Malone," Kaitlin said.

He kept walking.

"Dammit, *stop*."

Malone obeyed only because he'd reached the female cop. She was still breathing, her face ashen. Turning to Kaitlin, he saw she'd shifted the barrel from Smith and was pointing it at him. He searched her face for an indication of feeling, some connection to the past she believed they'd shared.

But there was nothing except an icy stare.

"You do what you have to do," he said. "But remember one thing, Christina . . ."

He looked into her eyes. "I loved you."

Three little words. Would they work?

Several tense seconds passed until Malone got his answer. Almost imperceptibly, Kaitlin's expression began to thaw. Then a smile tugged at her lips, and when she spoke, her voice was tight with emotion. "I never cared for Ralston. I only pretended to. You know that it was always you. There's never been anyone but you."

"I know."

"All these years, I wanted to call you, tell you. But I was afraid you wouldn't understand."

"I do understand."

She smiled shyly. "When this is over, maybe we can go away. Just the two of us."

"I'd like that."

"Now," she said. "Let's go now."

"I need to take care of the officer first. It'll just take a few minutes. Okay?"

Kaitlin hesitated, then nodded. "But first tell them to put down their guns."

"Not a chance," Canola said. "She could kill us all."

"Do it, Tom," Malone said wearily.

"Malone, our department's policy is—"

"Tom," Mother said, setting her pistol down. "Just put the guns down."

"Mother—"

"Do it, Tom, or she'll die."

Canola looked at the injured officer and back at Mother. "All right, but if she shoots us all, I hope to hell you're happy." He lowered his pistol to the floor, the other four officers following suit. Malone said, "You guys back there, too."

The security men reluctantly laid their weapons down.

"It's true?" Kaitlin said to Malone. "You did love me?"

"Yes. Very much."

"We'll go somewhere warm. To a beach. I always liked the beach."

"Anywhere you like. We'll leave for the airport from here."

Canola and Ray and Grace came over to pick up the female cop. As Malone bent to help, he saw Kaitlin's eyes were shiny with excitement. The reality of her situation didn't matter; nothing did except being with Malone. Turning away from her, he told himself that this was necessary, that he had no—

A gunshot.

Chapter 43

A DEAFENING CRACK FOLLOWED BY CRIES OF SUR-
prise. Malone had to will himself to look, afraid of what
he would see.

Crenshaw stood perhaps a dozen paces from Kaitlin,
the pistol pointed at her. She was turning toward him
with a bewildered expression, and for a moment,
Malone thought the general had missed. Then he realized Kaitlin had lost her grip on the pistol and it was
falling to the floor. Senator Smith stood trembling, saying, "Oh, God . . . Oh, God . . ." Kaitlin let go of his collar, but instead of escaping, the senator remained rigid
with fear. In a flash, Canola was upon him, pulling him
to safety, while Ray and another cop tackled Kaitlin.

"Cuffs," Canola ordered, joining in. "Get the cuffs on
her."

Malone and Mother hurried over and saw Kaitlin
bleeding from a wound in her forearm.

Seeing Malone, Kaitlin began to thrash wildly.
"Malone. Tell them to let me go. We're going away. You
promised. Tell them."

"Hold her," Canola said. "Dammit, hold her tight."

"I'm trying," Ray answered. "But Jesus, she's strong."

"Malone, get out of here," Canola ordered. "You're exciting her."

"What the hell?"

The third cop had pulled Kaitlin's wig loose. He stared at her in horror. Kaitlin kicked and shrieked, "Put it back. *Put it back.* Malone, don't look. Don't look."

But it was too late. Everyone was looking at her; they couldn't help it. Even though Malone knew what to expect, the sight shook him. Her bald scalp was mottled with wisps of hair and countless disfiguring scars and fresh scabs. It completely transformed her from a beauty into something hideous. Some kind of monster.

Kaitlin began to cry. "I told you not to look, Malone. Why did you look?"

She twisted and bucked with a crazed violence. The police fought to slip on cuffs, but she kept yanking her arms free, oblivious to the pain from her wound. "Leg cuffs," Canola said. "Grace, tell backup we need goddamn leg cuffs."

"Got it, Lieutenant. I'm talking to dispatch now." Grace was bending over the wounded detective, talking on a cell phone. Seconds later, she announced, "Backup units and paramedics are two minutes out."

"Will Jill make it?" Canola asked, panting from the struggle. "Will she make it?"

"She's got a chance, Lieutenant. Bullet missed her lungs, but she's losing blood."

Kaitlin continued to sob hysterically. "I told you

not to look, Malone. You ruined everything. I told you not to look . . ." The detectives finally managed to cuff her, but it still took three of them to keep her on the floor.

"Malone." Canola glanced up, his face streaked with Kaitlin's blood. "I told you to beat it."

"Kaitlin," Malone said loudly. "Come back. Tell Christina to go away. Come back, Kaitlin."

But his words had no effect. She continued to rage at him. She was lost in a world only she could understand.

"Malone, you're not helping. For the last time—"

"We're leaving, Tom," Mother said, pulling on Malone's arm. "C'mon. There's nothing you can do for her now."

Malone swallowed hard, nodding.

They crossed over to Crenshaw, who was watching Senator Smith and Marcy Dyers, seated in the front row. The senator was hugging himself, rocking back and forth, saying, "She's crazy. She would have killed me. You saw it. I almost died, Marcy. Kaitlin committed those murders. They'll blame me. You know they will. That bastard has a tape. It'll be misinterpreted . . ." The camera crews at the back of the room ran up and began taping him. Smith was so out of it, he didn't seem to notice. Someone must have passed the word that the situation was under control because more press streamed into the room.

When the camera flashes went off, Canola roared, "This is a crime scene. I want this room cleared. Reggie. Bill—"

Joined by security, the officers rushed toward the

reporters. "You heard the lieutenant. Everyone out. This is a crime scene. Move. You'll get a statement later."

But this was a huge story, and the press were determined to get what they could. As the reporters darted around to avoid the cops, several shouted questions to Crenshaw. He didn't seem to hear them; he was completely focused on Smith.

"Sir," Mother said gently to him, "you're wasting your time; he'll never thank you."

Crenshaw didn't reply; she had to touch his arm before he acknowledged her.

"It's not that, Mother. I couldn't give a damn if he thanks me." Crenshaw was still holding his gun, the one he'd hidden under his coat. This was the movement Malone and Mother had noticed. His attempt to show them he was armed.

"I suppose Canola will need this," he said, handing the pistol to Mother.

"And a statement, sir."

Crenshaw didn't answer her. He was staring at the downed officers with a pained expression. He sighed. "If I'd listened, none of this would have happened. But I gave in to my hate. I wanted to ruin Smith and a man died."

"Sir, the same thing might have happened if we'd picked her up outside."

"Except it didn't happen outside. It happened here."

"Sir, a little advice. This is baggage you don't need."

"I'm sorry, but I'm responsible."

"Now, sir. Let it go now. This minute. Because if you

don't . . ." Mother trailed off, looking toward Kaitlin in an ominous way.

"Come on, Mother," Crenshaw said, bristling slightly at the implication. "You think I could end up like her?"

"Guilt over her sister's death caused her to snap, sir."

"That's hardly comparable to my situation."

She gazed at him evenly. "Then why did you bring the gun, General?"

Crenshaw was silent.

"You were going to kill Kaitlin," Mother said quietly. "You ask me, that's a little crazy."

He gave her a hard look. "I didn't kill her."

"No," Mother admitted. "You didn't."

They were both quiet. Crenshaw was again looking at the downed officers, his face heavy with self-recrimination. Mother shook her head as if to say, *I tried.*

Before he realized it, Malone was moving toward Crenshaw. He said, "Sir, Mother's right. Let it go. All of it. The guilt you feel over Rachel's death, what happened here. You have to get past it, sir."

Crenshaw's jaw tightened. "Malone, I don't want to discuss—"

But the words poured from Malone with an intensity that surprised even himself. "We're all human, sir. That's not a simplistic observation, but a fact. We *all* make mistakes. Mistakes we can't correct no matter how much we want to. You can't change the kind of father you were or what happened here tonight. It's done, over. All you can do is move on. So do it, sir. *Move on.*"

Malone fell silent, breathing hard. Crenshaw and Mother stared at him. "Jesus," she said, "where'd that come from?"

"It appears," Crenshaw said, squinting at Malone, "you've done a great deal of thinking about this."

Malone hesitated. "Yes, sir."

"You must have serious skeletons in your closet?"

"Including being a terrible cadet."

Crenshaw smiled . . . almost.

"General," one of the last remaining reporters hollered out as he was being herded from the room. "That tape you mentioned? When are you going to release it?"

Crenshaw glanced to Smith, who had his head in his hands.

"There is no tape," he said.

Smith and Marcy looked to him in surprise.

"What?" the reporter said. "General, you told us you had a tape."

"There is no tape," Crenshaw repeated.

Smith gave Crenshaw an odd smile. The general returned it. Grace closed the door behind the reporter and the room became quiet except for Kaitlin's continual raging. Marcy Dyers coaxed an unsteady Smith to his feet and they left, escorted through the media swarm by security. Before the door shut behind them, the senator turned to look back at Crenshaw. And nodded once.

"Maybe I was wrong, sir," Mother said. "Maybe that was a thank-you."

"Maybe."

A minute later, uniformed officers finally arrived, accompanied by two teams of paramedics. The cops had plastic leg restraints and with some effort, Canola and Ray managed to immobilize Kaitlin and strap her to a gurney.

Crenshaw anxiously hovered over the paramedics as they treated the wounded officer. When they told him she would recover, the general's relief was evident, but only for a few moments. Looking at the dead cop, his face again became somber, a reflection of his difficulty in following Mother and Malone's advice.

"I want to know if he has a family, children," he said, "if there's anything they need."

Malone and Mother nodded.

Closing his eyes, Crenshaw mouthed a prayer. When he opened them, he looked suddenly tired. "I'd like to go home now," he said.

Since this was Canola's show, there wasn't any reason for them to stay. Because of the shooting, Crenshaw still needed to provide an official statement, but that could be done later. "I'll call you, Tom," Mother said to Canola, after giving him Crenshaw's gun. "Set up a time next week."

"Don't do me any more favors, Mother." Tom scowled at her, wiping his face with a handkerchief. He looked like hell; his hair was mussed, his shirt untucked and streaked with sweat and blood, and one of his jacket pockets had been torn off.

She winked at him. "Easy, tough guy. I've done you plenty of favors in the past and you never complained."

Canola reddened. He was smart enough to keep his mouth shut.

Mother grinned, trailing Crenshaw and Malone to the exit. "General," Malone said, "there's a question concerning Kaitlin I'd like cleared up."

"Why I didn't kill Kaitlin when I had the chance?"

"Yes, sir."

Crenshaw came to a stop, studying Malone. "You really don't know?"

Malone and Mother shook their heads.

"Look."

Crenshaw nodded their attention to Kaitlin, who was being wheeled out the other door. Even strapped down, she continued to thrash and scream. It was an unsettling image and Crenshaw shook his head pityingly. He said, "I wanted you to be wrong about her, Malone. But you weren't wrong. The footprints proved it. I had to ask myself if I could kill someone who didn't know what she was doing, a person whom we had a hand in creating. In the end, I couldn't and I'm glad. I gave in to my hate once tonight and look what happened." His eyes sought out Malone. "This is one aspect you neglected to mention. Along with mistakes, humans also have the capacity for doing what's right. Believe me, that's much easier to live with."

He opened the door and walked out into the hall. Immediately, the reporters converged, peppering him with questions. Drawing himself upright, Crenshaw moved through them with a regal grace, looking every inch a general.

Watching him, Mother said to Malone, "I still can't

believe he didn't kill her. I mean, that's why he came here."

"He's a man of character," Malone replied, as if that said it all.

In this case, it did.

Leaving the room, Malone could still hear Kaitlin's screams. He knew he would for the rest of his life.

Negotiating the media gauntlet, none of them intended to answer any questions. But there was one Malone couldn't ignore.

It was asked by a journalist who'd witnessed his confrontation with Kaitlin. "Agent Malone, you kept calling her Christina Barlow. Is that her real name or an alias?"

"Neither. Christina was her sister. She died a number of years ago."

"Why would you call her by her dead sister's name?" another reporter asked.

"Because that's who Ms. Barlow believed she was."

The faces walking beside him registered complete confusion. "Lieutenant Canola will brief you on the details," Malone said. "All you need to know now is her name is Kaitlin Barlow."

Chapter 44

On the return trip to the Academy, Crenshaw's character again manifested itself.

The general spent most of the time on the phone, first to the Com, giving him a heads-up and arranging a meeting, and then to the SECDEF, briefing him at length. During this second conversation, Crenshaw actually argued with the SECDEF. Initially, Malone and Mother assumed he was emboldened because his career was over and he had nothing to lose. But it soon became apparent the general would have pursued this issue even if he'd still been a player in the promotion game.

"Mr. Secretary," he said, "I don't profess to be a psychiatrist. But there's little doubt Kaitlin Barlow had a split personality and became her dead sister, Christina. Agent Malone initially considered this possibility when he recalled hearing her converse with someone even though she was apparently alone. There was also an odd phone call wherein Ms. Barlow was unusually docile and seemed fearful of— Fine, sir, I'll get to the point. It's this: Like it or not, we have some responsibility for

Kaitlin Barlow's crimes. Had we apprehended her sister's rapists, none of this would have happened. Sir, don't misunderstand me. I'm not saying we *caused* her insanity, at least not directly. But there's no denying we provided an outlet for it. Excuse me, sir?"

Crenshaw listened, scowling. "*Our* culpability, sir," he went on. "I'm asking for a public acknowledgment of our culpability. The investigator originally assigned to Christina Barlow's rape case was pressured to drop it." At this, Mother nodded emphatically. "Correct, sir. Coach Ralston had been suspected of being the rapists' ringleader. I understand your concerns about opening ourselves to more criticism, but considering the media scrutiny Ms. Barlow will receive, that point is moot. We're sure to be vilified over our handling of her sister's rape. Our only defense is to be seen as doing something proactive. I propose we determine whether there are other women similar to Ms. Barlow. Women whose cases occurred before the ten-year window of the Senate investigation— Mr. Secretary, please. Sir, if you'll let me— *Of course* we might uncover other cases. That's a risk we have to accept, Mr. Secretary. We have to be seen as genuinely trying to do the right thing. How else can we expect to negate criticism—"

Crenshaw shook his head in frustration. "Sir, that's your decision. But I'm retiring next month and when interviewed, I intend to be candid. *Completely* candid. I'll explain how the Academy does not have a system biased against women and never did. But in the same breath, I'm also going to admit we, as an institution, could have been more supportive of those who'd alleged sexual harassment in the past. Sir, I respectfully disagree; I don't consider it an admission of wrongdoing. Even if that's how it's interpreted, we are obligated to follow this course as a matter of conscience. As the superintendent I've tried to instill in cadets a code of honor and ethics. If leaders like you and me don't live up to that code, how can we expect them to adhere—"

Crenshaw broke off, listening. This time it appeared to be good news. He nodded and smiled. "Thank you, Mr. Secretary. In the long run, you'll see it will be to the military's benefit. Now, now, sir, please. That's a little strong. Blackmail? Since when is the truth considered blackmail? Of course, I don't question your integrity. Quite the contrary. I knew you'd agree because you do have integrity." He grinned. "No, I'm not shining up to you, sir, and I definitely have no interest in politics. Yes, sir, I'll be meeting with the commandant tonight to craft a press release. We'll send it to your office for approval. Good night, sir."

Clicking off, Crenshaw looked at Mother and Malone in the semidarkness. "You heard?" he asked.

"Enough, sir," Mother said. "We're going to reevaluate all the old rape and harassment allegations."

"In accordance with the procedures you've been following. Determine the validity of the charges and whether the cases were prematurely shelved."

"It'll be a waste of time, sir. We're batting zero as it is and you're talking going back twenty-nine years. If the investigators then couldn't find anything worth pursuing, we sure won't come up with anything now."

"You're preaching to the choir, Mother. I doubt if anything will be found."

"Then why go to all this trouble?"

"Ask Malone." Crenshaw gave him a knowing smile.

"Mistakes," Malone said to Mother. "The general wants to prove you can correct past mistakes."

"At least try," Crenshaw said with feeling. "I owe it to Rachel to try."

Settling back into his seat, he gazed into the darkness, saying nothing more.

It was after 11:00 P.M. when Malone rolled up to the superintendent's mansion. The Com's blue staff car was waiting for them in the circular driveway, parked behind Mother's pickup. The Com immediately got out and started over.

Crenshaw cracked his door. "Give me a minute, Tim."

The Com obediently stopped.

"You did a good job," Crenshaw said to Mother and Malone.

They nodded. "But it's not quite over, sir," Mother added.

"No . . ."

It was the single remaining loose end they had to tie up. They had to prove that Major Tupper had been Rachel Owen's lover. Crenshaw said, "You'll interview him Monday?"

"Yes, sir," Mother said. "If he doesn't confess, we'll take him to the hospital for a blood sample."

"Kaitlin," the general said. "She must have believed

Ralston was the father of Rachel's baby. That's why she killed her."

Malone and Mother nodded. If anything, this realization heightened the tragedy of Rachel's death. That it had been so senseless.

Crenshaw was quiet for a while, thinking about that.

He sighed. "Mother, you mind if I talk to Malone alone?"

"No, sir," she said, surprised. "Of course not. I'll call you tomorrow, Malone."

"Not too early."

She got out and closed the door. Malone waited expectantly, but Crenshaw was in no hurry to talk. They watched Mother briefly converse with the Com before she drove off. As her taillights faded, the Com focused impatiently on Crenshaw.

But he took no notice. He seemed content to sit quietly. Possibilities danced through Malone's head about the general's reluctance to speak. None were good. Surrendering to his anxiety, Malone finally said, "General, is it that . . . bad?"

"I'm very . . . ashamed."

Malone blinked. "Sir?"

Crenshaw looked at him. "I should have told you this years earlier, right after it happened. Do you know why I've always questioned your character?"

Malone knew this was too easy. "I thought . . . I thought it was because I quit on you, let you down— Then what, sir?" He saw the anticipated head shake.

"Your father," Crenshaw said. "Your father called me. He told me you'd gotten into trouble . . . serious trouble . . . and had no business being at the Academy."

Malone felt the air go out of him. "He . . . he told you about the arrests?"

"Among other things."

"What else, sir? What else did he say?"

"Malone, that's water under—"

"Sir, please. I want to know. I have a right to know."

Crenshaw hesitated, clearly reluctant. "Your father used words like *wild* and *spoiled*. You became involved with a group of young men he described as thugs and you stayed out of jail only because of your grandfather's influence. Your grandfather was desperate to get you discipline and essentially paid off a congressman to appoint you to the Academy—"

"Sir, that's enough."

Crenshaw became silent.

Malone had thought he could handle it, but he couldn't. He was furious and humiliated. As if walking out on him and his mother wasn't enough, his father had to sell him out to the one person whose opinion mattered. "Sir, there's nothing I can say except . . . except that my father is a son of a bitch."

"Malone, I didn't bring this up to discuss—"

But Malone was too angry to hold back. He went on bitterly, "As far as that bastard was concerned, I didn't exist. He had another family and another life. Sure, I was out of control for a while, but he was never around. You know what it's like when your own father doesn't give a damn—"

"Malone, this isn't about you. It's about *me*."

Malone frowned at him.

"My mistake, not yours." Crenshaw leaned close, speaking animatedly. "So you got into scrapes when you were young. Listen, I wasn't exactly a choirboy myself. My neighborhood, you couldn't be. What I'm trying to say is I unfairly prejudged you. I questioned your character and kept waiting for you to screw up, but you never did. At least not until you wanted to get us to throw you out." Malone was about to speak. Crenshaw said sharply, "Don't explain about the booze in your room. You obviously had your reasons for wanting to leave. Maybe I was a part of that reason. Probably was.

"You had potential, Malone. I saw it from the start and knew what you could be if you applied yourself. I should have encouraged you. It was my job to encourage you. But I couldn't get past the doubt your father implanted. And guess what? He was wrong and so was I. You have money; you didn't need to come back into the military. Yet you did, to prove yourself. And you have. You did a helluva job today. You didn't know how Kaitlin would react, how much of Christina was a part of her. Yet you put your life on the line tonight. You want, I'll call your father and tell him how wrong he was. Hell, I'd love to tell him."

He paused, smiling at Malone. "And you know something, you're right about him. He's a son of a bitch."

Malone was at a loss what to say. The magnanimity of Crenshaw's gesture overwhelmed him. This was a man who had lost a daughter and a career, yet still felt compelled to set the record straight.

"Thank you, sir," was all Malone could manage.

"I should thank you, Malone. You gave me a gift I could never repay. You gave me closure. I now know . . . why." He patted Malone on the shoulder and climbed from the car.

"General . . ."

Crenshaw leaned down.

Malone fought the impulse welling up within him. But there was nothing to be achieved by getting into this now.

"I'm sorry about Rachel, sir. I'm sorry about . . . everything."

Crenshaw smiled sadly. "Do me a favor, Malone. You try and move on and so will I. Deal?"

"Yes, sir."

"Good night, Malone."

"Good night, sir."

As Malone drove away, he was gripped by an unsettling realization. What if his father's call to Crenshaw hadn't been motivated by vindictiveness for his own son? What if his father thought he was doing the right thing?

What if his father knew?

Chapter 45

SOLITUDE.

Sitting on his patio in the dark and cold and sipping his second drink, Malone felt comforted by the solitude. He was exhausted and desperately wanted to decompress enough to sleep. He was tense and unsettled, the day's events swirling around in his mind, refusing to let go. So many deaths, too many . . .

He thought of the tragic irony that had led to the murders of Rachel Owen and Mary Zinnel, who died because they were convenient pawns in a twisted game of revenge. He thought of Mrs. Owen and the murdered security cop, and Cadet Jefferson and Agent Kranski, who were killed so the game could continue. And Laura Ralston, who so loved her husband that she ended both their lives to spare him the humiliation of a trial and prison. He thought about General Crenshaw's reassuring words to him and how he didn't deserve them. He thought about his own culpability and how he wished he could have prevented the killings, if only he'd known how.

As he sat drinking and contemplating the darkness, Malone thought about his childhood and his father and the nights he had spent as a kid, praying things could have been different. He thought about his past and his future and the man he wanted to be. He thought about a lot of things.

But mostly, he thought about Kaitlin. More than anyone, she manifested the theme of guilt and atonement. In a tragic accident, she'd taken Christina's life and reciprocated in the only way she knew how, by giving Christina hers. Not consciously, but at some level she offered the gift of her life and it was accepted. After that came the descent into a hate-fueled madness.

"I understand," Malone had told Kaitlin tonight.

And he did . . . finally.

As Crenshaw had concluded, if Christina's rapists had been caught, the focus of Kaitlin's hate would have been removed and there would have been no killing. But the rapists hadn't been caught and her hate had simmered year after year, until it reached a critical mass and exploded.

Malone dwelled on this ultimate irony. Specifically, on the possibility that there was another case similar to Christina's.

On this point, Crenshaw was mistaken. Malone had seen the old files. Most contained unprovable "he said, she said" harassment cases—a pinch in the ass, a lewd comment, a crude proposal. Less than a dozen involved actual rape charges, and those often followed consensual kissing and petting, invariably when both parties were drunk. None involved violence.

No, there weren't more cases like Christina's, because the Academy screening system generally worked. Eagle Scouts and student body presidents rarely became rapists. In fact, to Malone's knowledge, there was only one.

Shaking his head, he drained his drink and went inside for a refill. As he was about to return onto the patio, his phone rang. It was Mother; she couldn't sleep either.

"I knew you'd still be up. You doing okay?"

"No."

"You drunk?"

"Pretty close."

"You meant what you said? You really loved her? Christina, I mean?"

"I loved . . . the moments we had. When we first met, she had an innocence."

"Until you changed her."

She was stating a fact rather than criticizing him. Still, it stung. "Yes."

"What'd Crenshaw have to say?"

"Nothing much."

"Bullshit."

He sighed. "Mother, it was a private conversation. It had nothing to do with the case."

"Yeah, yeah. Quit stalling. You know you'll tell me. You always do."

"Sorry. Not this time."

"Have a heart; I'm dying here."

"I'll send flowers. 'Night, Mother."

"Just a sec. I meant to ask earlier. Kaitlin mentioned something that bothered me. She said you told her you reopened the case of Christina's rape. But that was me. I was the one who pushed for it."

"I was trying to gain her trust, get her to confide in me."

"That's all?"

"That's all."

A pause. He wasn't sure if she was buying it.

"Good night, Mother," Malone said firmly.

Cradling the phone, Malone felt a churning and knew what he had to do.

Character.

General Crenshaw had always defined character as the ultimate predictor of conduct. People with character did what was right no matter how hard it was or how much it cost them. It was a lesson Malone had learned only after leaving the Academy. Since then, he'd tried to live up to that standard and often failed.

Like tonight.

During his conversation with Crenshaw, Malone had been overcome with the sudden urge to do the right thing. But as always, self-preservation won out. It's why he'd joined the OSI and transferred to the Academy. He was determined to preserve the past and, by extension, himself.

And so far, he had.

The murders almost jeopardized everything, inviting scrutiny. Now that they were solved, Malone felt confident that the status quo would continue. But Mother was a concern. She was smart, and if Crenshaw ever mentioned Malone's history . . .

The odds were slim; the general would have no reason to do so. But for the first time in years, Malone felt uncertain about the future.

For the first time, he felt fear.

Walking into the living area, he built a fire in the fireplace and went upstairs to his loft. When he returned, he was carrying a metal box, the kind used for important papers. Placing it on the coffee table, he opened the lid, staring at the contents. Instantly, he was engulfed with self-loathing.

This was the reason he kept it, to remind himself of what he had once been.

The two other men . . . boys really . . . had been friends. Part of a loose gang of spoiled rich kids like himself, out for kicks and fun. That's why they went along.

For kicks and fun.

As Malone reached into the box, his hand shook as he thought about the cost of that night. Ten dead and one woman driven insane.

One victim had been bad enough. Could he live with the knowledge of all the others?

He didn't know. What he did know was that he couldn't tell the truth. Crenshaw and his father had been right from the beginning. He wasn't a man of character. Instead, he was a man who had allowed a blinding jealousy to propel him toward a single horrific act.

"I'm sorry, Christina," he murmured. "Christ, I'm so damned sorry."

Malone hurled the Mickey Mouse mask into the fire.

Epilogue

COLORADO SPRINGS GAZETTE,
Thursday, November 10

Air Force Academy Suffers Another Tragedy

COLORADO SPRINGS—On the heels of the horrific murders last weekend, Army Major Bradley Tupper, 34, apparently committed suicide while skydiving yesterday morning with the Academy's Wings of Blue parachute team. Major Tupper, an Air Officer Commanding supervising the 18th Cadet Squadron, was a member of the famed 82nd Airborne Division and a combat veteran with tours in Afghanistan and Iraq. According to stunned onlookers, Major Tupper, an advisor to the team, made no attempt to deploy either his main or reserve parachutes, both of which proved functional. "He didn't try to do anything," one shaken witness said. "He just fell and fell."

In a brief statement, the Academy said Major Tupper was an exemplary officer, but had been under a great deal of stress because of personal issues. While no details were given, an unnamed source confirmed that Major Tupper was under investigation for engaging in an illicit relationship with a female cadet. If true, he would have faced a court-martial and possible prison time.

The Academy Public Affairs Office and Lieutenant Tom Canola of the Colorado Springs Police Department would not comment on whether Major's Tupper's alleged suicide is connected to the recent murders. It is worth noting that all three of the cadets who were killed—Rachel Owen, 21, Mary Zinnel, 20, and Terry Jefferson, 21—were assigned to the squadron administered by Major Tupper.

Ms. Kaitlin Barlow, 34, a special assistant to Senator Smith and the lead investigator for the Senate panel investigating sexual harassment at the Academy, has been charged in the murders. According to District Attorney Dennis Hilley, it's uncertain when she'll face trial because of her mental instability. Ms. Barlow is currently incarcerated in the State Prison Hospital at Pueblo and has been diagnosed as an acute paranoid schizophrenic.

Brigadier General Tim Scully, the Commandant of Cadets and Acting Superintendent, remains confident the United States Air Force Academy will overcome this latest tragedy and regain its prominence as one of America's finest institutions. "We attract the best and the brightest young men and women in the country, patriots who want to serve their country. They define this school, not the terrible events we've recently experienced. If you talk to them [cadets], you'll understand why I'm so confident about the future. These young people are determined to honor the memory of their friends who passed away in the only way they can, by restoring the luster to the Academy's reputation. They'll succeed, too, much sooner than anyone expects. I only hope I'm still here when it happens."

In related news, a spokesman for Senator Smith has confirmed the Senate panel investigating the Academy's sexual harassment allegations has been disbanded. No determination has been made on whether it will reconvene. High-priced Denver defense attorney Dennis Stefanski has been retained to represent Ms. Barlow. In a press statement, Mr. Stefanski would say only that his fee is being paid by a party or parties who prefer to remain anonymous.

Major Tupper is survived by his wife and two small children.

Setting down the paper, Malone made a call he'd been delaying. He hadn't wanted to instill alarm unnecessarily.

"Richard," he said to his old friend, "it's Malone. Tell Dan we might be in trouble."

"*Might?* What the hell does that mean?"

"An investigator is starting to ask questions . . ."

NO MAN GETS LEFT BEHIND.

Catch all the nonstop action in these bestsellers from Pocket Books.

INTO THE TREELINE
A Men of Valor Novel
John F. Mullins

When Lieutenant James Carmichael is wounded in the Central Highlands of Vietnam, he finds himself surrounded and with only one choice: Fight or die.

NAPALM DREAMS
A Men of Valor Novel
John F. Mullins

Green Beret Captain Finn McCulloden and his troops are sent on a mission to protect a Special Forces border camp in danger of being overrun by the North Vietnamese. But they weren't counting on treachery from within...

THE COMMANDER
Patrick A. Davis

In South Korea, every freedom has a price...even murder.

WAR PLAN RED
Peter Sasgen

The submarine is stolen. The weapon is nuclear. The chase is on.

POCKET BOOKS
A Division of Simon & Schuster
A VIACOM COMPANY

www.simonsays.com

POCKET STAR BOOKS
A Division of Simon & Schuster
A VIACOM COMPANY

11224